SHIVER

LISA JACKSON

KENSINGTON
PUBLISHING CORP.

www.kensingtonbooks.com

KENSINGTON BOOKS are published by

Kensington Publishing Corp.
119 West 40th Street
New York, NY 10018

All Kensington titles, imprints, and distributed lines are available at special quantity discounts for bulk purchases for sales promotion, premiums, fundraising, educational, or institutional use.

Special book excerpts or customized printings can also be created to fit specific needs. For details, write or phone the office of the Kensington Sales Manager: Attn.: Sales Department. Kensington Publishing Corp., 119 West 40th Street, New York, NY 10018. Phone: 1-800-221-2647.

The K logo is a trademark of Kensington Publishing Corp.

First Kensington Hardcover Edition: April 2006

ISBN: 978-1-4201-1894-0 (ebook)

ISBN: 978-1-4967-3601-7

First Kensington Trade Paperback Edition: April 2006

10 9 8 7 6

Printed in the United States of America

Acknowledgments

There were many people involved in getting this book to print, all of whom were integral. I want to thank my editor, John Scognamiglio, for his insight, vision, input, support, and ultimate patience. Man, did he work hard on this one. As did my sister, Nancy Bush, who was not only my cheerleader and personal editor, she picked up the other balls of my life and juggled them effectively, never once losing her cool. Thanks, Nan.

Also, I have to thank my incredible agent, Robin Rue, and everyone at Kensington Books, especially Laurie Parkin, who also worked very hard on this one.

In addition, I would like to mention all the people here who helped me: Ken Bush, Kelly Bush, Matthew Crose, Michael Crose, Alexis Harrington, Danielle Katcher, Marilyn Katcher, Ken Melum, Roz Noonan, Kathy Okano, Samantha Santistevan, Mike Sidel, and Larry Sparks.

If I've forgotten anyone, my apologies. You've all been wonderful.

Author's Note

For the purposes of the story, I've bent some of the rules of police procedure and have also created my own fictitious police department.

This book was written pre-Hurricane Katrina, before the incredible city of New Orleans and the surrounding Gulf Coast were decimated by the storm. I hope I've captured the unique essence of New Orleans, what it once was and what it will be again.

Prologue

Twenty years earlier
Our Lady of Virtues Hospital
Near New Orleans, Louisiana

She felt his breath.
Warm.

Seductive.

Erotically evil.

A presence that caused the hairs on the back of her neck to lift, her skin to prickle, sweat to collect upon her spine.

Her heart thumped, and barely able to move, standing in the darkness, she searched the shadowed corners of her room frantically. Through the open window she heard the reverberating songs of the frogs in the nearby swamps and the rumble of a train upon faraway tracks.

But here, now, he was with her.

Go away, she tried to say, but held her tongue, hoping beyond hope that he wouldn't notice her standing near the window. On the other side of the panes, security lamps illuminated the grounds with pale, bluish light, and she realized belatedly that her body, shrouded only by a sheer nightgown, was silhouetted in their eerie glow.

Of course he could see her, find her in the darkness.

He always did.

Throat dry, she stepped backward, placing a hand on the window casing to steady herself. Maybe she had just imagined his presence. Maybe she hadn't heard the door open after all. Maybe she'd jumped up from a drug-induced sleep too quickly. After all, it wasn't late, only eight in the evening.

Maybe she was safe in this room, *her* room, on the third floor.

Maybe.

She was reaching for the bedside light when she heard the soft scrape of leather against hardwood.

Her throat closed on a silent scream.

Having adjusted to the half-light, her eyes took in the bed with its mussed sheets, evidence of her fitful rest. Upon the dressing table was the lamp and a bifold picture frame, one that held small portraits of her two daughters. Across the small room was a fireplace. She could see its decorative tile and cold grate and, above the mantel, a bare spot, faded now where a mirror had once hung.

So where was he? She glanced to the tall windows. Beyond, the October night was hot and sultry. In the panes she could see her wan reflection: petite, small-boned frame; sad gold eyes; high cheekbones; lustrous auburn hair pulled away from her face. And behind her . . . was that a shadow creeping near?

Or her imagination?

That was the trouble. Sometimes he hid.

But he was always nearby. Always. She could *feel* him, hear his soft, determined footsteps in the hallway, smell his scent—a mixture of male musk and sweat—catch a glimpse of a quick, darting shadow as he passed.

There was no getting away from him. Ever. Not even in the dead of night. He received great satisfaction in surprising her, sneaking up on her while she was sitting at her desk, leaning down behind her when she was kneeling at her bedside. He was always ready to press his face to the back of her neck, to reach around her and touch her breasts, arousing her though she loathed him, pulling her tightly against him so that she could feel his erection against her back. She wasn't safe when she was under the thin spray of the shower, nor while sleeping beneath the covers of her small bed.

How ironic that they had placed her here... for her own safety.

"Go away," she whispered, her head pounding, her thoughts disjointed. "Leave me alone!"

She blinked and tried to focus.

Where was he?

Nervously she trained her eyes on the one hiding place, the closet. She licked her lips. The wooden door was ajar, just slightly, enough that anyone inside could peer through the crack.

From the small sliver of darkness within the closet, something seemed to glimmer. A reflection. Eyes?

Oh, God.

Maybe he was inside. Waiting.

Gooseflesh broke out on her skin. She should call out to someone, but if she did, she would be restrained, medicated... or worse. *Stop it, Faith. Don't get paranoid!* But the glittering eyes in the closet watched her. She felt them. Wrapping one arm around her middle, the other folded over it, she scraped her nails on the skin of her elbow.

Scratch, scratch, scratch.

But maybe this was all a bad dream. A nightmare. Wasn't that what the sisters had assured her in their soft whispers as they gently patted her hands and stared at her with compassionate, disbelieving eyes? An ugly dream. Yes! A nightmare of vast, intense proportions. Even the nurse had agreed with the nuns, telling her that what she'd thought she'd seen wasn't real. And the doctor, cold, clinical, with the bedside manner of a stone monkey, had talked to her as if she were a small, stupid child.

"There, there, Faith, no one is following you," he'd said, wearing a thin, patronizing smile. "No one is watching you. You know that. You're... you're just confused. You're safe here. Remember, this is your home now."

Tears burned her eyes and she scratched more anxiously, her short fingernails running over the smooth skin of her forearm, encountering scabs. Home? This monstrous place? She closed her eyes, grabbed the headboard of the bed to steady herself.

Was she really as sick as they said? Did she really see people who weren't there? That's what they'd told her, time and time again, to the point that she was no longer certain what was real and what was not. Maybe that was the plot against her, to make her believe she was as crazy as they insisted she was.

She heard a footstep and looked up quickly.

The hairs on the backs of her arms rose.

She began to shake as she saw the door crack open a bit more.

"Sweet Jesus." Trembling, she backed up, her gaze fixed on the closet, her fingers scraping her forearm like mad. The door creaked open in slow motion. "Go away!" she whispered, her stomach knotting as full-blown terror took root.

A weapon! You need a weapon!

Anxiously, she looked around the near-dark room with its bed bolted to the floor.

Get your letter opener! Now!

She took one step toward the desk before she remembered that Sister Madeline had taken the letter opener away from her.

The lamp on the night table!

But it, too, was screwed down.

She pressed the switch.

Click.

No great wash of light. Frantically, she hit the switch again. Over and over.

Click! Click! Click! Click!

She looked up and saw him then. A tall man, looming in front of the door to the hallway. It was too dark to see his features but she knew his wicked smile was in place, his eyes glinting with an evil need.

He was Satan Incarnate. And there was no way to escape from him. There never was.

"Please don't," she begged, her voice sounding pathetic and weak as she backed up, her legs quivering.

"Please don't what?"

Don't touch me . . . don't place your fingers anywhere on my body . . . don't tell me I'm beautiful . . . don't kiss me . . .

"Leave now," she insisted. Dear God, was there no weapon, nothing to stop him?

"Leave now or what?"

"Or I'll scream and call the guards."

"The guards," he repeated in that low, amused, nearly hypnotic voice. "Here?" He clucked his tongue as if she were a disobedient child. "You've tried that before."

She knew for certain that her plight was futile. She would submit to him again.

As she always did.

"Did the guards believe you the last time?"

Of course they hadn't. Why would they? The two scrawny, pimply-faced boys hadn't hidden the fact they considered her mad. At least that's what they'd insinuated, though they'd used fancier words... *delusional... paranoid... schizophrenic...*

Or had they said anything at all? Maybe not. Maybe they'd just stared at her with their pitying, yet hungry, eyes. Hadn't one of them told her she was sexy? The other one cupping one cheek of her buttocks... or... or had that all been a horrid, vivid nightmare?

Scratch, scratch, scratch. She felt her nails break the skin.

Humiliation washed over her. She inched backward, away from her tormentor. What was happening to her was her own fault. She'd sinned somehow, brought this upon herself. She was the one who was evil. She had instigated God's wrath. She alone could atone. "Go away," she whispered again, clawing more frantically at her arm.

"Faith, don't," he warned, his voice horrifyingly soothing. "Mutilating yourself won't change anything. I'm here to help you. You know that."

Help her? No... no, no, no!

She wanted to crumple onto the floor, to shed her guilt, to get away from the itching.

Fight! an inner voice ordered her. *Don't let him force you into doing things that you know are wrong! You have will. You can't let him do this to you.*

But it was already too late.

Close to her now, he clucked his tongue again and she saw its pointy, wet, pink tip flicking against the back of his teeth.

In a rough whisper, he said, "Uh-oh, Faith, I think you've been a naughty girl again."

"No." She was whimpering. There it was...that horrid bit of excitement building inside her.

"Oh, Faith, don't you know it's a sin to lie?"

She glanced to the wall where the crucifix of Jesus was nailed into the plaster. Did it move? Blinking, she imagined Jesus staring at her, his eyes kind but silently reprimanding in the semidarkness.

No, Faith. That can't be. Get a grip, for God's sake.

It's a painted image, that's all.

Breathing rapidly, she dragged her gaze from Christ's tortured face to the fireplace...cold now, devoid of both ashes and the mirror above it, now an empty space, the outline visible against the rosebud wallpaper. They said she broke the mirror in a fit of rage, that she'd cut herself. That her own image had caused her to panic.

But he'd done it, hadn't he? This devil whose sole intent was to torture her? Hadn't she witnessed the act? She'd tried to refuse him, and he'd crashed his fist into the looking glass. Mirrored shards sprayed, hitting her, then crashed to the floor like glittery, deadly knives.

That's what had happened.

Right?

Or not? Now, feeling the blood beneath her nails, she wondered.

What's happening to me?

She stared at her bloodied hands. Her fingernails, once manicured and polished, were broken, her palms scratched, and farther up, upon her wrists, healed deep gashes. Had she done that to herself? In her mind's eye she saw her hands wrapped around a shard of glass and the blood dripping from her fingers...

Because you were going to kill him...trying to protect yourself!

She closed her eyes and let out a long, mewling cry. It was true. She didn't know what to believe any longer. Truth and lies blended, fact and fiction fused, her life, once so ordinary, so predictable, was fragmented. Frayed. At her own hands.

She edged backward, closer to the window, farther from him, from temptation, from sin.

Where was her husband...and her children, what had happened to her girls?

Terror burrowed deep into her soul. Confused and panic-stricken, she blinked rapidly, trying to think. They were safe. They had to be.

Concentrate, Faith. Get hold of yourself! Zoey and Abby are with Jacques. They're visiting tonight, remember? It's your birthday.

Or was that wrong? Was everything a lie? A macabre figment of her imagination?

She took another step backward.

"You're confused, Faith, but I can help you," he said quietly, as if nothing had happened between them, as if everything she'd conjured was her imagination, as if he'd never touched her.

Dear Lord, how mad was she?

She spun quickly, her toe catching on the edge of a rug. Pitching forward, she again caught her reflection in the window and this time she saw him rushing forward, felt his hands upon her.

"No!" she cried, falling.

Glass cracked.

Blew apart as her shoulder hit the pane.

The window broke, shattering. Giving way.

With a great twisting metal groan, the wrought-iron grate wrenched free of its bolts.

She screamed and flailed at the air, trying to reach the windowsill, the filigreed barricade that hung from one screw, the bricks, anything! But it was too late. Her body hurtled through the broken panes, pieces of glass and wood clawing at her arms, ripping her nightgown, slicing her bare legs.

In a split second, she knew that it was over. She would feel no more pain.

Closing her eyes, Faith Chastain pitched into the blackness of the hot Louisiana night.

CHAPTER 1

Twenty years later
Cambrai, Louisiana

"I just wanted to call and say 'Happy birthday,'" her sister said, leaving a message on the answering machine.

Abby stood in the middle of her small kitchen. Listening, she debated about picking up the phone, but decided against it. She just wasn't in the mood. She had spent most of the day at her studio in New Orleans, dealing with kids who had their own ideas about what a Christmas portrait should be. What she needed was a glass of wine. Maybe two. Not her sister's long-winded birthday message.

"So . . . give me a call back when you get in. It's still early here on the West Coast, you know. I, uh, I'd like to talk to you, Abby. Thirty-five years is a major milestone."

In more ways than one, Abby thought as she reached into her refrigerator and pulled out a bottle of Chardonnay she'd bought nearly a month earlier when she'd thought her friend Alicia was coming to Louisiana for a visit.

"Okay . . . so . . . when you get this, I mean, assuming you're not listening to it right now and still refusing to talk to me, give me a call, okay?" Zoey waited a beat. "It's been a long time, Abby. It's time to bury the hatchet."

Abby wasn't so sure. She turned on the faucet and heard the old pipes groan as she rinsed a wineglass that had been gathering dust in her cupboard for the past two years.

"You know, Abby, this isn't just about you," Zoey reminded her through the answering machine's tiny speaker.

Of course not. It's about you.

"It's a tough day for me, as well. She was my mother, too."

Abby set her jaw, reconsidered picking up the receiver, and once again determined not to. Talking to Zoey today would be a mistake. She could feel it in her bones. Digging in a drawer, she found a corkscrew she'd owned since college and began opening the bottle.

"Look, Abs, I really, really hope you're not home alone and listening to this . . . You should go out and celebrate."

I intend to.

The phone clicked as Zoey hung up. Abby let out a long breath and leaned against the counter. She probably should have answered, put up with all the falderal of birthday greetings, the fake cheer, the gee-aren't-we-just-one-big-happy-family, but she couldn't. Not today. Because Zoey wouldn't have let it go at that. There would have been the inevitable discussion of their mother, and what had happened twenty years ago, and then there would have been the awkward and uncomfortable questions about Luke.

She popped the cork.

It was just so damned hard to forgive her sister for sleeping with her husband. Yeah, it had been a long time ago, and before the marriage but there it was, the wedge that had been between them for five years, ever since Abby had learned of the affair.

But Zoey had dated him first, hadn't she?

So what? Abby poured the wine, watched the chilled, cool liquid splash into the glass. Her conscience twinged a little at that, even though she knew that Luke Gierman had proved to be no prize as a boyfriend and worse as a husband. No damned prize at all.

And though Abby had divorced him, Zoey was still her sister. There was no changing that. Maybe she should let bygones be bygones, Abby thought, staring out the partially opened window where a slight breeze, heavy with the scents of earth and water, wafted inside.

Twilight was just settling in this stretch of Louisiana, the crickets and cicadas were chirping, stars beginning to wink in a dusky, lavender sky. It was pretty here, if a little isolated, a place she and Luke had planned to add on to, to become an all-American family with 2.3 children, a white picket fence, and a minivan parked in the drive.

So much for dreams.

She pushed the window open a little farther, hoping for relief from the heat.

Happy birthday to you...

The wind seemed to sigh that damned funeral dirge of a song through the branches of the live oaks, causing the Spanish moss to shift as dusk settled deeper into the woods. Off in the distance she heard the rumble of a train. Closer in, at a neighbor's place down this winding country road, she heard a dog barking and through the trees she watched the ghostly image of a rising moon.

Her 35-millimeter camera was sitting on the counter near the back door and the dusk was so still and peaceful, so intriguing, she thought she might click off a few shots and kill the roll. The film inside the camera had been there for a long time as she used her digital more often than not. Leaving the wine on the counter, she turned on the camera and flash, then walked to the French doors off her dining room. Stepping outside, she positioned herself on the edge of the flagstones. Ansel, her cat, followed Abby outside and hopped onto a bench located under a magnolia tree. Abby focused then clicked off the last few shots of the tabby with the darkening woods as a backdrop. The cat faced away from the house, ears pricked forward, his eyes trained on the trees, his fur gilded by a few rays of a dying sun. "Hey, buddy," she said, and the cat looked over his shoulder as she took the last couple of shots with the flash flaring in Ansel's gold eyes. Why not have a few pictures of this, her thirty-fifth birthday? she thought as she turned to go inside.

Snap!

A twig cracked in the woods nearby.

Her heart jumped to her throat.

She spun around, half expecting to spy someone lurking in the deepening umbra. Eyes searching the coming darkness, she strained to see through the vines and brush and canopy of leafy trees. Her skin crawled, her pulse jack-hammering in her ears.

But no human shape suddenly appeared, no dark figure stepped into the patches of light cast from the windows.

Stop it, she thought, drawing in a shaky breath. *Just . . . stop it.* She'd been in a bad mood all day. Testy and on edge. Not because it was her birthday, not really. Who cared about the passing of another year? Thirty-five wasn't exactly ancient. But the fact that this was the twentieth anniversary of her mother's death, now *that* got to her.

Still jittery, she walked into the house and called to the cat through the open doors.

Ansel ignored her. He remained fixed and alert, his gaze trained on the dark shadows, where she expected a creature of the night might be staring back. The same creature who had stepped on and broken a twig. *A large creature.* "Come on, Ansel. Let's call it a day," she urged.

The cat hissed.

His striped fur suddenly stood straight on end. His ears flattened and his eyes rounded. Like a bolt of lightning, he shot across the verandah and around the corner toward the studio. There wasn't a chance in hell that she could catch him.

"Oh, ya big pussy," she teased, but as she latched the door behind her, she couldn't quite shake her own case of nerves. Though she'd never seen anyone on the grounds behind her place, there was always a first time. Leaving her camera on the dining room table, she made her way back to the kitchen, where the answering machine with its blinking red light caused her to think of Zoey again.

Abby and her sister had never been close, not for as long as she could remember.

Damn you, Zoey, she thought as she picked up her glass and took a long swallow. Why couldn't Abby have had that special bond with her sister, that best-friends kind of thing which everyone who did seemed to gush on and on about? Could it be because Zoey and Abby were so close in age, barely fourteen months apart?

Or maybe it was because Zoey was so damned competitive with her uncompromising I'll-do-*any*thing to win streak. Or maybe, just maybe, their antagonism was as much Abby's fault as her sister's.

"Blasphemy," she muttered, feeling the chilled wine slide easily down her throat, though it did little to cool her off.

It was hot. Humid. The fans in the nearly century-old house unable to keep up with the heat that sweltered in this part of the bayou. She dabbed at the sweat on her forehead with the corner of a kitchen towel.

Should she have answered the stupid phone?

Nope. Abby wasn't ready to go there. Not today. Probably not ever.

It was twenty years ago today . . .

The lyrics of an old Beatles tune, one of her mother's favorites, spun through Abby's head. "Don't," she told herself. No reason to replay the past as she had for the last two decades. It was time to move on. Tonight, she vowed, she'd start over. This was the beginning of Abby Chastain, Phase II. She'd try to forget that on this very day, twenty years ago, when her mother had turned thirty-five—just as Abby was doing today—Faith Chastain had ended her tormented life. Horribly. Tragically.

"Oh, God, Mom," she said now, closing her eyes. The memory that she'd tried so hard to repress emerged as if in slow motion. She recalled her father's sedan rolling through the open wrought-iron gates. Past manicured lawns toward the tall, red-brick building where the drive curved around a fountain—a fountain where three angels sprayed water upward toward the starlit heavens. Abby, already into boys at the time, and thinking of how she was going to ask Trey Hilliard to Friday night's Sadie Hawkins dance, had climbed out of the car just as her father had cut the engine. Carrying a box with a bright, fuchsia-colored bow, she'd looked up to the third story, to the windows of her mother's room.

But no warm light glowed through the panes.

Instead the room was dark.

And then Abby had felt an odd sensation, a soft breath that touched the back of her neck and nearly stopped her heart. Something was wrong. Very wrong. "Mama?" she whispered, using the name for her mother she hadn't spoken in a decade.

She'd started for the wide steps leading to the hospital's front door when she heard the crash.

Her head jerked up.

Glass sprayed. Tiny pieces catching in the bluish light.

A hideous shriek rose in the night. A dark body fell through the sky. It landed on the concrete with a heavy bone-cracking thud.

Fear tore through her.

Denial rose in her throat. "No! No! Noooo!" Abby dropped the box and flew down the steps to the small broken form lying faceup on the cement. Blood, dark and oozing, began to pool beneath her mother's head. Wide whiskey-colored eyes stared sightlessly upward.

Abby pitched herself toward the still, crumpled form.

"Abby!"

As if from the other side of a long tunnel she heard her name being called. Her father's desperate, tense voice. "Abby, don't! Oh, God! Help! Someone get help! Faith!"

She fell to her knees. Tears welled in her eyes and terror chilled her to the bottom of her soul. "Mama! Mama!" she cried, until strong hands and arms pulled her struggling body away.

Now, she blinked and gave herself a quick mental shake. "Jesus," she whispered, dispelling the horrific vision that had haunted her for all of twenty years. She was suddenly cognizant of water dripping from the faucet over the kitchen sink. Rather than shut off the pressure, she turned it on full, until water was rushing from the tap. Quickly, she cupped her hands under the stream, then splashed the water onto her face, cooling her cheeks, pushing back the soul-jarring memory and hoping to wash away the stain of that night forever.

Trembling, she snapped the dishtowel from the counter and swiped at her face. What was wrong with her? Hadn't she just told herself she wouldn't go down that painful path again? "Idiot," she murmured, folding the towel, noticing her half-full glass of wine on the counter, and feeling something about the memory wasn't quite right.

"Get over yourself," she rebuked as she picked up the glass, looked at the glimmering depths for a second.

"Happy birthday, Mom," she whispered to the empty room,

hoisting the stemmed glass as if Faith were in the room. She took a sip of the crisp Chardonnay. "Here's to us." Her mother had always told her she was special, that being born on her mother's birthday created a unique bond between them, that they were "two peas in a pod."

Well... not quite.

Not by a long shot.

A very long shot.

"Now, please... go away," she whispered. "Leave me alone."

She drained her glass, corked the bottle, and stuffed it into the refrigerator door. She had no more time for mind-numbing nightmares, for a past that sometimes nearly devoured her. Tonight, all that was over.

Determined to get her life on the right track, she set her glass onto the counter too quickly. It cracked, the stem breaking off, cutting the end of her thumb. "Great," she growled as blood began to surface. Just what she needed, she thought sourly. Opening a cupboard, she found a box of Band-Aids. As blood dripped onto the Formica, she undid the little carton and discovered only one jumbo-sized Band-Aid in the box. It would just have to do. Awkwardly she slipped it from its sterile packaging and wrapped it around her thumb twice.

She managed to swab the counter and toss the broken glass into the trash before walking through a mud room and slapping on the light of the garage. There, propped against a stack of wood, was a sign that said it all: FOR SALE BY OWNER. She picked it up then carried it to the end of her long drive. She hung the blue-and-white placard onto the hooks of the post she'd set into her yard late that afternoon.

"Perfect," she told herself, even though she did have one or two twinges of nostalgia about selling the place. Hadn't the little bungalow been the very spot where she'd tried once before to start over, a haven chosen as the ideal place to patch a broken marriage, a quiet retreat where she'd fostered so many hopes, so many dreams? She'd crossed her fingers when she and Luke had bought this house. She'd prayed that they would be able to find happiness here.

How foolish she'd been. Now, as dusk gathered and purple

shadows crawled across the grounds, she glanced at the cottage—a cozy little clapboard and shingle house that had been built nearly a hundred years earlier. It sat well back from this winding country road. The original structure had been renovated, added to, and improved to the point that the main house consisted of two small bedrooms, a single bath, and an attic with a skylight that she'd managed to turn into her in-home office. The attached building had once been a mother-in-law apartment, which Abby had converted into her photography studio, dark room, and second bathroom.

Five years earlier, she and Luke had found this property, declared it "perfect," and had spent several years here before everything had fallen apart. Eventually he'd moved out of the house and onto other women...no, wait. It was the other way around. The women came first. Starting with Zoey. Before the wedding.

Not that it mattered now.

Luke Gierman, once a respected newscaster and radio disk jockey, had become New Orleans's answer to Howard Stern as well as a chapter in her life that was finally and indelibly over. It had been more than a year since the final papers had been signed and a judge had declared the marriage officially dissolved.

Snagging the hammer from the ground where she'd left it earlier, Abby stepped back to study the sign, to make certain it hung evenly, to read once again the words and phone number indicating that this home was on the market.

She had been determined to set her life straight, had heeded what all the experts had suggested, though, in truth, she'd thought a lot of the advice had been useless. She'd tried to give their marriage a second chance but that hadn't worked. They'd split; she'd stayed with the house. Her friends had all warned her about suffering through the holidays and anniversaries and nostalgia alone, but those milestones had passed and they hadn't been all that bad. She'd survived just fine. Probably because she hadn't really handed her heart to Luke again. And she hadn't been all that surprised when his old tendencies for other women had resurfaced.

Luke would probably always suffer from an ongoing case of infidelity.

Snap!

A twig in the underbrush broke. Again! Glancing sharply toward the shrubbery, the direction where the sound had occurred, Abby expected to see a possum or raccoon or even a skunk amble into the weak light offered by the single bulb hanging in the garage.

But there was only silence. She realized, then, that the crickets had stopped their songs, the bullfrogs were no longer croaking. Her heart rate increased and involuntarily she strained to listen, to notice any other sounds that were out of the ordinary.

She suddenly felt very vulnerable in this isolated area of the road.

Peering into the darkness, she sensed unseen eyes studying her, watching her. A tiny shudder slid down her spine. She chided herself for her own case of nerves. It was her birthday, she was alone, and just thinking about her mother's death had left her edgy.

Relax, she told herself. *Go inside. It's dark now and the sign is finally up.*

From the corner of her eye, she caught movement in the bushes, a rustle of dry leaves. She froze, her nerves stretched taut.

A second later a dark shadow slid beneath the undergrowth. Her heart kicked hard.

Then Ansel scurried from his hiding spot beneath the branches of a leatherwood and buckthorn. At her feet, he turned, stared into the bushes from where he'd been hiding, and hissed loudly.

She jumped, startled. "For God's sake," she murmured, putting a hand over her racing heart. "Cut that out! What are you trying to do, give me a heart attack? Well, you just about succeeded!" She reached down and tried to pick him up. "I guess you're tense, too. How about a drink? Wine for me. Fresh H_2O for you."

Before she could grab him, Ansel raced the length of the driveway and through the open garage door. Nearly a quarter of a mile away, the neighbor's dog began putting up a racket that could raise the dead.

Anxiety ate at her. Her fingers tightened over the handle of the hammer, and ridiculously, she felt again as if someone was observing her. *Don't get paranoid. Don't. You're not like your mother… you're not crazy.* So the Pomeroys' Rottweiler was barking. So what?

Dismissing her case of nerves, she walked steadfastly toward the house, her shoes crushing the first few leaves of autumn. Inside the garage, she slapped the button to close the door, then walked through the mud room to the kitchen, where Ansel was seated on the windowsill over the sink, his eyes trained outside, his tail flicking nervously.

"What is it, buddy?" she asked.

The cat kept up his tense vigil.

"You know you're not supposed to be anywhere near the counters."

Still no reaction.

Abby stood at the sink and stared through the glass into the night. Looming black trees surrounded her small patio and garden. The window was open a bit, the sounds of the night and the breeze filtering inside.

Again the dog barked. At the same moment Abby's cottage settled, the old timbers creaking. Unnerved, Abby shooed the cat from the ledge, slammed the window shut, and flipped the lock. Though she wasn't easily frightened, every once in a while she felt edgy, the isolation of living alone getting to her.

But that was about to change.

If she accepted Alicia's invitation to move to San Francisco, they'd be roommates again, just like in college—except for the fact that they were both now divorced and Alicia had a five-year-old in kindergarten.

"Tempting, isn't it?" she asked the cat, who, rebuffed from his perch on the window, slunk to a hiding spot under the table. "Fine, Ansel, go ahead and pout. Hurt me some more."

The phone rang. Still feeling guilty about ignoring her sister's call, Abby swooped up the cordless receiver without checking caller ID. "Hello," she answered as she walked into the living room.

"Happy birthday."

She stopped short and her heart nearly dropped through the floor at the sound of Luke's voice. "Thanks."

"You're probably surprised to hear from me."

That was the understatement of the year. "More like stunned. You were the last person I expected to call."

"Abs," he said, drawing her nickname out so that it was almost an endearment. "Look, I know this is a difficult day for you because of your mom."

She wasn't buying it. She'd known him too long. "You called to make me feel better?"

"Yeah."

"I'm fine." She said it with complete conviction.

"Oh. Well. That's good," he said, surprised, as if he believed she might still be an emotional mess, falling into a bajillion pieces. "Real good."

"Thanks. Bye."

"Wait! Don't hang up."

She heard the urgency in his voice, imagined his free hand shooting out as if to physically stop her from dropping the receiver into its cradle. He'd made the same gesture every time he wanted something and thought she wasn't listening. "What, Luke?" She was standing in the living room now, the room where they'd once watched television, eaten popcorn, and discussed current events.

Or fought. They'd had more than their share of rip-roarers.

"Look, do you still have that stuff I left?" he finally asked, getting to the real point of his call.

"What stuff?"

"Oh, you know," he said casually, as if the items were just coming to mind. "My fishing poles and tackle box. An old set of golf clubs. Scuba gear."

"No."

"What?"

"It's gone. All of it."

She glanced to the bookcase where their wedding pictures were still tucked away with the rest of the photo albums.

There was a short pause and she knew she'd taken all the wind out of his sails.

"What do you mean 'gone'?" he asked and she imagined his blue eyes narrowing. "You didn't give my things away, did you?" His voice was suddenly cold. Suspicious. Accusing.

"Of course I gave them away," she responded without a shred of guilt. "I gave you six months to pick up your stuff, Luke. And that was way longer than I wanted to. Way longer. When you didn't show, I called the Salvation Army. They took everything, including the rest of your clothes and all that junk that was in the garage and the attic and the closets."

"Jesus, Abby! Some of that stuff was valuable! None of it's 'junk.'"

"Then you should have come for it."

There was a pause, just long enough for a heartbeat and she braced herself. "Wait a minute. You didn't get rid of my skis. You wouldn't do that. The Rossignols are still in the attic, right?" She heard the disbelief in his voice. Walking back to the kitchen, she threw open the refrigerator door and hauled out the wine bottle again. "Jesus, Abby, those things cost me an arm and a leg. I can't believe that you...oh, Christ, tell me that my board is in the garage. My surf board."

"I don't think so," she said, shaking her head. "I'm pretty sure that went, too."

"I bought it in Hawaii! And the canoe?"

"Actually I think that went to Our Lady of Virtues, a fund-raiser."

"Our Lady of Virtues? The hospital where your mother—"

"It was for the church," she cut in. "The hospital's been closed for years."

"You've completely flipped out, Abby," he accused. "You're as nuts as she was!"

Abby's stomach clenched, but she waited. Didn't respond. Wouldn't rise to the bait. Pulling out the cork while cradling the phone between her shoulder and ear, she felt her injured thumb throb. She wasn't crazy. No way. The only time she'd been close to mental illness was when she'd agreed to marry Luke. Those "I do's" were major points in the off-your-rocker column. But otherwise, knock wood, she was sane. Right? Despite the sense of creeping paranoia that lurked around her at times.

"This is a nightmare! A fuckin' nightmare. I suppose you even tossed my dad's thirty-eight?" When she didn't reply, he clarified, "You know, Abby, the gun?"

"I know what it is." She didn't bother with another wineglass, just pulled her favorite cracked coffee mug from the open shelf.

"That gun was my dad's! He—he had it for years. He was a cop, damn it, and . . . and it's got sentimental value. You wouldn't give it away!"

"Hmm." She poured the wine, didn't care that some splashed onto the counter. "Kinda makes you wonder what the Salvation Army would want with it."

"They *don't* take firearms."

"Is that so?" She took a long swallow of the wine. "Then maybe it was the nuns at Our Lady. I can't really remember."

"You don't even know?" He was aghast. "You gave my gun away and you don't know who has it! Jesus H. Christ, Abby, that pistol is registered to me! If it's used in a crime—"

"Now, I'm not sure about this, so don't quote me, but I don't think the Mother Superior is running a smuggling ring on the side."

"This isn't funny!"

"Sure it is, Luke. It's damned funny."

"I'm talking about my possessions. *Mine!*" She pictured him hooking a thumb at his chest and jabbing frantically, angrily. "You had no right to get rid of anything!"

"So sue me, Luke."

"I will," he said hotly.

"Look, my name isn't U-Store-It, okay? I'm not a holding tank for *your* things. If they were so valuable, you should have picked them up around the time we were splitting up, or, you know, in the next six or seven months, maybe?"

"I can't believe this!"

"Then don't, Luke. Don't believe it."

"Getting rid of my things is low, Abby. And you're going to hear about it. I think the topic of the next *Gierman's Groaners* is going to be about vindictive exes and how they should be handled."

"Do whatever you want. I won't be listening or calling in." She hung up, teeth clenched. She kicked herself for not checking caller ID before picking up the phone. "Never again," she promised herself, taking another sip of Chardonnay, wishing the wine would hurry up and dull the rage she felt boiling through her blood. Luke had the uncanny ability to make her see red when no one else could. She'd half expected to feel some sort of satisfaction when he finally learned that she'd tossed out his treasures; instead she felt empty. Hollow. How could two people who had sworn to love each other come down to this? "Don't let him get to you," she warned herself, walking into the living room, where, despite the heat, she grabbed a long-handled barbecue lighter and started the fire.

Flames immediately crackled and rose, consuming the newspaper and kindling she'd stacked earlier. She'd always kept logs in the grate, ready to light in case there was a sudden power loss, but tonight was different. She had a ritual she'd planned long before Luke's unexpected call. Though it was still sweltering outside, she had some trash to burn.

From the shelf near the stone fireplace, she pulled out her wedding album. Upon her friend Alicia's advice, she'd kept the photographic record of her big day for a year after the divorce, but now it was time to do the nasty and final deed. Luke's call had only reinforced her original plan.

She opened the leather-bound cover and her heart nose-dived as she stared at the first picture.

There they were, the newly wedded couple, preserved for all eternity under slick plastic. The bride and groom. Luke with his athletic good looks, twinkling blue eyes, and near-brilliant smile, one arm looped around Abby, who was nearly a foot shorter than he, her untamed red-blond hair framing a small heart-shaped face, her smile genuine, her eyes shining with hope for the future.

"Save me," Abby muttered, yanking the picture from its encasement and tossing it into the fire. As she slowly sipped wine from her cup, her thumb ached, its throbbing measuring out her heartbeats. She watched the edges of the paper bake and turn brown before curling and snapping into flame. The smiling, happy couple was quickly consumed by fire, literally going up in smoke. "Until death do us part," she mocked. "Yeah, right."

She glanced down at the album again. The next picture was of the family. A group shot. She with her father and sister; he with both proud parents and his two, shorter, not-as-successful, nor-as-handsome, brothers, Adam and Lex. His sister, Anna, and her husband were also in the picture.

"No time for nostalgia," she said as Ansel trotted into the room and hopped onto the sofa. She tossed the picture onto the logs. Eager flames found the new dry fuel and the page quickly curled and burned.

Another sip of wine and the next picture, this one of Luke alone, standing tall and proud in his black tuxedo. He was good-looking; she'd give him that. Frowning, she realized she'd loved him once, but it seemed a lifetime ago. He'd been a newscaster in Seattle, his popularity on the rise. He'd come into her little studio for a new head shot.

The attraction had been immediate. He'd joked and she'd been irreverent, not impressed that he was somewhat of a local celebrity. It had been her feigned disinterest that had intrigued him.

Only later, six months after their initial meeting, after he'd proposed and she'd accepted, did she learn the reason he'd shown up at her photography studio. He'd gotten her name from a coworker, an assistant producer, her sister, Zoey. No one had mentioned that they'd been lovers. Oh no. That had slipped out later, nearly a month after the nuptials—the nuptials where Zoey had caught Abby's bouquet. Abby had first learned of their affair in the bedroom no less, when Luke had uttered the wrong name. Though both Luke and Zoey had sworn the affair was over long before the wedding, Abby had never trusted either of them about that particular bit of shared history.

"Isn't that just perfect," she said now to Ansel. He climbed onto the back of the little couch and settled onto the afghan her grandmother had made. Yawning, he showed his thin teeth, and Abby quickly stripped the rest of the photographs from their jackets. One by one, she tossed the pictures into the fire, watched them curl, smoke, and burn.

"Ashes to ashes, dust to dust," she muttered as the fire began to die. Finishing her wine, she silently vowed that tonight her life was going to change forever.

Little did she know how right-on her words would be.

He slipped between the boards of the broken fence and stared up at the edifice where it had all happened so long ago. A surge of power sizzled through his bloodstream as he stepped through the overgrown bushes. Moist spiderwebs pressed against his face. He inhaled the humid, dank scent of earth and decay.

Insects thrummed and chirped, causing the night to feel alive. The wan light from a descending moon washed over the landscape of broken bricks, dry, chipped fountains, and overgrown lawns.

Where once there had been lush, clipped hedges and clear ponds covered with water lilies, there now was only ruin and disrepair. The ornate red brick building with its gargoyles on the downspouts and windows was now crumbling and dark, a desiccated skeleton of a once-great lady.

He closed his eyes for a second, remembering the sights and smells of the hospital with its grand facade and filthy, wicked secrets. Prayers had been whispered, screams stifled, a place where God and Satan met.

Home.

Opening his eyes, he walked swiftly along a weed-choked path that was, no doubt, long forgotten.

But not by him.

Twenty years was a generation.

Twenty years was a lifetime.

Twenty years was a sentence.

And twenty years was long enough to forget.

Now, it was time to remember.

From his pocket he withdrew a ring of keys and quickly walked to a back service door. One key slid into the rusted old lock and turned. Easily. He stepped inside and, using a small penlight, illuminated his way. He was getting used to it again, had returned nearly two months earlier. It had taken that long to establish himself, to prepare.

Silently he crept through a hallway to a locked door leading to the basement, but he passed it and turned right, walking two steps up to the old kitchen with its rusting industrial sinks and massive, blackened and ruined stove. Over the cracked tiles, he made his way through a large dining hall and then into the old foyer at the base of the stairs where a grandfather clock had once ticked off the seconds of his life.

It was dark inside, his penlight giving off poor illumination, but in the past few weeks he'd reacquainted himself with the dark, musty corridors, the warped wooden floors, the cracked and boarded-over windows. Quickly he hurried up the stairs, his footsteps light, his breathing quick as he reached the landing where the old stained glass window was miraculously still intact. Shining his light on the colored glass for just a second, he felt a quiver of memory, and for the briefest of seconds imagined her dark silhouette backlit by the stained glass Madonna.

He couldn't linger. Had to keep moving. Swiftly, he turned and hurried up the final flight of stairs to the third floor.

To her room.

His throat closed and he felt a zing sizzle through his blood as quick shards of memory pierced his brain. He bit his lip as he remembered her lush auburn hair, those luminous golden eyes that would round so seductively when he surprised her, the slope of her cheeks and the curve of her neck that he so longed to kiss and bite.

He remembered her breasts, large and firm, as they stretched the blouses she wore, straining the buttons, offering glimpses of rapturous cleavage. She wore slacks sometimes, but she had a skirt, in a color that reminded him of ripe peaches. Even now he recalled how the hem danced around her taut, muscular calves, hitting just below her knees, as she climbed the stairs.

He felt himself harden at the thought of the curve of her legs, the sway of that gauzy fabric, the way she would look over her shoulder to see him watching her as she ascended the old staircase, the fingers of one hand trailing along the polished banister as the old clock *tick, tick, ticked* away his life.

His lust had been powerful then.

Pounding through his blood.

Thundering in his brain.

He'd never wanted any one thing the way he'd wanted Faith.

He felt it again, that powerful ache that started between his legs and crawled steadily up his body. Beads of sweat emerged on his forehead and shoulders. The crotch of his pants was suddenly uncomfortable and tight.

He pressed on, to the upper level, his heart racing.

Room 307 was in the middle of the hallway, poised high over the turn of the circular drive, an intimate little space where his life had changed forever.

Carefully and quietly, he unlocked the door. He slipped inside to stand in the very room where it had all happened.

Starlight filtered through the window, adding an eerie cast to the familiar room. The heat of the day settled deep into the old crumbling bricks of a building that, in its century-long lifetime, had been the stage for many uses. Some had been good, others had been inherently and undeniably evil.

Not that long ago...

Closing his eyes and concentrating, he conjured up the sounds that had echoed through the corridors, the rattle of carts, scrape of slippers, the desperate moans and cries of the tormented souls who had unwillingly inhabited Our Lady of Virtues Hospital. Those noises had been muted by the chant of prayers and echoing chimes of the clock.

But Faith had been here. Beautiful Faith. Frightened Faith. Trembling Faith.

Again his memories assailed him.

Sharp.

Precise.

Not dulled by the passage of two decades.

In intricate detail, he recalled the scent of her skin, the naughty playfulness of her smile, the sweet, dark rumble of her voice, and the sexy way she walked, her buttocks shifting beneath her clothes.

His jaw tightened. The ache within him heated his blood, stirring old desires, pounding at his temples.

He shouldn't have wanted her.

It had been a sin.

He shouldn't have kissed her.

It had been a sin.

He shouldn't have pulled her shirt down to expose her bare breasts.

It had been a sin.

He shouldn't have lain with her, his muscles soaked in sweat, her hands gripping his shoulders as she'd cried out in pleasure and pain.

It had been heaven.

And hell.

Now, his fists balled at the agony of it all. To have wanted her so badly, so achingly, to have tasted the salt upon her skin, to have buried himself deep into the moist heat of her and then to have all that sweet, sweet paradise wrenched away so violently, had been excruciating. His teeth gnashed to the point his jaw ached.

He walked across the room, his hands at his sides, the tips of his gloved fingers rubbing anxiously together. *Faith. Oh, Faith. You shall be avenged.*

Carefully, almost reverently, he ran his fingers along the swollen wood casing of the window and looked at the spot where her bed had been. He remembered how this small room had smelled faintly of lilacs and roses, how sunshine had streamed through the tall, arched window where gauzy curtains often fluttered in the warm Louisiana breeze.

Now, the small space was bare.

He ran his penlight over the rusted grooves where the metal castings of the bed had dug into the floor. Tiny brittle carcasses and droppings of dead insects littered the floor or were caught in ancient webs. Dust covered every surface and the paint around the windows and baseboards had peeled. The floral wallpaper had faded and begun to curl away from the walls, deep brown stains running from the ceiling and down the separating seams.

So much pain. So much fear. Still lingering. His lip curled as he sensed silent recriminations where vile acts had occurred between these four walls. So many wrongs had taken place here, so many evil deeds.

Anger, deep and dark, stole through his veins.

Finally, he could right all the wrongs.

Take his own revenge.

And it would happen.

Starting tonight.

CHAPTER 2

Abby pushed the speed limit. She was running late and trying to make up time as she drove into the city.

When the going gets tough, the tough get going.

Jacques Chastain's personal credo ran through her head as the windshield wipers scraped rain from the windshield of her Honda. She turned on her headlights to cut through the sheets of water and the darkness of the storm.

She had tried to adopt her father's attitude, just as Zoey had, but the truth of the matter was she'd just never been as strong as her father or older sister... Again, she was more like her mother, not only in looks but in temperament.

Now, however, as she eased onto the freeway toward New Orleans, she was stupidly listening to the radio and her ex-husband's show. She'd warned herself not to, but tuning into the program was a test for her. How much could she stomach, she wondered, and decided she could use a little of her father's toughness just about now.

True to his word, Luke had centered his call-in show on bitter ex-wives, women who, he contended, had never gotten over the despair and anger of their rejection. They were "losers" in the matrimonial game, females who were desperate to marry again but didn't have a snowball's chance in hell of doing so. Fat women. Ugly women. Type-A bitches who didn't know their place in the world.

Luke was obviously still pissed by their conversation the night of her birthday and was on a roll, really going for the jugular today. He didn't seem to care who he offended. Divorced women bashing was the mode of the day.

Seething, Abby itched to call in, to tell him how wrong he was, but deep down, he knew it. His "viewpoint" was all about gaining listeners, and both he and the radio station didn't care if his audience liked him, hated him, or was merely fascinated with his outrageous opinions.

It made her sick.

Yep, it sure as hell was time to get out of New Orleans. Way past time. She just had a little unfinished business in town and then she was outta here.

Her tires sang over the wet pavement. A flock of pelicans flew across the steel-colored clouds as the skyline of New Orleans became visible.

She was only listening to the program today to witness him make an ass of himself over the airwaves. Since he'd warned her in their phone conversation that he was going to rake her over the proverbial coals, she wanted to hear the program herself rather than have some friend phone her with the ugly play-by-play.

For the life of her, she couldn't figure out the appeal of his show, but supposedly his audience was growing by exponential numbers. Luke Gierman was a household name in New Orleans, his radio program soon to be syndicated, if the rumors she'd heard were true. Inwardly she groaned. She could now be humiliated not only at a local level, but nationally as well.

It was a sad commentary on the American public's taste.

You've tuned in, haven't you? She chastised herself. Since the divorce, she had studiously avoided listening to Luke the Liar. In the past year, she'd only heard his rants a few times while surfing through the stations.

"Yeah, my ex is a real piece of work," he was saying, the tone of his voice incredulous. "She makes Mata Hari look like the Virgin Mary."

More uproarious laughter.

"You're so funny, Luke," Abby growled, her fingers gripping

the wheel until her knuckles showed white. How could she have ever thought she loved the creep?

"She really took me to the cleaners in the divorce and then had the nerve to be bitter about it! What's up with that? I guess ninety-eight percent of the assets weren't enough."

"She wants your ass, too," his side-kick, Maury, chimed in.

She should sue the son of a bitch for slander, but he'd just make a circus of that as well, somehow get more publicity for himself, paint himself as a victim and, in the process, mortify her.

She glanced down at her purse and considered grabbing her cell phone, calling in and defending herself. She'd always been able to verbally handle him, and she wanted like hell to stand up for herself and every other divorced woman or man on the planet who had dealt with a cheating, lying spouse.

The wheels of her Honda slid a little as she took a corner a bit too fast. "Don't let him get to you." She was more angry with herself than anything else and yet Luke's voice, the one that had once whispered endearments, cracked funny jokes, even risen in heated political debates for the downtrodden, was now loud and crass.

"...you know," he was saying to the audience, "I think all divorced people go crazy for a while. And women are worse than men. Some of them, like my ex, become sociopaths or else extremely delusional. Paranoid."

Maury the Moron laughed.

"You won't believe what my ex did."

Here it comes. Her gut tightened. "She had the gall to get rid of everything I cared about. Guy stuff. Skis—Rossignols, no less, my golf clubs, a handcrafted surfboard from Hawaii ... and she gave them all to the Salvation Army."

"No!" Maury breathed into the mike. Abby pictured the short, balding guy throwing a hand over his heart in mock horror.

"Yep. And it worries me, you know?"

Yeah, right. Abby looked in her rearview mirror, saw a cop car, and felt her heart sink. She'd been so into the show, she hadn't known that she was speeding, but one glance at the speedometer told her that she was nearly ten miles over the limit. She slowed just as the cop hit his lights and siren. *Great.* Just her luck! She pulled into the right lane, searching for a place to pull over. The police car, colored lights flashing, siren wailing, screamed past.

She lucked out. Let out a long breath.

That's what you get for listening to Luke's stupid program!

She started to switch stations when Luke said, "Don't get me wrong. She's a beautiful woman. Sexy as hell. And smart. But sometimes I think she's got more than one screw loose."

"She married you, didn't she?" the co-host joked, all in good fun.

"Idiots," Abby muttered as she increased her speed.

Luke laughed. "Well, yeah, there's that, and her mother was certifiable, you know. No kidding."

"You cheap, sick bastard!" Abby was stunned. This was beyond low.

"Okay, how about this, and you listeners, call in and let me know if your ex has ever done anything this nuts. When I called my ex the other night to wish her happy birthday and tell her I was going to pick up the things I'd left there...guess what? That's when she told me she'd given it all away! Including my Rossignol skis...now she knew I was planning a ski trip this winter, so how's that for vindictive?"

"Ouch." Maury was in his element, adding a little punch. "Aren't you taking your girlfriend on that trip?"

"Of course."

"Isn't she about twenty years younger than your ex?"

"Fifteen."

"Double-ouch."

Abby's hands clenched on the wheel.

Luke continued, "So the deal was, we had an agreement that she would store some of my things, including the skis, until I got a bigger place since, in the divorce, she ended up with the house, the car, the studio, and just about everything else we ever owned."

"You lying son of a bitch," Abby said through gritted teeth. She'd paid him for his share of the house and studio and she had the title to *her* car, this little Honda, while he owned a Lexus SUV! Just about everything had been split right down the middle. She gnashed her teeth and fumed. If she had any brains, she'd turn off the radio or find a station with smooth jazz or some calming classical music.

"So, get this, my ex claims she gave everything she was keeping for me away, including a family heirloom, which just happens to be a handgun. She says she donated it all, lock, stock, and barrel so to speak, to a charity."

"A charity?" More mock horror on the moron's part.

What a crock!

"Like I'm supposed to believe that any charitable organization would take a gun. Of course it was a lie. But how safe does that make me feel? Knowing that my psychotic ex-wife is literally gunning for me with my father's sidearm, the weapon he was issued from the police department."

"You'd better change your address."

"Or start packin' my own heat," Luke said as Maury cackled uproariously.

Abby couldn't stand it another second. She scrounged in her purse, dug out her cell phone, flipped it open, and quickly dialed the station, the direct line to the radio show.

An even-toned female voice answered the call, "WSLJ. *Gierman's Groaners.*"

Abby caught herself just in time. Before she said a word, she snapped the flip phone closed. *Don't engage him. Do not let him know that you heard the show. Do* not *listen to that pathetic drivel he calls entertainment or social commentary. Otherwise he wins.*

Muttering under her breath, she turned off the radio in disgust, then realized she'd missed her exit off the freeway. She simmered all the way into the city, where she was scheduled for a consultation for a wedding. Having to backtrack made her nearly ten minutes late by the time she pulled into the driveway of a gracious two-hundred-year-old home in the Garden District. Painted a soft green, accented by black shutters, and surrounded by flowerbeds still ablaze with color, the house stood a full three stories amid its tended grounds.

As she was climbing out of her car, her cell phone rang and she looked at the luminous display. Another real estate company. Probably the twentieth who had contacted her since she'd placed her *For Sale by Owner* advertisement in the paper and hammered her sign into her yard two nights earlier.

She let the call go to voice mail, and turned off the phone. Then grabbing her portfolio from the backseat, she ducked her head against the warm rain and headed up the brick walkway to the front door to meet with the bride, groom, and no doubt the bride's mother.

How ironic, she thought, that she'd burned her own pictures while she carefully staged, planned, and snapped pictures of dozens of other newlyweds.

Who said God didn't have a sense of humor?

Where was he taking her?
Bound, blindfolded, and gagged, Mary LaBelle sent up prayer after prayer to God.

For help.

For freedom.

For salvation.

Tears rained from her eyes, soaking the cloth wrapped tightly over her head, and lower still onto the gag that had been thrust so violently into her mouth. She felt as if she might retch, her stomach heaved, but somehow she managed to force the urge back. She didn't want to drown in her own vomit.

It was dark. She couldn't see a thing. She sensed she was in a vehicle of some kind, a truck she guessed from the ride and sound of the engine. She hadn't seen it, but he'd managed to push her into a cramped backseat that was covered in plastic. The driver, the guy who had jumped her from behind as she'd been jogging on the trails of the All Saints campus, had appeared out of nowhere, leaping from behind a hedge running from the commons just as the rain had really started to pour. Anxious to return to her dorm, Mary hadn't seen him, had never caught so much as a glimpse of his face, just felt his weight as he'd tackled her from the back, thrown a bag over her head, and subdued her by twisting her arm upward and dropping her to her knees. She'd tried to scream, but he'd held a gun to her temple; she could still feel the cold round impression against her skin. She'd closed her mouth and accepted her fate.

God would save her.

He always did.

If not, then it was because He was calling her home. Her faith would sustain her... and yet as she listened to the tires hum against the pavement and splash through water, she sensed that she was doomed.

Please, Father, not yet. I'm young...I have so much to offer. So much of Your holy work to do.

She bit back sobs when she thought of her mother and father. She loved them both so much. She couldn't die tonight. No! She was a fighter and, though small, was athletic. She had been on the tennis team in high school and kept herself in shape. Hence the jogging.

But as the truck drove farther into the night, her hopes died. Where was this lunatic taking her? Why had he singled her out? Or had it been random? Had she just been in the wrong place at the wrong time? All her parents' warnings, all their suggestions about safety, she'd ignored them because she'd known God would take care of her. And now...now what?

She wasn't naive enough not to understand what he probably wanted, that he intended to rape and kill her. And she couldn't allow that. Wouldn't. Fighting tears and panic, she quietly struggled against the tape that bound her hands behind her back and held her ankles together. If she could only get free, she'd find a way to reach over the top of the front seat and wound him, maybe strangle him with the tape he'd used to subdue her.

But murder is a sin, Mary...remember. And if you try to harm him, he might lose control of the car. You, too, could be injured.

So what if they wrecked, she thought wildly. And if she killed a man in self-defense, surely God would understand. Please, Jesus, please.

Even risking injury and a collision was better than what he had planned.

Mary was certain of it.

But her bonds wouldn't move, not so much as shift a fraction of an inch, no matter how much pressure she put on them, how desperately she struggled.

Panic rose inside her.

She was running out of time. He wouldn't drive forever. She kept at it, straining against the rope and tape while the miles, the damning miles, rolled past beneath the wheels of this big truck. They were driving farther and farther away from Baton Rouge. Farther and farther away from any chance she would be saved.

Fear chilled her to the bone.

Her arms ached, her legs were cramped and useless.

Mama, I love you, and I'd wanted to make you proud by joining the order.

Daddy, forgive me for being stupid and letting this maniac grab me. You warned me to always take my cell and never run after dark. You gave me a weapon and I refused it... I'm sorry...

She felt the truck slow as he exited off a main road, probably a freeway, and so, he was, no doubt, getting closer to his ultimate destination. New terror surged through her and she frantically tried again to slide one hand from the grip of the duct tape. Her heart was knocking, sweat running down her body, fear sizzling down every nerve ending.

Free yourself, Mary. God helps those who help themselves!

"It's no use," he said, jolting her. He hadn't said a word since the attack. Not one. His voice was surprisingly calm. Steady. Creating a fear that cut straight to her heart. "You can't get away."

Again she thought she might throw up. Who was this madman? Why had he chosen her? His voice was unfamiliar, she thought, and yet she wasn't certain of anything anymore. She was barely staving off full-blown panic.

"Only a few more minutes."

Dear Father, no. Please stop this. Intervene on my behalf. If you want me with you, please let me come to you some other way, not by the hand of a sadist, not so cruelly, not by a madman.

Trembling, she thought of all the martyred saints, how horridly they'd died for their beliefs. She tried to steel herself, to find her faith. If this was a test, or truly God's will, then so be it. She would die stoically, putting all her faith in the Father.

Hail Mary, full of grace, the Lord is with thee...

She felt the truck slow, then turn quickly, as if maneuvering off a smooth road. The wheels began to jump and shimmy, as if going over stones or cracked pavement. She strained to hear over the grind of the engine, hoping for the sounds of traffic, for signs that they weren't as isolated and alone as she feared. But the familiar rush of passing cars, of shouts, or horns had disappeared, and any hope she had left sank like a stone.

Blessed art thou among women, and blessed is the fruit of thy womb, Jesus...

For what seemed like hours, but was probably less than five minutes, he continued to drive, and finally, at last, he braked hard and the big rig slammed to a stop. She slid forward, then back.

Her heart jammed into her throat. She began to quiver from the inside out. Terror slid through her veins.

Holy Mary, Mother of God, Pray for us sinners, now and at the hour of our death...

He cut the engine. Rain peppered the roof of the car. Mary could barely breathe. *Amen.*

A door clicked open and she felt the sticky heat of the night seeping into the interior as he climbed outside. She heard the squish of his boots or shoes into the mud. Heard a thunk—the front seat being pulled forward?

A second later she was dragged roughly out of the car.

Her running shoes sank into deep loam and she nearly fell over. The musky odor of the swamp assailed her and she thought of snakes and alligators, merciless predators who were nothing compared to the monster who had abducted her. She squirmed, trying to wrestle away.

"Stop moving!" he yelled and she felt a new fear. If he wasn't afraid of speaking so loudly or sharply, they were alone...totally alone. Oh, God, this was it! She was going to die here in the darkness, in what seemed like a bayou of sorts. "I'm cutting your feet free, but if you try to run..." Again he pressed the muzzle of steel against her temple. "...I'll kill you." She nearly peed in her jogging shorts. He was going to murder her anyway. She knew it. If she got the chance, she was going to run. Better to be shot in the back than raped for hours and brutalized in a dozen sickening ways. She had to get away. Had to. The minute he cut her feet free...

But he had anticipated her plan. In one swift motion, he cut away the tape on her ankles. Then he stood and sliced through the tape binding her wrists and quickly grabbed hold of her arm in a grip that was punishing and intense. Her shoulder sockets still hurt from her arms being twisted behind her back but this, his touch, was much, much worse. "Don't even think about it," he warned as if he sensed she was about to bolt, then applied such painful pressure to her arm that she squealed through the gag and dropped to her knees.

He yanked her up roughly. "Let's go." Prodding her with the cold muzzle of the gun and holding on to her arm with strong fingers, he forced her forward.

She heard the sound of frogs and crickets, sensed the soft dirt and leaves compact beneath her feet, felt the drizzle of warm rainwater run down the back of her neck and drip from the tip of her ponytail.

She thought she smelled a river nearby, but wasn't certain and broke down altogether, sobbing wretchedly as she nearly stumbled against something hard and unmoving. A tree? Rock? This was a bad dream, it had to be. A horrid nightmare.

And yet she was wide awake.

"Step up," he ordered against her ear and she obeyed, her feet catching a little as she climbed two steps, then heard him open a screen door. A key clicked in a lock. "Inside."

Oh, dear God, this was the spot where he intended to kill her.

Her throat closed as she smelled the dry, musty interior of this hidden place. She thought she heard the sound of frantic tiny claws, like rats scurrying for cover, and her skin prickled in newfound fear.

The screen door slapped behind her and she jumped.

She wanted to scream, to rail against him and God for abandoning her—like Jesus cried in agony upon the cross—as her kidnapper pushed and prodded her farther into a room that smelled unused, dirty, and forgotten. As if this cabin or whatever it was hadn't been used in years. Boards creaked under her feet. Her throat was so dry she couldn't call up any spit.

Dread inched up her spine as she heard him close the heavy door. He pushed her forward and she wondered if she'd fall off a ledge, be thrown into some dark hole, a deep exposed cellar, and be left here to die. Whimpering, barely holding on to her bladder, she stepped tenuously forward and then she heard it...a muffled noise, as if someone else were in the room.

She nearly passed out.

Dear God, he hadn't brought her to a place where other men were waiting, had he? Fear pounded a new, frantic tattoo in her heart. Her stomach curdled and yet she smelled something, some-*one* else.

A mixture of sweat, musk, and cold, stark terror trembled over her skin.

She'd heard of barbaric rites against women and braced herself for whatever sick fate awaited her.

"Okay, now, be a good girl," he whispered into the shell of her ear, his hot breath fanning the nape of her neck. "Do everything just as I say and I won't hurt you. You'll be safe."

She didn't believe him for an instant.

His silky words were a trap. A trick she wasn't going to fall for.

"Strip."

She froze. Thought she would be sick.

He pressed the gun to her chest and she thought for a minute of disobeying, but in the end, she did what he suggested. Knowing the gun was trained on her, she pulled off her T-shirt and slid out of her shorts. Shaking, she'd never felt more vulnerable in her life. Tears rained from her eyes. Fear clenched her gut. How many people, men, were watching her? How many were going to touch her? Her stomach retched and she thought she might pass out.

"That's good."

She froze in her jog bra and panties.

She didn't have to get completely naked?

"Now, put this on." She heard a zipper hiss downward and then she was handed something soft and silky—a dress? Fumbling, her fingers nearly useless, she hurriedly bunched the smooth fabric and found a way to step into it. She didn't know what it was, but it would cover her nakedness, and right now that was all that mattered. "Turn it around," he ordered and blindly she gathered and rotated the fabric, then pulled the bodice of the dress upward, over her waist and higher to cover her breasts. Awkwardly, she found the long sleeves and pushed her hands through. Then he was behind her and he held one of her arms again as he slowly pulled the zipper upward where it stopped near her shoulders. His breath was hot. Nasty. Nearly wet as it touched the nape of her neck.

Now…if she could just find a way to stop him. But that was impossible.

Slowly, still holding her with one hand, he trailed the barrel of the gun against her skin, so that the cold metal caressed her neck.

Goose pimples rose on her skin.

If she spun around quickly now, she might catch him unaware, be able to knock the weapon from his hand, rip off her blindfold, and run like crazy. She was fast. And with the adrenalin pumping through her bloodstream, she could run five or six miles without stopping to catch her breath.

"Uh, uh, uuuuh," he murmured so close that she felt his chest against her back, his erection, through the soft folds of the dress, pressed into the cleft of her rump.

Her chin wobbled. He was going to rape her…and probably the silent others in the room would have their turns with her, too.

Why? Oh, Father, why?

Run, Mary! Take a chance! So what if the gun goes off?

The arm holding her shoulder snaked around her waist, drawing her tight against him. "Now, Mary," he rasped and she nearly wilted when she realized he knew her name. She hadn't been a random target. He'd wanted *her* for whatever evil purpose he had planned. "Here's what you're going to do to save yourself. Are you listening?"

She nodded, hating herself. Hating him.

"You're going to take this gun and you're going to shoot it into a pillow."

What?

"That's right, I'm going to put it into your hand, but you're not going to turn around and kill me with it, okay? I won't let that happen. My hand will be over yours. Like this, see…" He pressed the gun into her shaking, sweating hand and curled her index finger over the trigger. His strong grip guided hers, and when she tried to turn it, he forced the hand forward.

"All you have to do is squeeze."

Her whole body trembled. This was insane. Crazy. She wasn't going to shoot blindly into the dark. For a second she wondered if this was some nutty college prank, the kind sororities and fraternities were famous for, but she didn't believe it. She hadn't pledged any house on campus and was going to drop out of All Saints College soon. Besides, this overriding sense of pure, malicious evil didn't have a drop of fun or jest in it.

It was no prank.

"Come on," he urged, his breath whispered out in excited little bursts. She heard it again, that muffled cry—laughter? Terror? Where was it? Nearby? Far away? Someone hiding in a closet, or watching her? One person? Two? A dozen?

So scared she physically shook, she knew that if it weren't for the steely fingers pressed intimately over hers, the weapon in her hand would have clattered to the floor.

If only this was a nightmare!

If only she would wake up in her dorm room!

"You've got five seconds."

No! Again the muffled noise.

"Five."

Please, Father help me.

"Four."

Do not abandon me, I beg of you.

"Three."

I am your humble servant.

"Two."

Have mercy on my soul!

"One."

He squeezed the trigger for her.

Bam! The gun blasted, jerked in her hand.

A muted squeal came from somewhere nearby.

She smelled cordite and burning material and something else . . . the stringent odor of urine?

Another tortured, strangled groan.

New terror crystalized.

Dear God, had she just shot another human being?

Please, please, no!

What was this? She started shrieking in terror behind her gag, struggling to get away, but the lunatic held her tighter, kept his hand over hers and quickly untied her blindfold.

She immediately retched, just as her abductor yanked the gag from her face.

In the glow of a single small lantern she witnessed what she'd done. A man who was vaguely familiar was seated in a chair, a thin pillow strapped around his torso. His hands were bound behind him, his ankles strapped to the metal legs of the chair. He was slumped forward, and beneath him, in an ever-widening pool, was the blood draining from his body. Feathers were still drifting toward the floor, like wispy snowflakes, slowly settling into the oozing reddish stain.

Mary lost the full contents of her stomach and she threw up on the floor and the front of the white dress he'd forced her to wear. She was crying, trembling as she watched the man die. His eyes glazed in the soft golden light, and Mary, tears tracking from her eyes, sobs erupting from her throat, was certain she saw his spirit leave his body.

Dear God, she'd murdered an innocent person, tied to the chair. She moved her gaze to focus on the small gun still clutched in her hand...her gun....the little pistol her father had given her for protection.

And with it she'd killed a man.

No, Mary. Not you. The monster who kidnapped you. Take the gun. It's still in your hand. Turn it on him. God would never punish you for taking his filthy, sin-filled life.

Just as the thought reached her, his grip on her hand tightened. "You killed him, Mary," he said almost endearingly, as if he wanted to caress her.

She shivered, started to protest, but felt the pressure in his grip increase. He yanked her backward so that her body was pressed to the hard wall of his chest, the back of her legs wedged against his thighs and shins, her rump nestled against his crotch, his erection bulging against her cleft again. Her heart hammered wildly. Sheer terror paralyzed her.

"Killing's a sin." His breath was hot and silky, the air filled with his depravity. "But you know that, don't you?"

She didn't respond, just felt the rain of her own tears against her cheeks. It didn't matter what she said. She was doomed. She knew it. There was no escape.

"You just sinned, Mary," he whispered seductively and she swallowed hard. Searched desperately in her soul for her inner strength. Knew what was coming.

Father, forgive me...

"And we all know the wages of sin is death..."

Slowly he rotated her hand in his, then pushed the muzzle of her own pistol to her temple.

CHAPTER 3

"Three o'clock would work out," Abby said, cradling her cell phone between her shoulder and ear. Two days after she'd listened to Luke on the radio and made a pitch for the Nolan-Smythe nuptials, Abby was carrying a sack of groceries in one arm and her portfolio in the other. She'd spent most of the day before and the early hours of this morning at her studio in town, going through her bills and consulting with some college seniors for their graduation pictures, before stopping at the store, then racing back home.

She dropped the sack onto the kitchen counter where Ansel was seated by the window, his tail switching as he watched birds flutter near the feeder hanging from the eave. "Shoo," she whispered as the woman on the other end of the line made arrangements to view her house.

Her FOR SALE BY OWNER sign had been up less than seventy-two hours and she'd already received several calls from potential buyers, this being the first who actually wanted to "view the property," after hearing the price and details.

As Ansel stretched on the counter and patently ignored her command to hop onto the floor, Abby walked into the living room, where she placed her portfolio onto a gate-legged table.

"What was your name again? And your number?" she asked as she hurried back to the kitchen, retrieved a pen from her purse, and began scribbling the pertinent information onto a note pad she kept near the phone. "Okay, see you at three."

Abby hung up and glanced at her watch. The potential buyer would be here in less than four hours.

Not that the place was in too bad a shape. Unless you spied the film of gray cat hair that clumped everywhere and collected in the corners. Despite her best efforts with the vacuum, she could barely keep ahead of the fur as Ansel was in full shed mode. "Maybe what I need is an electric razor for you rather than a vacuum cleaner for the house, hmmm?" She plucked the heavy cat from his perch near the windowsill and held him close to her for a second. Petting his soft fur, she whispered into his ear, "I love you anyway. Even though you and I both know that you can be a real pain in the backside when you want to be." He rubbed the top of his head against the underside of her chin and purred so loudly that she felt vibrations from his body to hers.

It felt right to just spend a second saying stupid things to the cat.

The last two days had been so hectic, she hadn't had a chance to catch her breath. She'd gone from sitting to sitting and fortunately hadn't had time to stew about Luke or his public annihilation of her character.

Abby had decided not to let Luke's diatribe over the airwaves get to her.

"It's just not worth it." She kissed the cat between his ears then set him on the floor and checked his water dish. Still half-full. He trotted to the back door, circled, and cried until she opened it. Darting outside, Ansel made straight for the tree near the bird feeder where chickadees and nuthatches fluttered. The warmth of October, caught on a gentle breeze fragrant with the earthy smell of the swamp, swept inside.

Abby stepped onto the porch. Sunlight was struggling to peek through a wash of gray clouds. For a second she thought she saw the pale arc of a rainbow, but as quickly as the image appeared, it faded.

"Wishful thinking," she told herself and closed the door behind her as she walked inside. Glancing around, she realized she'd have to spruce things up before the showing.

In her bedroom Abby peeled off her slacks and blouse, then

yanked on her "cleaning clothes," a favorite pair of tattered jeans and a T-shirt that showed off not only old coffee stains, but bleach spatters as well. After snapping her unruly hair into a ponytail, she went to work, polishing tables, cleaning windows, scrubbing counters, and washing the old plank floors.

Turning on the television for background noise, she listened to warnings about a tropical storm forming in the Atlantic, one poised to enter the gulf within days. After much meteorological speculation, there was a break for a commercial, and when the news resumed, Abby, swabbing a windowsill, heard a phrase that always caused her heart to freeze.

"*Our Lady of Virtues...*"

Abby's head snapped up. She turned her attention to the little set balanced on a bookcase shelf. On the screen, a willowy reporter with perfect makeup and short dark hair stood in front of the grounds of the old hospital where Faith Chastain's life had ended.

"...the hospital has been a landmark in the area for nearly a hundred years," the twenty-something reporter was saying as wind feathered her hair. "This building behind me has gone through several different incarnations in its long, and sometimes scandal-riddled, history."

Oh, God, they weren't going to bring up her mother's death again, were they?

Abby felt every muscle in her body tense, as if waiting for a blow.

"Originally built as an orphanage, the main building was converted to a full-fledged hospital after World War Two, and has been, from its inception, run by an order of Catholic nuns." The camera panned away from the reporter to capture the full view of the once-stately building.

Abby's heart clutched as she looked at the hospital where a wide concrete drive, now buckled and weed-choked, had cut through once-tended lawns to curve around the fountain. Long ago Abby had sat on the edge of the pool and watched koi darting beneath thick lily pads as sunlight had spangled the water and the spray from the fountain had kissed her skin. She'd been able, from that vantage point, to look up to her mother's room situated on the third floor behind the tall, arched window.

Abby swallowed hard. How many hours had she spent by the fountain? Now the pond was dry and cracked, the sculptured angels streaked with a green, slimy moss that seemed to track from their eyes like tears.

"Most recently Our Lady of Virtues was used as a hospital for the mentally ill, and though it was privately owned, it, too, suffered when federal funds dried up. Amid allegations of abuse and the apparent suicide of one patient, the facility closed nearly eighteen years ago..."

Abby's throat tightened. She dropped the sponge and watched the news bite that seemed surreal.

Above the television, mounted on the shelves near the fireplace, was an eight-by-ten picture of her mother, smiling, dark auburn hair pulled away from a beautiful face, no trace of the tortured soul who had hidden behind those wide, amber-colored eyes.

Swallowing hard, Abby walked to the bookcase and took the picture from its resting place. A deep sadness swept through her and she felt a stab of longing to once again see her mother's frail smile, feel her cool hands holding Abby's, smell the gentle, clean scent of her perfume.

"...scheduled for demolition, sometime next year if all goes as planned."

Abby's head swiveled back to the television screen. They were tearing the old hospital down?

A schematic drawing of a two-story building, very similar in appearance to the old one, but newer, brighter, with more modern touches, flashed onto the screen. Gone were the beveled glass windows, gargoyles on the downspouts, and wide, covered flagstone verandahs. The brick would become stucco, the windows wider, the fountain of angels replaced by a metal-and-stone "water feature."

The screen returned to the newsroom, where the anchor, Mel Isely, sat behind a wide curving desk. In the corner of the screen was an insert of the reporter on the hospital grounds. She was still speaking.

"The plan is that this facility will become a graduated elder care home, starting with assisted-living apartments and including a full-care facility."

"Thanks, Daria," the anchor said as the inset of the reporter disappeared and all cameras were focused again on the news desk and Isely, a man Abby had met a few times while she'd still been married to Luke. A smarmy suck-up, she'd thought at the time. He was good-looking, but a little too *GQ*-esque to suit Abby's taste in men. "Coming up...sports," Isely was saying, while smiling broadly into the camera. She thought he might even wink. She recalled one Christmas charity event when, after a few too many drinks, he'd actually made a pass at her. Now, he picked up the papers on his desk and said, "After the break, we'll be back with news about the Saints!"

"Save me." Abby switched off the set and Mel's face with its startling blue eyes ringed in thick lashes disappeared.

She let out her breath and considered the news report.

So what if the facility where her mother had died was scheduled to be razed? So what if a new building would replace the old? That was progress, right?

Leaving her mother's picture on the shelf, she walked into the kitchen and opened the refrigerator. No bottled water. "Oh, hell." She grabbed a glass from the cupboard, then turned on the tap and listened as the old pipes groaned in protest. Resting a hip against the counter, she filled the glass and thought of all the reasons she'd agreed to return to Louisiana in the first place.

She hadn't been keen on moving back here.

In fact, she'd thought Seattle—with its vibrant waterfront, cooler climate, rugged snow-capped mountains within driving distance, rough-and-tumble history, and most importantly, the over two thousand miles of distance from there to Louisiana—had been a perfect place to settle down.

Well...aside from Zoey and that nasty little indiscretion with Luke. She took a long swallow from her glass.

Be fair, Abby, her conscience argued, *Luke's involvement with Zoey hadn't been a little indiscretion, it had been a full-blown, heart-wrenching, mortifying affair!*

"Bastard," she growled, then drained the glass and shoved it into the dishwasher.

She should have divorced Luke when she'd learned he'd cheated during their engagement, but oh, no, she'd been stupid enough to give the marriage another chance. He'd sworn to change his ways if she'd just move with him to New Orleans.

She'd been dubious of the marriage being able to resurrect again, of course, but the temptation for a new start had been hard to resist, and at that point, she'd been foolish enough to think that she still loved her husband.

"Idiot," she muttered under her breath, returning to the living room and the dust rag sitting on the windowsill. There had been other reasons for moving to New Orleans, or the area surrounding it. Hadn't she always promised herself that she'd return to the place where her life had changed forever when Faith Chastain had fallen to her death? Hadn't Abby decided that the only way to put the ghosts of the past to rest was to visit the hospital, take pictures of it, reexamine that night that was so fragmented in her mind?

"Oh, Mama," she said, once again picking up the framed head shot and staring into eyes so like her own. She glanced at the fireplace where, only a few nights earlier, she'd burned the photos of her marriage. Black curled ashes still clung to the grate.

Her cell phone rang. She could hear it singing inside her purse, which sat in the dining room next to her portfolio. She hurried to the purse, snatched up the slim phone, and flipped it open. "Hello?"

"Hi, Abby, this is Maury," the caller said. Abby's heart sank. "Maury Taylor. You remember. I work with Luke."

"Of course I remember you." Her voice grew cool. Maury the Moron.

"Look, I don't suppose you've heard from Luke, have you?"

"No," she said slowly, sensing a trap. Maybe this was one of her ex-husband's pranks. He was known for setting people up while he was on the air, then letting the whole listening world laugh at the victim's expense. Even if the show wasn't airing at the moment, he would tape his victim's responses and replay them over and over again when the show was broadcasting. Her stomach tightened.

"You're sure?"

"Of course I'm sure. Why would I hear from him?"

"I don't know." There was an edge to Maury's voice. Worry? Panic? "He, uh, he didn't show up at the station yesterday. Missed the program completely. We had to air an old program we had on tape from last summer."

She wasn't buying it and really didn't care. She was finished with Luke Gierman. "So why do you think I'd know where he was?"

"I don't know. I thought you might have heard the show we aired earlier this week, the one on ex-spouses."

She didn't respond, but felt heat climb steadily up her neck. *Bastard,* she thought, imagining Luke at the microphone, spewing his lies. Her fingers clenched over the phone.

"He, uh, well, you probably already heard, he really ripped you up one side and down the other."

"And that would make me want to talk to him?" she mocked, somehow managing to hold her temper in check. She still wasn't convinced this wasn't a setup. "What a charmer. I have no idea where he is. Good-bye."

"No, look! Abby," he said anxiously, as if afraid she would hang up on him. "I'm sorry. The program was...over the top, I know, but that's what his audience likes, what they connect to."

"So?"

"So...after that program, Luke disappeared. He didn't show up at his health club and you know he always works out after the show."

She remembered. Didn't comment about Luke's obsession with staying in shape. It wasn't just about looking or feeling good, it was some kind of rabid mania.

"No one has heard from him. I went over to his town house, but no one answered the door. I've called his home phone and his cell and he's not answering."

"He'll surface," she said, refusing to be sucked into Luke's antics.

"But—"

"I haven't seen him. Okay? And as he so publicly made certain of, I'm not his wife anymore." She was angry now, and her tongue wanted to go wild. "I don't keep tabs on him. Why don't you talk to his girlfriend?"

"Nia...yeah...Luke and Nia..."

When he trailed off, she asked impatiently, "What?"

"Nia doesn't know where he is."

She could tell he'd been going to say something else. Whatever it was, she didn't care. "Maybe she does and she's not saying."

"This isn't like him." Maury sounded worried. Really worried.

Good. Let him stew about Luke's whereabouts. To her surprise,

Abby didn't care about Luke's shenanigans or his love life at all. And she wasn't worried about him. Luke was known to pull all kinds of publicity stunts. He was just the kind of guy to fake his own death to give the ratings a shot in the arm. "I haven't seen Luke since last weekend when he picked up Hershey, the dog we share custody of. Sorry, I can't help you. And he'd better be taking care of my dog."

"Okay, okay, but if you do hear from him, have him call the station immediately. The producer's ready to tear Luke a new one."

"Oh, great." Just what she needed to hear. She hung up and refused to consider what Luke was up to. It didn't matter anymore. They were divorced. Period.

And his things were out of the garage.

Still, she walked into the bedroom and opened the second drawer of her nightstand, on what had once been Luke's side of the bed.

There, as it had been for years, was his father's service revolver. Picking up the .38, she felt a pang of guilt for having lied to her ex about the weapon, but her remorse was short-lived.

For now, she was keeping the gun.

"Okay . . . so what have we got here?" Detective Reuben Montoya, in jeans, T-shirt, and a black leather jacket, stepped carefully toward the door of the small, dilapidated cabin in the bayou. Morning sunlight was crawling through the trees and brush, burning off the last of the night fog. The smell of the swamp was thick in his nostrils: slow-moving water, rotting vegetation, and something else, a stench he recognized as that of decaying flesh. His stomach turned a bit but he contained it. For the most part he'd always been able to button down his emotions, work the scene, and not lose his lunch.

"It looks like a murder-suicide," the deputy, Don Spencer, theorized. He was short, with pale blue eyes and reddish hair buzzed into a military cut. "But not everything adds up. We're still figuring it out. Crime-scene team's been at it for an hour."

Montoya nodded and looked around. Several officers had already roped off the crime scene with yellow tape and were positioned around the perimeter of the little cabin stuck in the middle of no-damned-where. "You the first on the scene?" Montoya asked as he signed the security log.

"Yep. Got the call into dispatch from a local—a fisherman who admits to trespassing. He was on his way to the river, noticed the door hanging open, and walked in."

"He still here?"

The officer nodded. "In his truck, over there." Spencer hitched his chin in the direction of an old, battered Dodge that had once been red, but had faded after years of abuse by the hot Louisiana sun. In the bed was a small canoe and fishing gear. Montoya glanced at the cab of the truck, noticed the black man seated inside. "His name is Ray Watson. Lives about six miles upriver. No record."

"Is he the only witness?"

"So far."

"Have him stick around. I'll want to ask him some questions."

"You got it."

Hankering for a smoke, Montoya slipped on covers for his shoes, and made his way toward the house, careful not to disturb an investigator snapping pictures of the overgrown path to the door. Weeds had been crushed, leaves pulverized, and it was evident that several sets of footprints led to the steps.

Montoya made his way through the open door and stopped dead in his tracks.

"What the hell is this?" he said, looking at the crime scene and feeling his stomach clench.

Harsh lights illuminated the small room where blood, feathers, vomit, and dirt vied for floor space. The air was punctuated with the smells of cordite, blood, puke, urine, and dust. Investigators were filming and measuring, lifting latent fingerprints, and searching for trace evidence.

In the center of it all was the crime scene where two victims had died. One of the victims, a white man in good shape, who looked to be in his early forties, was lying naked as the day he was born and staring faceup. Blood had trickled from the hole in his chest, but not as much blood as Montoya would have expected. The man had died quickly.

"Jesus," Montoya muttered.

The second victim, a young woman wearing a white silk and lace wedding gown, was lying atop the dead guy. She appeared to have fallen over him from what looked like a single gunshot wound to her head. Her long ponytail was splayed across her bare back where the neckline of the dress scooped low. Some of the blond strands were bloody and tangled from the wound at her temple.

A photographer clipped off shot after shot, his flash strobing the already macabre scene while Bonita Washington, the lead crime-scene investigator, was busily taking measurements around the bodies. Her black hair was pulled into a tight bun at the base of her skull, her eyes trained on the floor as she squatted near the vics.

"You sign the log, Montoya?" she asked. Wearing half-glasses and a sour expression, she looked up from the sketch she was drawing. She skewered him with a don't-mess-with-me look. African-American and proud of it, Bonita ran the criminologists team with an iron fist and a keen eye.

"What do you think?"

"Just checkin'. No one gets in here without signin' my security log. I need to know everyone who comes in here and keep a record of it." One dark eyebrow arched, and above her rimless glasses, her intense brown eyes didn't so much as flinch as she stared at him. "You have been known to bend more than your share of rules." She was absolutely not taking one ounce of crap today.

"I signed in. Okay?"

"Good. Where's Bentz?"

"On vacation with his wife. Vegas." Rick Bentz was Montoya's partner. Had been for years, ever since Bentz had moved from L.A. and Montoya had been a junior detective. The only time they'd not worked together was a few months when Montoya had taken a leave of absence from New Orleans to work a case in Savannah. A sour taste filled the back of his throat as he thought of those painful weeks, but he pushed any memory aside and concentrated on the here and now. And it was bad. "Bentz will be back in a few days," he said, rubbing the goatee that covered his chin. He flashed Washington a grin. "For now, you get to deal with me."

"How could I be so lucky?" she said with the slightest trace of humor, then, her expression turning stern again, pointed at the two bodies with the eraser end of her pencil. "Careful where you step, what you touch. We're still collecting fingerprints and trace."

Montoya shot her a look as he pulled a notepad from the back pocket of his pants. "I've been at dozens of scenes, Washington."

"Okay." She was still frowning, but gave him a quick nod as she slipped into a more companionable mode. "I did the preliminary walk-through. Everything appears to have happened in this room. From the blood splatter and body position, it looks like both vics were killed right here." She jabbed a gloved finger at the floor of the cabin. She was obviously convinced of where the crime had happened, but her brow was still furrowed, her frown intense. "But it's been staged."

"Staged?"

"Um-hmm. What we have here is either a murder-suicide or a double murder. Haven't figured that out yet. But I will."

He didn't doubt it.

"I think the man was tied to that chair over there." She indicated an old metal and plastic dinette chair that had been shoved into a corner of the room. "Traces of blood on it, and you can see that it was dragged through the dust...footprints beside the tracks. Shoes. Our boy here"—she motioned toward the dead man staring sightlessly upward, his eyes glazed, his face bloated—"isn't wearing any. And we can't find a pair. They're too big for the girl, so I'm thinkin' we've got a third party. A big man from the footprints around. We'll just call him Size Twelve."

"The killer."

"Yeah, the male vic is a size nine and a half, maybe a ten. This whole scene appears staged to me, but not done well enough that we wouldn't figure it out immediately. As I said, either the killer's an idiot, or he wants us to know that he's behind it; he's just showing off." Her eyes narrowed as she looked at Montoya over the tops of her half-glasses. "There is gunshot residue on the female vic's hands, and a little blood, but this whole place feels off."

"Who threw up?"

"Her, by the looks of her clothes."

"A wedding dress? She was a bride?"

"Don't know. Don't think so...over there in the pile? Running shorts and T-shirt. She changed. Or was changed. Premortem, the blood spatter is all over the wedding dress."

"Why would she change?"

"Beats me." Dark lines creased her forehead and she tapped her pencil to her lips as she thought. "But whoever our killer is, he wants us to notice that the guy is stripped bare, naked to the world, and the girl is on her way to her own wedding . . . or something like that. Go figure . . ."

Montoya didn't like what she was suggesting. He stared at the man lying faceup, the woman's body draped over his. Something about him . . .

"You recognize the male vic?" she asked, again pointing with her pencil at the dead man with the thinning brown hair.

"Should I?"

"Luke Gierman. Local celebrity of sorts. Shock jock."

"Gierman's Groaners," Montoya said, remembering the controversial radio personality. He'd never met Gierman but had seen his photo in the newspapers a few times.

"ID was on him. Cash and credit cards undisturbed, or so it seems. He had two hundred and six dollars on him and a receipt from an ATM from First Congressional Bank on Decatur Street for two hundred dated the night before last at 6:36 P.M."

"He could have been abducted about that time." He decided to review the cameras at the bank.

"Maybe. As for her . . ." She pointed a finger at the dead woman lying atop Gierman. "Courtney LaBelle, according to the student identification card in her wallet. She wasn't carrying a purse, just one of those slim card holders she'd stuffed into a small pocket of her running shorts. No credit card and only five bucks with her. But she did have a driver's license that indicates she's from the city, address is in the Garden District." She clucked her tongue sadly and shook her head. "Eighteen years old." The edge of Washington's jaw hardened. "The ME took a preliminary look, thinks from the lividity, flaccid stage of rigor, and body temperature, the TOD was the night before last, probably between ten P.M. and three A.M. He can't get any closer than that."

"Not long after Gierman's ATM transaction."

"Yep."

"Did she know Gierman?" Montoya said, glancing at the corpse of the girl. Her skin was waxy, her face bloated, but he guessed she had been beautiful just a few days earlier.

"That's what you need to find out. Gierman allegedly had a thing for younger girls and she would definitely qualify."

Montoya was already taking notes. Bonita Washington bugged the hell out of him sometimes, but she was good at her job. Damned good. Making it hard to argue with her, harder still to rib. "We got the weapon?"

"Yep. Bagged and tagged. Twenty-two pistol. Found in the female victim's hand."

He took in the floor again. Feathers, dust, mud, and blood covered the old planks. "What's with the feathers?"

"A pillow. Probably strapped to Gierman. Maybe to mute the sound, I don't know, but it was left by the chair." She pointed and Montoya examined the flaccid bag of an old stained pillowcase. A hole was blown in its center, the faded fabric and feathers within singed and darkened with blood. "Shot at close range."

Montoya stared at the bodies, tried to imagine their places before death and how they ended up almost in a lover's embrace.

"As I said, I'm guessing from the marks on Gierman's legs and arms, that he was bound, maybe his ankles tied to the legs of the chair that would match the bruising on his body. Though it's missing now, I think there had been tape over his mouth. There are still traces of some adherent on his face."

Montoya looked closer, noticed the flecks of grayish matter sticking to Gierman's whiskers and cheeks. A rectangular red mark was visible against his pale skin and even his lips were raw looking, as if the tape had stuck to them before being roughly ripped away.

"They aren't married?"

"He's single. Divorced, I think. And I don't know about her, but she's got a hell of a scrape on her left ring finger. Looks like a ring was pulled off and took a lot of skin and flesh with it."

"Jesus," Montoya muttered, spying the girl's bruised and raw finger.

"I guess the 'I do's' didn't go easily," Washington muttered, a sick joke to lighten the scene.

Montoya had seen more than his share of bizarre killings since

joining the force, but this was right up there with the best of them.
He straightened. "Do you think this was some kind of mock wedding...that our killer was the preacher and the ring was forced on,
then yanked off...did we find it?"

"No jewelry other than the necklace still on the vic." She pointed
at the intricate gold chain with its small cross of what appeared to
be diamonds.

"No shoes?" he asked, noting the dead woman's bare feet.

"Just the running shoes for both of them. For what it's worth, it
looks like they were each either on their way to or from a workout.
Both were originally dressed in shorts, T-shirts, running shoes, but
he"—she jabbed her pencil at the dead man—"ends up stark naked
and she"—Washington indicated the dead woman—"is wearing a
wedding dress. No shoes, hose, no veil, and no ring...Bizarre as
hell if you ask me."

"Won't argue that."

Washington held her notepad to her chest and tapped the eraser
end of her pencil against her mouth as she stared down at Gierman.
"You know, this guy pissed off a lot of people. A lot. Church
groups. Parent groups. He even had the FCC on his ass. For all his
popularity, he was hated as well." Her lips folded in on themselves.
"To say he wasn't PC would be a gross understatement."

"You didn't like him."

"I'd be in that category, yes, but"—she turned her gaze to the
girl—"who would hate him so much as to want him dead?"

"Courtney LaBelle?" Montoya offered.

"Nah. Don't think so. Why would a college student bring him
here, hold him hostage, it looks like, then off both him and herself?"

"Sex games?" Montoya asked, stating the obvious.

"He's naked, but she isn't. He was tied to the chair, I think, in
the submissive position." Brown eyes looked at him again. "And
the white bridal dress isn't the usual dominatrix attire."

Montoya asked, "How would you know?"

"Hey, Montoya, there are a lot of things about me that you don't
know. Dog collars, whips, lace-up gloves are only part of 'em." She
flashed him a smile suggesting she was joking, then double-checked
her drawing, her expression turning professional again. "I'm still

banking on Mr. Size Twelve, but we'll know more when we finish processing the scene."

"Good."

"So I suggest you find out everything you can about our victims."

That went without saying, but rather than pick a fight with her, he asked, "What about the rest of the house?"

"Looks undisturbed, but we're checking every room, including the attic."

"The lock on the door?"

"Old and rusted. Broken. The fingerprint and tool guys are going over it."

"Anyone know who owns this place?"

She shot him another don't-mess-with-me look over the tops of her half-glasses. "Someone does, but it's not me. Another thing you'd better check out." She began drawing again and careful to disturb nothing, he took one last look at the victims in their macabre position dead center in the middle of the small room before checking his watch, logging out, and walking outside. Though the morning air was still thick and sticky, it felt crisp compared to the stagnant, foul atmosphere inside the cabin. Picking his way around an investigator making casts of tire tracks and footprints, he headed to the old red pickup.

A barrel-chested black man was seated on the driver's side, his radio turned on, his thick fingers tapping against the steering wheel in an impatient rhythm.

"Ray Watson?" Montoya asked and flipped his ID in front of the open driver's window. He cast a glance at the back of the truck. Beside the canoe was a fishing creel and a few poles, tackle box, oars, safety vest, and bucket of bait. Everything was strapped down as the tailgate of the truck was open to accommodate the length of the canoe.

"That's me." Watson was around fifty. He had a flat face with dark skin, wide-set eyes, and teeth that, when he talked, showed off a bit of gold. A tattered Saints cap was pulled low over nappy salt-and-pepper hair. Wearing big overalls over a T-shirt, he seemed agitated and tired. On the seat next to him were a pair of hip waders, a flashlight, and a tin of chewing tobacco.

"Mr. Watson, can you tell me what you found? How it happened?"

"You saw for yourself," Watson said, his big eyes rounding. "I didn't touch nothin'. That place"—he pointed past the bug-splattered windshield toward the house—"is just like when I first opened the door. I came up here fishin' like always, but this time, somethin' looked different about the place. Just kinda...I dunno...not right. I checked, noticed the door open, and stepped inside. That's when I saw them, the dead people." He shook his head. "I couldn't believe it. I mean the guy's naked as a jay bird and the woman's dressed up as if she's goin' to her own damned wedding." He glanced away from the cabin and straight into Montoya's eyes. "I took one look, saw that they were dead, then I came back to my car and used the wife's cell phone to dial 911."

"Do you know either of the victims?"

"No, sir," he said emphatically and shook his head.

"What time was that?"

"About an hour and a half earlier," he said, checking his watch. "Five A.M. So I can start fishing at dawn. I come early before breakfast. It was still dark when I passed by the house, but I shined my flashlight on it, like I always do, and as I said, somethin' looked strange, gave me a weird feelin', you know? Can't really explain it, but I come up here quite a bit and I could tell things weren't right. Thought I'd better check it out."

"So that's when you went in?"

"That's right." Watson's nose wrinkled as if remembering the rank odor. "Never seen nothin' like that before. No sir, nothing like that at all."

"You know who owns this place?"

"Not anymore. It used to belong to a guy named Bud Oxbow, a fella I used to fish with."

"Where's Oxbow now?"

"Retired from the Mobile post office and moved up north, somewhere around Chicago, I think, five or six years ago. He never lived here, just came out fishin' once in a while and hung out at Lottie's Diner, that's where we first got to talkin'. Had a place in Mobile where he worked." Watson scratched his chin. "I think he told me he inherited this place from an uncle, but I can't really say."

Montoya ran Watson through it one more time and Watson recounted his discovery without adding anything new. He agreed that he'd be available for further questioning and would call the station if he thought of anything else that might help.

Montoya released the witness, patting the fender twice as Watson flipped on the ignition and backed down the leaf-strewn drive. The sun was climbing higher in the sky, the surrounding woods already warm, but he saw dark clouds on the horizon. After a few more minutes of talking with several of the investigators, Montoya decided he'd found out all he could here. He slid into his car and started back to the city.

It was going to be a helluva day. Two dead bodies and it wasn't yet noon.

CHAPTER 4

"Only half a mile more," Abby promised herself as she ran along the side of the road, her heart pounding, her calves beginning to protest, the bottoms of her shoes slapping the asphalt. Sweat ran into her eyes, and though the weather had changed quickly, sunlight chased away by burgeoning, purple clouds, she'd decided to chance the jog. It had been three weeks since the last time and her muscles weren't used to the punishment. She set her jaw and kept at it.

While she'd lived in Seattle, she'd run at least three times a week, but in New Orleans with the humidity in the stratosphere, the heat oppressive, and the road on which she lived narrow enough that two cars could barely pass without one set of tires touching the shoulder, she'd found more than enough excuses to let her exercise routine slip.

No more.

Her birthday had been a milestone and propelled her into getting into a regimen again. Whether she lived here or with Alicia in the Bay Area, she wasn't going to let her body slide out of shape. Too bad that right now her lungs burned and she'd developed a stitch in her side. She pushed the pain out of her mind and kept jogging until she reached the Pomeroys' mailbox, the three-mile mark.

Slowing as she passed the massive gates, she barely cast a look through the expensive wrought-iron-and-brick barricade that shuttered Asa Pomeroy, a local multimillionaire, from the curious. Married to his fourth wife and secluded in an antebellum home reminiscent of Tara in *Gone with the Wind*, he opened his estate to the public twice a year, once at Christmas, the other time on Fat Tuesday. Otherwise, even though she was a neighbor, she'd not been inside.

She and Vanessa Pomeroy didn't run in the same social circles.

She heard a low growl and glanced at the fence. The Pomeroys' Rottweiler paced on the other side of the grillwork. He was a huge animal, with a head as broad as a bear's. From the other side of the fence he barked madly, loud enough to raise the dead from here to the city.

Give me a break, Abby thought. Breathing hard, sweating so much that her hair was wet and damp tendrils escaped her ponytail to curl around her face, she walked briskly toward her own place around a curve about a quarter of a mile down the road. Her pink T-shirt was plastered to her body; even her shorts were damp with her perspiration. She tugged at the hem of the shirt and leaned over, dabbed at her face with the faded T's hem, but as soon as she swiped away the droplets, more appeared.

She gave up and, at her own driveway, she leaned against the FOR SALE BY OWNER sign, stretching her calves and the backs of her thighs. Despite the pain, she felt good, as if she'd actually done something positive for herself.

Maury's call about Luke had put her on edge. What the hell was her damned ex up to? "None of your business," she said aloud, her hands on the back of her hips as she curved her spine slowly forward, then back, feeling all her muscles stretch and relax.

She'd spent the morning doing more housecleaning, fielding calls about viewing the cottage, and had sneaked in the three-mile jog before she met with her first clients in the studio at one-thirty. After that, she had two more photography sessions and two more showings of the house. One couple had already seen it the night before and wanted a second look. The second potential buyer was a single man.

Good news.

She grabbed the newspaper from her box as Ansel, a mouse in his mouth, slunk around the corner. "Oh, geez, what have you got?" she asked, seeing that the little rodent was still alive and squirming, its beady eyes fixed in fright. "Oh, Ansel," Abby whispered, not wanting to deal with the field mouse alive or dead. "Let him go. Now! And don't catch him again or bring him back to me without a head! Ansel!" The cat started to dart away as she heard the sound of a car's engine. She turned just as a police cruiser pulled into the driveway. Her heart nose-dived. What was it her father used to say? The police only stop for two reasons, neither one good.

Either someone is dead.

Or you're about to be arrested.

The spit dried in her mouth.

From the corner of her eye, she saw the mouse somehow wiggle free and scamper quickly through the underbrush, Ansel in hot pursuit. Abby barely noticed. She was focused on the police car and the man who was climbing out.

He was five-ten or -eleven with an athletic build, jet-black hair, and chiseled features that suggested a bit of Native American tossed into his Latino gene pool. A trimmed goatee surrounded his mouth, and in one ear, a gold ring winked in the sunlight.

"Abby Gierman?" he asked and slid off his shades to reveal dark, intense eyes guarded by thick black eyebrows. Though he wasn't exactly Hollywood handsome, he was good looking and there was something about him that hinted at danger. He hooked the shades on the neckline of his open-collared shirt where a few dark chest hairs were visible.

"I'm Abby."

Though he was staring hard directly at her, squinting against the last of the sunlight, she figured he saw everything that was going on around him. His expression said it all: he was delivering bad news. Probably the worst.

She thought of her father . . . dying by inches from complications of emphysema and cancer. No, dear God, please, don't let Dad be dead! Her heart was beating like a drum, her nerves strung tight as high wires.

"My name's Chastain. Abby Chastain."

He reached into a pocket and withdrew his badge. "But it was Gierman," he said and added, "Detective Reuben Montoya, New Orleans Police Department." His badge, glittering in the poor sunlight, confirmed his identity.

"Are you looking for me?" she asked, bracing herself.

"Unfortunately, yes. Maybe we should go inside."

"What is it, Detective?" she asked, then remembered the conversation with Maury Taylor the day before. Maury had been worried about Luke. And the cop had called her by her married name. It wasn't her father, after all! "Oh, God, it's Luke," she whispered, her hand flying to her mouth. "What happened?"

"Ms. Chastain, he's dead. I'm sorry."

She let out a gasp, and though she didn't realize it, her knees began to buckle. Quick as lightning, Montoya grabbed hold of her arm. His strong grip helped her stay on her feet.

Her mind stalled. She felt disconnected. Then images of Luke flashed like quicksilver behind her eyes. Luke sailing on Puget Sound, his hair flying around his face as he tacked into the wind. Luke giving her a single rose when he asked her to marry him while they were hiking in the Olympic Mountains. Luke hurrying out the door before dawn to report the news on the Seattle radio station. Luke, disheveled, coming home late, his eyes bright, his excuses lame. Luke, drunk, telling her about Zoey...

She closed her eyes. Fought tears. Her stomach lurched and she thought she might be sick.

Dead? He was dead? Luke? No way! He couldn't be. It was impossible. She'd just talked with him, argued with him on the phone a couple of nights ago. She blinked rapidly against hot, unlikely tears. "I—I don't believe it."

Montoya's face said it all. This was no prank, no publicity stunt set up by the master of self-promotion himself. "I'm sorry," he repeated.

She let out her breath, shoved her hair out of her eyes, and saw that Montoya's strong fingers were still around her arm. As if he, too, suddenly realized he was holding her upright and recognized the fact that she wasn't going to faint dead away, he released her.

"Why did you think I was talking about Luke Gierman?"

She lifted a shoulder and silently wished their last conversation hadn't been in anger. "Because Maury Taylor called here yesterday looking for him. Maury was worried that something bad had happened. But I blew him off. I thought it was just one of Luke's tricks..." She squeezed her eyes shut and pulled in a deep breath. This was wrong. So very wrong. "I can't believe it. There must be some mistake."

"No mistake." Montoya's voice was firm, his expression convincing.

"Sweet Jesus." Luke...dead? She fought a sudden rush of tears for a man she no longer loved. "What happened?" she asked, and her own voice sounded distant and detached, the words coming out right and yet seeming as if they were from someone else. He must have been in an accident...his damned car, that was it.

"I think we should go inside."

"Why?" she asked and then saw something in Montoya's eyes, something dark and suspicious and frightening. Her heart started pounding double-time again. "What happened, Detective?" she demanded, her voice stronger, her mind racing.

"Gunshot wound. Close range."

"*What?*"

"He was murdered."

"No! Wait!" She took a couple of steps backward. No, no, no! "Someone shot and *killed* him?"

"That's right."

She heard him, but the words sounded as if they'd come from a long distance, through a deep tunnel.

"Dear God. I—I thought it had to be a car accident..." Automatically she reverted to her youth and deftly made the sign of the cross over her chest while her brain pounded with the news and bile crawled up her throat. Rain began to fall in fat drops that peppered the ground and ran down her face. "Who?" she asked. "Why?"

"We don't know yet."

"Oh, God." She rolled her eyes toward the sky, unaware of the raindrops splashing against her cheeks, running down her neck.

"Ms. Chastain," he said, motioning toward the front porch. She looked up, saw the clear drops catch in his hair and trickling past his collar, darkening the shoulders of his shirt.

"Oh, yes...of course," she said, finally realizing that they were both getting soaked. "Let's go inside." Dazed, she walked to the garage door, where she punched an electronic code into the keypad. The keypad blinked in error. She tried again. Rain was already gurgling in the gutters, gathering on her eyelashes. Again the keypad flashed and didn't unlock the door. "Damn," she muttered. On the third try the heavy door rolled noisily upward, and before it had settled, she ducked beneath it and led the detective inside. Dripping, she walked between her parked hatchback and shelves filled with cans of paint, gardening supplies, and bags of cat litter, then kicked off her shoes as she opened the back door. With Montoya only a step or two behind, she headed straight for the sink, twisted on the faucets, and splashed more water over her face.

Luke was dead. Dead! *Oh, Jesus.*

She couldn't believe it. Everything seemed surreal, blurred around the edges.

Snagging a kitchen towel from the counter, she swiped her face and all the while the words *Luke's dead. Luke's dead. Luke's dead!* pounded through her brain, creating a headache that began to throb.

"Are you all right?" Montoya's voice was soft. As if he cared for her, for her feelings. He'd done this before. Probably dozens of times. Was used to giving out bad news. And yet his brown eyes missed nothing. Sexy and dark, they observed her every reaction. She felt it, and didn't trust it. At all.

She exhaled a little disbelieving puff of air. "Okay?" she repeated. "No. I'm definitely *not* okay." Shaking her head, feeling her wet ponytail rub against the back of her neck, she leaned a hip against the counter for support and offered him the towel.

"No, thanks. I'm okay."

"I can't believe it," she went on as she folded the towel. "I know I said that before, but it's just so damned hard to accept." Her heartbeat was slowing but she was still stunned beyond belief. "I mean . . . we just talked the other night." She remembered the fight about her getting rid of Luke's things, and her face, which she was certain had drained of all color, suddenly flushed hot. A stab of regret cut through her at the thought that their final words had been accusing and spat in anger. She refolded the towel automatically.

"What did you talk about?" From out of nowhere it seemed he had extracted a notepad.

"Oh..." She let out her breath and shook her head, remembering. "We fought. Of course. We always did. Couldn't ever seem to get past the divorce. This time it was about the things he'd left here after he moved out. He was pissed that I got rid of them." She looked away, not wanting to stare into those knowing eyes. She realized then that she should be careful about what she said to this intense man. He wasn't a friend or a preacher, or even an acquaintance. He was a cop. In her hands was the dish towel. How many times had she folded and refolded it? Four? Five? She hadn't been aware of her actions. "Anyway, it's been impossible to get along."

"Do you have children?"

She shook her head and tried not to show any sign of regret as she dabbed at the sweat that had collected on the back of her neck. She'd wanted kids, had thought, fleetingly, that they could be a happy family. Two miscarriages had devastated her, but as her marriage had unraveled, she'd decided her inability to carry a child past the third month of pregnancy had been a blessing in disguise. "Just a cat and a dog," she said, shaking off the bitter memory. "When we split up, I got Ansel, the tabby, and Luke ended up with Hershey, our chocolate Lab. Losing the dog was bad enough; I can't imagine what would have happened if we'd had children." At the thought of the dog, panic swept through her. "What about Hershey?" she demanded. "Where is she?"

"We've got people at Gierman's town house now."

"I want my dog back," she said emphatically.

"A big dog for an apartment."

"I know, I know. I wanted to keep both the animals, but Luke wouldn't hear of it. He was supposed to be moving into a bigger place, a house with a yard...soon, I think." Her eyebrows slammed together as she tried to remember. "How do I get my dog back? I'll drive over there now."

"No." He shook his head. "Gierman's place is still being processed."

"What? But Hershey—"

"I'll see to it."

"Would you?"

"Yeah. It'll be later today."

Something inside her sagged. The single act of kindness by this hard-edged policeman got to her. "Thank you," she whispered, shoving a hand over her damp, pulled-back hair. She blinked and sniffed before she shed any tears. The shock of it all was settling in.

"Are there people at the town house now? Can you call and find out that Hershey's okay?"

"I was there earlier. The dog's fine." His eyes held hers. "Someone from the department took her outside and walked her, then put her in a kennel, but she's fine." When she started to protest, he added, "Really."

"Okay, okay. This is all just so...weird. Disturbing. Do you have any idea who did this?"

"That's what we're trying to find out."

"So where was he, you said you were processing his apartment, did someone break in?"

Her head was pounding with a million questions and she felt disengaged from her body, as if this were a bad dream, and through it all, she sensed the detective scrutinizing her, as if she had something to hide. His eyes never left her face. Well, let him look all he wanted. "Let's sit down."

She nodded, and though her legs were rubbery, she managed to lead him the few steps to the living room, where she sank into her favorite chair, a rocker her grandmother had left her. Abby had positioned the chair in the corner near the window and often retreated to it whenever she wanted to think. She would rock for hours, staring out the window at the wildlife, or into the blackness of the night.

Now, though, the rocker remained motionless. She bit her lip and observed the detective with his jaded, I've-seen-it-all eyes; tense, razor-sharp lips; and straight white teeth. His nose was long, a little crooked, and she guessed it had been broken at least once, probably a couple of times. His hands were big, like an athlete's, his shirtsleeves pushed up over his elbows to show off golden skin with a dusting of black hair.

He was handsome, no doubt about it, and he probably knew it. There was something about him that suggested he used that innate sexiness to his advantage, as a tool.

Not your typical detective in pushed-up sleeves, jeans, and an earring.

Not on a typical mission.

So why would she even notice?

"Could I get you a glass of water or something?" he offered and she shook her head.

"I'll be fine." That was a lie and they both knew it, but she added, "Now, tell me, Detective, what happened to Luke?"

He took a seat in the corner of her couch and sketched out a story of finding Luke in an isolated cabin in a swamp about ten miles from Abby's house. Some fisherman had noticed that the place wasn't locked properly, went in to investigate, and found Luke dead.

"... the thing is," Montoya went on, hands clasped between his knees, "your husband wasn't—"

"Ex-husband," she clarified quickly, though the scene was surreal, Montoya's words sounding far away, as if she were in a cave.

Montoya cleared his throat, and if anything, his gaze became more intense, more focused. "Your ex wasn't alone. There was another body in the cabin."

"What?" she asked, staring at him. "*Two* people were killed?"

"Yes." He nodded curtly.

Her insides froze. More bad news was on the way. "*Another* person was murdered, too?"

He hesitated. "It looks that way."

"How?"

"We're not exactly certain how it went down. Still working on it. The scene was staged, we think, made to look like a murder-suicide. At this point it appears to be a double murder, that the victims were taken to a small cabin in the woods about fifteen miles out of town."

"You don't know?"

"Not yet, no. Until we go through all the evidence, we'll be exploring all possibilities."

She was floored. "So... what do you think happened?"

"As I said, we're not completely cer—"

"I know what you said, Detective, but you've got a gut feeling, don't you? Isn't that what everyone talks about? Hunches? A policeman who's been around a lot of crime scenes and murder investigations usually has some idea of what went down."

"We'll know soon."

"This is unbelievable," she whispered, feeling a chill run through her bones despite the warm temperature. Bracing herself, she asked, "Who was the other person?" Was she about to hear that someone else she knew, someone she was close to, had been murdered as well? Her fingers gripped the arms of the rocker so hard her knuckles showed white.

"An eighteen-year-old woman by the name of Courtney La-Belle." He paused a second, near-black eyes searching her face for some kind of reaction. "She was a student, a freshman, at All Saints College in Baton Rouge."

Courtney LaBelle? Had she heard the name before? Something about it teased her mind, but she couldn't remember why.

"Do you know her?"

"No." Abby shook her head slowly, rolling the name around in her brain and coming up with nothing. *Eighteen? The girl was barely an adult? Oh, Luke . . . You stupid idiot!*

"Did she know your ex-husband?"

"I don't know." Abby was thinking hard, trying to come up with a name and face that matched, a girl they'd both known, or she'd been introduced to at parties, but that was impossible . . . the girl was just too young. "I'm sorry. Luke and I have been divorced for over a year. I don't keep up with whom he's dating . . . or . . . or even seeing as a friend or acquaintance. He has a girlfriend, Nia Something-or-other."

"Nia Penne," he responded without checking his notes. "She appears to be an ex-girlfriend. She's in Toronto. Has been for the last week."

She thought back to the phone call from Maury. So that's what he'd been going to say to her. Luke and Nia had broken up. She grimaced, remembering the panic in Luke's friend's voice and how she'd blown him off, certain Luke was involved in some kind of sick publicity stunt.

Abby shook her head, trying to make sense of it. "Maury didn't tell me when he called yesterday. Maury Taylor works with Luke. He was looking for him."

"Any particular reason he thought Luke would contact you?"

"I have no idea. He must've already talked to all of Luke's friends...but I'm not sure of that. You'll have to ask him."

"I will."

Abby didn't doubt it. From the glint of determination in Montoya's eyes, she was certain he was going to get to the bottom of Luke's death.

"Did your ex-husband have any enemies?" he asked, and she looked at him as if he'd sprouted horns.

She almost laughed. "He made enemies for a living, Detective. You know that. I'm sure if you check with the station manager or producer of the show, they'll have a list a mile long of people who have complained about him."

"What about personal enemies?"

She shrugged and tried to concentrate, but the fact that Luke was dead, that someone had killed him, made it impossible to think. "Probably. I...I can't think of anyone in particular. Not now." And even if she had, she wasn't certain that she would tell him. There was something about Montoya that put her on edge; something that seemed relentless and suspicious; something slightly dangerous, that suggested he knew what it meant to be on both sides of the law; and something sensual and dark, as if he might be able to guess just what made her tick. As a woman. As a suspect. And she didn't kid herself. Ex-wives made damned good suspects. She warned herself to tread gently, say the truth, but be careful.

It was almost as if staring at her so intently, he was searching for signs of deception, and in the pauses in the conversation, she thought he expected her to fill the space, to say something she might later regret.

Or was she just imagining things? Had the shock of Luke's death put her over the edge?

"I really think we should call someone to be with you. A friend? Relative? Maybe a neighbor."

She thought of Vanessa Pomeroy next door, or her sister in Seattle, or Alicia on the West Coast, or her father, or Tanisha, the student who worked part-time in Abby's studio in the city. "No. I'll be fine. Really. It's not as if I was still in love with him."

One of his dark eyebrows quirked and she regretted her words immediately. She felt compelled to explain herself. "Listen, Detective, just because he left me for another woman, one quite a bit younger, doesn't mean that I'm still pining for him or that I'll break into a million pieces once you leave. What I'd felt for Luke died a long time ago. Sad, but true." She looked down at her hands and gnawed at her lower lip a second. The lag in the conversation made the sounds of the house, the creaking timbers, a squirrel scampering across the roof, the steady gurgle of rain washing through the gutters, more noticeable. "The marriage was probably over before we moved here from Seattle. We were trying to make a second stab at it, but we failed." She nodded as if to herself and the confession of her true feelings felt good. "Nonetheless, I just can't believe he's dead." It was her turn to stare at him. "You're certain of this, right? When I first heard he was missing, I thought it was a publicity stunt."

"If it is, it went seriously wrong. Luke Gierman is dead. Trust me."

A deep sadness welled inside her. As much as she and Luke had been at odds, she hated the thought that he'd been killed, his life snuffed before he reached forty.

Montoya rose and reached into his back pocket for his wallet. She watched his movement, noticed how his jeans hugged his butt, then looked quickly away. Geez, what was wrong with her? Yeah, the guy's hips were right in her line of vision, but so what? Had Luke's violent death kicked in her libido? How sick was that? What was she thinking, looking at the detective's buttocks?

That was the problem, she wasn't thinking. Hadn't been. Despite all her protests of being okay with the news of her ex-husband's death, she was still in shock.

So she'd noticed the detective was sexy. So what? It wasn't a big deal. She also knew that she couldn't trust him within an inch of her life.

He scribbled something on the back of a card, and if he'd caught her checking him out, he had the decency not to show it. "My cell phone number," he explained. "If you think of anything else, contact me."

"You, too." She stood and took the white business card he handed her before a horrifying thought struck her. "Please tell me I don't have to go to the morgue and identify the body," she asked, suddenly weak in the knees again.

"No. His parents are coming into town."

She nodded, didn't want to think about her former in-laws and the grief they were enduring.

"So... I saw the FOR SALE sign out front. Are you getting ready to move?"

"After I sell this, yes," she said and wondered why she felt defensive about it, as if the question was one he might ask a suspect. She half expected him to wink at her and advise her not to leave town, but he dropped the subject, only asking once again if he could call someone to be with her and, when she declined, promising to return with her dog.

She walked him to the door. The rain had stopped, leaving puddles in the drive and only a few drops still dripping from the trees. From the porch she watched as he folded his muscular frame behind the steering wheel of his cruiser, his black hair shining like ebony in the dismal rays from a cloud-covered sun. He backed the vehicle out of her long drive, his tires splashing in the water that had collected, then he nosed the cruiser onto the road.

As he drove out of sight, she collapsed onto the porch, dissolving into tears that streaked down her face. It was stupid, really, she didn't love Luke, hadn't for a long, long time, but still, knowing that he'd been murdered, that he was gone forever, left a hole in her life.

Who had murdered him? Had he known his attacker? Had the woman pulled the trigger? Or had someone decided to kill them both?

Montoya had been a little vague about the details of the slayings, and now, after some of the shock had dissipated, she had questions, lots of them. Who had killed Luke? Granted, he had dozens, maybe hundreds, of enemies, but who had been so outraged, so deadly furious, as to have shot him?

And why the girl?

Unless they were involved romantically. Sexually.

Sick as it was, she could imagine Luke being fascinated by a coed with her bright, innocent smile and young, supple body. He'd always had a thing for young women and now it may have cost him his life. How had someone overpowered him? Where had he been abducted? And why?

Slapping the stupid tears away, she forced herself to her feet and into the house. *Get a grip, Abby. Pull yourself together! He was no longer your husband, and face it, sometimes you didn't even like the guy!*

With a twist of the deadbolt, she locked the front door and headed for the shower. She had to focus. There was nothing more she could do. She checked her watch. She had just enough time to clean up, swab out the tub, then face the single guy who had expressed an interest in seeing her house.

Peeling off her clothes, she headed for the bathroom. Her heart was heavy, but she gritted her teeth and told herself life went on. As bad as she felt, she wasn't going to change her plans.

Not this time.

Her father's mantra started all over again. *When the going gets tough . . .*

"Yeah, yeah, I know," she said as she twisted on the faucets and the shower spat and coughed before thin needles of hot water started spraying over her body, washing away the sweat, the tears, the shock. Adjusting the temperature, she let the water pour over her body and reached for the bottle of shampoo. For the moment she would push all thoughts about Luke and his murder out of her head.

CHAPTER 5

There was something about Abby Chastain that didn't ring true, Montoya thought as he drove into the city. Worse yet, she was sexy as hell and didn't seem to know it. Even without a trace of makeup, her hair scraped away from her face, exertion evidenced in the sweat that had stained her T-shirt, she pulled at his senses.

He hadn't liked the awareness that had built within him as he'd watched raindrops shimmer in her hair, then plaster her shirt against her body. He'd caught a glimpse of her cleavage in the V-necked T-shirt, seen a raindrop drizzle its way between her breasts, noticed how her wet hair, slick and pulled back, framed a heart-shaped face, and he'd thought, stupidly and dangerously, of what she might look like coming out of a shower.

Shit.

His thoughts, though fleeting, had been totally unprofessional. Completely out of line.

He'd been too long without a woman, that was it. Ever since Marta's death...Instantly his gut clenched and his fingers curled around the steering wheel. Flipping on his siren and lights, he stomped on the accelerator, as if he could outrun his thoughts, his grief.

It had been nearly two years since Marta had been killed and it was time to get over it. Maybe his interest in the ex–Mrs. Gierman was a good thing, a signal that he was back to his old self.

And yet, he had to watch his step.

Abby Chastain Gierman was off-limits. Way off-limits. Even though the evidence pointed to a man being at the scene of the crime, that didn't mean she couldn't be involved; if not actually having set up the crime, then a behind-the-scenes player. It didn't seem that way, but until all the evidence was in, he wasn't crossing anyone off the suspect list. Especially an ex-wife.

Who knew what kind of personal ax Abby Chastain had to grind?

Angry at himself, Montoya forced himself to decelerate. He switched off his lights. Hell! What had he been thinking?

As he drove into the Garden District, his police band crackled, the windshield wipers slapping time at the fitful rain. Checking his rearview mirror, he saw the irritation in the narrowing of his eyes. He didn't think Abby had out-and-out lied. She seemed too smart for that. But she'd known more than she was saying. Even if he gave her a break for the shock of learning that her ex-husband was dead, she still hadn't come clean. He could feel it.

And it bugged the hell out of him.

He slowed for a stoplight on St. Charles Avenue. Drumming the tips of his fingers on the steering wheel, he saw the raindrops reflect red from the signal, the only illumination in this gray, soggy afternoon. As he waited for the light to change, he watched as pedestrians with umbrellas and hats climbed off the street car and made a mad dash across the street to the cobblestoned, tree-lined sidewalks.

Students on their way to classes at Tulane and Loyola, two old universities resting side by side facing St. Charles Avenue, crossed in groups. Laughing, talking, carrying paper coffee cups and wearing backpacks, they hurried onto the paths and broad lawns of the universities that were within minutes of Courtney LaBelle's home. If she'd decided to attend classes at Loyola, the red brick Catholic college with its turrets and crenels that resembled a medieval castle, would she be alive today? Set here in the Garden District, Loyola was within walking distance of her family. Of safety.

Seeing other young students blissfully unaware of what had happened to Courtney LaBelle, he ground his back teeth. Man, this case was a pisser.

What he needed was a smoke. Just to take the edge off his nerves. He considered stopping at the next convenience store for a pack of Marlboros. Shit, he'd love to draw in a lungful of nicotine about now. Quitting the habit was harder than he'd imagined and he remembered giving Bentz a hard time about giving up smoking a few years back. He'd accused him of being a wuss for leaning on gum or the patch or anything Montoya had considered a crutch.

Now, he understood.

Hell.

It was times like these, when he really wanted to think, to mull over his recent conversation with a witness, that he felt the urge to light up.

The traffic light turned green. The crosswalk was clear. He trod on the gas, water spraying from the Crown Vic's tires as he hit puddles from the recent shower. His mind wandered to Abby Chastain again.

Seeing her had hit him hard.

Where it counted.

If she hadn't been out-and-out lying, then she'd been holding something back. There was a mystery in her gold eyes, some kind of secret. She hadn't been coy, seemed straightforward, but something was off. Or maybe he'd been distracted, surprised at how she'd affected him. He'd expected to walk up to her house, give her the bad news, watch her reaction, and find someone to stay with her, to help her get over the shock.

But that's not what had happened.

The woman had gotten to him.

And he, blindsided, had let her.

Petite, packed tight, curves in all the right places.

He flipped on the radio and told himself he had to stop thinking about Abby Chastain's body. Jesus, hadn't he learned anything in the last five years? His jaw tightened as he slowed for a corner. He'd always been accused of being a player and it was true enough that he enjoyed women, a variety of women. The one time he'd thought of settling down, the situation had gone from bad to worse.

His guts twisted as he thought of Marta again...God, she'd been beautiful, with a sharp tongue and flashing dark eyes that had held him captive.

He'd thought she was the one, if there was such a thing. He hadn't believed it before and he didn't believe it now, but for that one short period of his life, he'd been certain that he'd wanted Marta Vasquez for his bride.

"Son of a bitch!" he growled as a guy in a red Mazda RX7 cut in front of him. Montoya slammed on the brakes. As the driver glanced in his mirror and obviously realized he'd nearly collided with a cop car, he shifted down, slowing to the speed limit, and immediately became Mr. Good Citizen, the epitome of the perfect driver. "Yeah, right," Montoya muttered. If he had any balls, he would pull the guy over and read him the riot act, maybe scare the bejeezus out of him by slamming him up against the side of the car and pulling out his cuffs before slapping him with a ticket and a fine that would make the guy's eyes bulge.

Montoya smiled at the thought, then checked his watch as it began to rain again.

No time to spare.

"Next time, buddy," Montoya said as the sports car turned into a bank parking lot.

With a sigh, he forced himself to concentrate on the task ahead: informing Mr. and Mrs. Clyde LaBelle that their daughter wasn't ever coming home. "Damn it all to hell."

This was the part of his job he detested the most.

"...I don't know," Sean Erwin said as he walked slowly through Abby's house. Behind sleek black-framed glasses, his eyes darted from one side of the living room to the other as he and Abby walked toward the dining area. It was the third pass through and Sean, a tall, lean man with spiky hair, patrician nose, and thin black brows over expressive eyes, wasn't happy. Yet he wasn't going away. "I just don't think this is big enough." Tapping one long finger against his mouth, he frowned, pursing his lips as if he'd just sucked on a lemon. "I have a lot of oversized pieces. An armoire from my grandmother, an overstuffed couch, a small piano...and my bed is a king." He strode quickly down the short hallway where the bathroom separated the two bedrooms. He poked his head into Abby's room again. "No. Don't think so. Your bedroom doesn't look like it could accommodate my bed, the two night tables, *and* my dresser." Sighing dramatically, he pulled a small tape measure from his pocket. "I'd better take some measurements."

"Go ahead. I'll be in the kitchen if you need me." It was all Abby could do to keep her cool. While this art dealer from the city walked through her house as if he already owned it, and didn't like what he saw, she was thinking of Luke's murder. Somehow Sean Erwin's furniture arrangement didn't seem so important today. The couple who'd stopped by an hour earlier had wandered through for the second time, but hadn't seemed all that interested either. They'd left without asking any more questions.

The phone rang and she picked up in the kitchen where Ansel was cowering under one of the chairs.

"Hello?"

"Oh my God. Tell me it's not true!" Zoey's voice shrilled through the wires. "Tell me Luke's okay!"

"I can't."

"He was murdered? He and some girl?"

Abby nodded, though her sister couldn't see her. "I found out, less than two hours ago. A detective from the police department came by."

"Are you all right?"

"No, but then who would be?" Abby said, trying to keep her voice low as she heard Erwin in the bathroom, opening closet doors and closing them. "How did you find out?"

"I work in the news business, remember."

"But you're on the West Coast."

"Seattle isn't exactly Timbuktu and we do get feeds, you know, running streams of news from all over the world. I just happened to see information about a double homicide or maybe homicide-suicide in New Orleans and then...then I called a local station. They said the next of kin were just being notified, but someone at the station has a contact in the department. He let the identities out. Officially, the police aren't releasing information about who was killed until the next of kin have been notified, but I figured that was you and Luke's parents." She exhaled shakily. "I just can't believe it."

"You and me both," Abby said.

"So how're you holding up?"

"Still in shock, but I'll be okay."

"You're sure?" Zoey's voice was filled with worry.

"Of course I am," Abby said a little hotly. Her feelings for Luke were ambivalent, but to deny that she had any was ridiculous. She heard Erwin walk out of the bathroom and test the cupboard door in the hallway, the one that always squeaked. "Look, I've got to go. I've got someone looking at the house right now. I'll call you back."

"You'd better give Dad a ring. He'll want to know. He always liked Luke."

One of the few in the family, Abby thought, gritting her teeth. "I will," she promised just as Sean Erwin poked his gelled head into the kitchen. Tape measure at the ready, forehead creased, he eyed the doorway to the back porch. "You don't have a pantry, do you?" he asked, oblivious to the fact that she was still on the phone.

"I'll call you back," she said to her sister and Erwin finally saw the receiver.

His head ducked back into his shoulders like a scared turtle. "Sorry," he mouthed, but she was already hanging up.

"No problem." *Oh, Abby, you're such a liar.* She was irritated and couldn't help saying, "And no, I don't have a pantry. Nor a piano, so space for one isn't really a concern for me and my smaller bed works out just fine."

He blinked as if shocked, and she decided it was a good thing that she made her living in photography rather than by trying to sell real estate. But she was steamed and Erwin's questions seemed not just curious but kind of pointedly snarky.

"I understand," he said, stung, "but I'm just trying to work with what you've got here."

"Then go for it. But there's only so much space unless you want to add on, or connect the main house to the studio." She walked to the back door and opened it. Ansel streaked outside like a shot. "It's unlocked if you want to see it, just on the other side of this porch."

"I will. Thanks." He hurried out of the kitchen and Abby wished he'd just go away. As much as she wanted to sell the house, today was not the day.

"...oh, God, no. No! No! No! Not Mary. Please, please, you must be wrong!" Virginia LaBelle was trembling, her blue eyes wide, her head shaking violently from side to side as she stood next to her husband. Her face had turned white, her legs wobbled, and if not for the steady arm of her husband, she, no doubt, would have crumpled into a heap onto the glossy marble floor of her three-storied Victorian home. Tears rained from her eyes. "Not my baby," she cried and Montoya's guts twisted as he looked up the curved wooden staircase to the landing, where a huge gold-framed picture of a vibrant, beautiful girl had been hung. Bright blue eyes, gold hair that curled past her shoulders, dimples visible around a radiant smile. A beautiful girl. In his mind's eye he saw the female victim with her bloated face and waxy complexion and felt sick.

"I'm sorry," Montoya said and he meant it. This was the worst part of his job. The worst. Dealing with the dead was preferable to informing the living of the loss of a loved one. Especially a child. "Her identification said Courtney."

"She goes by Mary. Has from the time she was old enough to decide, somewhere around the fourth or fifth grade, I think," the father, Clyde, said. Tall, with a large frame, ruddy cheeks over a short-cropped silver beard that matched his thinning hair, Clyde LaBelle aged before Montoya's eyes. His shoulders drooped beneath his tan sport coat, the color washed away from his skin, leaving his complexion pasty, and his blue eyes, behind gold-rimmed spectacles, seemed to fade.

"Third. She had Sister Penelope for a teacher," Virginia said, still blinking against her tears, denial etched on her face.

"You're certain this is our child?" Clyde asked softly.

"Yes, but I'll need someone to identify the body."

Another piercing wail from Courtney's mother as she lost control of herself.

"There has to be a mistake."

"I'll do it." A muscle tightened in Clyde's jaw and Montoya witnessed him physically stiffening his spine.

"It can't be, it just can't be," Virginia muttered.

"Shh...honey...shh." He pressed his lips into her hair but he didn't say the obvious lie of *everything's going to be all right*.

Because it wouldn't be. For the rest of their lives this well-to-do couple would mourn their daughter and nothing else would matter. Everything they'd worked for, dreamed of having—this stately old house, the tended grounds, the silver Cadillac parked in the driveway—would be meaningless.

"Perhaps you should lie down," Clyde suggested to his wife, but she would have none of it.

Wiping at the bottoms of her eyes with a long, manicured finger, she whispered, "I want to hear what the officer has to say. It's wrong, of course, but I need to hear it."

"Ginny, Detective Montoya wouldn't come here if he wasn't certain—"

"But it has to be a mistake. We both know it." She drew in a slow, shuddering breath and extracted herself from her husband's grip. Her legs were unsteady but she managed to stay upright, her spine suddenly ramrod straight. "Please, give me a second." Touching her hair as if realizing it had become mussed, she walked to what appeared to be a nearby bathroom, her gold sandals clicking across the veined marble floor.

"I'm a psychiatrist," Clyde said. "I'll prescribe something to calm her down." He glanced nervously at the closed powder room door. "And I'll call our parish priest. Father Michael has a way of soothing her."

Montoya took note of the carved wooden cross mounted above the archway that led to the back of the house. A heavy leather-bound Bible rested prominently upon a small occasional table near the foot of the staircase. The ceiling of this entry hall rose two full stories, allowing the foyer to open to a gallery on the floor above where more pictures of the LaBelles' only daughter had been artfully arranged.

The door to the powder room opened and Virginia LaBelle, her makeup restored, her frosted hair no longer mussed, managed a wan smile that didn't quite reach her eyes. "Please, Officer, if you would follow me into the parlor." Her voice wobbled and for a second she seemed about to dissolve again, but she tugged on the hems of her sleeves, gathered her breath, and said, "We could discuss this matter further. I'm certain that there has been a vast, horrible mistake."

Clyde sent Montoya a look but followed his wife into a cozy room filled with peach-colored chintz, ornate antique tables, and lamps that dripped with crystal. Flipping a switch, Virginia turned the fire on, though it had to be eighty degrees in the house, then she sat on the edge of a small settee. She folded her hands in her lap and tried like hell to appear composed, to slip back into the world of Southern gentility to which, Montoya guessed, she'd been born. "Would you like something to drink? I could have Ada get us some sweet tea."

"I'm fine," Montoya said.

As her husband joined her, Montoya took a quick survey of the room. Over the fireplace was another huge portrait of Courtney and upon the wide marble mantel was a gallery of pictures of the girl in various phases of her life: photos of her as a towheaded toddler, others in the awkward age when braces glinted in her mouth and small granny glasses covered her eyes, still other shots that were more recent, pictures of a young woman with a fresh face and placid smile.

"She's going to be a nun," Virginia said with a touch of pride as she fingered a diamond cross at her throat, so similar to the one found around her daughter's neck.

A nun?

That was a curve ball Montoya hadn't expected. Montoya eyed the mother carefully, wondering if she'd gone off her rocker. "She was going to join an order?"

"We know it's not a common calling for a young woman these days and goodness knows her father and I tried to dissuade her." She sent her husband a knowing glance. "We want grandchildren, you see . . ." Her voice drifted off again as she looked up at the mantel to the pictures of her only child. A single tear drizzled from the corner of her eye.

Montoya's stomach soured. As gently as possible, he explained what he knew, what he could tell them. About the cabin. About Gierman. About the gun that had been found in their daughter's hand. About the wedding dress.

Throughout it all, Courtney Mary LaBelle's parents listened. Raptly. Sadly. Without comment. Rain splashed against the tall paned windows and the gas logs hissed, but Clyde and Virginia huddled together on the tiny couch, holding hands, wedding rings catching the firelight, and didn't say a word. It was almost as if he were talking to mannequins. Only when he mentioned the pistol did the father wince and blink, guilt stealing through his eyes.

"I gave her that gun for protection," he whispered, his voice thick. "I never thought... Oh Jesus." He buried his face in one hand and his shoulders began to shake.

Surprisingly, his wife touched Clyde's shoulder with her free hand, as if to offer him strength.

"I shouldn't have done it. If I hadn't, then she might be alive today," he said.

"Shhh. No. Clyde. Whatever happened, it's not your fault. You'll see. This is a mistake." She turned her sad eyes on Montoya again. "Mary doesn't know Luke Gierman, I'm sure. He's the man with that horrible program on the radio, isn't he? The one who's being banned everywhere?"

"He worked at WSLJ. Was known as their shock jock."

"Well, there you go. Mary doesn't know him. Wouldn't. And she doesn't own a wedding gown, believe me. You've got the wrong girl. Someone who just happened to have our daughter's ID with her."

"Have you talked to your daughter in the last two days?" Montoya asked and thought of the picture he was carrying, the one of the dead girl, but he couldn't bring himself to take it from his pocket.

"Well, no."

"The picture on her student ID and driver's license is of the same woman we found."

A small high-pitched sound of protest came from Virginia's throat.

"I could call Father Michael for you," Montoya offered, knowing that he would get nothing more from these tortured parents today.

"No, no... I'll take care of it." Virginia offered up a tremulous smile, then walked to a desk where she picked up a phone and pushed a speed-dial number. She spoke into the phone for a few minutes and then hung up, her hand resting on the receiver a second longer than necessary, as if she was hesitant to break the connection.

"You mentioned that Courtney, er, Mary had decided to become a nun," Montoya said as the girl's mother returned to her spot on the settee, found her purse, and retrieved a tissue from within. "When did she decide to join an order?"

Clyde frowned. "Six, maybe eight months ago, I think." He glanced at his wife for confirmation.

"Last Christmas." Virginia twisted the tissue and looked out the window as if she could will her daughter to appear on the front walk. "She visited the order at Our Lady of Virtues."

Montoya felt something inside him click.

"At least it was close by," the mother said again and Montoya's gut tightened. "And I guess, we have some affinity for the order. Clyde was a doctor on staff of the hospital and I was a social worker. We met there." Her smile was quick, tremulous, and dissolved instantly. "They're tearing down that old hospital, but the sisters are still going to live in the convent. I hear they're going to build new apartments and an assisted-living facility, and as the nuns age, they're guaranteed living and care expenses free of charge. This is after they can no longer care for themselves, or the order can't care for them any longer." She closed her eyes and sighed, still winding and unwinding the tissue in her hands.

Montoya had heard about the renovations to the old hospital. His own aunt had joined the order years earlier. Was still there.

Clyde said, "We just asked that she spend a year at college before she actually took her vows, but...she'd already made up her mind."

"Do you know why?"

He hesitated. Tugged at his silver beard and cast a glance in his wife's direction. "She felt as if God had spoken to her."

"Personally?"

"Yes." He nodded and looked away.

So would-be Sister Mary, aka Courtney, might not have been so normal after all.

"I know how it sounds, Detective. I work with people who hear voices all the time—"

"This wasn't the same!" Virginia intervened. "Mary...she just thought God was answering her prayers, that's all. She wasn't schizophrenic, for God's sake!" Her lips pulled into a tiny knot of disapproval. "She is a normal, sane, lovable girl."

Right. Like Joan of Arc.

Clyde slipped his arm around his wife's shoulders.

Montoya asked, "Did she have any boyfriends?"

"Nothing serious."

"You're certain?"

"Yes." The wife answered but both parents nodded.

"Could there have been someone who might have been interested in her, but she wasn't returning the favor?"

"Mary gets along with everyone, Officer," Virginia said. "Though she could have dated a lot of boys, a *lot,* she hasn't. She's already promised herself to God. That's what the ring is for."

"The ring?"

"The one she wears on her left hand," Clyde offered and Montoya's mind flashed to the battered and bruised ring finger of the victim.

Virginia added, "Where other girls wear their boyfriend's class ring, or an engagement or wedding ring, Mary wears a promise ring. It's something she picked out herself on her eighteenth birthday, the day she promised herself to the Father."

"As in God."

"Of course." Virginia's shoulders stiffened as if she were girding herself to defend her child.

Montoya didn't know what to say. Things were getting weirder by the minute. He glanced up at the portrait again. It was a posed shot where the girl's hands were folded over the back of a couch. Sure enough, on the ring finger of her left hand, she wore a filigreed gold band with a single square-cut red stone.

"So she wasn't getting married?"

"What? No! Of course not." Virginia let out a disgusted sigh.

"Did she own a bridal gown?"

"No...why would she? I told you, she didn't even date!"

"Did she pick All Saints for a reason?"

Clyde said, "We did. We wanted her to be close enough to reach her, but far enough away that she would experience college life. She could have gone to Loyola, of course, the Jesuits there do a wonderful job. It's an institution around here, I know. I even spent a few years on the staff there."

Virginia started shredding the tissue. "Clyde felt it would be good for her to get away from under our wing, meet new people, even if she were going to join an order." She blinked rapidly and sniffed. Her chin trembled. "Clyde wanted her to experience a bit of the world."

Courtney's father's face drew together in anguish. "I just wanted what was best for her."

"We both did." Virginia sniffed, then dabbed at her nose.

"I understand," Montoya said, lying because he didn't understand it at all. These days eighteen-year-old girls didn't run off to nunneries. Beautiful, supposedly popular girls dated boys. Unless they were gay. Then they dated girls, and if Courtney "Mary" La-belle was into girls, then what the hell had she been doing with Luke Gierman?

By all accounts the two victims couldn't have been more unalike.

Montoya talked to the LaBelles until he spied a bronze-colored sedan pull up to the curb outside the house. It was Montoya's cue to leave. To let the grieving parents have some time alone with a priest. A tall man, maybe six-two or six-three, wearing a black suit, black shirt, and stark white clerical collar, stretched out of the car. Thick white hair, rimless eyeglasses, and a few lines on a weather-beaten face suggested he was near seventy, yet he stood straight and with a quick, sure stride he walked to the door.

The doorbell pealed in soft, dulcet tones.

Mrs. LaBelle was on her feet, and once the priest entered, her tenuous facade fell completely away in a wash of tears and sobs.

Montoya was glad to get away from the perfect house, a near shrine to a daughter who wasn't returning. He strode to his cruiser, climbed inside, and fired the engine. Before he backed into the street, he called the station on his cell phone and was connected to

Lynn Zaroster, a junior detective who happened to be manning the phones.

"Hey. It's Montoya. Can you check with the crime lab, see if there was any jewelry found on Courtney LaBelle, the female vic who was found with Luke Gierman this morning? Also, find out if Gierman was wearing any jewelry."

"I think he was *au naturel*. Weren't you there?"

"Yeah, and that's the way it looked to me, too." Montoya did a quick U-turn, then hit the gas. "I didn't see that he was wearing anything, but double-check and get back to me, would ya? The girl, she supposedly never went without her promise ring."

"Got it."

"Is anyone still at Gierman's town house?"

"Brinkman and an investigator from the crime-scene team."

"Call and tell them to crate the dog. I'll be by to pick her up."

"The dog?"

"Yeah. Gierman's ex wants the dog back. Seems as if she lost her in the divorce."

"The dog?" Zaroster repeated.

"That's what I said."

She said something about lunatic, fanatic dog lovers under her breath, then more loudly added, "I don't suppose you've heard about the calls into the radio station the other day?"

Montoya wheeled around a corner and cut through two lanes of traffic. "No. What?"

"It was the day they aired a show on vindictive exes."

Montoya's hands tightened over the wheel. "What about it?"

"The station keeps a log of anyone who phones in. The telephone numbers flash onto the computer display."

"Who called?"

"Lots of people. Irate. Or ones who had stories to share with old Luke. The thing is, one of the people who phoned in hung up before she said anything."

Montoya felt it coming.

"That caller just happened to be his ex. Abby Chastain. She didn't bother saying anything, probably thought better of talking to her ex-husband on the air. If it were me, I would have held my tongue, too. But she had definitely been listening and I just heard a replay of the program. He reamed her, but good. If I would have heard that and it had been my ex, I'm thinkin' I might have killed him."

"You're saying Abby Chastain might have offed her husband and Courtney LaBelle?" No, that didn't seem quite right. Not with the bridal gown and the size twelve shoes.

"Don't know about the girl, but man, oh, man, that Gierman, what a piece of work. He gave his ex-wife a powerful motive. That's all I'm suggesting."

"Save the tape. I want to hear it."

"Got it right here," she said and he heard a couple of raps, as if she were patting something for emphasis.

"Has his car been found yet?"

"Not that I know of."

"Let me know when it's located," Montoya said before hanging up and driving to Luke Gierman's town house, located in the French Quarter. Gierman's end unit was a full two stories of old, painted brick and decorated with tall, paned windows, hurricane shutters, and fancy wrought-iron balconies. The private entrance, a small courtyard, was cordoned off with crime-scene tape.

Eyeing the place, Montoya pushed open the door. One of Bonita's investigators, Inez Santiago, was closing up her evidence collection kit. She looked up at Montoya as he stepped into the foyer.

"Well, look what the cat dragged in," she teased, her teeth flashing white against golden skin. Santiago was a looker, blessed with a dancer's body and long, coffee-colored hair that she highlighted with streaks of red, and when she was working, scraped away from her face in a crisp, professional knot. Her eyes were green, intelligent, and didn't miss a damned thing.

"You through here?"

"That's right."

"Find anything?"

"Some fingerprints, but who knows who they belong to. We'll check them with the Automated Fingerprint Identification System and see what we come up with. Brinkman took some personal stuff, files and the computer, the trash, and the answering machine. I think we got everything we could. You can poke around all you want. Just don't mess up anything until I get the final word from Washington." Santiago's smile flashed again.

Fingerprint powder was everywhere and a few drawers still hung open, but underlying what the police crime department had done while investigating, the place was neat. Tidy. Clean. "I'm here for the dog."

"Does the dog know that? She might not approve."

"Oooh, where do you get off today?"

With a naughty wink, she said, "Wouldn't you like to know?" She clicked her kit closed and nodded toward the kitchen. "The dog's in there. I tried to pawn her off on Brinkman, but he said 'no way'; seems to be paranoid around most animals."

"He leave?"

"About fifteen minutes ago. Said to meet him at the station and you could ride up to Baton Rouge together to check out the girl's dorm room."

Montoya didn't comment. He could only stand so many hours in the car cooped up with Brinkman. Today he had no choice but to put up with the irritating detective, but he couldn't wait until Bentz returned to duty. Rick Bentz was his regular partner, and though Montoya had kidded around that Bentz was old for his years, he beat the hell out of Brinkman, the Know-It-All.

Santiago walked through the kitchen to a small laundry area, where dog dishes were placed by the dryer and a large crate was wedged beneath a closet with one of those pull-down ironing boards. Through the mesh of the crate, a brown Lab peered intently. "She's been waiting," Santiago said.

"I'll bet." Montoya squatted. "How are ya, girl?" he asked and the Lab gave up a quick yip. "Guess she wants out." He opened the door and the dog shot from its kennel in a bounding rush of warm brown fur. Wiggling crazily, Hershey knocked over her water dish and panted expectantly, hoping for attention.

"Good thing I already processed this room," Santiago muttered.

"You're done, aren't you?"

"Yeah, but I don't know what more Washington might want. Better get her"—she motioned to the dog—"outside quick and not just in the courtyard."

"Got it," Montoya agreed and then, when the dog began jumping up on him, said, "Hey, hey, slow down." Montoya grabbed a leash hanging from a hook in the wall and snapped the lead onto the rambunctious dog's collar. "Chill!" he ordered but the anxious Lab pulled at the tether, nearly choking herself in the process. "I think I'll take her outside."

"Good idea," Santiago said with a little, mocking nod of her head. "Yep, damned brilliant, Montoya. And for the record, the command isn't 'chill' or 'calm down' or 'freeze.'" I think you'd better stick with 'sit' or 'stay,' you know, your basic commands from Puppy 101."

"Funny."

"I thought so."

"You're just full of yourself, aren't you? Good night, last night?"

"As a matter of fact it was," she said, her eyes gleaming. "But not what you think. I went out on the town. With a friend. Dancing. Didn't get home until one A.M. Innocent fun and games." Again the smile. "Get your mind out of the gutter, Montoya. Don't be such a guy." They walked outside, and after the dog had relieved herself near the curb, Montoya managed to get her into the back of the cruiser.

"Better crack a window."

"I was just about to do that," he muttered, already opening the driver's side, turning on the ignition, and letting the front windows down several inches. He'd parked in the shade, but the heat was still oppressive. After climbing out of the car, he rested his hips against a fender.

"Find anything interesting inside?" he asked, hiking his chin toward the courtyard.

"Not much. You were here earlier. No signs of a struggle."

"And his car is still missing." It was a statement, not a question. The single-car garage had been empty. Montoya had checked.

"Yep."

"What about his personal things? Clothes. Jewelry."

"Nothing looked disturbed. In fact, the place was...kind of classy...or tasteful. You know, I've listened to Gierman's show a few times and figured him for some kind of obscene slob. All his talk radio pushes the envelope. I figured he was a racist, a homophobe, a misogynist, and a card-carrying member of the NRA, but as far as I can tell from what I found, I'm probably only right about the guns."

"So that rules out the gays and members of the NAACP as suspects," he said, but the joke fell flat.

"He had lots of enemies."

"So I keep hearing."

"He incited people. Loved to feed the fire, y'know?" Her forehead wrinkled. "But maybe it was all for the show. For ratings. For the almighty buck."

"Maybe we'll find out."

"Too late for Gierman. Hey, do you want me to drop the dog off?" she offered.

"I think I can handle it."

"Oh?" Santiago looked confused for a second before her chin came up and she looked at Montoya with a slow nod. "Don't tell me, Gierman's ex is single and a looker? Jesus, Montoya, when will you learn?"

"Learn what?" he asked and she just laughed.

"Fine. Take the dog!" Santiago was already unlocking her own vehicle, parked at the corner just in front of Montoya's cruiser.

Montoya ignored her comments and made his way into the town house one more time for a final quick look around the place Gierman had called home for more than a year.

Santiago was right; the place was neat, or had been before the fingerprint and trace crew had been through. Polished wooden floors, modern furniture in muted tones, and abstract art in splashes of bold color were the mainstays of Gierman's furnishings.

Upstairs in the master bedroom, his clothes were all pressed, folded, or hung, his jewelry in one box that was filled with tie clips, cuff links, and several rings. Pictures of himself in sailing or ski gear were arranged on his dresser. Montoya recognized Puget Sound, the Space Needle on one end, a downtown skyline farther away, and a big mother of a mountain—was it Mt. Rainier?—in the background as Gierman tacked his craft into what appeared to be a bracing wind.

Because of the location and Gierman's apparent age, Montoya figured the picture must've been taken in the time Gierman was either married to or courting Abby Chastain. They seemed an unlikely couple, Montoya thought, remembering Abby Chastain's fresh face and, despite the shock of her ex-husband's death, her wry sense of humor. She seemed to have a genteel facade while Gierman's was crude and crass.

But then they both could be fakes.

Montoya hadn't dug deep enough to rely on his first impressions.

Yet.

The upstairs bathroom was clean, Gierman's shaving gear neat despite the investigative team's search. The shower stall, tub, even the toilet, had been scrubbed, either by a girlfriend, cleaning service, or Gierman did the dirty jobs himself.

Seemed unlikely.

Montoya opened a cabinet. No kinky sex magazines. Not even a single issue of *Playboy.* Instead Montoya found copies of catalogs from upscale furniture shops and art galleries, even the most recent issues of a skiing magazine, *Golf Digest,* and *Men's Health.* As it appeared that Gierman lived alone, it looked like his loud-mouthed, boorish public persona was a fraud. Or more likely, he was a complex guy.

Down a short hallway of gleaming hardwood, Montoya made his way to the second bedroom, which was used exclusively as a den and workout room. No daybed or foldout couch, just a desk, computer, file cabinet, and television with a DVD and VCR and Bose music system. As Gierman had in the bedroom and the living area. A media freak. Against one wall was a set of weights and bench; in a bookcase a CD library of classical, jazz, and old rock 'n' roll.

Any guests had to sleep with Gierman or on the olive green couch in the living room.

Now, because of the investigation, the guts of the computer had been taken away, cords left dangling where they had once been attached to the hard drive. File drawers had been left hanging open and had been stripped of a lot of the information inside, those files now, no doubt, piled upon Montoya's desk at the station.

Brinkman was thorough, he thought, but still a prick.

Water dripped from the old pipes.

The smell of earth seeped in past tiles and bricks that had long ago lost their seals. Without care and resealing, the ancient mortar and grout had crumbled, letting in the dank, moist scent of dirt.

He didn't care.

It didn't matter.

Didn't cloud his purpose.

If he stood very still and closed his eyes, he could remember the pungent odors of antiseptic and ammonia masking the acrid human scents of urine, sweat, and fear.

Above the smells were the sounds. If he listened very carefully, straining his ears, he could still hear the hushed whispers, the muted prayers, and the soft, unending moans. Metal carts rattled, the clock struck the hour, and everywhere there was the faint sense of depravity and decay, all washed over with a gloss of wellness and sunshine and false hope.

Now, standing in the labyrinthine corridors of the basement, he imagined how it had once been. So clearly he could see the lies... the shining eyes, the patient smiles, the concerned knit eyebrows, but everything had been untrue.

He opened his eyes, and spurred by all those falsehoods, those dark, hidden sins, sins his mother had warned him about, sins for which he'd been brutally punished, he slipped through the shadowy corridors and felt again that he'd finally come home, had returned to make things right.

He moved noiselessly, leaving lanterns burning at critical junctures, golden light from tiny flames washing up against what had once been gleaming, pristine walls. Now black mold was evident, dark stains encroaching on dusty, dirty squares of the tile that had covered the walls of this area of the hospital basement. This was the part that had always been locked and kept secret, a place where the light of day never shone, where few knew what travesties had occurred down here. Those who had known had held their tongues and had expected the treachery and vile acts to have been forgotten.

Oh, how wrong they were.

Nothing was forgotten.

Nor was it forgiven.

His mother had taught him these valuable lessons.

He lit another lantern and turned a last corner. With his key, he unlocked a final door and stepped into the windowless room where his belongings were stashed. He lit candles and walked to the small secretary-desk with its peekaboo cabinets. It was unlocked. Pressing a small lever, he watched as the writing table unfolded, revealing hidden little niches, perfect cubicles for secreting his treasures. From his pocket, he withdrew the ring, a tiny gold band with a winking red stone. For a second he rubbed the metal circle between his forefinger and thumb, feeling its warmth, remembering the girl who had worn it. Heat thrummed through his bloodstream and he licked his lips. So perfect was she...so unaware. He noticed the blood on the perfect gold circle. Her blood. So much the better.

He relived the act of placing the pistol into her fingers, of squeezing the trigger, of feeling her smooth, supple back pressed into his abdomen, then fall away as death took her.

She had been so frightened and he knew he could have forced her into submission. It had been all he could do not to give into the urge. Her buttocks had fit so beautifully and intimately against his rock-hard cock. Mounting her would have been easy. Claiming her virginal body an act of pure indulgence. He'd imagined ramming himself into her tight little untouched cunt, of breaking that thin barrier that separated woman from child.

But it would have been wrong.

Ruined all his carefully laid plans.

Now, thinking of her warm, trembling body, he felt the need for release, for the hot, urgent ache within him to be assuaged as he grew hard again.

But he knew his torment was part of his own atonement.

He let out his breath slowly, found that he'd gripped the ring so hard it had cut into his skin, and he mentally berated himself. It wasn't time. Not yet.

Angry with himself for his weakness, he placed the gold band into a special cranny, then he removed the watch from his pocket and set the expensive timepiece next to the ring.

Perfect, he thought as the candles burned and water dripped in the hallway. This was the first step, though he was far from finished. His work would take time; there were so many who had to pay. From an upper shelf, he withdrew a black bound photograph album and began flipping slowly through the pages of posed photographs, newspaper clippings, snapshots, and magazine articles.

He smiled as he stared down at the lifeless pictures and read the stories he'd memorized long ago. But his smile fell away as he came to Faith Chastain's photograph, a studio shot in black and white that caught her looking nearly lasciviously at the camera's eye. He touched the photograph, outlining the curve of her jaw. His chest tightened as he remembered her in life. In death.

Angrily he snapped the album closed and stuffed it into its special slot of the desk. Then he slammed the top of the secretary closed. He didn't have time for this. There was so much work to do.

The deaths of the other night were just the beginning.

CHAPTER 6

"We're all in shock here at WSLJ," the disk jockey was saying, "everyone's going to miss Luke Gierman. I mean, the guy was like a legend around here..."

Oh, save me, Abby thought.

"...as a tribute to Luke and the contribution he made to free speech, WSLJ has decided to replay some of his most popular shows and we'd like your opinion about which ones you'd like to hear again. You can either call in or log on to our website." The DJ rattled off phone numbers and the website address with such enthusiasm that Abby felt sick. She clicked off the radio.

"So now they're going to canonize him," she said to Ansel, who was seated on the back of the couch and staring hungrily at a hummingbird hovering near the feeder. "Unbelievable. It gives a whole new meaning to St. Luke, don't ya think?" But despite her flippant words, she felt more than a little regret about their last conversation and the fact she'd lied about his father's gun.

"Don't even think about it," she chided herself just as she heard the sound of tires crunching on the drive. Ansel, no longer mesmerized by the hummingbird, hopped down from the couch and strolled to the door, only to stop dead in his tracks.

"What?" Abby asked as she looked out the window. Detective Montoya had arrived. With Hershey. Abby's heart leapt. Damn, she'd missed that dog. Opening the front door, she let in a rush of warm October air as she stepped outside.

Hershey was straining at her leash, kicking up leaves. Detective Montoya, rather than yank the eager dog back, was jogging to keep up with her. He glanced up, caught sight of Abby on the front porch, and flashed a smile.

A sincere smile that was crookedly boyish and caught Abby off guard.

"I think she missed you," he said as Hershey bounded up the steps. Leaping, jumping, wiggling, and wagging her tail, she demanded every bit of Abby's attention.

"Yeah, you're good. You're so, so good," Abby assured her, petting her sleek coat and bending down to have her face washed by Hershey's tongue. "I missed you so much, Hersh."

The Lab barked loudly and Abby laughed. Though she hated the circumstances by which she'd inherited Hershey, she was glad to have the dog back home. "Thanks for bringing her back," she said to Montoya as she took the leash from him.

"No problem."

She raised an eyebrow. "I don't exactly live around the corner from the police station. At least let me offer you a beer or a Coke— oh, I've only got Diet..."

"Nothing, really."

She unsnapped the leash and Hershey, spying Ansel, shot inside. "Uh-oh. Watch out." The cat puffed up to twice his size, hissed, then took off, streaking out through the open door, across the porch, and up the trunk of a live oak. The dog was inches behind and stopped short at the tree, only to bark wildly as Ansel sat on a low branch and looked down.

Abby couldn't help grinning. "It's their favorite game."

Hershey whined and barked until she caught wind of some other animal and started sniffing the bushes. "It never fails," Abby said, shaking her head as she watched her pets. "Every time Luke brought the dog over, Hershey would go berserk and Ansel would hiss and run. The dog always gave chase and then, twenty minutes later, they'd both be lying in the living room, Ansel on the back of the couch, Hershey in her bed by the fire, both curled up and sleeping dead to the world, as if they didn't know the other animal was in the room." Abby shoved her hair from her eyes. "Sometimes it's a regular three-ring circus around here."

"Did your ex leave the dog here often?"

"Just about every weekend," she said, thinking of the absurdity of the situation. "As much as he fought for Hershey in the divorce, the responsibility of having a dog really cramped his style. He was gone a lot between his hours at the station and his other activities." She slid Montoya a look. "Luke was an outdoor enthusiast, and when he couldn't be fishing or hunting, or skiing or whatever, he spent hours in the gym. He was rarely home and so the dog was in his way. But I didn't mind—as I said, I've missed Hershey." She felt an unlikely tug on her heart. "I feel badly about Luke, really. We didn't get along very well and our last conversation . . . it was really bad, awful, in fact . . . and then he really gave me some shots on his program the next day."

"You listened?"

She rolled her eyes. "Yeah. I guess I was curious, or deep down I have masochistic tendencies, I don't know, but yes, I tuned in. It was a mistake." She stared at the dog and absently rubbed a forearm with her opposing hand. "Luke really went for the jugular that day."

"Did it make you angry?"

"Damned straight," she admitted, then looked at him. "It would have made anyone angry, but no, not that you're asking, but you're hinting that I might have been mad enough to kill him. I didn't."

"What about Courtney LaBelle. Any luck remembering her?"

"No . . . But there's something about her name that seems familiar."

"Famous singer named LaBelle," he offered. "And a disk jockey over at WNAB."

"No . . . Something more." She'd wondered about it all day, had felt uneasy ever since hearing the girl's name. "But she's too young, I wouldn't have known her."

"She went by Mary."

"Mary LaBelle." Abby rubbed the back of her neck and drew her lips into a knot as she tossed the name around in her head. She came up with nothing, just a vague uneasiness that she should remember something. Something important. "Sorry. It's probably nothing."

"Do you know if your ex wore any piece of jewelry that was important to him?"

"Like what? A nose ring?"

He snorted a laugh. "I don't know, but let's start with a ring, you know, for his finger."

She crossed her arms. "He never even wore his wedding band after about six months into the marriage. He had an accident when he was sailing, the ring got caught on something, or so he claimed. Anyway, he quit wearing it. Later, I figured he just didn't want to advertise the fact that he was married. I still have it, in my jewelry box," she admitted, embarrassed. "I guess I was saving it for an anniversary or something so I could hurl it into the Mississippi, but I never got around to it."

He was staring at her with those damned dark eyes that seemed to see more than she wanted him to. She felt foolish, as if she were sentimental for a marriage that had died a natural death long ago, long before the divorce proceedings had been started.

"So...no wedding ring or ring of any kind?"

"I never saw him wearing one." She looked pointedly at the gold ring in Montoya's ear. "No earrings, either, or...ID bracelets or gold chains...the only piece of jewelry, if you could call it that, was a watch. Never without it." Her stomach curdled when she remembered the day she'd dashed outside, trying to avoid big drops of rain, to the spot where he'd parked the BMW. She'd been on a mission of mercy, to close the sun roof and to find his auto insurance documents as there was some question about coverage on the new car. What she'd discovered, locked in the glove box of the shiny black sports car, was an expensive watch, a card signed by initials she recognized as belonging to Connie Hastings, the owner of a rival radio station that was trying to lure Luke away from his job at WSLJ, and the singularly devastating knowledge that her husband had been cheating on her. Again. Her hands had shaken as she'd read the cute, overtly suggestive card. Her stomach had boiled with acid when she opened the padded box wherein lay the Rolex. The whole experience was tantamount to a blow to the solar plexus. She'd felt as if she couldn't draw a breath and she'd been totally unaware that the passenger side door was still open, the warning bell dinging insistently, rain blowing into the interior, drenching her and the stupid proof of insurance.

God, she'd been such a fool. If she hadn't been pregnant at the time, she would have divorced him on the spot. Instead she'd left the sun roof open, the card and gift on the passenger seat, the door open in hopes that the interior of the car would be ruined, the battery drained, and the precious new watch stolen. She'd vomited in the bushes, delighting Hershey, then gone inside and waited for Luke to step out of the shower.

Now, she looked up and found Montoya waiting. "Oh, well. The watch. It's a Rolex, one that he could use scuba diving, if you can believe that. It still ran under so many pounds of pressure and could withstand decompression...and it was cool enough looking that he never took it off. At least he didn't while we were married."

"Did he have it insured?"

"I don't know," she admitted. "But since you're asking, I assume it's missing."

"Just taking an inventory of all of his stuff."

"But if he had been wearing the watch, you'd know about it, right?" she asked. "You wouldn't have to ask me."

"We can never rule out robbery as a motive."

"If Courtney killed him, she didn't rob him. If it was someone else, why go to all the trouble to take them both out to the middle of nowhere?" Abby asked, angry that the detective was holding out on her. "Thieves usually rob people on the street, in a car, at work, at home. They don't go to the trouble and time of getting two victims together to stage some bizarre murder-suicide."

"Unless they were into it," Montoya said.

"Is there a reason you've not told me more about what happened the other night?" she asked, deciding to air her worst fears. "Am I under suspicion or something?"

"Everyone is."

"Especially ex-wives who are publicly humiliated on the day of the murder, right?"

Something in Montoya's expression changed. Hardened. "I'll

be back," he promised, "and I'll bring another detective with me, then we'll interview you and you can ask all the questions you like."

"And you'll answer them?"

He offered a hint of a smile. "That I can't promise. Just that I won't lie to you."

"I wouldn't expect you to, Detective."

He gave a quick nod. "In the meantime if you suddenly remember, or think of anything, give me a call."

"I will," she promised, irritated, watching as he hurried down the two steps of the porch to his car. He was younger than she was by a couple of years, she guessed, though she couldn't be certain, and there was something about him that exuded a natural brooding sexuality, as if he knew he was attractive to women, almost expected it to be so.

Great. Just what she needed, a sexy-as-hell cop who probably had her pinned to the top of his murder suspect list. She whistled for the dog and Hershey bounded inside, dragging some mud and leaves with her. "Sit!" Abby commanded and the Lab dropped her rear end onto the floor just inside the door. Abby opened the door to the closet and found a towel hanging on a peg she kept for just such occasions, then, while Hershey whined in protest, she cleaned all four of her damp paws. "You're gonna be a problem, aren't you?" she teased, then dropped the towel over the dog's head.

Hershey shook herself, tossed off the towel, then bit at it, snagging one end in her mouth and pulling backward in a quick game of tug of war. Abby laughed as she played with the dog, the first real joy she'd felt since hearing the news about her ex-husband. The phone rang and she left the dog growling and shaking the tattered piece of terry cloth.

"Hello?" she said, still chuckling at Hershey's antics as she lifted the phone to her ear.

"Abby Chastain?"

"Yes."

"Beth Ann Wright with the *New Orleans Sentinel*."

Abby's heart plummeted. The press. *Just what she needed.*

"You were Luke Gierman's wife, right?"

"What's this about?" Abby asked warily as Hershey padded

into the kitchen and looked expectantly at the back door leading to her studio. "In a second," she mouthed to the Lab. Hershey slowly wagged her tail.

"Oh, I'm sorry," Beth Ann said, sounding sincerely rueful. "I should have explained. The paper's running a series of articles on Luke, as he was a local celebrity, and I'd like to interview you for the piece. I was thinking we could meet tomorrow morning?"

"Luke and I were divorced."

"Yes, I know, but I would like to give some insight to the man behind the mike, you know. He had a certain public persona, but I'm sure my readers would like to know more about him, his history, his hopes, his dreams, you know, the human-interest angle."

"It's kind of late for that," Abby said, not bothering to keep the ice out of her voice.

"But you knew him intimately. I thought you could come up with some anecdotes, let people see the real Luke Gierman."

"I don't think so."

"I realize you and he had some unresolved issues."

"Pardon me?"

"I caught his program the other day."

Abby tensed, her fingers holding the phone in a death grip.

"So this is probably harder for you than most, but I still would like to ask you some questions."

"Maybe another time," she hedged and Beth Ann didn't miss a beat.

"Anytime you'd like. You're a native Louisianan, aren't you?" Abby's neck muscles tightened. "Born and raised, but you met Luke in Seattle when he was working for a radio station...what's the call sign, I know I've got it somewhere."

"KCTY." It was a matter of public record.

"Oh, that's right. Country in the City. But you grew up here and went to local schools, right? Your mother and father are from around here?"

Warning bells clanged in Abby's head. She felt a headache forming in the base of her skull.

"I don't want to talk about it."

"Jacques and Faith Chastain."

"Luke was their son-in-law for a few years, nothing more," Abby said tightly.

"Wait a minute..." Beth Ann muttered, as if searching through some notes, though Abby suspected she had all the information at her fingertips. "Your mother probably never met him, right? Wasn't your mother, Faith Chastain, the woman who died at Our Lady of Virtues Hospital, the one they're planning to tear down?"

The woman had certainly done her homework.

"So, she never really knew Luke as a son-in-law?"

Abby hung up. Slammed the receiver down and vowed if it rang again, she'd just let the answering machine pick up. She would screen her calls. Anyone who wanted an appointment to see the house or for a photography session would leave a message.

She stared at the phone for a second, half expecting it to ring again, then she let out a long breath. *Get used to it,* her mind warned her, *this is just the beginning. Until they find Luke's killer and even afterward, the press, police, and the just-plain-curious will be calling.*

There was just no getting around it.

The drive to Baton Rouge was fairly tolerable, Montoya thought. Brinkman wasn't as irritating as usual and he kept the conversation on the crime. So far the lab had come up with nothing, but Gierman's car had been found in an alley near his athletic club, the ATM where he'd gotten money only a block away. The trouble was, according to Brinkman, no one at the club had seen Gierman at the facility working out. He hadn't shown up for his personal training session nor the rock climbing he liked to do on the fake stone wall that was built into the place.

At first glance Gierman's BMW seemed clean, but the techs at the police garage were still going over it.

"I also had a chat with the ex-girlfriend, Nia Penne," Brinkman said, cracking his window as Montoya drove northwest on Highway 10. It was twilight, headlights punctuating the gathering darkness, the air thick with the promise of more rain.

"What did she say?"

"Mainly that Gierman was a ladies' man. Had the old wandering eye, but she thinks he was still in love with his ex-wife all the same." He shot Montoya a look across the darkened front seat of the Crown Victoria.

"This is the same guy who bad-mouthed her on his program."

"Yep. That's what she claims. I asked about it but she said his show was all an act, if you can believe it."

Montoya didn't.

"Anyway, if you ask me, airing all your dirty laundry ain't exactly a way back into a lady's good graces, or the sack." He cackled as he fished in his inside jacket pocket and came up with a crumpled pack of cigarettes. "Go figure." He shook out a filter tip, rammed it into the corner of his mouth, and searched his pockets for his lighter.

Montoya didn't have too much trouble figuring at all. He eased the car around a broad corner and decided it might be tough to get over a woman like Abby Chastain.

"I'm lookin' into the money." The cigarette wobbled in his mouth as he spoke. "Who gets what, assuming Gierman still has some after his divorce. Usually the wife, she makes out like a bandit."

Montoya wasn't buying it. However, he hadn't gone through three divorces like Brinkman had. And he had a sense that Abby Chastain wasn't about the money. But then, he could be wrong. It wasn't as if he hadn't made mistakes of character in the past. "Back to Gierman. So he was a player. We already knew that. What about the girlfriend's alibi?"

"Iron tight. Like a damned locked chastity belt." Brinkman found the lighter and fired up his cigarette. "She's been in Toronto with friends, a couple with a ten-month-old baby." He shot a stream of smoke toward the passenger window. "When Gierman was killed, she was with her friends, drinking wine and playing cards at their house until one-thirty in the morning. Noise woke up the neighbors, who called the police. Took everyone's names."

"Maybe she hired someone."

"Doesn't sound like it." Brinkman shook his head and wrinkled his nose. "She was a little pissed off at him. Seems he had a fling with some waitress at a hotel restaurant on Bourbon Street and Nia found out about it. Threw a hissy fit and quit seeing him. They hadn't been cohabiting, so she just broke it off. If anything, she seemed relieved."

"And the waitress?"

He took another deep drag. "Haven't got that far yet. Hey, ain't this the exit?"

Montoya was already braking. He flipped on his turn signal and drove through the rain-washed streets of Baton Rouge. Though it wasn't quite yet night, the street lamps, guided by the thickening twilight, had begun to glow, casting a shimmering light on the wet asphalt. Pedestrians scurried under awnings or beneath umbrellas, and a few bicyclists sped through the puddles. Neon lights offered sizzling splashes of color from windows of bars and restaurants lining the streets.

"What about the radio station? Anyone there who would like to put Gierman off the air permanently?"

"Still lookin' into it. Spoke with a couple of coworkers, so far everyone's talkin' nicey-nice about the dead. To hear them tell it, Gierman was a helluva guy. A goddamned prince." He snorted, smoke curling out of his nostrils. "Nice guy, my ass. Still got a few more people to talk to. Last to see him, so far, was his sidekick, Maury Taylor, who seems genuinely upset. Could be an act." He tossed the butt of his cigarette out the window. "Radio guys," he said derisively. "Bunch of whack jobs."

Montoya eased the cruiser through a residential district where the houses became larger and grander as they approached the university. Landscaped lawns, wide verandahs, gingerbread accents, fresh paint, and the look of affluence surrounded the gated entrance to All Saints College.

"You know where you're going?" Brinkman asked as they passed the unguarded gate.

"Cramer Hall."

"You've been there before?"

Montoya nodded. "Bentz's kid, Kristi, lived in that dorm when she went to school here." He didn't go into the reasons he'd been here, the terror that Kristi and her father had lived through, but Brinkman had been around at that time. Knew the score.

"Oh, yeah," he said now, nodding. "That case with that serial killer who called himself the Chosen One or some such shit. Jesus, there was a nut job."

Aren't they all? Montoya found a parking spot designated for visitors, then he and Brinkman piled out of the car. Ducking their heads, they made their way inside the dorm to where the Dean of Students, Dr. Sharon Usher, who had been called earlier, waited. The dean was a small-shouldered, nervous woman with short brown hair shot with silver, no makeup, and thin, pinched lips. She looked about forty-five, but the gray hair could have added some extra years. She was every bit a part of cliché academia with her owlish glasses, long tweed skirt, and brown sweater.

They shook hands all around and she, clutching a large key ring as if it held the keys to the kingdom, led them up the old stairs of the brick building—a building that smelled of perfume, sweaty running gear, and enthusiasm. Girls in groups of three or four, chatting wildly, wearing headsets or clutching cell phones, passed by, barely noticing the older men.

But the third floor was quiet. Any students still around were either locked behind their doors or out. Crime-scene tape barred the door to Room 534.

"I hope you clear this up quickly," Dr. Usher said, as if the police department would intentionally drag its heels.

"That's the general plan," Brinkman acknowledged with a conspiring glance at Montoya.

"Good. Good. As you asked, I've got Courtney's class schedule, a list of the students in those classes as well as everyone here in the dorm, by room number. I also think you should know that Mr. Gierman was here, just three weeks ago. He was a guest speaker in Dr. Starr's Personal Communications 101. Courtney was in that class."

Montoya stopped and his focus sharpened. Finally a connection between the two victims.

"Luke Gierman was here?" he clarified.

"That's right." She sifted through the keys.

"Did Courtney speak with him?"

"I don't think so, but I really don't know. I've talked to Dr. Starr. The administration wasn't pleased at his choice of speakers." She slipped one of the keys into the lock of the dorm room. "As much as we preach diversity and freedom of speech and everything else, this is still a pretty conservative school."

"We'll need to talk to Starr, too."

"I know. He'll meet with you later, when we're finished," she said with the efficiency with which, he guessed, Dean Usher tackled any assignment. "I've included his cell phone number along with everything else in a file in my office. You can pick the file up when you're through here."

Montoya glanced at Brinkman. Maybe they'd caught a break. Usher unlocked the door and, without another word, let it swing open.

Montoya stepped inside and, for a second, felt as if he'd been propelled into another world. "What the hell is all this?" he asked, flipping on the light and staring at the walls. One side of the room was painted stark white and covered with crucifixes, pictures of the Holy Mother, Mary, and portraits of Jesus upon the cross. The other side was painted black as night and was starkly bare. No wall hangings, no pictures, nothing to reveal anything about the occupant. The desk on the white side of the room was littered with Lucite cubes and framed pictures of Courtney Mary LaBelle along with an open Bible and a rosary that hung from the knob of her closet door. The other side of the room was nearly empty aside from a small printer and several books on a bookcase, novels by Anne Rice and others about vampires, werewolves, and the paranormal.

"I don't get it," Brinkman said, and for once, Montoya agreed.

"This room belongs to Courtney LaBelle"—Dr. Usher motioned toward the cluttered side of the room—"as well as Ophelia Ketterling." The dean's hand waved toward the stark black walls.

"Roommates?" Brinkman said.

"We encourage our students to be individuals and some of them, well, they take it to the max." To prove her point more clearly, Dr. Usher snapped down the window shade, allowing no fading light into the room, flipped on a single lamp that sat on the desk in the dark side of the room, then turned off the overhead light.

"Holy shit," Brinkman said as the dark room transformed instantly. Instead of flat black, the wall was suddenly crawling with designs that were only apparent when the black lightbulb glowed with its eerie purple light. Weird, nearly abstract pictures of gargoyles, vampires, and creatures with long teeth, tails, and tongues appeared as if they'd erupted from the very bowels of hell. "Jesus H. Christ," Brinkman muttered. "Would you look at this."

"Ophelia is an art student. A talented one, though some question her subject matter." Usher snapped on the overhead again and the grotesque images disappeared.

"How did Courtney get along with her roommate?"

"They didn't."

Big surprise, Montoya thought.

"She, uh, complain about the weirdo decorations?" Brinkman asked.

"Not to me, nor the resident advisor," the dean said, biting her lower lip. "It's fall term, actually the year has barely started. I only heard about this"—she motioned toward the black walls—"after word of the tragedy hit." She sighed and wrapped her arms around her slim waist, the key ring jingling in her fingers. "It's all so horrible."

Amen to that, Montoya thought. "Did the two girls know each other before they came to All Saints?" Montoya asked.

"Courtney and Ophelia? Oh, no." She shook her head.

Montoya believed it. "Then how did they get together?"

"Computer random pairing," the dean said.

"As different as they are?" Montoya asked.

"Maybe not so different. Both into art, both nonsmokers, both come from religious families, Courtney from New Orleans, Ophelia from Lafayette. Both their mothers went to college here, both from the upper middle class. Both went to private Catholic high schools. Yes, they're very different, but they had a lot in common." Her smile was wan. "Obviously, it didn't work out."

"Can we talk to Ms. Ketterling?" Montoya asked.

"She's downstairs in the office."

Brinkman was already poking around. Montoya said, "We'll just be a few minutes."

"I'll be there as well." The dean clipped off in hard-soled shoes that echoed through the tile floors of the hallway and down the stairs.

"What a freak fest," Brinkman muttered. "The weird art... the vampire books, the black walls. This chick is disturbed. Extremely disturbed. We might want to find out where she was on the night her roommate bit it."

"Lots of people read vampire books. It's cool these days."

"Just cuz it's considered cool, doesn't mean it's a good idea."

Painstakingly they searched the small room, barely speaking to each other, finding nothing of interest. Courtney Mary's side of the room held textbooks, a few pairs of jeans, T-shirts and sweaters, one dress, and a drawer for her bras and underwear. Crammed onto the desk was typical college stuff: iPod, notebook computer, cell phone, makeup, and toiletries. It was odd she hadn't taken her cell phone with her, Montoya thought, and bagged it. He eyed the religious symbols. Pictures of angels, reprints of religious paintings—some Montoya recognized—crucifixes and statues of the Madonna. One rosary was looped over the handle of her closet door, another draped over her bedpost. Saints cards and medals were kept in a special box.

He wondered about her obsession. Had being forced to live with a girl who seemed more interested in the dark arts than getting into heaven caused Courtney to take an even deeper interest in her religion? She'd already thought she'd been called, had heard God's voice. What had being with this roommate done to her?

"Weirder and weirder..." Brinkman finally said. "Isn't that from an old book?"

"I think it's 'curiouser and curiouser.' From *Alice in Wonderland.*"

"Close enough." Brinkman hooked a thumb to the dark side of the room. "And speaking of Wonderland. This chick is off." Then he glanced at Courtney Mary's side. "Well, they both are."

"Maybe that's why the computer connected them," Montoya said. "Yin and yang."

"Whatever. I need a smoke." He was already scrounging into the inside pocket of his jacket. "How about we finish here, I go outside, and I meet you in the office?"

"Works for me."

The dog would be a problem.
They always were.

He mentally berated himself as he stood in the woods, darkness closing in, the smell of the swamp thick and dank in his nostrils. Through the dripping Spanish moss and swamp oak and sycamore trees, he stared at the cottage with its broad bank of windows.

Rain gurgled and ran in the gutters as the wind gusted away from the house, carrying his scent in the opposite direction. From these ever-darkening shadows he could, as he had before, follow her movements as she walked through her home. He knew where she kept her hand cream, in the small bathroom near the stairs. He'd seen her coming out of that doorway, rubbing her hands together. He'd watched as she stretched upward to a top shelf in the hallway where her holiday decorations were stashed and seen a flash of smooth hard abdomen as her knit shirt had risen upward, away from the waistband of her jeans. And he knew that in a drawer near the bed, the side of the bed where she didn't sleep, there was a gun in the drawer; he'd seen her pull it out, study it, then replace it and shut the drawer quickly.

Her husband's father's service weapon, he'd learned from Luke Gierman's last radio broadcast.

Now, she was inside. He caught her image as he stared through her windows, where the warm patches of light were like beacons in the gathering twilight. She'd made herself a pot of coffee and was sipping from a cup as she moved from one room to the next, talking to her animals, turning on the television, working at the table where she'd laid out negatives and pictures. Though he'd barely heard the ringing of her phone, he'd watched as she'd picked up the kitchen extension and talked without a hint of a smile.

The conversation was probably about her dead husband.

Studying her, he wondered how she could have married a man as base as Gierman, a man who had publicly cheated on her and had belittled her on the air.

Mary did you a favor, he thought, remembering the feel of the gun blast in the girl's hand as she'd killed Gierman, who had been frantic, his eyes bulging in fear, his head shaking wildly as if in so doing he could stop the inevitable.

Gierman's body had jerked when the gun had gone off. Instantly blood had begun to pump the life from him. Yes, Mary, the virgin, had done the world a favor in taking Gierman's life. And then she'd made the ultimate sacrifice herself.

He felt a little buzz in his blood as he remembered the feeling of power, of justice, that had swept over him.

From his hiding spot he saw Abby throw out a hip and wrap one arm under her breasts as she cocked her head and held the phone against her ear. Curling, red-gold hair fell to her shoulders, not the dark mahogany color of Faith's, but just as inviting. Hot. Fiery.

He swallowed hard as rain caught in his eyelashes and dripped down his nose.

She twisted her head, as if rotating the kinks from her neck, and his erection sprouted as he looked at the column of her throat, the circle of bones at its base.

He rubbed the tips of his gloved fingers together in anticipation and licked his lips, tasting his own sweat and the wash of rainwater. God, she was beautiful. So much like Faith. For a second, he closed his eyes, let the ache within, the wanting control him; felt the rain, God's tears wash over him, bless him on his mission.

I will not fail, he silently vowed, then opened his eyes to look at her beautiful face, but she'd moved. She wasn't framed in the living room window any longer.

Where was she?

Panic jetted through him as he checked every window...no sign of her. Had she decided to step outside? But he wasn't ready. He reached into his pocket, felt the handle of the hunting knife and wondered if he'd have to use it.

Heart pumping, his fingers surrounding the hilt, he started to move.

Suddenly she appeared, walking toward the windows from an interior room near the central hallway. He relaxed a second. She was heading into the dining area, but she abruptly stopped, as if she'd heard something. She turned, her eyes staring straight at him. A frown pulled at the corners of her mouth. Her eyebrows drew together. She walked unerringly to the window and stared into the darkness.

He froze.

Caught his breath.

Ignored the thrum through his body as she squinted, gold eyes narrowing.

She was utterly beautiful. He watched as she bit the corner of her lip, her eyes trained on the very spot where he was hiding. Had he moved? Caught her attention somehow? Then maybe it was time... her time...

No, no! Stay with the plan! You've worked too many years to change things now. Do NOT *follow your instincts... not yet.*

But she was so like the other one; nearly a replica of Faith. He stared straight into her intense eyes, willing her to see him. Daring her.

Absently she scratched her nape and he studied the movement, thought of the soft skin at her hairline. He considered what she might taste like, what she would feel like, facedown, unaware until his weight pressed her deeper into the mattress...

She moved and his inward vision died. Now, she was walking the length of the house, talking to someone, heading toward the door that led to the little walkway separating the main house from her studio. As she passed the French doors, he understood. The damned dog was trotting eagerly beside her, nose upward as if the blasted animal were listening and understanding every word. In a few seconds she'd be at the back door and would probably let the fool dog out. The stupid beast would come barking and leaping after him.

He reached into his jacket pocket, withdrew the stolen cell phone, and knowing that he'd blocked caller ID from any transmission, hit speed dial. For her number. The number he'd programed in earlier after lifting the phone out of an unlocked car. He was already moving away from the house, cutting through the heavy cypress, pines, and underbrush, not checking to see if she was going to pick up.

One ring.

Sweating, he hurdled a small log in his path.

Two rings.

Oh, fuck, was she letting the damned dog out?

Three rings.

She wasn't answering. Damn it, she was probably already at the door. He increased his speed.

Four rings.

Shit!

Click.

His heart nearly stopped.

"Hi, this is Abby. Leave a message."

He slapped his phone shut, jammed it into his pocket, and silently raced through the dense foliage. He was swift, his body honed from exercise, but he didn't want to blow his cover by allowing an idiot dog to find him. He'd parked the car over a mile away behind the shed of an abandoned sawmill.

Even in the gathering darkness he didn't need a flashlight; he'd traveled this way many times. At the fence of the Pomeroy property, he slowed, carefully walking the perimeter, past a small utility gate far from the road. Breathing hard, he half expected Asa's damned Rottweiler to charge at the fence.

Another stupid dog to deal with.

But there was no growling, no barking, no thundering paws, no snarling, drooling jaws snapping at him from behind the iron bars sealing off Pomeroy's acres. He turned on the speed again, crossed the road, and slipped onto a deer trail that cut behind the old mill.

Minutes later he vaulted the rusted chain-link fence and landed behind the dilapidated drying shed where his truck was parked.

By the time he slid behind the steering wheel, he was soaked from running through the damp underbrush and his own sweat. His head was pounding, his breathing irregular, not from the run, but from the knowledge that he had come close to being discovered.

Not yet. Oh, no, not yet.

As he switched on the ignition, he let out his breath. Pulling out from behind the old drying shed, he flipped on his wipers to push aside the drops that had collected. He didn't bother with headlights. Just in case anyone was nearby.

The truck bounced and jostled over the pitted road. He had to stop to open the gate, drive through, then stop and close the gate behind him again, securing the hiding place for another time. He even secured the damned thing with his own lock. He'd already dispensed with the original one by snipping it with bolt cutters a few weeks earlier.

Because this was the perfect location to hide his vehicle.

Once inside the King Cab again, he eased toward the main road and, seeing no car coming, eased onto the highway and turned on his headlights. His heart was still pounding out of control, his nerves stretched to the breaking point. He rolled a window down to help with the fog inside, then once he'd put a few miles between himself and Abby Chastain's cottage, he switched on the radio and hit the button for WSLJ.

"... continuing our tribute to Luke Gierman tonight. All of us here at WSLJ, well, and I'm sure everyone in New Orleans, too, is outraged and saddened by what happened to Luke and we urge everyone who's listening, if they know anything that might help the police solve this crime, to call in. We don't have a lot of details as to exactly what happened yet, but it seems that the murder-suicide theory has been scrapped, and that the police believe the double murder was staged to make it appear as if the female victim, Courtney LaBelle, shot Luke then turned the gun on herself. Local, state, and federal authorities are now searching for the killer of both Luke Gierman and Courtney Mary LaBelle. The minute we get any more information about this sick crime, we'll let you know, of course.

"Now, we've got several of his personal favorite shows and we'll run them back to back with a half an hour between each one where you, the listeners, Luke's fans, can call in with your comments, or if you'd rather, e-mail them to the station and we'll read them on the air. The first show will be taken from last summer, right before the Fourth of July, and it will be replayed at nine P.M. ...."

Satisfied, he snapped off the radio. The tribute to Gierman was pathetic, but it also kept the public aware of Gierman's death and that was important. So the citizens of New Orleans were "outraged and saddened." Good. It was time. Long past.

Tune in tomorrow, he thought as he considered his next act of retribution, his next victims.

They were out there.

Just waiting for him.

CHAPTER 7

Montoya locked the door to the dorm room, then he and Brinkman clomped down four flights to the main reception area of Cramer Hall. While Brinkman peeled off to go outside and light up, Montoya found the small office behind the bank of mailboxes where Dean Usher sat behind a wide oak desk. A heavyset girl with obviously dyed black hair and a bad complexion that was partially hidden by white, ghoulish makeup glowered from a side chair. She was wearing a long black dress, black lacy gloves without fingers, black boots, and a bad attitude as she sat cross-legged, one booted foot bouncing nervously.

"Ophelia, this is Detective Montoya." Usher looked past him to the doorway, obviously expecting Brinkman to follow. "Detective Montoya, Ophelia Ketterling."

"Just O," the girl corrected without a hint of a smile. "I go by O."

Montoya took the only remaining chair, near the girl. "Detective Brinkman will be here in a second," he explained. "But we should get started. I'll be recording this interview. That okay with you?"

A lift of one shoulder. As if she just didn't give a damn and was waiting for the ordeal to be over. "Whatever."

"Good." He set the pocket recorder on the corner of the big desk.

Dean Usher eyed the tiny machine with its slow-moving tape as if it were a rabid dog, but she didn't argue. "Both detectives are with the New Orleans Police Department and want to ask you some questions about Courtney."

"You mean 'Mary,' don't you?" the girl shot back, coming to life a bit. "She was pretty insistent about her name."

The dean's irritation was visible in the tightening of the corners of her mouth. "Just answer the questions."

"What are they?" Looking past layers of mascara, she managed to appear bored to tears.

"First of all, was she dating anyone?"

Ophelia snorted derisively and folded her arms across her chest, thus increasing her cleavage. Which, he figured, was intentional. Montoya had seen dozens of kids with the same kind of attitude as this girl, so hung up on being "bad" and "different" he could read her like a book. "No one, okay?"

"No boyfriend?"

She rolled her expressive eyes, as if she thought him a thick-headed idiot. "Not unless you count Jesus."

"Ophelia!" The dean came unglued. "This is an interview, you're being recorded."

"Well, it's true. It's all she ever talked about. God, Jesus, and the damned Holy Spirit. She was a freak. Went on and on about promising herself to God and being married to Him and how she couldn't wait to join an order of nuns, that she was just in college to appease her parents."

"How'd that sit with you?"

"How do you think?" she said and Montoya noticed a small red stone pierced into one nostril as well as a necklace that was really a long leather cord that encircled her neck. Hanging from the thin, twisted strap was a tiny glass vial that was dark from the liquid inside.

Using the exposed fingers of one gloved hand, she plucked up the end of the necklace and held the small bottle to the light. "Are you looking at this? Wanna know what it is?" She lifted one dark eyebrow in a vampish, sexy come-on. "It's blood, okay."

"That's enough!" the dean said, reaching for the recorder. "Let's turn this off, at least for the moment."

Ophelia actually smiled, her glistening purple-colored lips stretching. "Don't turn it off. I want to get this over with, and for the record, we're on the record, right, isn't that what the recorder is all about? This is not only blood." She wiggled the tiny little jar with its dark liquid contents splashing against the glass. "It's human."

At that point Brinkman, reeking of smoke, walked in, glanced around, and took up his vigil by the door.

Ophelia was in full shock mode now. Montoya waited, showed no emotion, let her run her game.

"Of course it's not human blood," the dean said, but her own face had whitened and one of her hands had curled into an anxious fist. "We have rules about these kind of things."

"No, you don't. It's *my* blood and I can carry it around however I want, whether it's in my body, or in a test tube or in this." She wiggled the leather strands. "It's rare blood, too," Ophelia added proudly. "AB negative."

Brinkman cleared his throat. Looked uncomfortable as hell.

"About your roommate," Montoya said, refusing to be derailed. The shock show was over as far as he was concerned. "Can you tell me the last time you saw Courtney LaBelle?"

Ophelia didn't bother correcting him on the victim's name this time. "Okay, on the day she was killed, nothing big was happening. I saw her getting ready to go to the library like she always does... did. She had her backpack with her and had changed into her jogging clothes, the ones she always wore when she was going to study and then run afterward."

"She seemed normal?"

"Oh, whoa. No way. She *never* seemed normal to me," Ophelia said, twisting the vial in her fingers. "She was at least ten beads shy of a full rosary, to put it in her vernacular. But if you mean did she seem any different than usual? No. She was the same. Weird and holy as shit as ever."

"Ophelia," the dean warned.

"It's O, remember?"

Montoya asked, "What time did she leave that day?"

Ophelia dropped the vial and shifted in the chair. Her cleavage disappeared. "I'm not sure, but it was after dinner, if that's what you call the food they serve in the dorm." She shuddered and pulled a face.

"So it was night?"

"Yeah. Dark. Like . . . seven, seven-thirty, in there somewhere."

"What time did she usually come back?"

"Before midnight, I guess," she said, then looked out the window, where the reflection of her pale face was visible.

"Do you know if she met anyone?"

Ophelia shook her head, wound a finger in a strand of her straight black hair. "I don't know. Don't think so. She was like a loner. I told you. Extremely odd. Ultrareligious. A real nut case."

"She must've had friends."

Ophelia shrugged. "Maybe through the church. I don't really know. There's a youth group and then she knew someone, a nun, I think, in an order somewhere . . . hell, what was her name? Melinda or Margaret, maybe. No . . ."

"Maria?" Montoya asked and a feeling of dread settled deep in his gut.

"Yeah! That was it."

"From Our Lady of Virtues?" He felt cold inside, cold as death.

"Could be. Yeah, maybe." She chewed on a small black fingernail, then sighed and trained her eyes on Montoya again. "I didn't pay a whole lot of attention, y'know. I can't remember."

"And as far as you know, she wasn't dating anyone special," Montoya asked.

Ophelia let out a puff of exasperation. "I think we covered that. She was married to God, remember? No dates with mortal males. I guess that was out. It wasn't an open marriage."

Ignoring the comments, Montoya pressed on, "Did she wear a ring?"

"Oh, yeah. Always. The virgin ring."

"What?"

"That's what I call it. It's what some kids do who are really into the God-thing. They get a ring, or someone important gives it to them, like, I dunno, a parent or something, and they, the girl, she, like promises not to do the wild thing, you know. Have sex? It's like some kind of a covenant between the girl who gets the ring and

God. She swears to remain a virgin until she gets married, or...
maybe forever in Mary's case, you know, since she was married to
God and all." Ophelia rolled both palms toward the ceiling.
"What's that all about? Virginity forever? Give me a break." She
shook her head as if ridding it of obscene ideas. "See what I mean?
Mary was really, really fuck...messed up."

"Did she ever mention Luke Gierman?" Montoya asked.

"Yeah, I guess so," Ophelia said dismissively. "Once, maybe,
twice when she'd overheard part of his show and was"—she held
up her hands and made air quotes with her fingers—"'shocked' by
what he said. Jesus, wasn't that the whole point?"

Montoya felt a little jolt of electricity, that bit of adrenalin rush
he always experienced when he hit on the first glimmerings of a
connection. "Did she know him?"

"Nah. I don't think so."

"She ever call his program?"

Ophelia opened her mouth to answer, then closed it quickly and
thought for a second. "I was gonna say 'no' for sure, but I don't
know. She never said she called and I never heard her phone in.
She wasn't like that. Didn't have the balls. Was kinda mousy. But
hey, stranger things have happened. She could have phoned, I
guess. I just never heard about it."

"But she did talk about him?"

"Not really. Oh, wait, no...she maybe said something to me
once, maybe twice. About him needing to find Jesus. But then, she
thought everyone did, including me, so I didn't really think too
much about it."

"But you don't know if she ever talked to him about it," Brinkman clarified and O shook her head.

"Let's back up a second," Montoya suggested. "Courtney, Mary,
did go out with friends, though? She did things, had a social life?"

"I guess, if you could call it that. But it wasn't the normal stuff.
She didn't hang out at the local pub or go to concerts or games or
anything like that."

"Isn't she too young for the pub?" Brinkman asked and Dean
Usher tensed another notch.

Ophelia sent Brinkman an exasperated, don't-play-dumb, we-
both-know-about-fake-IDs look. "She usually went to the library

after we ate, then she'd jog back, change clothes, and go to the chapel for an hour or two to pray or whatever it was she did there."

"The chapel on campus?"

"Yeah, but I don't think she got that far that night," Ophelia said, her foot no longer bouncing. "She didn't come back to change like she always does and she wouldn't have gone to the chapel in her running gear."

"You keep tabs on her?" Brinkman asked.

Another bored glance his way. "No way. After the first week of school, I didn't ask her anything. She had a way of twisting everything and I mean *every*thing to God. It didn't matter if I was studying or on the phone or going to the shower, she was right there, always with a cheery face and a suggestion that I find Jesus. You know, I was raised Catholic, went to St. Theresa's in Santa Lucia. That's in California, by the way."

"I thought you were from Lafayette," Montoya said.

"I mean when I was younger. My dad was transferred to Lafayette during my junior year. It was a real pisser. Anyway, all that Catholic school, and I never had to go and beat the bushes to find someone to convert. Most of the kids I went to school with at St. Theresa's were cool about it; kept all the God-stuff to themselves. No way were they out on some kind of mission to save the world. But Mary, she's like one of those born-agains. Avid. Rabid. All of the above. So, no, I did *not* keep tabs on her. In fact, I tried to avoid her. She was a real freak-out. I'd already put in a request for a new roommate."

Montoya glanced at Dean Usher, who nodded.

"Let me get this straight," Brinkman said, folding his arms over his chest. "*She* freaked *you* out?"

O nodded. "Amen and end of story."

They questioned her a little more, then, after securing the file from Dean Usher of all of Courtney's classes, they visited the chapel and met with Dr. Starr, a man in his early thirties. Fit and lean, Starr blinked as if his contacts were ill-fitting. He showed them into his tiny office, a room barely larger than a closet, which was situated on the second floor in one of the massive stone and brick buildings that surrounded the quad. There were two padded folding chairs on one side of his chipped wooden desk and on the other, a rolling executive-type chair upholstered in oxblood leather. "Please, have a seat," he suggested after introductions were made. His desk was huge, but neat, as if he spent his days patting the piles of essays and phone messages into precise stacks. The bookcase behind him was carefully arranged, not one bound volume out of place, and Montoya, though he didn't say it, thought the room looked as if it were more for show than work. At the station, Montoya's own desk was organized, but functioning, and always changing with the reports, files, and messages that landed in his in basket. Bentz's was cluttered, in an order only he could decipher, and Brinkman's was a pigsty, with seven or eight coffee cups in the litter of reports, newspapers, messages, and jumbles of pens.

But this guy's . . . it just looked too perfect.

"I know this is about Mary," Starr said as he snapped on a desk lamp that glowed in soft gold tones. Montoya made a note that he was familiar enough to call her by the name she preferred. "What a tragedy. It's shocked the faculty and student body, I assure you."

"How well did you know her?" Brinkman asked, getting right to the point.

"Enough to see that she was a talented writer. Her essays were insightful, her observations in class deep, though theologically narrow." He smiled and slid a glance at his watch.

"Small class?" Montoya asked. "Enough that in the first few weeks of school you know all of your students?"

"This one was," he said patiently. "And yes . . . eight in the morning isn't a popular time for most students. The class is only twenty-six." He blinked. Frowned. "Or was."

Brinkman said, "We were told you had Luke Gierman come and speak to the class."

"Luke Gierman, yes, I know, the shock jock who was killed. His body was found with Mary's. I saw it on the news." Some of Starr's cool facade slipped and Montoya thought a few beads of sweat showed at his hairline. "I asked Gierman to speak to PC 101 because—"

"PC 101?" Brinkman asked. "As in Politically Correct?"

"Personal Communications," Starr explained, a slight edge to his voice. "I thought the kids would like him and that it would shake up the system here a little. The only time he could make it

122 • *Lisa Jackson*

was the eight o'clock, so we set it up." Starr glanced away, looked through the tiny window in his office. "Of course, I had no idea what would happen."

"Of course," Brinkman said, and Starr looked up at him sharply.

"I assure you, all I did was invite a speaker from a radio station." He rearranged his pens around the ink blotter covering the wood desk. "You know, I would appreciate your keeping my name out of this investigation as much as possible ... I'm fairly new here and though I wanted to, you know, create some interest by bringing a radio personality to the classroom, I ... I, well ... I don't need this kind of trouble."

"We're investigating a double homicide," Montoya said, unable to hide his irritation. "We're not trying to mess with anyone's reputation, but we have a job to do and we're going to do it."

"I understand, but—"

"Have you had trouble with the law before?" Montoya asked and the man paled.

"A little, yes," Starr admitted, then was quick to add, "It wasn't anything serious. Some eco-terror stuff. I didn't do anything, was just involved in a protest, but ... this is a very conservative school."

"And they don't know?"

He shook his head. "I don't think so, no."

"If you've done nothing wrong, then you've got nothing to hide," Montoya said, sick of the theatrics. One of his students had been killed and Starr was worried about his reputation. What a dick.

From that point on, the interview was straightforward, and they didn't learn anything that would help. If Starr was to be believed, and Montoya wasn't convinced the guy was being completely honest, the professor had landed in the middle of a murder investigation through circumstance.

Starr was obviously relieved when the detectives left.

As they walked across the quad, Brinkman lit up and said, "The jury's still out on that guy. You see how he played with his pens? Nervous Nellie. Means guilt to me."

"Of what?"

"Don't know, but I'd like to run him in for being a pompous ass. Too bad that ain't a crime."

For once, Montoya agreed.

They stopped at the chapel, found the priest on duty, Father Stephen, a small, slight man with thick glasses and a hearing aid that he kept adjusting. They learned nothing more than the elderly priest thought of Mary LaBelle as a "breath of fresh air," or a "good girl," or any and all the antiquated clichés about young women who had chosen "a path of devotion over a more selfish and material lifestyle."

All in all, it made Montoya's blood boil, but he held his tongue and let the tired old man ramble on without learning much. When Luke Gierman's name came up, Father Stephen clucked his tongue, but didn't comment.

On the way back to the car, Brinkman muttered, "Jesus, can you believe that guy? Was he born in the sixth century or what?"

Montoya couldn't help smiling. Maybe Brinkman wasn't such a jerk after all, but in the car ride home, the older detective reverted to his usual, aggravating ways.

"That roommate was one weird chick," Brinkman said as Montoya drove through the gates of the university and headed past the grand estates on his way to the freeway. The night had cleared, and he only had to use his windshield wipers sparingly when trucks drove past.

"Ophelia?"

"Oh, wait... don't call her that. She's 'O' and Courtney's 'Mary.' Christ, doesn't anyone use their given names anymore? Shit. Did I hear the tail end of that conversation right? She wears her own blood in a little teardrop thing hanging around her neck?"

"So she claims." Montoya eased the Crown Vic toward the freeway heading east.

"Freakoid, that's what she is." Brinkman cracked his window, pulled out his pack of cigarettes. He fired up his last Marlboro and crushed the pack in his fist. "Can you imagine banging her? Jesus. Probably bite your damned neck just before you came!" He drew hard on the cigarette.

"She's just a kid. Trying to get a reaction."

"By wearin' a fucking thimbleful of blood?" Shooting a stream of smoke from the corner of his mouth, he muttered, "Maybe she did it."

"Killed Gierman?"

"The girl's weird."

"She has an alibi."

"Yeah, freakoid friends like her." Smoke drifted out of his nostrils. "They all could have been in on it. A cult of some kind."

"No evidence that there was anyone there but the two vics and maybe one other person. The guy with the big feet."

"We don't know yet. I'm telling you that loony girl hasn't got all her marbles. That getup. The dark lipstick, the white face, those gloves without fingers."

"You've seen worse, man. A lot worse. You work in New Orleans. Haven't you been on Bourbon Street?" Where was this coming from?

"Yeah, yeah, but this sick-o crap isn't in the Quarter. No way, José. It's at some frickin' Catholic college."

"Kids are kids."

"I'm just sayin' she could be involved." Another long drag on his smoke. "Damned crazy chick."

Anyone could be involved, Montoya thought; that was the problem. His jaw slid to the side as he flipped on his blinker and accelerated onto the freeway ramp while the police band radio crackled and the tires sang. Brinkman studied the end of his cigarette. "But the more I think about it, my money's still on the ex-wife." He slid Montoya a look. "Just you wait and see, I bet she stands to inherit whatever Gierman had."

"They were divorced."

"Doesn't matter." Brinkman took one last drag, then slid the butt through the window. "My money says Mrs. Ex-shock-jock is gonna end up with some cash from this, I tell ya, and when she does, she'll become suspect *numero uno.*"

Montoya didn't want to believe it, but as he drove through the night watching the stream of red taillights, he knew Brinkman was right. Abby Chastain was a suspect. Whether he liked it or not.

Abby stared out the window. The night was black and wet, a growing wind whistling through the trees. And something outside was bugging the hell out of Hershey. The Lab was nervous, whining and growling at the back door. But that wasn't unusual. Every time Luke had brought the dog over for a visit, Hershey had been eager and anxious, wound tight with pent-up energy. Now, the dog danced and whined, ready to rip outside and tear into whatever night creature had the misfortune to wander too close to the house. Not that Hershey was that big a threat. In a fight with a raccoon or opossum, Abby suspected Hershey would end up the loser.

"Cool it," she said to the Lab. Hershey's antics made her jumpy, and for the first time in a long, long while she wondered what was outside peering in.

Or who?

She felt suddenly cold and rubbed her arms.

It hadn't helped that while the dog was going berserk to get outside, she'd received a phone call. Caller ID had identified the person on the other end as PRIVATE CALLER, so Abby hadn't picked up.

Whoever was on the other end hadn't bothered with a message.

Probably a telemarketer. Or a reporter.

And yet, she'd had a feeling...a sensation that there was something more to the phone call, something that bordered on sinister. The skin on the back of her arms prickled.

"Get over it," she muttered, but all the same, she closed the blinds on the windows that ran across the rear of the house. She then poured a cup of coffee from what was left in the pot and warmed it in the microwave.

She was jittery because of the murders. That was it. The dog wasn't helping matters, nor was the rush of wind that rattled the branches of the trees and whistled around the corners of the house. She told herself there wasn't anyone hiding outside, that whatever she'd sensed, whatever the dog had heard, had been of the four-footed variety. Skunks, opossums, raccoons, even a rare porcupine wandered these woods.

It was ironic, she thought, because part of the original attraction of this isolated cottage had been the nature that surrounded it. When she'd first viewed the place, she'd noticed a snowy egret and minutes later a deer. She'd been sold. When they'd first bought the house, she'd sat in her grandmother's rocker by the window, or on the back verandah, and loved to watch the wildlife, the herons and pelicans, the squirrels and deer...but that had been before things had gone bad, when she'd still had hope.

Well, she had no room for nostalgia.

The microwave dinged. Using a potholder, she removed the cup and took a tentative sip that nearly scalded her lips.

The phone rang again and she jumped, sloshing some of the hot liquid onto her arm. "Damn it," she growled, dropping the cup. It shattered, shards of blue ceramic smashing against the floor. Coffee sprayed up against the cabinets and ran on the floorboards.

Hershey, tail between her legs, studied the mess and the damned phone jangled again. Abby yanked up the receiver, read the number on caller ID, and braced herself. "Hi, Dad," she said, dabbing at her sleeve with the potholder and cradling the phone between her ear and shoulder.

"Hi, honey." Jacques Chastain's voice was a rasp, a whisper of what it once had been, and she imagined him sitting in his chair, his oxygen tank at his side, plastic tubes running into his nose. Cancer and emphysema had slowly and determinedly taken their tolls upon his body. Surgery had removed part of his throat and chemotherapy had zapped him of his strength. He was better now, improving even, but he would never again be the tall, robust, full-of-life man he'd once been. A mountain climber, a white-water rafter, a tennis player.

No more.

"Hey, Dad, how're you doing?" she asked and tried to keep the catch out of her throat.

"Still kickin', so I guess I'm all right. How about you?"

"Okay."

"I heard about Luke," he said. "A shame. I'm sorry."

"Me, too." She ignored the red welt on her hand where the coffee had burned.

"I know things weren't good between you, but... I liked him."

"I did, too. Once." And she felt betrayed that her father would even say the words, admit to feelings that hurt her. Jacques, always the dreamer, had thought she should have stayed married to her ex-husband, that Luke would have eventually "come to his senses" if she would have just given him another chance. Abby had disagreed. She'd been of the opinion that she should finally cut her losses. She'd tried reconciliation once. It hadn't worked.

But then, her father had never known about Luke's fascination and affair with Zoey. And he never would. There was just no reason to ruin Jacques's relationship with his firstborn. Besides, as they say, it was water under the bridge now. Old, stagnant water.

"Do you know when the funeral is? I'd like to come."

"I don't. I don't think the police have even released his body yet. But when I find out, I'll let you know." Her hand was beginning to sting, so she leapt across the mess of coffee and pottery, turned on the cold water, and let it cascade over her wrist.

"The girl that was found with him, did you know her?"

"No."

A second's hesitation and Abby guessed what was coming. "I hate to ask, but was he involved with her?"

"I don't know, Dad."

"No, I suppose not," he said as she ripped a kitchen towel from the handle of the oven door, bent down, and while holding the receiver to her ear in one hand, picked up the biggest pieces of the cup and tossed them into the trash can under the sink.

"But it was a double murder, right? Not the murder-suicide that was first reported?"

"I'm not certain of anything," she admitted. Carefully, she swabbed at the floor where the coffee had spilled onto the hardwood. How could she answer his questions about Luke? She wasn't even sure of the truth herself and the police weren't talking. No one seemed to know for certain what had happened, least of all her.

"Oh...well," Jacques continued as she finished mopping the floor and threw the stained, dripping towel into the sink. "So how are *you* doing? This has got to be difficult."

"Still kickin', so I guess I'm all right," she said, repeating his answer.

Her father chuckled.

"How's Charlene?" she asked, though she'd never been close to her stepmother, a vain woman who was pushing sixty, looked fifty, and claimed to be in her "late forties." Where nature had failed her, plastic surgeons had come to the rescue, which was no big deal if she would just own up to it. She didn't. These days, who cared? The woman bugged Abby.

"Char's fine, fine. Keeping busy," he said and his voice brightened with hope. "As soon as the doctor says it's okay, she's going to bring me back home."

A lump tightened Abby's throat. "And when will that be?"

"Oh, soon, I think."

It was a lie. They both knew it. But Abby wasn't going to call her father on it now. Let him hold on to some false hope that he would return home to be with his wife in their rambling house on half an acre in Shreveport. Why take away his dreams? Maybe there was a chance that he would get better. As she talked to him, she crossed her fingers and fought tears.

"Well, I was just checkin' on you, honey. You let me know if you need anything, okay?"

"Sure, Dad. You, too."

"And let me know about that funeral."

"I'm not the one who'll be making the arrangements. It'll probably be one of Luke's brothers, or his parents."

"But they'll call and give you the information," he said steadfastly, as if they were all still one happy family.

"I'm sure I'll find out."

"Good, good. You take care, honey."

"Will do. You, too, Dad." She hung up depressed, thinking of her small family and how disconnected it was. Her father was alone in an assisted-care facility. She knew that each day he hoped to return home and probably never would. Zoey was in Seattle, still trying to mend fences, but thousands of miles away. Abby was here, in southern Louisiana in a house that she would soon sell so that she could move away.

Or run away, her mind taunted.

She mopped the floor and washed down the cabinets before trying to clean the stain from the sleeve of her shirt. Impossible. The skin over her wrist hurt like crazy. She ignored the pain and, with Hershey at her heels, walked into the living room, where Ansel was dozing in his favorite spot above the couch. Abby sat on a corner of the love seat and the dog hopped up onto the cushions without waiting for an invitation.

Abby started to scold the Lab, then thought better of it. She scratched Hershey behind her ears and the dog placed her lower jaw on Abby's leg, rolling her expressive brown eyes upward to stare at Abby's face. "You know just how to get to me, don't you?" Abby said and chuckled. On the nearby couch, Ansel stretched and yawned, showing off needle-sharp teeth and black lips.

Life could be worse, she thought, wondering about taking both animals to the West Coast. She glanced to the fireplace, where the ashes of her last burning were still black and curled in the charred firebox.

Pictures of Luke.

It was too bad that he'd been killed, but the truth of the matter was that he'd been a louse of a husband. She wasn't buying into the Luke Gierman local town hero.

But then, she knew better.

CHAPTER 8

"Listen to this," Lynn Zaroster said. She was sitting at her desk in a wide room filled with cubicles where other detectives and uniformed officers were walking, talking, reviewing files, or clicking away at computer keyboards. Lynn, all of twenty-five with an athletic body, mop of short black curls, and enough idealism to right the world on its axis, hit the play button on the tape recorder that was sitting square in the middle of her desk.

Gierman's voice boomed through the recorder. "...my ex claims she gave everything she was keeping for me away, including a family heirloom, which just happens to be a handgun."

Montoya's gut tightened. He rested a hip on the edge of Lynn's desk and listened.

"She says she donated it all, lock, stock, and barrel, so to speak, to a charity."

"A charity?" Another male voice, registering disbelief.

"That's the sidekick, sometimes billed as the cohost of the show," Zaroster clarified. "Maury Taylor."

Gierman was raging. "Like I'm supposed to believe that any charitable organization would take a gun. Of course it was a lie. But how safe does that make me feel? Knowing that my psychotic ex-wife is literally gunning for me with my father's sidearm, the weapon he was issued from the police department."

Psychotic. Interesting term.

Maury Taylor suggested slyly, "You'd better change your address."

"Or start packin' my own heat," Luke confided to all of New Orleans and the surrounding area as the other man in the booth with him laughed.

The program continued in the same vein until Lynn could stand it no longer. She hit the stop button and looked up at Montoya. "What a jackass," she muttered through clenched teeth. "I'm telling you, if I was his ex-wife, I think I would have killed him and done it on the air." She made a gun out of her right hand, extending her index finger and cocking her thumb as if it were the hammer. "Ka-pow," she said, the "gun" kicking back as she pretended to shoot the recorder. "Just blow him the hell away." She lifted her finger to her lips, blew across it, then faked holstering the "gun." Frowning sourly, she added, "Good riddance." She glanced up at Montoya. "And one more lying, cheating son of a bitch of an ex-husband would disappear. How would you like all your dirty laundry aired in public?"

"Maybe that's why she's moving."

"The ex-wife?"

"Uh-huh."

He heard steps behind him. "Great timing," Brinkman said. "I just went through Gierman's papers. Found his will and insurance policies. Guess who's listed as the only beneficiary?"

The muscles in the back of Montoya's neck tightened. Just the way Brinkman posed the question boded bad news.

"The ex-wife," Zaroster said again, her blue eyes narrowing.

"Bingo. Give the little lady a Kewpie doll!" Brinkman's smile was wide. "You saw the preliminary forensic reports, right?" he said to Montoya. "Looks like there definitely was a third person in the room with Gierman and LaBelle. And the blood spatter and GRS suggest that someone had his or her hand over the girl's when the trigger was pulled. There were traces of adhesive from some kind of tape around her mouth, wrists, and legs. Bruising, too, suggests that she had been bound at one point. Someone set the whole thing up."

"Why would Abby Chastain go to the trouble of killing the second victim? Why not just off her ex?" Montoya posed.

"To throw us off." Brinkman looked at him as if he were thick as cement. "I'm not sayin' she did such a good job of it, but she's an amateur, probably doesn't know about forensics."

"Everyone who has a television knows about forensics," Montoya pointed out. He climbed to his feet, so that he was eye-to-eye with Brinkman.

"I'm not talking that CSI junk that's on TV. I'm talkin' the real thing," Brinkman said.

"She doesn't wear a size twelve men's shoe."

"So she had help."

"Can it, Brinkman, you're barking up the wrong tree. Motive or not, she didn't do it."

"How do you know?" Brinkman asked irritably, and Lynn Zaroster lifted an eyebrow, waiting for the explanation, too. "Let's just say, she knows her ex was up at All Saints, and finds out who was in the class. Or maybe she thinks he was doin' this girl."

"The Virgin Mary?" Montoya said. "The autopsy report came back that her hymen was still intact." Montoya was still thinking about that one. Courtney LaBelle. Ultrareligious. Went by her middle name.

"Well, the ex-wife, she doesn't know that, does she?"

"This isn't a woman's crime," Zaroster insisted. "All this staging. Nuh-uh." She leaned back in her chair. "You know, my uncle teaches up at All Saints. Religion classes. He might have known the victim or some of her friends."

"We were already up there," Brinkman pointed out. "She didn't have many friends. Just a roommate straight out of a coven."

Zaroster looked quizzically at Montoya.

"She's a Goth," Montoya explained.

"Jesus, Brinkman. Have you been to the Quarter lately? Goth is like, I don't know, real, real tame there." She laughed. "Maybe I should ask my uncle if he knows of anyone involved in a local coven."

"Check on vampires, too. This chick, she carries around her own blood on a necklace."

Again the raised eyebrow. "Beyond Goth," Zaroster said.

"Over the top," Montoya admitted, then added, "Yeah, check with your uncle." The more information, the better.

In the meantime he had his own relative to contact. He'd put a call into his Aunt Maria. So far he hadn't heard back. But they weren't exactly high-tech out at the nunnery. One phone, no cells, one computer, he thought. A visit might be easier. His aunt definitely believed in the human touch over technological communication.

Brinkman snorted and ran a hand through what little hair he had left. "Talkin' to your uncle, you'll just be spinnin' your wheels."

"Mine to spin," Zaroster shot back. "As I said, this doesn't look like a woman's crime to me."

"We're not talking about a woman. We're talking about a pissed-off ex-wife who is set to inherit a shitload of money." His smile was oily and smug. He cocked his head toward the exit. "Let's have a word with the new heiress."

So this was it. The "official" interview. Abby sat stiff-backed at her dining room table with Montoya and another detective. The first time he'd stopped by, Montoya had come alone, to tell her about Luke's death. The second time to deliver the dog. On each occasion, he'd asked a few questions, all very casually. After all, she'd been in shock.

But now he was back and this time she sensed the gloves were off.

Brinkman, the balding guy with him, didn't even try to be friendly. His eyes were suspicious, his manner polite but cold, his expression hinting that he knew more about her than she knew herself.

All of which bugged the hell out of her.

He stood by the French doors and stared outside while Montoya sat across from her at the dining table. Separating them was a colorful centerpiece of small pumpkins, gourds, leaves, and candles. It seemed ridiculously festive and out of place, especially with a pocket recorder balanced on the edge of the table, Montoya taking notes, and the generally grim and sober tone of the conversation.

Almost accusatory.

Almost.

She shot a hard look at Detective Brinkman with his soft gut, balding pate, and hard-ass attitude. If Brinkman was what they meant by backup, she thought Montoya was better off flying solo.

The two cops had arrived half an hour earlier, much to Hershey's delight and Ansel's dismay. The Lab had barked and danced excitedly at the appearance of company while Ansel had streaked into the living room to hide beneath the couch and peer out suspiciously.

Abby had offered coffee and now three cups sat virtually untouched as the questions kept coming. They'd already gone over all the information she'd shared with Montoya on his last visit and now were venturing into new, uncharted territory.

Abby told herself this was routine, that they were talking to anyone who had known Luke and the girl who had been with him, yet she couldn't help feeling that she was under suspicion, that the police thought she was somehow involved in the tragedy, which was ludicrous. True, she'd lost all love and most of her respect for Luke Gierman, but she wouldn't have done anything to kill him and she hoped Montoya, at least, knew it.

She tried not to fidget, but she was on edge, slightly intimidated by the recorder and the necessity of two men to double-team her and ask questions. She'd thought they were about finished when Brinkman, rotating to face her, no doubt to judge her reaction, asked, "So, did you know that you were still listed as the beneficiary on your ex-husband's life insurance policy?"

"What?" She was floored. "Life insurance?"

"That's right. A half a million dollars." He gave her a fake smile. "Quite a bit of cash."

"There must be some mistake."

"Nope. I found the policy in his personal papers and checked with the insurance company."

"I can't believe it." Never in her wildest dreams would she have guessed she might receive another dime from Luke.

"I guess he never got around to changing it, eh?" he asked.

"I didn't even know he had that kind of insurance," she said honestly. "I mean, yes, when we were first married, we each took out policies, but small ones. Term insurance."

"Is he still your beneficiary?"

"No." She shook her head. "I let the policy lapse and changed my will immediately." All she owned would go to her father, and in the event he predeceased her, then Zoey would get whatever assets she'd amassed. Abby had made certain that Luke would never get anything. She had assumed he would do the same. Now, hearing this from the detective, she felt as if she might have maligned him.

"As I said, a lot of money." Brinkman rubbed the back of his neck as if deep in thought. "Half a mil. How about that? And then there's his checking account, a few stocks in his retirement account, no house, you already got that, but all his assets add up to just over six hundred grand."

"That can't be right," she said, looking over at Montoya. He hadn't said a word since the announcement but was leaning forward, his forearms resting on the tabletop. "Luke has family. His parents and brothers."

"I double-checked with the lawyer." Brinkman lifted a shoulder. "Unless your ex found himself a new attorney and drew up a new will that no one knows about, the one he signed five years ago is still in effect. Which means you're a rich woman." He cocked his head to one side. "But you didn't know about the will, is that what you're saying?"

"I assumed he changed his, and he never told me about any life insurance policy, I swear." Abby didn't know what else to say, so she just stared at the two detectives, who seemed hell-bent to connect her to Luke's murder.

"Looks like you just won the lottery."

"It doesn't feel that way, okay?"

"If you say so."

"Look, I don't like all your insinuations." She turned her attention to Montoya, who, for this last round, had been mostly silent. "Do you have any other questions?" she asked, and tried to hang on to her cool. Brinkman was just trying to rattle her and she knew it.

"No, that's about it," Montoya said.

"Good. Because I was beginning to think I might need a lawyer."

"Why would you think that?" Brinkman asked, his smile meant to be disarming. She didn't trust it for a minute.

She asked Montoya, "Is there anything else?"

"Just that we found a connection between Luke and Courtney LaBelle. He was the guest speaker at one of her classes at All Saints College."

"So he knew her?"

"We don't know that they even met. Just that they happened to be in the same place at the same time."

"Which would be one helluva coincidence."

"If you believe in 'em," Brinkman said. "Me, personally? I don't."

Abby felt that same old gut tightening she always did when it came to her ex-husband and younger women. "But they didn't hook up?"

"That's the weird thing. No indication that they even talked to each other."

"Hard to think it was a coincidence," Brinkman said. "But you"—he gestured in Abby's direction—"you never met her before."

"That's right," she said evenly. Getting to her feet, she glared at both men. "You seem to think that I had something to do with my ex-husband's murder. The plain damn truth is that I didn't and I have no idea who did. I've never met Courtney LaBelle, had never even heard of her. I don't know how, or if, she knew my ex-husband. I made it a point to stay out of his business and asked that he do the same for me."

Brinkman said, "Except you called the station the day of the program where he went off on ex-spouses."

"No...oh, yes, I did call, but I didn't say a word. Just hung up. I realized Luke was baiting me. He was really, really ticked, Detective. He'd called asking for his things and I had to tell him that I'd given them away, that I'd gotten tired of hanging on to them. After repeated attempts to get him to come and take them, I gave them all away. He was furious. The next day I heard him crucify me on the airwaves, and I did call in, but I didn't speak to him or anyone else. Didn't want to say anything I would regret in the long run."

She was livid now, her cheeks burning, her old rage boiling to the surface. "What the fight with Luke on the phone and the subsequent radio show did was convince me that I needed to get the hell out of Dodge, or in this case, New Orleans. To put as much distance between my ex and myself as possible."

"Seems like death might do that," Brinkman observed.

"Are you kidding? The man's looked upon as a saint now! I'm getting phone calls from reporters day and night. People who want to talk to me to get to know, and I quote, 'the real Luke Gierman.' It's a joke. All Luke ever wanted was to get his fifteen minutes of fame and maybe stretch them out to a full half an hour. Being killed got him what he couldn't get while he was alive. Unfortunately, some people still think I'm the link to him."

Brinkman snorted out a laugh. "Like Priscilla Presley is to Elvis."

"It's not quite the same," she said through her teeth, trying to tamp back her temper. She knew Brinkman was goading her on purpose, hoping for a reaction, but she couldn't help herself. "I just want to move on. To start over."

"I thought that's why you came back here in the first place, to return home and start fresh with the husband. You're a local girl, right?"

She was instantly wary and looked over at Montoya. He was still seated at the table, watching her. She heard a rush in her ears. "What does this have to do with anything?"

"Grew up here, went to school here, and weren't your parents Jacques and Faith Chastain?"

"They *are* my parents. My father's still alive." The rush was getting louder.

"And your mother?"

"Is dead." She skewered the fatter detective with her eyes. "But you knew that, didn't you? You're just trying to bait me. Why?" She turned her angry gaze on Montoya. "What is this?"

"We found a link between the victims. Courtney LaBelle's parents worked at Our Lady of Virtues Hospital at the same time your mother was a patient there. Clyde LaBelle was a psychiatrist and Virginia Simmons was a social worker."

Abby gazed at him in confusion.

Montoya added, "On top of that, Courtney, who went by Mary,

was only going to college to appease her parents. She'd already decided to become a nun."

"I thought the church was struggling for people to join the orders."

"Courtney LaBelle apparently wanted to join. She'd already talked to the Mother Superior at Our Lady of Virtues. They're tearing the old hospital down, but the convent stays."

"This is your 'link'?" she asked. "The hospital? But Luke had nothing to do with it. He'd never even been there that I know of. We were married after my mother died."

"Do you remember Courtney's parents?" Montoya asked.

Abby shook her head. "Virginia...Simmons, did you say her name was?"

Montoya nodded. "Yeah."

"No." Try as she might, she couldn't call up an image of the woman, but distorted images of the doctors at the hospital played in her mind. She remembered a tall, nearly gaunt man with a trimmed beard and oversized glasses that magnified his eyes. He always stood a little hunched and he'd reminded Abby of a praying mantis.

"But Dr. LaBelle, I think...he might have treated my mother at one time." She closed her eyes for a second, bit her lip, tried to roll back the years to the time before the tragedy, when she and her father and Zoey had visited the hospital. She remembered the angel fountain, and making a wish, catching sight of the brightly colored fish swimming beneath thick water lilies. Dragonflies, their wings humming, had flitted over the surface of the pool. Bullfrogs had croaked, squirrels scolding the old calico cat that had wandered the grounds. Older people in wheelchairs had sat on broad verandahs, or in the shade of colorful umbrella-topped tables, or beneath the fragrant branches of huge, gnarled magnolia trees.

There had been staff as well, nurses in crisp uniforms and doctors with white lab coats flapping in the breeze, stethoscopes swinging from their necks, and impatience in their gazes until their eyes landed upon her or Zoey or her father. Then a calm and warmth had appeared, the icy resolve she'd witnessed fading with a wide smile and handshake and words of encouragement.

"She's doing fine...yes, well...one episode...responding well to the new medication...shouldn't be too much longer...we have several different ways to go...new treatments every time we turn around..."

In her mind's eye, Abby saw herself as a child, walking up the broad front porch with its terra-cotta pots overflowing with pink and white petunias and yellow black-eyed Susans. Wasps and hornets had buzzed in the eaves, and conversation had whispered across the broad, manicured lawns.

She recalled the huge door swinging open to a yawning darkness within. That's where everything changed. Even as a young child as she'd set foot over the threshold, where the noises of the outside had been cordoned off, and the sunlight only filtered through windows with thick shades or the stained glass on the staircase landing, she'd felt fear. Anxiety. Sensed that something had been very wrong.

The hushed words, the prayers intoned, the soft, but certain sounds of moaning and dismay had crept through long, narrow corridors with dark, walnut wainscoting and hunter green wallpaper. The smells of urine and vomit and human decay had been disguised by antiseptic, bleach, and pine-scented cleanser, but Abby had smelled the odors that had never disappeared, had only been masked.

There had been a doctor who had treated her mother, but his name had been something else, not LaBelle. What was it? Holman? or Hellman? No, Heller! An unpleasant taste rose in the back of her mouth at the thought of him, but she couldn't remember much. Heller had been just one of the members of the vast staff. She thought hard. LaBelle?

Abby's insides seemed to crush in on themselves as she remembered Dr. LaBelle hurrying down the stairs, his gaze drifting to Abby, then jetting quickly away. She had a vision of him signing papers on a clipboard, what she thought was a patient's chart, then looking up from his paperwork to talk to her father. He'd appeared impatient, as if Jacques's questions about his wife had been asinine, or mundane, or a complete waste of time. Dr. LaBelle had carried with him the air of superiority and the put-upon tone of someone who had tirelessly gone over the same questions time and time again. He'd given the impression that he was far too busy to spend much time with a patient's family, that he'd had more important things to do. It had been as if Jacques and his two daughters were an imposition, one more chore he'd been forced to deal with.

Now, she opened her eyes and felt a chill as cold as December settle in her stomach.

"Yes...I remember him now," she said, a bad taste filling her mouth. It was hard to think of LaBelle as a father, a man who was hurting at the loss of his child.

"But you never met his daughter."

"No. I didn't know anything about him. Once my mother died, I never went back to the hospital again, never talked to anyone who had worked there or been a patient." She met Montoya's steady gaze. "I tried to forget everything that ever happened there." She was still grappling with the fact that Luke had been killed with a girl who was connected, even loosely, to Our Lady of Virtues. "Does Dr. LaBelle remember Mom?"

"We're checking into that."

Abby was blindsided. All of this had to be a coincidence, that was all. The police were being thorough, checking every lead they could find. The connection to the hospital was thin, weak at best, and she was grateful when the interview was over and Montoya clicked the recorder off. "I think we've got all we need." He offered her the hint of a smile. "We appreciate your time. If you think of anything else, just give me a call." He pressed a card into her hand and she curled her fingers around it.

"Of course."

She walked them both to the door and watched as Brinkman, the minute he was outside, shook a cigarette from his pack and lit up.

Montoya had just stepped onto the porch when she grabbed his arm impulsively. "Detective."

He paused. Glanced down at the fingers surrounding his forearm, then looked up at her face. Dark eyes searched hers, and for a second, under such intense male scrutiny, her breath caught in her throat.

"Look," she said, but didn't let go. "Off the record, despite any amount of money I might inherit from Luke, he was a jerk, okay? I wasn't in love with him any longer and I did want to get away from here, from him." Her fingers tightened a bit. "But I didn't kill him and I'm sorry he's dead." She held his gaze and inched her chin up a fraction. "And your link to the victims, through the hospital, that's pretty damned thin."

"Maybe the link isn't the hospital," he said in a low voice that caused her heart to knock.

"But—"

"Maybe it's you."

"What do you mean?"

He wasn't smiling, his thin lips compressed. "Be careful, Abby," he suggested. "Lock your doors. Set your alarm, if you've got one. If you don't, then call a security company and have one installed ASAP." His eyebrows pulled into a single dark line. "Watch your back."

She felt herself pale.

"You think I'm the link? Me? No." She shook her head. "That's crazy, Detective."

"Just be aware." He touched her shoulder and the gesture, as the first drops of rain began to fall, seemed somehow intimate. "I'll call," he promised and ridiculously she felt her heart surge.

Then he was gone, hunching his shoulders against the rain, climbing behind the wheel of the cruiser and driving off, taillights disappearing at the end of the drive.

Abby shut the door and leaned against it, Montoya's warning echoing through her mind.

She stood there, frozen, a long time.

The numbers on the door of the room looked funny and uneven, but Abby knew this was her mother's room: 307. That was it. Mama was always in the room. Abby tried the door, expected it to be locked, but it opened easily and she stepped inside.

"Mom?" she called and saw Faith Chastain at the window. She smiled, beatifically as always.

"Baby." Her grin widened. "You came."

But then Faith's gaze shifted, moving past Abby to the door hanging open and the dark hallway beyond.

There was something in her mother's gaze. Fear? Then a slight tightening of her neck muscles.

"Mom? Is something wrong?" Abby asked, dread mounting as she stepped inside. "Mom?"

Suddenly her mother's face changed. Faith's smile fell away. Panic distorted her features. She started walking backward, her eyes fixed on the open door, her steps taking her closer and closer to the window. "No," she whispered. "Sweet Jesus, no."

"Mom?" Abby called again. Dear God, what was happening? "Mom, be careful!"

But apparently her mother couldn't hear her.

A deep male voice seemed to rain from heaven above. "What are you doing here? Get out!"

Who was this guy? Another visitor? A patient? A doctor? One of the guards?

"Leave, now!"

Heart pounding, nerves stretched to the breaking point, Abby turned to face the man but he wasn't behind her. The door to the hallway seemed to sag. She glanced into all of the shadowy corners. Was he concealing himself in the darkness? Or in the closet, where the door was open just a crack? Or in the cedar chest at the foot of her mother's bed . . . the bed! Was he hiding under it, secreting himself in the darkness beneath the thin mattress? Were those eyes peering out . . . hideous, damning eyes staring at her?

Her throat closed as she tried to see the image, but it came and went, a wraith with stark, cold features, the very face of the devil?

Her blood froze.

She had to get out of here now. With her mother. This room was evil, the very den of death.

She made the sign of the cross over her chest and looked up to the crucifix hanging at an angle over the bed. The painted blood on Christ's ceramic hands, feet, side, and face began to ooze, running down the peeling wallpaper.

"Mama?" Abby whispered, using her little-girl voice and spying her mother's reflection in the mirror hanging over the mantel. Tall, thin, ravaged, her clothes torn, bruises on her face, blood flowing from her wrists, Faith seemed to wither before her eyes.

The mirror suddenly shattered, distorting her mother's image into thousands of tiny reflective shards that showered into the room.

Abby flung herself backward, away from the splintering glass, stumbling as she tried to get away from the tiny biting slivers.

"It's not your fault," her mother whispered into her ear.

"What?" Abby spun around, searching. But her mother was shriveling, disappearing. "Mama, what's not my fault? Mama?" she cried desperately.

An earsplitting crack cut through the room.

Her mother's bony arms were suddenly around her, holding her close, crushing her.

More glass shattered and the floor gave way. Together, they hurtled through the night, tumbling and falling.

"It's not your fault," Faith whispered again and again as they fell into the darkness, straight, Abby was certain, into the yawning gates of hell. "It's not your fault . . ."

Abby's eyes flew open.

She sat bolt upright.

She was in bed. Her bed. Hershey beside her burrowing into the covers. Sweat soaked her body despite the paddle fan whirring softly overhead. Heart pounding, head thundering, she gasped as she tried to catch her breath.

The dog lifted her head and yawned as Abby slapped on the bedside lamp. Her small bedroom was suddenly awash with soft illumination, headboard gleaming, shutters closed, her robe tossed carelessly over the foot of her bed where Ansel, curled into a ball of feline comfort, opened one eye.

"Oh, God," she whispered, sinking back into the pillows. It had been a dream. A nightmare.

Always the same.

Whenever she was stressed, she dreamed about her mother and the hospital. Sometimes it was an out-of-body experience and she was actually looking down upon her younger self climbing the old staircase of the hospital, lingering at the stained-glass window at the landing, walking through the darkened hallway on the third floor, then opening the door to find her mother at the window. Other times, like tonight, she was actually a part of the drama, walking through the corridors herself, though always, she was young again. Fifteen.

Involuntarily, as she always did when she was startled awake by the dream, she made the sign of the cross over her chest and gathered in several deep breaths. Her heart rate began to slow thankfully as the nightmare slowly faded, shrinking back into her subconscious, but lurking, ready to strike again.

This was all that damned Montoya's fault, she thought churlishly. If he hadn't brought up the hospital and her mother... if he hadn't been so damned sexy and disturbing...

Wrong-o, Abby. You can't blame the man for doing his job, or for being appealing. Nuh-uh.

"Damn!" She tossed off the covers.

She glanced at the clock. Four-sixteen. Almost too early to get up.

Montoya's warning echoed through her brain. *Lock your doors. Set your alarm, if you've got one. If you don't, then call a security company and have one installed ASAP.*

"Well, I don't have one," she muttered under her breath.

Still agitated, she rolled out of bed and padded barefoot through the house, testing the doors and making certain each window was securely locked. Hershey followed after her, toenails clicking on the hardwood.

Maybe Montoya had a point. As it was, her security depended upon a friendly Lab who wouldn't harm a damned flea, a revolver she'd never fired, and her own wits. "You're doomed, Abby," she chided herself. She also had stickers glued to the inside of the windows claiming that the house was protected by an alarm system connected to the sheriff's department, but that was a lie, one perpetrated by the previous owner. If anyone broke into her house, she was on her own.

"Get a grip," she told herself and walked to the kitchen, where she grabbed a glass from the cupboard and turned on the faucet. She stared through the window as she first held the glass to her forehead to cool off, then drank half the water. As she swallowed, she saw her pale reflection in the window over the sink, beyond which the thick darkness of the forest shrouded any and all who might be lurking outside and watching her.

And who would that be, Abby?
Are you getting paranoid now?
Like her?

Like Faith?

Remember, your mother's disease started as simple distrust and moved quickly into general suspicion and thoughts of persecution. Is that what's happening to you, too?

"No!" Angrily, she tossed the last swallow of water into the sink.

Like mother, like daughter.

"Oh, shut up!"

Talking to yourself, Abby? Isn't that what she used to do? Didn't you see her in the kitchen, mumbling to herself, having conversations with herself? Isn't that what customers at the antique shop used to accuse her of?

Leaving the empty glass on the counter, Abby refused to listen to the voice in her head. She was *not* like her mother.

Still wound up, she knew she couldn't sleep, so she decided to go to the darkroom and check the prints she'd developed.

More to prove that she wasn't afraid of living in this house than anything else, she threw on a pair of jeans and a long-sleeved Hard Rock Cafe T-shirt, then grabbed her keys. Whistling to the dog, she walked through the kitchen and outside, where the bullfrogs croaked and crickets chirped, and she caught a glimpse of a cloud-shrouded moon. She locked the door behind her, leaving Hershey to guard the house. In ten short steps she was across the walkway and into the little studio.

The darkroom was little more than a closet with water piped to it. Shelves stored paper, bottles, tongs, chemicals, and trays marked for the various stages in the process.

These days she didn't develop many of her own pictures because she had use of the lab next door to her shop off Jackson Square. For commercial work she primarily used her digital camera and computer. But for her personal black-and-white photos she liked to develop her own film.

It was soothing. Calming. And lately she needed all the soothing and calming she could get.

Several days earlier she'd processed the negatives from the roll of film she'd found in her old 35mm camera, which she'd replaced some time after her divorce from Luke. Curious about what was on the film, she'd clicked off the remainder of the roll the other day, filming Ansel on the verandah with the late autumn light fading through the trees. Later, she'd developed the negatives and created a contact print of the small pictures. She'd left that print clothespinned to a cord strung across the darkroom.

Intending to get back to the contact print after it had dried, she'd been derailed by Detective Montoya's initial visit telling her about Luke's murder. The news had knocked thoughts of the print from her head. Only now, in the wee hours of the morning, after that horrendous, recurring nightmare, had she remembered. Deep down she suspected that it was more than a need to see what was on the print, that she'd really been looking for an excuse to get out of bed and stay up, that the thought of falling into another fitful sleep might bring back the terrifying nightmare.

"Chicken," she muttered under her breath, bending to her work.

She removed the contact print from the cord and carried it out of the darkroom to her desk in the main part of the studio. Adjusting a tension lamp for the best viewing, she found her favorite magnifying glass in a desk drawer and began carefully viewing each shot, smiling when she caught images of Ansel sleeping, or hunting, or hiding under the sofa. Slowly she checked each image to see that the subject was clear, the light right.

On the third strip, she gasped. "Oh, God." She nearly dropped her magnifying glass.

Her dead ex-husband's face looked up at her.

Smiling easily, showing just a bit of teeth, a hint of a dimple and a sexy twist of his lips, he stared up at her in bold black and white.

"Damn." How had she missed it when eyeing the negatives?

She took a step back, as if she expected the image to suddenly morph into the man.

She'd forgotten she'd taken the shot, having snapped it before deciding to use her digital camera. Luke had wanted new head shots and she'd agreed to photograph him.

Shortly after that session she'd found out about Connie Hastings. She'd called her lawyer that afternoon, told Luke to move out, erased the images in her digital camera, and started the legal proceedings to end her marriage. She'd forgotten this one final shot.

How long had it been since she'd taken those pictures? Eighteen months ago? Two years? It didn't matter.

"Time flies when you're having fun," she muttered to herself and noted that the picture was good. It captured Luke's fun-loving, devil-may-care spirit, brought out the boyishness that she'd fallen in love with so many years ago.

And now it was useless.

Unless she wanted to give it to his parents.

Or did she even want to open that can of worms? His mother had never believed her son to be a womanizer, had hinted that a strong woman could hold on to "her man."

"Forget it," she said and made an X through the shot. There were other pictures, taken of Hershey, Ansel, and some of the wildlife she'd caught around her house. She would enlarge those later. She'd had enough fun for the night.

She locked the studio behind her and walked the few steps to the house. It was still dark outside, the frogs and insects making noise, dawn not yet streaking the sky.

Hershey was waiting at the door, resting on the mat, her paws supporting her big brown head. "You *are* a good girl," Abby whispered, scratching the dog behind her ears and then saying, "I shouldn't do this, so don't tell anyone, okay?" Reaching into the pantry, she found a box of dog biscuits and tossed one to the Lab. Hershey caught it on the fly, then carried it into the living room, where she crunched the bone to bits.

"Come on, let's go back to bed and see if we can get a few more hours of sleep." The clock on the mantel showed that it was after five. Abby groaned. Sleep now would be nearly impossible and she had a nine o'clock consultation at the office, so she'd have to be up by seven-thirty at the latest. She headed off to bed again but Hershey, following after her, stopped short at the French doors.

"You need to go out?"

The dog just stared and slowly the hackles on the back of her neck rose. She growled low in her throat.

"Oh, don't do this," she whispered, Montoya's warnings running through her brain. Had she locked the door behind her when she'd returned to the kitchen?

Abby turned off the lights so that the house was in darkness. She, too, peered through the window, but all she saw was the dark, dark night.

"It's just a raccoon," she said and the dog growled again. Low. Rumbling. A warning.

"Come on, Hersh, you're freaking me out." She thought of the gun in the bedside table and wondered if she would ever have the nerve to use it, to blow some intruder away.

Without snapping on a single light, she returned to the door leading to the studio and found it locked. She was safe. Right? She stared through the glass panels toward her studio and saw a shadow slip beneath the pooling light from the security lamp near the smaller building.

Her heart nearly stopped.

She froze, half expecting a man's face to appear in the window on the door, the barest of inches from hers, only a thin pane of glass separating them.

But nothing happened. No face appeared. No dark figure scuttled through her line of vision. The shadow she'd seen didn't return.

Get a grip, Abby.

No one's out there.

No one at all.

The dog growled again and she felt a fear dark as the night.

And with it came a sense of foreboding.

A knowledge that whatever had begun with Luke's death was far from over.

Chapter 9

"Pedro!" Sister Maria called, smiling and waving upon sight of her nephew.

Montoya was already feeling out of place in the foyer of the convent; hearing his confirmation name only made him more so. *"Tia Maria."*

"What a surprise!" She slipped her arm through his and hugged him. She'd aged since he'd last seen her, and her once vibrant skin was now lined, her lips thin, her hands spotted, but she still had a strength to her, a vitality that snapped in her dark eyes. "Come on, come on, let's sit in the garden and you can tell me what it is that brings you here. Though I'd love to think that you were just missing your old aunt, I have the feeling that there's something more to your visit." She patted his arm as she teased him, just as she had for as long as he could remember.

She led him through the long hallway, past mullioned and tracery windows that allowed the gloomy day to seep inside. At the bottom of a carved wooden staircase she pushed open a door to a courtyard where flowers in large cement pots had begun to fade. A center fountain sprayed water upward only to cascade down on an angel holding two vessels from which streams of water poured into a large square pool. Water lilies floated on the surface and goldfish swam in the shimmering depths.

Maria sat next to him on a stone bench under the protection of the cloister roof. In her profile he caught a glimpse of the girl she'd once been, a frightened teenager who, he'd overheard from gossiping family members, had found herself pregnant before she was twenty. Whoever had been her lover had remained her secret, guarded for nearly forty years, and what had happened to the baby, Montoya had never learned through the whispers of his mother and her sisters. Maria had never married. Instead she had joined this order of nuns where she'd sought refuge, solace, and, he supposed, forgiveness.

As clouds collected in the sky and the wind buffeted the Spanish moss draping from tall oaks rising on the outside of the cloister walls, they shared small talk about the family for a few minutes, catching up on relatives and sharing a laugh about the time when Sister Maria had caught him with his first girlfriend.

"But you're all grown up now," she said, angling her head to stare at him, the hem of her wimple falling over her shoulder. "And have you finally forgiven yourself for what happened to your...friend?"

"I'm not here about Marta," he said quietly as a cloud passed over the sun.

"No? Why did you come here, Pedro? Is it something to do with the hospital being torn down?"

"Maria, my name's Reuben, or sometimes I go by my middle name, Diego. No one calls me Pedro."

"Just me," she said with a smile. "And I'm not going to change. It's a good name, you know. Pedro—Peter—is my favorite of all the saints." She grinned. "You know what they say about old dogs."

"I think you could learn new tricks if you wanted to."

She laughed. "Okay, maybe. Just, please, don't ask me to dance."

"It's a deal." He relaxed a little. He'd always loved being around her.

She touched his knee. "So what is it? What do you want to know?"

"I'm not here specifically about the hospital's demolition," he said, "but I do have some questions about it. You worked over there, didn't you?" He hitched his chin in the general direction of the sanitarium. "Around twenty years ago?"

Plucking at her sleeve, she nodded and watched the birds, a fly-catcher and titmouse fluttering near the fountain. "I had an office there, yes. Shared it with a social worker."

"Virginia Simmons?"

His aunt turned to face him. "She was one of them. Ended up quitting and marrying one of the doctors. Dr. Heller, I think it was." She frowned at the mention of Heller, as if the very thought of him was distasteful. "No... I've got that wrong. It was Dr. La-Belle." Her face registered her surprise as she put two and two together. "Oh, my stars. She's the mother of Courtney Mary LaBelle, the girl who was killed the other night!"

"That's right."

Sadness touched Maria's eyes. "I heard that she'd been murdered," she said softly, resting her hands over the black folds of her skirt. "Such a shame. So that's why you're here. You're investigating her murder. I think you should probably talk to Mother Superior. She knows more about Mary becoming a novitiate. I didn't realize... how silly of me... I'd heard her name, met her, but it never registered that she was Virginia's daughter." She smiled sadly and said, "Sometimes... well, sometimes I forget."

This wasn't a surprise. He'd heard from his own mother that she was worried about her sister's "confusion" or her "forgetfulness" and there was a question, though no one said it aloud, of Alzheimer's disease or some other form of dementia.

Clearing her throat, Maria fingered the cross hanging from her neck and looked up when a gate on the far side of the cloister opened and a tall man with broad shoulders walked inside. He pushed a wheelbarrow while balancing a rake and broom across the empty pan.

"Who's he?" Montoya asked, eyeing the man who wore dark glasses and a baseball cap pulled low over his eyes. Around his neck was a headset for listening to music. A long, looping wire attached it to his pocket, where a small CD player or iPod lay hidden.

"The groundskeeper. Lawrence." She patted her nephew's hand as Lawrence, plugged into his music, began sweeping leaves from the courtyard. "Don't tell me you're suspicious of him?"

"I was just surprised to see a man here."

She chuckled. "Well, they do come in handy now and again, you know. As self-sufficient as we are here, most of us aren't as young as we used to be and there are some duties that are more suited for men than a bunch of old nuns." She grabbed his hand. "Sometimes, Pedro...er, Reuben, I think the world has become a very ugly place. Then I remember the words of the Father and they are a balm to me. Settle me down. Give me back my faith in humankind. That might be difficult for you, I know, because of what you do for a living."

"Is that the reason?"

She gave his hand a squeeze. "You look like you could use a little of that faith now."

"Probably," he said, thinking he could use more than a little, but then faith for him was in short supply these days. He turned the conversation back to the path he was interested in: Abby Chastain's mother. "Let's go back about twenty years ago. You remember a patient named Faith Chastain?"

Maria's face seemed to fold in upon itself. The lines in her forehead deepened. She locked her fingers. "A few days ago was the twentieth anniversary of her death," she said, surprising him that her memory of the tragedy was so clear. "I'll never forget it. I was the first one at her side. I'd been just starting out the door to the convent when I heard the sounds of groaning metal and shattering glass. And then the scream. That horrible, soul-jarring shriek of pure terror." Maria rubbed her throat. "Faith's family had just pulled up in their car. One of the girls was already inside, perhaps even up the stairs, yes, I think I passed her on the landing as I was coming down. The other daughter and Faith's husband were still outside, fussing with a present for her, I think...though it was so long ago..." Her eyes clouded, and though she looked across the courtyard to the groundskeeper busy with his broom, Montoya knew she was seeing something else in her mind's eye.

Her skin seemed paper thin. Softly, she said, "It was awful. I heard screams and shouts as I was just coming out the front door and there she was...poor thing, lying all twisted and broken on the concrete." She quickly made the sign of the cross over her bosom. "The girl was there and the husband...Jacques. It was awful, so awful." She shuddered and blinked rapidly against suddenly glistening eyes. "One of the girls had brought a gift. It was Faith's birthday, that day. A strange thing, you see, to come into this world and leave it on the very same day of the year." She frowned. "And it was the birthday of one of the daughters as well, the younger one, I think, but I'm not really certain."

"What can you tell me about Faith?" Montoya asked.

"About her condition? Not much, I'm afraid. Patient records are confidential."

"I know, but she's dead, *Tia*. Has been for a long time."

"Nonetheless, I can't release any information to you."

"I could get a court order."

"And if I defy it, would you send me to jail?" She pushed herself upright and walked to the eave of the porch, from which a mossy basket hung. Flowers and fern fronds spilled over the edge. With her thin fingers she began plucking the dead, brown fronds and leaves from the basket.

"*Tia* Maria, please," he said, trying to keep the exasperation from his voice. "Help me here, I'm trying to catch Courtney's killer."

"By asking questions about Faith Chastain?" She clearly didn't believe him.

"Everything you say will be held in confidence, you know that."

"There are laws protecting patients and doctors," she said, keeping her voice low as she, crushing the dead leaves, walked back to the bench. She bit her lip and let the dry pieces of foliage fall from her fingers. Across the way the gardener kept sweeping, his head down, as if he hadn't noticed them seated together on the bench.

She sighed. "I guess it's no secret that Faith was in and out of the hospital several times. Different doctors diagnosed different conditions. Of course, it all happened years ago and the medical profession didn't know as much about mental illness then as it does today." She dusted her hands. "I can tell you my opinion: Faith Chastain was a very misunderstood and disturbed woman. That's not a professional, medical diagnosis, but it's the truth. As for her disease? Schizophrenia? Possibly. Paranoia? Certainly. It was as if she were fighting some inner demons. I tried to help her through prayer, and hoped she would find some consolation, some peace through God. Did she? I don't know..." Maria's eyes clouded over.

"What happened to her? What forced her to leap to her death?"

"I don't know. I'm not sure that anyone does. It's one of the great mysteries surrounding the hospital. But Faith is with God now. She's no longer plagued and tormented by the demons in her mind. That's all that matters."

"Except that Courtney LaBelle and Luke Gierman were murdered and the obvious link between them is that they each had family members who were associated with the hospital."

"Luke Gierman? The radio disk jockey? He had family here?" She frowned, thinking hard.

"Not him. His ex-wife is Abby Chastain. Faith's youngest daughter."

"Oh...I didn't realize." She looked off into space. "That poor girl. What she saw that day..."

"You see why I need your help."

She glanced at him, touched his cheek with her cool hand. "I appreciate what you're doing. I know your job is difficult. You often see the gruesome and gritty side of life, but I don't know anything more that would help you." She smiled. "I'm sorry, Pedro." She glanced at her watch and stood. "I have kitchen duty in a few minutes, but it's been so good to see you again. Give my best to your mother."

"I will."

"And here." She reached into her deep pockets and came up with a rosary, the decades made up of blood-red beads. "Take this."

"I can't," he said.

She folded the rosary into his hand. "Of course you can. Use it, Pedro. Remember the saint you were named for. Capture his strength, his conviction." She wrapped her hand around his. "You'll be surprised at the power of God."

"'The power of God'?" he repeated. "Wait a minute, Maria, you're starting to sound like one of those born-again preachers. You know, like what's his name?" He snapped his fingers. "Billy Ray Furlough. Isn't 'the power of God be with you' his catchphrase?"

She looked away. "Is it?"

"I think so. You're scarin' me, *Tia.* I'd hate to think that you were straying from the order and starting to watch one of those fire-and-brimstone televangelists."

"That's highly unlikely." But she didn't laugh as he'd expected and the lines of worry around her eyes seemed to grow deeper rather than lessen as they walked out of the courtyard.

Montoya left the cloister and, with his aunt as his usher, wended his way through the dark, hushed hallways to the parking area. He drove through the gates of the convent but, rather than continue to the main road, turned at the fork in the road and onto what was left of the driveway that had been the entrance to the hospital.

He could get no farther than the fence. The old iron gates were closed, reinforced with a rusted chain and padlock, but he let the cruiser idle as he climbed out. With the damned alarm dinging a gentle reminder that he hadn't bothered to close the door, he walked to the barricade to peer through the iron bars and toward the decrepit building beyond.

The cement driveway was buckled, weeds growing through the cracks. The lawn was knee high and above it all the brick building rose a full three stories. The roof was missing some tiles and many of the windows had been boarded over. In the center of the edifice, squarely over the front door and above the broken fountain, a dormer with a round, colorful window jutted out from the otherwise unbroken roof line. What had once been a wide verandah with short stone walls flanked one side of the building. It was now covered with vines and brambles, and on the other end antiquated, rusted fire escape stairs began creaking as a gust of wind rattled through.

This was the link between the murder victims?

This tired, dilapidated building?

He thought of Abby as a young girl coming here to visit a mother who was out of touch with reality, a "troubled" woman fighting her own inner "demons," if Maria's estimation was to be believed. He considered his own family: poor, but united and, for the most part, happy. Five hellions of brothers and two sisters. His family had struggled against poverty and all the temptations and frustrations lack of money caused, but the family unit had been strong, his parents firm in their faith and determined to make the most of their lives. He'd been encouraged to become an athlete, and his soccer skills and streetsmarts had helped him get through college.

All of the class struggles and racial barriers that he'd overcome seemed small in comparison with dealing with a weak-minded mother who had ended up flinging herself from an upper-story window to land on the cement in front of her daughter. What a helluva thing for a kid to witness.

No one was paying attention.

The police were running around like rats in a maze.

The reporters had found other stories to keep them busy, and though there were occasional mentions of the "bizarre double murder" involving Luke Gierman and a coed, the story had slipped off page one and was beginning to go unnoticed.

Which was just *not* right.

Didn't they understand that this was a matter of importance? That finally, retribution was being had?

He slid through the corridors of the old asylum, for that's what it had been no matter what fancy, kind, reverent, or even lofty name the building had been christened. He walked swiftly, running his gloved fingers intimately over the walls, trying to find some peace of mind. But even here, in his sanctuary, as he crept silently through the dark hallways, he felt no comfort, no calm. And the high that he'd experienced, the rush of blood and adrenalin that had come with the killings, was fading.

He moved onward, easing through rooms few remembered and those who did would rather forget. The smell of dust and misuse clung to the walls and settled upon the chipped tile floors. The ceilings leaked but he didn't care.

This was where he would work.

This would be his home.

This was the place he had always remembered.

This was where he would make things right.

Setting a lantern in the corner of one of the private windowless rooms, he viewed the old equipment that was still hung on hooks in the walls or packed away and forgotten on tilted shelves. Slowly he ran a finger over a straitjacket, its straps dangling almost to the floor as it hung suspended from a rusted hook. The jacket had once been white but had turned gray and smelled of mold. Standing alone in a corner where it had been tucked over a decade before was an electric prod, an instrument of torture that had been outlawed for use on humans, he thought, but used it had once been. He walked to a metal cart parked against the wall. The top was stainless steel, the drawers shallow. He opened the top drawer and spied surgical instruments, no longer shiny and razor sharp, dulled with the passage of time, but organized by size and shape.

He swallowed hard. Remembered. Oh, yes, he remembered.

With a gloved hand he picked up a scalpel and held the slim blade close to his face, so that he could see his own reflection in the slender reflective surface. His eyes narrowed in the dim light and he thought for a moment that he could hear the horrible, tortured screams of those who had once been brought to this room, a place where practices and surgeries no longer deemed ethical had occurred.

He'd seen so many, the out-of-control and loud, all sedated and quietly wheeled into this very room.

Remembered each and every patient who had lived through the archaic, Machiavellian practices as well as those who had not.

He slipped the scalpel and a few other surgical tools into his backpack.

No one knew that he had survived.

No one knew that he was alive.

And no one cared.

But they would, he thought, feeling a warmth of anticipation steal through him, oh, they would.

CHAPTER 10

The afternoon sky darkened as Montoya made his way back to his cruiser and climbed inside. He executed a quick U-turn to leave the decaying old hospital behind. As he headed toward New Orleans, his cell phone rang.

"Montoya," he said, flipping on his headlights while Bonita Washington updated him on the Gierman-LaBelle murders. The upshot of the conversation was that there were no skin scrapings under Courtney LaBelle's fingernails, no DNA evidence whatsoever. None of the fingerprints they'd pulled from the scene came up with any matches using AFIS, so either the killer hadn't left prints or he wasn't in the database. Courtney LaBelle's backpack had been recovered, but it was empty and pretty much a bust. No evidence collected from it.

Washington went on to say that the autopsy report showed nothing unexpected. Both victims had died from single gunshot wounds at close range. Both looked as if they'd been bound and gagged, most likely abducted.

"So," Montoya said as he accelerated onto the freeway and the damned rain started up again. "Aside from the size twelve shoe prints and one short dark hair on the wedding dress, we don't have a lot to go on."

"At least it's something."

"I guess. The hair's at the DNA lab now. I'll let you know when we get the report back. There is one other thing," she added as he flipped on his wipers. "The wedding dress that the female victim was wearing had all the tags cut from it but it looks damned expensive to me. The fabric's imported silk and there's intricate beadwork along the sleeves and neckline. I'd bet that it's a designer gown, not that I'm an expert, but I know someone who is. Maybe she can give us a clue as to where it was purchased or who designed it."

"Somehow I don't see our killer visiting bridal shows or meeting with dress designers."

"Me neither. It was probably stolen. Maybe bought at a second-hand shop, or on eBay. But it wasn't Courtney's. Aside from the whole 'giving herself to God' thing, the wedding dress is a couple of sizes too big. Courtney was a four or possibly a six, maybe, pretty small. The dress is an eight, I'd guess, and made for a taller woman. The hem's dirty where Courtney stepped on it."

"She wasn't wearing shoes. A bride would be in heels."

"Yeah, but probably not six-inch heels . . . this dress looks like it was made to order, especially designed, but not for Courtney La-Belle or anyone her size."

"So we need to know for whom."

"That would help. As I said, I'm talking to my expert, and if we find out where that fabric or the beads came from, we might find our dressmaker. It's not much," she admitted, "but at least it's a start."

"Hey, right now, I'll take anything. Thanks."

He hung up, drove for about three miles, then dialed Brinkman. "Yeah?"

"Have we come up with the last people to see our vics alive?"

"Yeah . . . well, we think so . . . let me see . . . yeah, okay, I got my notes right here. Let's start with the Virgin Mary, okay? I followed her steps that night as well as I could, and the last people to see her alive were two girls who were going into the library about the time she was coming out, around nine-thirty. They're pretty certain that they know it was Mary. One of the girls, Jenny Ray, had her in the same communications class. Jenny, too, caught Gierman's act at All Saints."

So did a lot of other students.

"So these two, they spied her, dressed in her running gear with her backpack. She was headed across campus toward the dorm."

"Her usual routine."

"According to the freakoid roommate, yes."

Montoya switched lanes. "What about Gierman?"

"We haven't found anyone who saw him after he left the radio station. But someone picked up his mail from the box and put it on the kitchen counter of his town house. I found it on the day we searched his place, so I figure he left the station, went home, hung out, maybe ate—as the autopsy report shows he had the remnants of lasagna in his stomach and I found the empty box of frozen lasagna in the trash. Then, I'm thinking he must've headed for the gym. But he was low on cash so he stopped at the ATM first.

"Now, before you ask, yes, I saw the bank's videotape from the ATM. Got him front and center in his workout clothes as he withdrew the cash. It's Gierman, all right. No one with him. I even checked the people who stopped at that ATM the hours before and after Gierman. Nothin' out of place. All legit."

"So we've got nothing?"

"Not much."

"Son of a bitch," Montoya grumbled, glaring at the minivan in front of him. A bumper sticker was slapped onto the back bragging about the owner's kid. "What about word on the street? Anybody see anything? Hear about something big going down?"

"Not from the regular snitches...whoever did this is keeping his mouth shut. Or hers."

"I agree with Zaroster—not a woman's crime," Montoya said, irritated that Brinkman, as good a cop as he was, was still keeping Abby Chastain in the pool of suspects.

"Yeah, well, time will tell."

Frustrated, Montoya hung up. He drove toward the heart of the city, watching the New Orleans skyline come into view, tall buildings knifing into the gray day. But his thoughts were elsewhere, on the damned case. He felt the hours slipping away, as if some unseen clock was ticking, and he realized it was because of Abby with her seductive smile, intelligent eyes, and body that wouldn't quit. Damn the woman, she was getting to him, something that hadn't happened in a long, long while. There had been a time when any beautiful woman had caught his eye, but now...oh, hell. His fingers tightened over the steering wheel and he swore under his breath. It was imperative that he remain completely clearheaded and impartial, but Ms. Chastain, the ex–Mrs. Gierman, was definitely clouding his judgment.

He hadn't liked how Brinkman had pushed her in the interview. For the first time ever, Montoya had considered the interrogation brashness out of line, which was damned ludicrous. He'd hate to count how many times he himself had done his own share of leaning on a witness, shaken 'em up a bit, waited for the truth to sift out. In Abby's case, it had been all Montoya could do to hold his tongue, to not step in, to goddamned defend her. And yet, he'd forced himself to go along with Brinkman's tactics and hated every minute of it. The session had seemed more like an inquisition rather than an interrogation.

But then, his judgment wasn't as clear as it should be.

He probably should remove himself from the case, but couldn't stomach the idea of Brinkman running roughshod over Abby again, or teaming up with Bentz when he returned.

A helluva time for Rick Bentz and his wife to take a honeymoon.

Montoya turned off the freeway, slowed as he entered the city and wound his way to the French Quarter. The city was teeming with people, as usual. Pedestrians vied with cars, buses, trucks, and mule-drawn carriages while jaywalking through the thick traffic. Even in the rain, street musicians played, their instrument cases open as they hoped for tips, people walked bareheaded or huddled under umbrellas, and the aromas from the local restaurants mingled with those of gasoline and oil.

And still his thoughts were with the case and Abby Chastain.

The bottom line, he thought, as he wheeled around a corner, was that whether he wanted to admit it or not, he was attracted to the woman. Physically and even emotionally. The first woman since Marta. And the worst choice possible.

Luke Gierman's ex, for crying out loud. And if not a suspect in his death, then certainly a person of interest.

She had the means and opportunity. And the motive? Over half a million dollars was a good start. The fact that Gierman had publicly ridiculed her didn't hurt.

But how could she pull a well-planned killing like that in so little time? And what about Courtney LaBelle? No, it couldn't happen. Even if she had wanted Gierman dead because of what he'd said on the radio, there just wasn't enough time to hire an assassin, set up the abduction and killings to make it look like...what? A lover's quarrel? Nah, no paid hit-man would do what was done to Gierman and LaBelle, despite the time.

Brinkman's theory was bullshit. Plain and simple.

"Damn it all to hell," he growled, catching sight of his reflection in the rearview mirror. He saw his own dark eyes, the purse of his lips, the determination in the set of his jaw. "Stay objective," he ordered. As the light changed, he drove the final two streets to the station's parking lot and nosed the cruiser into an open spot. Still irritated with himself, the case, and the whole damned world, he climbed out of the Crown Vic and took his foul mood up the main steps of the station.

Women had always been his problem.

He liked them.

And they liked him.

Plain and simple.

His stupid libido had a way of working overtime, or at least it had, until Marta. For a while he'd been a one-woman man, changing his womanizing ways for Ms. Vasquez.

But that was all over now, he thought as he climbed the stairs and walked into the offices of the homicide division. Computer keyboards clattered, phones rang, and there was a sense of urgency in the nest of cubicles and offices that spread out over the floor. Somewhere a copy machine was whirring out pages, and near Zaroster's desk a handcuffed and shackled suspect, his dreadlocks disheveled to his shoulders, his face unshaven, was talking with great animation. In jeans and a denim jacket with the sleeves cut out, he was speaking fast and jerkily, coming off of something, protesting his innocence vigorously to Zaroster and another detective.

Montoya nearly ran into Brinkman, who was heading out the main doors while slipping his arms through the sleeves of his jacket. "Get a load of that," he said, sliding a look at the suspect. "Involved in a knifing down off of Esplanade and Royal. Scumbag

One here," he explained, hooking his thumb at his dreadlocks, "didn't like the fact that Scumbag Two was gettin' it on with Scum One's old lady. Grabbed a kitchen knife and that was the end of Scum Two." He made a theatrical slice across his neck with his thumb. "Ooops. I mean he 'allegedly' nearly sliced the guy's head off in front of the lady, and I use the term 'lady' loosely, considering the piece of ass in question."

"Why isn't he in an interrogation room?"

"Full to capacity. A shooting on Decatur and an accident on the waterfront. Been a busy day. This scumbag already said his piece in the interrogation room, we've got it on tape, but he wanted to make a statement. Waived his right to a lawyer. We needed the space, so..." He shrugged as if to say "all in a day's work." He then found his pack of Marlboros in his inside jacket pocket, fished one out, jabbing the cigarette into the corner of his mouth.

"You know what I'm wonderin'?" he said, the filter tip bobbing. "Why the hell everyone in the damned Gierman case has another name? Courtney goes by Mary, the freakoid calls herself O... what the hell is that all about?"

"Beats me."

"Hey, even you used to call yourself 'Diego,' didn't ya? When you were out prowlin' around for the ladies?"

Montoya figured he wouldn't mention that his aunt referred to him as Pedro in honor of St. Peter. Things were confusing enough as it was.

Brinkman, patting his pants pockets in search of his lighter, started down the stairs. "Oh, by the way. Bentz is back," he called over his shoulder. "Lookin' for you. Guess I've been replaced." He said it without a drip of acrimony. Montoya figured Brinkman didn't like him either. It was a mutual thing.

As the paunchy detective disappeared down the stairs, Montoya made his way to his cubicle, checked his messages, printed out Bonita Washington's reports, and placed them into an ever-expanding file. Tucking the file under his arm, he grabbed a couple of cups of coffee from the pot in the small kitchen, then made his way to Bentz's office.

He didn't bother to knock, just shouldered open the door that was already ajar and found Rick Bentz seated at his desk, papers strewn in front of him, pictures of his wife and kid shoved to the corners. He looked up as Montoya walked in.

"*Hola, mi amiga,*" Bentz said, grinning. He was a big man who fought his weight by pummeling the hell out of a punching bag daily. He spied the coffee and waved Montoya over. Seemingly easygoing by nature, Bentz had been known to explode, especially if anyone messed with his daughter, Kristi, now nearly twenty-five, or his wife of a few years, Olivia. "*¿Cómo está usted?*"

"Jesus, Bentz, that's *amigo.* With an 'o.' I'm a male. *Varón!* Got it? *Soy un hombre, para el motivo del Dios!* Translation? 'I'm a man, for God's sake!'"

The corners of Bentz's lips twitched and he stared pointedly at Montoya's earring. "If you say so."

"Hell, man, let's not go there, okay?"

"Just breakin' the ice, *hombre.* Gettin' back into the swing of things here," Bentz said, sipping from his cup then hoisting it into the air. "*Gracias.*" In his mid-forties, he had a blocky body, an ex–football player's build. At his age, the few gray hairs and lines in his face added character, or so he'd told Montoya time and time again when the younger man had flung him some crap about aging. And he was a helluva cop, despite what had happened in L.A.

"And here I thought you probably broke the banks in Vegas." Montoya sipped his coffee and leaned against a file cabinet upon which a Christmas cactus was dying. "I figured you won a few mil on the craps table and decided to drop in just to pick up your things and say 'good-bye.'"

Bentz snorted. "Yeah, that's what happened. Only it was roulette. I'm so rich, I could buy and sell Asa Pomeroy *and* Billy Ray Furlough put together."

Montoya laughed. Asa Pomeroy was a wealthy industrialist, had made his fortune in arming the world, and Billy Ray Furlough a televangelist spreading God's word via the tube while collecting donations from wherever the airwaves cast his sermons. Asa Pomeroy's money was tied up in ex-wives, trust funds, and land development. Billy Ray "the power of God be with you" Furlough's was spent to help the poor, bring the word of God to underdeveloped nations, and fill the coffers of tax-sheltered foundations which provided him with a lifestyle befitting royalty.

"So, since you're the new Mr. Trump—"

"Here it comes." Bentz leaned back in his chair until it creaked.

Montoya flashed a grin. "You know Trump goes by 'The Donald,' right? So, I'm thinkin' from now on we'll all call you 'The Rick' ... No!" He snapped his fingers. "I like 'The Dick' even better."

Bentz barked out a laugh. "And I don't suppose you're talking about my job with the department?"

"Hell, no!" Montoya felt better than he had since this whole double homicide mess had started. Dealing with Brinkman had been a pain; Bentz was easier. Smarter. Calmer. A good balance for Montoya's more explosive personality. "So, The Dick," he said, "if you're in a generous mood, I could use a new set of wheels. A Ferrari would be nice, but I'd settle for a Porsche, as long as it was tricked out."

"Aren't they all?" Bentz asked as phones outside his office jangled and footsteps pounded past his doorway. "I'll remember that. Christmas is coming." He reached into his drawer for a bottle of antacids, popped a few, and motioned toward his computer screen, where images of the Gierman-LaBelle murder scene were visible. "So how about bringing me up to speed on the double? I've seen the preliminary reports. What else have you got?"

Montoya handed over the file and gave Bentz his version of what he thought had gone down. "We've got no suspects on the one hand," he said, "because no one was holding a grudge, at least not that we can find, against Courtney Mary LaBelle. She was a virgin, for God's sake, planned on joining the order at Our Lady of Virtues."

Bentz was way ahead of him. "But on the other hand, you've got Luke Gierman, who has every feminist, or PTA member, or socially conscious group wanting him dead because he does a lot of shows on weird sex, odd behavior, pushes the envelope to entertain and offend."

"You got it."

"What about the murder weapon?"

"Given to Courtney by her father for protection and definitely a taboo on campus. I double-checked today. Even her roommate, who goes by the name of O and has an affinity for Goth culture and blood, didn't know about the piece."

"Someone did," Bentz said.

"Yep." Montoya scratched his goatee. "You know, it's funny. The girl wears a promise ring and vows her virginity to God as some kind of sacred rite and her dad gives her a handgun for protection." He frowned. "I never think of God and weaponry as things that go together."

"You're wrong. Look at the Crusades, or what's happening in the Middle East. Religion and money are the source of all wars."

"So now you're a philosopher."

"A philosopher who just happened to win a fortune at the roulette wheel," Bentz said, flashing his smile as he reached onto the desk for his reading glasses. He thumbed through the file, his eyes scanning the pages. "What else have you got?"

Montoya filled him in on the alibis of just about everyone close to either of the victims, and the lack of evidence found at the crime scene. The forensics department was still separating out tire tracks near the cabin at the woods while also trying to find product matches for the shoe tread of the size twelve prints they'd discovered. Once they found the company who made the shoe, they could find the local distributors and start searching through the names of purchasers of size twelves in the last few years. A tedious process but a necessary one.

He told Bentz about the wedding dress and the single, short dark hair found on the fabric.

"It's at the DNA lab now. Hopefully it'll come back and match up with someone who knows the victims."

Bentz frowned. They both were aware that finding that individual would take a lot of time. DNA samples from all the potential suspects would have to be taken, and if the suspects balked and wouldn't give up a swab voluntarily, court orders would have to be issued.

That was a whole new ball of wax.

As Bentz listened, Montoya explained about the wedding dress, the fact that it might have been custom made, and that the blood-stained gown had already been photographed, the fabric analyzed. Copies of the photos were already being circulated to the local dressmakers and bridal gown shops throughout the state.

Montoya and Bentz talked over the list of suspects—who was

close to the victims and who might want them dead. They narrowed the field by who, within the time constraints of their schedules, could accost both Gierman and LaBelle and not be seen. Then they talked over where the victims had been abducted and why they'd been chosen.

Neither man believed either of the victims had been a random choice. The murders had been too well planned.

"That's the big question, isn't it? Who would want Courtney LaBelle and Luke Gierman dead?" Bentz said, thinking aloud. He reached into the top drawer of his desk and found a pack of Doublemint gum, pulled out a stick, and offered the pack to Montoya.

"No thanks."

"Still goin' cold turkey?" he asked as he folded his stick of gum and slid it into his mouth.

"Yeah."

"And how is that?"

"Fine," Montoya snapped. No way was he admitting to Bentz that he would have killed for a drag about now.

Bentz lifted an eyebrow in disbelief but didn't comment. "So let's go through this again. The last to see Courtney alive were some kids walking into the library as she was going out, right?"

"Can't find anyone else," Montoya admitted.

"And the last person to see Gierman was Maury Taylor at WSLJ."

Montoya nodded, explained Brinkman's theory and what they found on the bank's ATM tape as Bentz finished his coffee and Montoya's grew cold.

"I know some people over at the radio station. I think I'll poke around over there, see if I can turn up anything Brinkman might have missed." He crushed the paper cup in his fist and tossed it into the trash. "So it looks like whoever abducted them grabbed Gierman around six-forty, probably, and the girl three hours later."

"In Baton Rouge. An hour and a half away. What's he do? Keep Gierman locked in the trunk while he waits for the girl?"

"The cabin's not far from the west side of Lake Pontchartrain."

"Twenty miles off of Highway 10."

"So where does our guy live?" Bentz wondered aloud. "And how did he know about that empty cabin?"

"No connection between the owners and any of the victims. Already checked." Montoya took a final sip of his coffee, scowled, and poured the rest into the pot holding the near-dead plant.

"And the only link between the two victims that you can find is a class where Gierman spoke and the fact that Gierman's ex-wife's mother was a patient where Courtney LaBelle's mother and father worked and Courtney intended to become a novitiate."

"It's thin," Montoya admitted.

"Nearly invisible."

"So you think it's a coincidence?"

Bentz leaned back in his chair until it creaked, chewing his gum thoughtfully. "You know how I feel about coincidences," he said and glanced over at the graphic pictures visible on his computer monitor.

"That there are none. Same as Brinkman." Montoya studied the images on the screen. Luke Gierman's naked body, partially covered by the girl in the bloodstained bridal dress. Obviously posed. A statement. From a sick, twisted mind.

"You agree?"

"Yep."

Bentz rubbed his neck and frowned. "A guy who does something like this, he's looking for attention."

Montoya knew where this was going. "You think he'll do it again?"

A muscle worked in the older man's jaw and his face hardened. He looked up at Montoya. "I hope to God not."

CHAPTER 11

"I want to come to the funeral," Zoey insisted from the other side of the continent. "When is it?"

"I don't know." Maneuvering through traffic, Abby was holding her cell phone to her ear while driving, and hating it. She was just no good at juggling her attention. Teenagers seemed to buzz in and out of lanes, cell phones to their ears, as if the two tasks, talking on the phone and handling a car, were second nature.

It was raining, the sky dark even though it was closing in on noon. At sixty miles per hour, her Honda seemed to skate over the puddles of water that had collected in the low part of the road. Trucks, sending up sprays of water from beneath their massive eighteen wheels, were flying past her as if she were standing still. "Look, I'm in the car now, let me call you back."

"I'm in the car, too. So what?"

"I can't concentrate on the conversation and the traffic."

"Come on. I do it all the time. Piece of cake."

"Right," Abby said sarcastically as a silver Toyota from the inside lane cut in front of her and she had to touch the brakes. "Jerk!"

"Me?"

"No. Well, at least not today."

"Thank God," Zoey said. "So when are you going to call?"

"When I'm done. Promise."

"What's on the agenda? Photo shoot?"

"Yeah," Abby hedged. It wasn't really a lie. Not a big one. But she knew Zoey would have a heart attack if she knew that Abby was on her way to Our Lady of Virtues intending to finally put the past to rest. Yesterday she'd spent the hours with clients or showing the house, or trying to catch up on her sleep. She'd dragged around all day, forcing herself to go on a three-mile run that had left her winded and her muscles aching. After a microwave dinner and a long, hot bubble bath which had included sipping a glass of wine, she'd slept like the dead. No eerie, returning nightmares had woken her up, no images of her dead ex-husband peppering her sleep. She'd awakened surprisingly revitalized and refreshed.

So today, she had planned to take charge of her life. First on the agenda: visiting the hospital. Laying the past to rest. It was time. Long past time. But Zoey wouldn't understand.

"Okay, just let me know when Luke's service is."

"Oh, Zoe—"

"Look, you'll need some support. Luke's family isn't exactly warm and fuzzy. No Ozzie and Harriet, if you know what I mean. Mom, baseball, and apple pie don't exist in that bunch of loons!"

Abby couldn't help smiling. Sometimes Zoey could be funny as all get-out; other times she was a royal pain in the backside. "Okay, okay, I'll let you know."

"Abby?"

"What?" she asked, checking her rearview and seeing that a semi had nearly attached itself to her bumper.

"Are you okay?"

"What? Yeah, fine," she snapped, though of course that was a lie. "Just hunky-dory."

"I mean it. I know Luke's death is difficult and—"

"Gotta go, this is my exit," Abby cut in, steamed. She hung up before Zoey asked another damned question. She was tired of the whole overly concerned older sister bit from her nosy sister. Sheesh. She hadn't heard from Zoey for months and now she called all the time. *All* the time. It was almost as if her sister had some kind of sick fascination with Luke's murder, or she needed to be close to the action.

Or she's just genuinely concerned. How about that, Abby? Get over what happened in Seattle; Zoey is probably just worried. "Fat chance," Abby muttered and clicked the damned cell phone off. Anyone else who wanted to call her could bloody well leave a message on voice mail. She glanced in her rearview, noticed the semi was still on her ass, and wanted to slow to a crawl to really piss the guy off. Why didn't the damned driver just pass her if she was going too slow?

"Idiot," she muttered, slowing as she eased onto the exit ramp. The eighteen-wheeler gunned it past her, engine roaring, his HOW'S MY DRIVING? sign on his back bumper mocking her. If she had the time, she'd phone the number listed and give whoever answered an earful. As it was, he was already past; she couldn't read the 1-800 number anyway.

By memory, she found her way along the twisted road to Our Lady of Virtues. Of course the landscape had changed and where there once had been fields with cattle grazing or forests skirting the road, there were now clusters of houses in little pockets of farmland that developers had found.

Eventually the houses thinned and the terrain was more familiar with the stands of live oak or swamp holly. Her pulse accelerated and her hands were sweaty on the steering wheel. Several times she considered turning around.

When the going gets tough…

"Yeah, yeah, Dad, I know," she muttered under her breath, ignoring an underlying sense of panic that had grown with each mile she'd driven closer to this, the place where her life had changed irrevocably.

She bit her lip.

You can do it.

One final turn and the narrow lane with its weatherbeaten sign was visible. OUR LADY OF VIRTUES. EST. 1843.

Abby's fingers locked, her knuckles showing white as the wheels of her car rolled into the grounds owned by Our Lady of Virtues convent: thirty acres of lush, valuable gardens, buildings and forests that developers had been salivating over for years. As the suburbs had grown, inching ever closer to the secluded property owned by the order of nuns still living there, the land had doubled, then tripled in worth, even though many of the buildings were decayed and destined for the wrecking ball.

Abby took a fork in the private road and drove to the entrance of the hospital grounds. The gate, of course, was locked, a chain reinforcing the original bolts, a stern, faded NO TRESPASSING sign warning anyone who chose to ignore it that they would be prosecuted "to the full extent of the law."

"Nice," she muttered sarcastically. "Real Christian." She had expected that the entrance would be barred and had formed a backup plan on the drive over. No way would she be thwarted. No way was she going to go through this emotional turmoil more than once. She unzipped her camera from its case, snapped a strap to it, then climbed out of her car. With more than a trace of sadness that she hadn't expected, she noted the ever-declining state of the grounds and lawns and buildings beyond. Her heart nearly stopped as she viewed the old hospital, a building that had survived the War between the States, two world wars, and all the skirmishes in between. For a hundred and fifty years it had been maintained and kept alive, even flourished, but hadn't been able to weather the most recent of times.

Everything has a life span.
Everything and everyone dies.

Ignoring her unexpected case of nostalgia, Abby pushed her camera's lens through the bars and snapped off half a dozen shots in the fading light.

As she stared through the viewfinder, she felt an overwhelming sadness at the crumbling mortar, missing bricks, and lengths of plywood nailed over once grand windows. Graffiti sprayed in neon orange was visible under a layer of black that someone, probably hired by the sisters themselves, had used to try and cover up the profanity.

Dear God, what was wrong with her? She hated this place. So why a sense of sorrow or wistful sentimentality for a place she detested, a building on whose grave she should be dancing?

Maybe she was more screwed up than she'd thought.

"Stop," she ordered. This was getting her nowhere fast.

Abby tried the gates. Felt raindrops in her hair. The old metal rattled and groaned, but the lock and chain held. Of course. She'd expected as much. She could turn back now. At least from a distance she'd seen the spot where her mother had died. Still, she wasn't satisfied. And this, she promised herself, was her last trip to Our Lady of Virtues. If she couldn't lay the ghosts to rest today, they were destined to be with her for the rest of her life.

What a depressing thought.

She had to give this her best shot.

She climbed into her Honda again, but instead of taking the fork to the main road, she veered toward the convent. Once near the gates, she turned onto a small access road, to a lower parking lot which, in the past, had been used primarily by maintenance workers.

As a child she'd found this small parking lot while exploring the grounds of the hospital. She and Zoey had discovered the path leading between the hospital and convent long ago, when they'd been grade-schoolers, searching the grounds, chasing butterflies and broken dreams through the sun-dappled woods.

Today the sky was gloomy and gray, another rain shower appearing inevitable if the heavy clouds scudding across the sky were to be believed.

Snagging her camera again from the passenger seat, Abby stepped into the warmth and solitude of the afternoon. She heard birds chirping and the chattering of a squirrel, but no sound of prayers or music or conversation seeped through the thick walls surrounding the convent itself. Good. She didn't want any of the nuns to witness what she was about to do.

Feeling more than a little nervous that she was not only breaking the law, but perhaps making a mistake of insurmountable emotional proportions, she ignored her second-guesses, locked her car, then walked to the side of one of the garages where mowers and gardening equipment were kept.

A row of twelve-foot-tall arborvitaes flanked a chain fence that loomed over Abby's head. The fencing curved inward, toward the hospital, making it nearly impossible for anyone to climb out, at least not easily, though Abby knew it could be done if one was agile enough.

At ten, she had been.

Now, though, the task seemed daunting. Could she climb over

the fencing, drop ten feet to the ground below, and then somehow climb out again? As a child she was monkey-like in her ability to scale trees, fences, and balconies. Now, nearly twenty-five years later and forty pounds heavier than her pre-pubescent weight, it would be extremely difficult. But there had been a gate, she remembered, one that allowed the nuns and hospital staff to go between the two facilities. She searched the area and found what had once been some kind of entrance, though now the scratchy, moist, unclipped branches of the shrubbery had nearly grown together. She had a fleeting thought of the thorns and bracken surrounding the castle of Sleeping Beauty, a story her mother had read to her often when she was a child. In the bedtime tale the prince had found a way through the horrible, thorny branches to the castle to rescue his princess. Abby didn't expect anything so grand or romantic. Even if she did manage to get to the hospital and face the past, as her last shrink had advised, what then? Would she feel this great uplifting of her spirit? Would all the problems in her life suddenly and miraculously disappear?

Not hardly.

Nonetheless, she pushed through the wall of greenery to the gate and found, to her utter amazement, that it not only was unlocked, but swung open easily.

Why?

She hesitated. This was too easy. Something wasn't right. Why lock and chain the main gates and put up threatening placards, only to leave this one swinging free? That didn't make any sense... unless the nuns still needed access, or the maintenance guys or groundskeepers still checked on the old building. That had to be it.

Then why let the arborvitaes grow out of control? Why not trim them here and keep the path clear? Inside the gate, on the hospital grounds, there was some evidence that others had trod through the grass and bushes... some bent blades, and for no reason other than to calm herself, she took a picture of the overgrown path she'd followed as a child.

Her heart raced a little faster as she hurried through the trees where grass, vines, and weeds had nearly obliterated the trail and her shoes squished in the mud. As she walked, she remembered running through this thin forest of bayberry and pine and oak.

Zoey had often hidden in the branches of a swamp willow and sometimes the sweet scent of magnolia and jasmine in bloom had scented the air.

She saw herself as if it were an old movie, she and her sister running in sepia tones through this bit of forest, finding a hollowed-out oak and a nest of honeybees, spying jack rabbits and skunk. All the while she'd pretended that Faith Chastain was normal, that all the kids in the private Catholic school they attended only saw their own mothers every Sunday after church, or on Wednesday evenings in the long hot summers. She'd tried, as a child sprinting toward the looming hospital, to convince herself that her classmates' mothers, too, suffered from splitting headaches that changed their personalities. Surely, too, those mothers had spent the long hours of the day in bed with the shades drawn and occupied their nights by pacing the hallways, just as Faith Chastain had. Abby remembered the sporadic times when her mother had lived at home.

Those long nights, lying in her twin bed, Abby had felt the breath of wind stir through the screened windows, seen the sweep of the paddle fan mounted on the ceiling. She'd listened to the sound of traffic, watched as the splash of headlights traversed around the pine-paneled walls of the room as cars passed, heard the lonely sound of a solitary owl while her sister, in the next bed, slept blissfully unaware of their mother's ritual.

But Abby had known.

She had watched the slim crack of light beneath the doorway, seen the shadows moving slowly back and forth as Faith Chastain had paced the halls; she'd smelled the scent of smoke from her mother's ever-lit cigarette.

It had been on one of those nights, when Jacques, a lumber broker, had been out of town, when Abby had been awake, listening to the hum of the crickets and cicadas while watching the shadow pass under the doorway, that she felt it . . . a strangeness in the air.

She'd been around ten at the time and she'd heard the bathtub filling, water rushing through the pipes, and had noticed that the pacing had stopped.

The bathroom door clicked shut. Locked.

She'd wondered why her mother was going to take a bath at three in the morning.

Abby had lain in bed, waiting, though she didn't know for what, all the while listening as the water ran and ran and ran.

Finally, she'd been unable to lie still another second and had thrown back the thin sheets. By the time she'd left her room and stood in the hallway, water was seeping from under the bathroom door, running along the old plank floors in slow rivulets tinged red...

Now, as she hurried through the thickets surrounding what had once been manicured lawns, Abby's throat tightened and raindrops slid beneath her collar. In the back of her mind, she'd always thought her mother's first stay at the hospital had been her fault... that if she'd been braver, if she'd gotten out of bed earlier, if she'd somehow stopped Faith Chastain from locking herself inside that bathroom, some of the tragedy that had become her mother's life might have been averted.

I forgive you...Abby Hannah, I forgive you... Her mother's voice, soft and whispery as it always was in the dream, slipped through her mind. She felt the first cool drops of rain fall from the sky and she stepped around a weed-infested hedgerow to look at the back side of the hospital.

How many times had she stood in this very spot, anxious as she'd slipped away from the shadows of the woods, hoping beyond hope that none of the nuns, especially stern-faced Sister Rebecca or ever-exasperated Sister Madeline, would catch her?

Again she lifted her camera, took pictures of this side of the old building, the willow tree and the long, open verandah where now only one forgotten chaise, rusted and broken, lay on the splintered flagstones.

Creeaaaakkk!

Looking up, she spied a gutter, bleeding rust and heavy with years of debris, leaning away from the roof, the metal being pushed from its eave by the wind. A gargoyle, eyes bulging over its spillway of an open mouth, glared down at her.

God, how those stony, medieval monsters had scared her as a child. She'd been certain any bird or squirrel foolish enough to step close to that gaping, dark mouth would be snagged and swallowed by the evil creature.

Of course, it had all been her childish imagination, she thought now as she walked to the front of the building.

She glanced to the upper floors and the third-story window poised directly over this spot. That window, shattered when Faith had flung herself through the old panes, had been replaced and was one of the few sheets of glass still intact. No bullet hole, no cracks, no graying plywood tacked over it.

Once Faith Chastain had fallen through, the window had been replaced quickly and now remained. Abby turned her camera to the window, and stepped back toward the end of the drive to make certain that the entire building and the fountain were included in the picture. Shadows moved and shifted, the dark reflection of the surrounding trees in the gloomy light. For a heartbeat, looking through the camera, focusing and snapping the first shot, she thought she saw a dark figure standing in the window of her mother's room. She lowered the camera and studied the panels of glass with the circular, stained wheel of glass above them, but no one stood behind the panes.

"Of course," she growled at herself. She was determined not to allow her own wild imagination to take hold of her. Yes, this was a depressing place, the very spot where her mother had lost her life, the building where Abby's life had shifted forever, but it was time to deal with it.

Setting her jaw, she forced her heart rate to slow and clicked off several shots of Faith's room, getting lost in the play of shadows, shapes, and images she saw through the viewfinder. She took pictures of the hospital as a whole, then separate shots of the component parts, the lifeless fountain with its mossy weeping angels, the skeletal remains of the ancient fire escape, and the large, looming front door where she had raced, eager to see her mother, her heart pumping with excitement as she was anxious to confide her latest crush to Faith on their shared birthday...

Or had she?

Her brow knit as she thought, the years tumbling backward. Was that what had happened? Or just the way she wanted to remember that day?

The rain increased as she stopped at the very spot in the cracked, wet concrete where her mother's body had landed with a heart-stopping and sickening thud.

"Oh, Mama," she whispered.

Her throat closed in on itself. She felt slightly ill remembering the horrifying scream and turning to spy her mother land, head cracking, bones breaking, blood pooling a thick, dark red.

"Jesus," she whispered now and sketched the sign of the cross deftly over her chest. She knew the exact spot where her mother had landed, and when she closed her eyes, she still heard the rush of noise, her father's shout, the cries and thunder of footsteps as others rushed to help.

Too little, too late.

Even the shriek of the ambulance's sirens was just useless loud noise, part of the cacophony that seemed to announce to the world that Faith Chastain had finally escaped from her pain.

Abby backed up, away from the precise point, where, if she let herself, she could still see the blood flowing, her mother's face, turned at an impossible angle. Staring up at her...as if from a far distance...as if Abby were on a mountaintop. Her mind, as always, played tricks on her as she, still staring at that horrid place, forced herself backward.

Her heels hit the steps leading to the main door. Abby tore her gaze away from the area where Faith had lost her life. There was no use standing in the rain, reliving the tragedy. If seeing that precise slab of concrete had been the point, she'd accomplished it. She turned and mounted the stairs at the door, she reached for the handle, then pushed with her shoulders.

Locked.

Of course.

The clouds were beginning to open up, raindrops bouncing on the ground, the sky as dark as twilight. She should just go back, call it a day, hope that just being here was enough to satisfy whatever psychological and emotional need was necessary to find the closure of her mother's death. But as she glanced up toward the window of Faith's room, she knew she would always have questions, be plagued with doubts if she didn't find her way into the bedroom where her mother's madness had escalated to suicide.

And she was here, wasn't she?

She walked the perimeter of the building, testing doors and finding them all locked, the French doors to the verandah, the kitchen door where deliveries had been made, the two opposing hallway doors beneath the old fire escapes... all locked tight.

She was about to give up, deciding the Fates were against her, when, at the back of the building near a service parking area, she noticed an unlatched window, one where the glass hadn't yet been shattered.

Maybe the Fates had changed their collective mind.

She stepped onto the crumbling stoop leading to the kitchen and tried pushing the window upward. It gave slightly. Slinging her camera to her back, she pressed closer and, using two hands, shoved hard. Nothing happened. It didn't even budge. "Come on, come on," she urged, wondering how many laws she was breaking and, ludicrously, imagining herself explaining to Detective Montoya why she was breaking and entering. *That* wasn't a pleasant thought. After taking several deep breaths, she tried again. This time she strained so hard, the muscles in the backs of her arms burned and her shoulders and upper back began to ache. She gritted her teeth. Pressed harder.

Suddenly, without warning, the window slid upward and Abby nearly tumbled off the stoop. Stale air escaped and she had another moment's indecision before thinking, *In for a penny, in for a pound.* Using the strap on the camera to lower it, she set the Minolta inside. Now it was her turn. With more agility than she had expected, she pushed herself up and through, using her hands to catch herself as she landed on the dusty floor of what had once been a dining hall. It was empty now, the three chandeliers dark, the floor stained from water that had oozed through the window, down the wall, and into the cracks between the once-glossy planks.

It was dark inside, not only from the gloomy day but because she didn't dare try any lights. She suspected the electricity had been turned off a decade earlier. The few windows that were still intact let in some natural light, but as she crept through the old dining area, she tried to be as quiet as possible, as if in making any noise, she might alert whatever ghosts and spirits abided here.

Which was just plain stupid.

She didn't believe in ghosts.

So then why not run through the old hallways shouting? Did

she think someone could hear her? Who? The nuns cloistered in their convent a quarter of a mile away? Did she feel the need to remain quiet out of reverence for the dead? Or fear? Of what? Possibly scaring up a snake that had taken up residence and now was coiled in some dark corner? Seeing a rat streak across the dusty floor?

Or simply because she knew she shouldn't be here. Not only was she trespassing, but if she was honest with herself, she was afraid.

Of what she would find.

Within herself.

When the going gets tough, the tough get going . . . Her father's words again echoed through her mind, replaying like a mantra as she stepped from the dining room and through a butler's pantry that separated the eating area from the kitchen. She remembered being here as a child, the gleaming china, the glistening glassware that guests and patients, if they could be trusted, were allowed to use.

The kitchen was dark and dingy, the old stove covered with grease and a decade of dirt and, she assumed from the droppings she spied, home to any manner of rodents that had obviously scampered across the counters and into the drains. She tried the door to the basement, but it was locked solidly and she felt instant relief that there was at least one dark place she didn't feel compelled to explore.

Enough with the facing of demons here in the kitchen, she thought and made her way to the foyer where, she remembered, an ornate grandfather's clock had stood at the base of the stairs. The spot it had occupied was now empty, the reception desk unmanned and forgotten, the offices behind like small, airless tombs.

The parlor, with its high ceilings, had once seemed elegant and grand. It now reeked of decay and disrepair, its faded velvet curtains tattered and torn, the one remaining chair once a deep maroon now a dull orange, its batting spewing out of the cushions and littering the floor.

The whole damned place was depressing. If she were supposed to find any great epiphany of the soul here, it had yet to arrive.

But then you haven't visited her room yet, have you, Abby?

Nothing else matters, does it?

You need to see the room where she lived, the room where she spent her sleepless nights, the room where she finally cast herself through the glass and gave up her life.

"Damn it," she whispered and walked to the stairs. She climbed each riser slowly, as she had as a child, when Sister Rebecca had insisted that there was to be "No running. No jumping. No scampering about like wild hooligans."

At the second floor she stopped and looked down the dark corridor. All of the doors to the private rooms were open, sagging against old hinges.

She grabbed the rail, started toward the third floor, and stopped when she thought she heard something—footsteps?—on the floor below? Or above? Holding her breath, she waited. Listened. But there was no sound save for the rain falling against the roof and water running through the gutters. The rest of the old hospital remained silent aside from the sound of her own footsteps creaking up the staircase.

Get hold of yourself, she silently admonished, her heart hammering as, at the final landing, she looked at the stained-glass window and wondered how it had survived. Why hadn't it been sold? What had saved it from being broken? She remembered staring at the image of the Madonna when bright summer sunlight had streamed through the colored glass, illuminating Mary's golden halo so that it seemed to glow as if touched by heaven. Now it was dim and dark, no sparkling reds, blues, or greens on this dreary day.

She turned and walked up the final few stairs to the third-floor hallway and froze, her heart squeezing painfully. Every door was shut, not one open as they had been on the floor below.

"How odd," she whispered and wished she'd had the presence of mind to bring her flashlight with her instead of leaving it in the glove box of the car. *Just do this. Get it over with.* She stepped into the hallway and walked directly to the door of her mother's room. The numbers 307 were intact, and only when she slid a glance at the room next door did she find it strange. The neighboring room had no numbers on its door at all, and the one across the hall was missing the zero, so it looked like Room 36 with a gap between the digits.

So what?

Big deal.

Go on, Abby, quit being such a wimp! What do you expect to find in there anyway?

Mentally pumping herself up, she reached for the handle and tried to turn the knob.

It didn't move.

She tried again. The door was probably just stuck, swollen against its frame from years of neglect. She tried again. The knob didn't turn. It wasn't the door that wasn't moving; the lock had been turned.

"Great."

She rationalized that there must be some valuables left on this floor, so the rooms had been locked. The stained-glass window was proof enough of that. Obviously whoever was cleaning out this old place had . . .

Again she heard a noise, a shuffling, and her heart lurched painfully. Was someone walking downstairs? Slipping through a door? Shutting it behind him? *Oh, God.*

She melted against the neighboring door.

It gave way.

Opened under her weight.

She fell, stumbling loudly into the empty room. A gasp flew from her lungs as she caught herself. Over the knocking of her heart, she strained to hear any noises in this huge, nearly empty building.

She heard nothing.

Or did she?

She licked her lips. Was there the slightest click of a door latch? Her hair nearly stood on end.

It's your damned nerves, Abby. Nothing more. You're paranoid. Just like she was!

A tiny sound of protest formed in her mouth, but she didn't let it out. She wasn't paranoid; wasn't falling to pieces . . . no way! She was mentally strong. Had to be. *When the going gets tough . . .*

Click.

Abby's heart thumped hard and fast. Was that another muffled noise? The nearly indecipherable sound of a lock turning?

She wanted to call out, but didn't. Instead she shriveled into the shadows, fear pumping in her eardrums.

This is stupid, Abby! Pull yourself together. Do not let the settling and creaking of a condemned building scare you out of your wits!

She forced her heart rate to slow and sagged against the wall, closing her eyes. She heard nothing. Her imagination had gotten the better of her. Again. Letting out a long breath, she fought the fear spreading through her, convinced herself that she was alone.

Do this now and get it over with! Do it now!

Stiffening her back, she moved to the door of her mother's room again. She rattled the damned knob and pushed her body against the panels.

It didn't budge an inch.

She walked to another room in the hallway and turned the handle. The door swung open as easily as if it had been freshly oiled to another empty, dirty, forgotten room. She tried another one, on the opposite side of the hallway. It, too, opened without any effort on her part. So did the next.

But 307 was locked tight. The only room on the floor. Her mother's bedroom. The supposedly safe haven from which Faith had flung herself to her death . . .

Or had it really happened as she'd believed all these years?

In her mind's eye Abby observed her mother at the window . . . Had Faith been looking outside, making the sign of the cross over her thin chest, mentally preparing to leap through the glass?

That's what she'd always thought, but in her dreams Faith, frightened and shivering, was always staring away from the window and toward the open door . . .

Thump, thump, thump!

Footsteps!

This time Abby heard the tread clearly. Someone was mounting the steps. Her lungs constricted and she gazed around in panic. Quickly, she shrank into the shadows, slowly sliding back into the room across the hall from 307.

Who would be here now?

Had someone seen her?

Or did they have their own reasons for entering this decaying asylum? For climbing to the third floor?

But why?

The entire building looked as if it hadn't been entered in years.

She was drawing in shallow breaths, trying to make no noise whatsoever, hoping desperately that whoever was coming hadn't heard her, didn't know she was hiding.

Still the footsteps echoed through the stairwell.

Closer.

Almost to the landing.

Oh, God. She swallowed hard and prayed.

Steadily the tread neared, the floorboards of the upper hallway groaning in protest.

She closed her eyes. Hardly dared to breathe.

Nearer.

Oh, sweet Jesus!

The footsteps stopped.

She opened her eyes and nearly screamed.

Looming in the shadows was a dark, bulky figure.

CHAPTER 12

Abby gasped and stepped backward.

"You're the girl, aren't you?" a soft voice demanded. "Faith's daughter." The figure moved closer, out of the shadows and Abby nearly collapsed as she saw the old nun's face, a countenance she thought she recognized.

"Yes . . ."

"What are you doing here?"

I wish I knew! "I was told, by my shrink, that I should come back here. You know, to resolve some issues I have."

"Did he also tell you to trespass and break in?"

Heat climbed up her neck. "That was my idea."

"You could have asked."

"Would anyone have let me in?"

The nun smiled and shook her head sharply. "Probably not. I'm Sister Maria, by the way."

Sister Maria. Of course. Abby stared at the old nun in the dark shadows and imagined how she would have appeared twenty years earlier with smoother skin, a healthy glow, more robust . . .

"I thought I saw someone heading over here, so I followed," Sister Maria went on. "I'm just not as quick as I used to be, so it took me a while to catch up to you." She cocked her head to one side. "So, then, Faith, I assume you found what you needed?"

"I'm Abby. Faith was my mother."

"Oh...yes, of course. That's what I meant." She blinked as if to clear her mind.

Abby asked, "Why is the door to my mother's room locked?"

"Locked?" the older woman repeated. "I don't think so. None of these doors have been locked since we closed the hospital. What's it been, nearly fifteen years? The main doors, yes, of course they're secured, but nothing inside."

"I couldn't open it."

"Swollen shut, I imagine..."

"Don't think so." They walked across the hall to 307. "And all the doors on this floor were closed, every last one of them, though, as you said, unlocked."

"Really?"

"But the doors to the room on the floor below were open."

"Isn't that odd," Sister Maria said distractedly, seemingly unconcerned as she tested the door. It didn't open. "Oh, come on." She tried again. The door held fast. "Well, I'll be." She gave it one more shot before giving up. "You're absolutely right," she finally admitted. "It's definitely locked. How strange."

She sighed and looked to the side.

In Sister Maria's profile Abby witnessed a younger woman, hurrying past, skirts billowing as twilight descended and Abby passed her on the stairs... "You were there," she said, realizing for the first time that this was the nun who had rushed to her mother's side, felt for a nonexistent pulse in Faith's throat. "The day my mother died. I saw you."

"I worked here at the hospital, then. Yes."

"I was visiting...it was her birthday," Abby said. "I—I was bringing a gift to her."

The old nun frowned. "You?" She focused on Abby's hair, then her eyes. Confusion drew Sister Maria's eyebrows into one. "That was you with the gold box and pink ribbon?"

"Yes. It was my birthday, too," Abby said, feeling the old sadness running through her. "I'd found this afghan in a little shop on Toulouse Street. It was white with a silver thread running through it and I knew my mother would love it..." Fragmented images of that long-ago night cut through her mind. The package. The gauzy ribbon. The blood-freezing scream. Her mother's body lying broken by the fountain as she stared down at her...

"I'm sorry I didn't recognize you. I thought it was your sister, the girl with the black hair, who was carrying the box that day." The nun was clearly puzzled. "Hadn't you run by me on the stairs, near the landing? You were racing up as I was hurrying down, on my way to the convent. I'm sure of it."

"No." Abby shook her head, but felt something dark and insidious run through her mind. "That's impossible." Or was it? And yet she repeated her story, the one she'd been so certain was true. "I'd just gotten out of the car when it happened." Goose bumps crawled across her skin.

As if she'd had a premonition.

But of what?

Why was the old nun staring at her so hard? What was with the unspoken accusations Abby suddenly felt simmering between them? As if she were lying. About what? The gift box? But that was silly. Abby remembered holding the bulky thing and fighting with Zoey in the car about who would actually get to carry it inside. As if it mattered. Abby had been impatient, her mind running forward to the upcoming dance and Trey Hilliard and...that was right, wasn't it?

The nun was confused, that was all. Sister Maria had made a mistake.

And yet there was a sharpness to the woman's dark eyes, as if she understood Abby more than she did herself. Abby cleared her throat. Forced a smile. "So you knew her, my mother?"

"I didn't know her well," Sister Maria answered cautiously, "I'm not certain anyone really did." She paused and looked at the door to Room 307. "If it's answers you're seeking, I'm afraid you're not going to find them in here. At least not today." Sighing, she touched Abby on the arm. "Your mother had a strong faith, child. Perhaps instead of searching through old hallways and dark rooms, you should look to God." She motioned to the murky hallway. "This isn't where you'll find what you seek. You need to look inside yourself, into your heart. The Father will help you."

Abby thought about all the hours of prayer, the sleepless nights when she'd cried and reached out to God, especially right after her mother's accident. Where had He been then? She'd searched her heart, her mind, her soul, and all she had come up with was an overwhelming sense of despair laced with more than a tinge of guilt.

"Come now, there's nothing more for you here. And besides, this building has been condemned."

By whom?

The State of Louisiana?

Or the tormented souls who had resided here?

Abby hadn't come this far to be thwarted. "I know, Sister, but I really need to visit my mother's room before the wrecking ball destroys it forever. It's part of my personal quest, my attempt at moving on with my life, of getting some closure about my mother's death." The nun hesitated. "I've prayed, Sister Maria, believe me. And I think God has led me here." That was a bit of a lie, really, but Abby wasn't beyond stretching the truth a bit, even to a nun, to get this behind her.

Maria stared at her, sizing her up. "All right, then," she said slowly as if she wasn't quite sure what to believe. "I'll see what I can do."

With this assurance, Abby allowed the older woman to shepherd her toward the stairs.

"We have a caretaker for the grounds," Sister Maria said. "I'll ask him to come and check the door, see if he can find a way to open it." She offered Abby a kind, understanding smile that Abby thought was odd. How could this woman know anything about her? Or was it just her communion with the Lord that made her seem so calm, serene, and understanding? "It may take some time, Mr. DuLoc has a lot of work taking care of the convent, but he's a very resourceful man. I'm sure he'll be able to help." They had descended to the second floor and the old woman stopped to squint down the darkened hallway. "I thought you said all these doors were open."

Abby couldn't move a muscle. She looked down the corridor and her heartbeat deafened her ears.

Every door was closed.

Shut tight.

"Isn't that curious," Sister Maria thought aloud and walked to the first door. "Hello? Is anyone here?" she called out, obviously irritated.

"Who would be here?"

"I don't know, but let's find out."

"No, wait!" Abby stepped forward, not certain who or what she thought would be behind the door, but she couldn't stop the nun from yanking on the handle of 206. The door opened easily, allowing some light from a single cracked window to spill through the room and into the hallway.

Abby let out her breath. Next, Sister Maria reached for the handle of 205 and pulled it open.

No bogeyman jumped out. No one screamed, "Gotcha!" No ghost or monster or wraith appeared in a greenish cloud only to disappear.

"You're certain these doors were open?" Sister Maria asked.

"Absolutely."

The old nun raised an eyebrow, obviously disbelieving.

"Did you notice when you came up the stairs?" Abby asked and tried one of the doors herself. It swung open without catching. Room 204 was empty.

"I really didn't pay attention."

"What? But you were following me."

Sister Maria nodded. "And I knew where you'd go, didn't I? My eyesight isn't as good as it once was, the hallway was dark...darker than this. I think the doors were as they are now, Abby."

But that couldn't be. Abby's fear dissolved and she marched down the hallway opening doors and peering inside, leaving the one directly under her mother's room for last. She walked to that final door, set her jaw, and yanked hard.

The door stuck.

"Come on!" Angry, she threw all her weight against the old panels. The door suddenly flew inward to reveal a room that was nearly identical to her mother's. There was nothing in it, of course, the furnishings missing, the walls drab where the wallpaper had long ago been stripped away. A closet was cut into the wall in the same position as the room above, and a similar fireplace, some of the decorative tiles around the grate having fallen to the floor, dominated the same wall as the room above. The only significant difference was the window. This one was tall and narrow, but it was different in that there was no circular, stained-glass window mounted over the tall panes. That decorative panel, sometimes called a rose window or compass window, was only on the top floor, set into a dormer that broke up the roof line directly over the front door.

As a child in the backseat of her father's Ford, Abby had easily picked out her mother's room as Jacques had driven through the main gates of the hospital. That special arch in the roof and circle of colored glass below had been her beacon.

"You're certain you didn't close these doors yourself," Abby said as she reentered the hallway.

Sister Maria appeared wounded. "Of course not. Listen, my memory might fail me at times, but not to that point, and I wouldn't have lied about it or pulled some kind of prank on you. What is in question is your own perception! Come on. It's time to go."

Abby followed the nun to the stairs, but as she glanced over her shoulder and looked down the corridor one last time, she experienced a cold feeling against her spine, like the sharpened talon of a demon scraping down her backbone.

On the first floor, some of Sister Maria's anger dissipated. She grabbed Abby's hand and looked into her eyes. "You look tired."

And she was. After waking up refreshed from the dreamless sleep, she'd thought she would be able to set the world on fire today, but this place, this dreary, old asylum with its dingy walls and dark memories, had drained the energy from her, zapped her of her strength.

Sister Maria walked her through the main door and locked it behind her. Together, hunched against the wind and rain, they started around the building, but as they reached the corner, Abby looked over her shoulder, for one last glimpse of her mother's room.

There, standing on the other side of the glass, was a man. A big man, his features hidden in shadow. Her heart almost stopped. She spun, squinting through the sheeting rain.

"What?"

"In the window," she whispered, pointing.

But the image was gone as suddenly as it had appeared.

Sister Maria scowled upward. "I don't see anything. Now, come along," she insisted in exasperation. "We're both getting soaked."

Abby wanted to tell the nun what she'd seen, but it seemed impossible. Rain was plastering her hair to her head and it was so dark . . .

"Is something wrong?" the older woman asked. "Come on!"

Abby felt as if the devil himself had grabbed hold of her heart and squeezed. Her chin chattered though she wasn't cold. Who was the man in the window? An apparition? Just a shifting shadow that her fertile mind had conjured up as an evil being?

"Abby?"

Sister Maria was several steps ahead of her.

Turning quickly, Abby caught up with the nun.

"What is it?" the nun asked, sliding her a glance. "You look like you've seen a ghost."

"It . . . it's nothing," Abby replied. "I just had to take another look." Quickly, her Nikes splashing through puddles, she hurried along the overgrown path, through the trees, startling a squirrel that dashed into the underbrush.

Once they were through the forest, Sister Maria held open the unlocked gate, then the two moved rapidly along the fence line to the parking lot. "We don't use that gate very often," Maria explained. "Except when the gardener has work to do, or one of the people who are planning to tear the hospital down wants access, or when we need to chase down trespassers."

Abby flushed. "I'm sorry. Next time I'll ask."

"Will there be a next time?"

She thought about the figure she'd seen lurking in the window of her mother's room. Her imagination? A trick in the play of light? Then what about all those suddenly closed doors on the second floor? "I hope so. As I said, I think I need to see Mom's room one more time," Abby said, pushing aside her fears. There was no one in the old hospital. No one.

But the doors were shut!

And you saw someone staring at you! You did, Abby! You're not imagining things. You are not cracking up!

"Who knows about this gate?" she asked.

Maria shrugged. "Except for the Sisters, not too many. As I said, there are a few who have access to the hospital now, but that's about it. When the hospital was open, some of the staff used it, of course, but only a few of those people are still around." She chuckled, swiping a drop of rain from her nose with the back of her hand. "You know, there was a time when we had trouble keeping people locked inside the gates, not the other way around."

"Why don't the people who are buying the hospital just go through the main gate?"

"Oh. That." Sister Maria stopped as they reached the parking lot, seeking protection from the rain beneath the overhang from the garage. "They will. But the sale isn't exactly a 'done deal' yet. Until all the snags are worked out through the parish and the archdiocese and the engineers and architects and the Mother Superior here, nothing will happen."

"The hospital's not sold?" Abby asked.

"Let's just say 'we're in negotiations' and leave it at that because I've probably said more than I should." She looked at Abby again. "Are you certain you're all right?"

I'll never be all right, Abby thought. *My mother was a paranoid schizophrenic who committed suicide by throwing herself through a window, my father is slowly dying from disease, my sister slept with my fiancé who cheated on me with several women after we were married. Once Luke became my ex, he publicly humiliated me and now he and some coed are dead in a macabre, staged death scene. Oh, no, I will never be all right.*

"I'm fine."

Concern drew lines across Sister Maria's forehead. "Maybe you should come inside." She glanced up at the heavy clouds. "I think I could scare up a cup of tea."

"Not necessary. Really." Now that she was out of the creepy old hospital, she was ready to make tracks, and fast.

Sister Maria's gaze was skeptical.

"Would you call me when the lock's been fixed and I can get into my mother's room again?"

"You're certain that's what you want to do?"

"Yes!" Abby said with renewed conviction, gazing over her shoulder to the fence and woods beyond. From here she couldn't see the red bricks of the hospital, cosseted as it was by acres of forest, where, the idea had been, the gentle sounds, smells, and sights of nature would help soothe the tortured minds of the patients within.

"Then of course I'll call." The rain began to pour even more heavily, slanting with the wind.

"I'll phone the convent later with my number."

At the nun's nod, Abby waved a good-bye and dashed to her car, sliding behind the wheel. Through the foggy windshield she watched an amazingly spry Sister Maria sprint toward a doorway cut into the wall surrounding the convent.

Abby twisted on the ignition of her little Honda and pulled a quick one-eighty, then nosed the car toward the main road.

She didn't bother taking the fork that jogged to the old hospital. She'd seen more than enough for one day.

He waited as she drove away.

From the third-floor window he could see over the gates, and at one point, where the trees parted, there was an eagle's eye view of the road. Just a short glimpse, maybe two seconds, when her car would pass, turning the corner to the main road. But it was enough. For now. Taking up his vigil, he lifted his powerful binoculars so that he was ready, would be able to catch her expression as she drove by.

It took a little longer than he'd figured, probably because of that prattling nun, the one who had a few dark secrets of her own, secrets that were so close to his own. His lips twitched at that thought. The meek woman, draped in her black habit, might seem holy to some, but he knew better.

Soon, her secret would be exposed.

As would those of the others.

He had to work fast and so he intended to step up his time schedule. Through the field glasses, he saw a flash of silver in the rain. His heart pounded and anticipation thrummed through his body. A hot rush slid through his veins as he caught a glimpse of her taking the corner too fast. In the driving rain, the Honda's tires slid, the back of the hatchback fishtailing.

He imagined her fear as she struggled with the steering wheel.

He licked his lips as she managed to right the Honda and drive out of sight.

His heart pumped wildly and he felt a bit of sweat upon his upper lip. She looked so much like Faith...his throat went dry and lust slid like a hot, determined snake through his veins.

Faith...oh, beautiful...

His head pounded and he remembered the sweet, welcoming warmth of her, the way she gasped as he entered her, the glimmer of fear beneath the hot, anxious look in her eyes. His body thrummed as he thought of her seduction, her ultimate surrender, the need that had caused her to pant beneath him and press her teeth into his shoulder.

His lips curled back as he sucked in his breath. God, how he wanted her now, ached to feel the hot, urgent suppleness of her body clinging to his.

All in good time, he reminded himself as he squeezed his eyes closed. Faith's face came to him...her hot eyes, her throaty laugh, the naughty invitation of her slick lips. And as he imagined her, almost smelled her, her features altered slightly and the memory of the mother became a vision of the daughter.

CHAPTER 13

"Look, I'm telling ya, it was the last time I saw him," Maury Taylor insisted as they stood in the reception area of the radio station. Bentz, having called in advance, had shown up about the time that Maury, spending extra hours in Luke Gierman's chair, was free. The Gierman show was being played at various times in the afternoon and evening and apparently, from the latest poll, skyrocketing in the ratings.

That's what being killed did for a person. Instant fame. Or infamy. In Gierman's case, it was probably the latter.

"I explained this all to that other detective. What was his name?" Maury asked, then snapped his fingers. "Brinkman, the big guy with the gut."

Bentz nodded. "I know, but I was out of town and I'm just double-checking a few details," he said, which was pure garbage. Brinkman had done a decent enough job talking to everyone at the station, but Bentz just wanted his own "hit" about how things were going down here.

Besides, this was familiar territory. He'd been here often enough a few years back when Father John, a psycho of the worst order, was haunting the streets of the city. The killer's fascination with Dr. Sam, a late-night radio psychologist, had been a grisly nightmare.

The radio station, a block off Decatur Street and close to Jackson Square, looked pretty much the same as it had then, the reception area with its padded benches, one wall covered by a glass case filled with awards and news items, pictures of celebrities, and even an authentic voodoo doll. Melba, the receptionist, seemed forever on the phone.

"I don't know anything else except Luke was really pissed, and I mean *really* pissed at his ex-wife," Maury explained. "She'd thrown away some of his stuff and he let her have it on the show that day." He pulled a face. "I know we do some pretty off-the-wall things here, but usually Luke didn't overdo the personal shit, you know, he wasn't into bringing up his own personal dirty laundry. He had kind of an...unwritten rule or code of ethics about that."

"Code of ethics?" Bentz didn't buy it. He figured Gierman would have done anything including moon his own grandmother if he thought it would boost the ratings for his show as well as his own inflated ego.

"It was, I don't know, and he'd deny it to the death but...oh, hell," Maury said when he heard himself.

"But what?"

Taylor glanced away, toward a colorful neon display that reflected pink and blue on his face, then returned his gaze to the policeman's. "But I think he was still in love with her." At the quirk of Bentz's eyebrow, he quickly added. "Oh, yeah, yeah, I know. He liked the young ones. Hell, don't we all? The way he told it, he couldn't get enough...was a regular man-slut. I don't know all the women he banged, but he told me about a few and I gave that information to the other cop. The only one I remember, and Luke only mentioned it once, when he'd had a few too many, was his wife's sister."

"What?"

"Yeah...it didn't sit too well with the wife, if ya know what I mean. The minute Luke confided in me, even though he was drunk, he clammed up about it, laughed it off, like he was joking, but I don't think so."

Bentz made a mental note and felt an old pang of anger. He'd been there. Man, oh, man had he been there. He didn't know what it meant to Abby Chastain to know that her husband had cheated with her sister, but it couldn't be good.

"It really didn't matter if the fling with his sister-in-law was true or not."

Like hell. It mattered a lot.

"I just always had this feeling that he really never got over his ex-wife."

"Did he say so?"

"Luke? Admit to being hung up on a woman who would have nothing to do with him? Nah. Not his style." Maury raised his slim shoulders and shook his head. "But then who knows, maybe I got it all wrong."

"The ex-wife couldn't have liked the attraction to her sister."

"Ooh, no. Ouch! You know what they say about love and hate."

Bentz didn't disagree, but he knew from personal experience that the line between love and hate was so thin as to be invisible at times. Passion was a hair-trigger emotion.

"Anyone mind if I look through his desk and his closet?"

"Knock yourself out, but that other cop—"

"Brinkman?"

"Yeah! Geez, why can't I remember that guy's name?" Taylor snorted. "Not a good sign. I need my memory, man, need to think fast on my feet or in my seat." He offered up a proud, toothy smile. The high school geek who'd just made a touchdown. "The station manager's talking about making me the next Gierman. How 'bout that?"

Bentz figured the station manager wasn't doing the listening public of New Orleans any great favors. "What about Brinkman?"

"Oh. Right. He already looked through Luke's stuff. Took what he wanted. Luke's desk is this way." Maury guided Bentz down the main hallway, known as "the aorta," through the labyrinthine corridors of the old building. They passed other employees as well as glassed-in sound booths and editing rooms. "What about Gierman's girlfriend?"

"Nia?" Taylor snorted. "Nice ass. But not much upstairs, if ya get my drift." He tapped his temple with two fingers. "Not exactly a brainiac, and Luke, he'd get bored quickly if the woman couldn't keep up with him. The physical chemistry was nice, always got him goin', but that only lasts awhile, y'know."

As if this guy were Casanova or Dr. Phil. The trouble was, in

Bentz's opinion, this time Maury Taylor was right. Wasn't Bentz, himself, a prime example? He'd never planned to remarry after his first wife, but in Olivia Benchet he'd found a woman who was, he'd discovered, his mental match as well as drop-dead gorgeous. What combination was sexier than that?

Taylor, passing by a showcase of vintage LPs, was still rambling on, "Nia and Luke broke up—I guess you know that. From what I heard, she'd already found some new guy, a jock...even more of a workout nut than Luke, if ya can believe that. 'Tall, dark, and handsome,' she told Luke, then really stuck it to him. Claimed this guy was the best lover she'd ever had. Can you beat that? Ouch!" He looked over his shoulder at Bentz and gave him the we've-all-been-*there* look. "Turns out, little Nia had been seein' this guy on the sly for weeks. How's that for a turn of events? The cheater got cheated on. Some kind of cosmic justice."

"Except that the cheater ended up dead."

"Yeah," Maury said, grimacing. "Except for that. Double ouch! Sucks, ya know?"

"Big time." They reached the back of the building, where a rack of built-in desks vied for wall space with lockers. "What about Gierman? Did he have any other girlfriends, or exes that he might have teed off?"

"Don't think so. On the air he always acted like he had a girl-friend whether he did or not. That was part of the routine," Maury said as he pointed out Gierman's desk, where Sharpie pens were kept in one of those personalized cups with a picture of a chocolate Lab on it. On the bulletin board over the desk were snapshots of Gierman sailing, skiing, playing tennis, leaning against the fender of a sporty BMW, or romping with the same brown dog that was on the coffee mug—a virtual shrine to himself and his hobbies. An egomaniac if Bentz had ever seen one. The only other photo was a small one of a woman Bentz recognized as Abby Chastain. In the picture she was staring out to sea, her curly red-gold hair was tangled in the wind, her lips parted into a sexy smile that showed a hint of dimple. She had the kind of eyes that seemed to delve straight into a man's soul.

Yep, he figured, Maury Taylor was right. No one would keep a picture like this unless he was seriously hung up on the woman.

Bentz glanced back at Taylor. The smaller man, too, was staring at the snapshot.

"What did I tell you?" Taylor said, his jaw sliding to one side. "The only woman Luke Gierman ever really gave a damn about was his ex-wife."

Montoya eyed the crowd, mentally checking off each of the mourners who had come to stand around the chapel door at All Saints College. A young priest, Father Anthony, stood straight-backed on the steps in front of the lancet-arched doorway. Flanking the fresh-faced priest was the old relic, Father Stephen, his bare head bent in prayer. Beside him was Dean Usher, the brim of her hat dripping in the rain.

Hundreds of students surrounded the chapel steps, each holding a candle, each listening raptly to the priest's smooth, calm voice at this, the vigil for Courtney Mary LaBelle.

Chapel bells tolled softly as Father Anthony, a rapt, fervent individual, recounted the joy of knowing "Mary" and the tragedy that she, who had pledged herself to the service of God, was struck down, so young. So innocent. So trusting in God. Father Anthony's white collar, a stark beacon in the night, stood in deep contrast to his black shirt and suit. The priest lifted his hands in supplication.

But he wore no vestments, Montoya noted, assuming the formal robes would be saved for the real funeral mass.

Wind rushed through the campus, causing the Spanish moss to dance from the branches of trees overhead, as Father Anthony warned that no one should be "heavy of heart" as Mary was with the Father now, she was safe and cared for, in a place far better than the rest of the crowd was.

Montoya listened with only half an ear.

The group of mourners prayed and cried, holding their candles in the darkness, and as they did, Montoya photographed them with a small, hidden camera. The pictures would be blurry at best, but they were at least something; he was certain Father Anthony would not approve a video camera with lights filming the students, faculty, and whoever else happened to stop by in his or her hour of grief.

Montoya only hoped that the killer would be hyped up enough to attend. Often times the murderer wanted to be a part of the investigation, to be close to the action, to revel in what he considered his superior intellect while the lowly police attempted to track him down. The killer would show up at the crime scene or the wake, or a vigil, joining with the others or hiding in the shadows, eager to be connected to the investigation and grief. It fed his ego to know that he was the mastermind behind the tragedy. It was usually only a matter of time before he showed his hand.

So, Montoya pretended to pray, to listen heedfully to the priest's words of wisdom, but all the while he was checking out the faces in the crowd, noting which seemed out of place... not that appearances would matter. Some killers had the innate ability to blend in, to look more than normal, to appear so boring and bland that no one would suspect them of being able to slice their wife's throat, or shoot the neighbor for scratching a borrowed lawn mower, or plan with meticulous detail the deaths of a string of victims.

At first no one had suspected serial killer Ted Bundy, a good-looking guy with a degree in psychology and a bright political future. Bundy had actually worked at a rape crisis center in Seattle. Then the BTK killer in Wichita was a compliance officer, a religious man who looked like an Average Joe. Closer to home there had been Father John and The Chosen One, neither of whom had raised anyone's suspicions as they'd gone on their gruesome killing sprees. Dr. John McDonald, a brilliant young surgeon, was serving time for butchering his family, though he still vehemently protested his innocence.

No one, by looks alone, could identify a killer.

Meticulously Montoya photographed each and every individual who either genuinely or fraudulently expressed grief for Courtney Mary LaBelle. Someone who felt so fervently about the killings that they'd ventured out on this miserable, wet, blustery night.

As if to reinforce his thoughts, the wind gusted, causing candles to flicker and die, umbrellas to be whipped out of clenched hands, and in one case turned completely inside out.

"Let us pray to the Father," the priest said, lifting his hands toward the heavens again, "and then come into the chapel for the rest of the service." He folded his hands and bowed his head.

Everyone standing near the chapel did the same.

Except for Montoya.

* * *

"You said you'd call back," Zoey accused as Abby answered the phone in the kitchen.

Abby's gaze darted around the room. She was still creeped out by her experience at Our Lady of Virtues and couldn't shake the feeling that she was being watched.

Which was just plain paranoid.

No, not paranoid, just overly cautious.

The refrigerator door was hanging open, Hershey standing expectantly beneath it, while Abby, with her free hand, searched through the bottles of half-used salad dressing and sauces to find a container of yogurt.

"I waited for hours," Zoey pouted.

Oh, get over yourself, Abby thought. "I know, I know, Zoe. I'm sorry...time got away from me." She was irritated that she felt the need to explain herself and apologize to her older sister. She was thirty-five, for crying out loud, not a baby, not a recalcitrant kid, not *Zoey's* child. "I was busy. And no, I haven't heard a word about Luke's funeral."

"It has to be soon, doesn't it?"

"I don't know when it 'has' to be. If his family decides to cremate him, they might hold a service later. Look, Zoey, I'm not sure what my role in this is. Or even if I have a role. Ex-wife isn't particularly high on the food chain, y'know. It doesn't exactly mean I have royal status or even real ties to the family. But that said, I'll pay my respects. It's just that I'm not sure I had any. Not in the end."

Zoey sucked air in through her teeth. "That bites, Abby."

"You didn't hear his last radio program." She opened the cap, then tugged off the plastic seal of her yogurt container. Her conscience twinging a bit, she decided there was no time like the present to fess up. "I went out there yesterday."

"Out where?"

"To the hospital."

There was a pause and the silence stretched thin. "Why?" Zoey finally asked.

"They're going to tear it down and—"

"Good!"

"—and I thought I should visit the place."

"Because some know-nothing shrink told you to?"

Abby felt her back bristle. She'd been to several psychiatrists since her mother's accident, some better than others, but all, she assumed, knew what they were talking about. "Because it felt like the thing to do."

Her sister mumbled something under her breath she didn't catch, then louder, asked, "So? How was it, Abby? A grand old time?"

"Not funny, Zoe," Abby said through her teeth. Why had she even brought it up? "To tell you the truth, it was weird as hell, okay? And spooky. Really spooky. The place is crumbling into total decay. I met a nun who used to work there. She saw me going over there because I had to park at the convent. Maybe you remember Sister Maria. She's tall. Pretty. Latina, I think."

"Yes, I remember her," Zoey said a trifle tersely.

"She was there the day that Mom died."

Zoey didn't respond.

"It was weird. She got me confused with you, I think. She seemed to think that I'd run into the hospital ahead of you and Dad, at least I think that's what she meant." Abby pulled open a drawer and found a spoon. "That I was running upstairs while she was coming down and that she met you with Mom's present...or something like that." Abby felt her eyebrows pulling into a knot. "At least I think that's what she was getting at. As I said, it was all weird." She dipped her spoon into the yogurt and took a small bite. Zoey still hadn't responded. "Zoe?"

"Yeah."

"What do you think of that?" The cool yogurt slid down her throat but she barely tasted it.

"I—I don't know why she would say anything of the sort. She must be pretty old. Probably confused."

"Most of the time she seemed pretty clear."

"Most of the time," Zoey repeated, seizing on her words. "It's been twenty years, Abby."

"Hey." She held up her spoon and wagged it at the window, as if she were pointing at her sister. "Why do I get the feeling that you're lying to me?"

"Because I'm uncomfortable discussing the hospital and Mom's death, that's why. I know you don't have closure on it, Abby, but I do and I *don't* need to revisit it every time you have a birthday on the anniversary of her death."

"And her birth," Abby reminded her sister.

"Yeah, yeah, I know. You had this special bond with her, this unique, God-granted karma or whatever you want to call it that no one but you understands. I get it. But I don't *get* it, and as far as I'm concerned, we should move on."

"To Luke's funeral?" Abby's voice was dry.

"Yes! Let's get some closure there, too. And once he's in the ground or cremated or whatever, then I say you and I, we have ourselves a couple of cosmopolitans, toast him—then bury him, the past, and the damned hatchet, okay?" She was talking faster and faster, her voice rising nearly an octave. When she'd finished, she was breathless.

"Okay. Fine."

"So I'm coming to New Orleans."

"Perfect," Abby said with a false smile, "then Zoey, we can talk about a lot of things before we have that drink, okay? Including Mom and the day she died. I think you know more about it than you've ever said. If you won't go back there with me, fine, but we're going to discuss it."

"Oh, Abby..."

"I need this, Zoe," she said, then hung up, hard. She tossed her uneaten yogurt into the sink. Where had *that* come from? She'd always had a feeling that her sister and father hadn't been completely honest with her about that day, but she'd never baldly questioned them. She'd been content to be wrapped in her little cocoon of innocence, afraid of what she might find if she ever emerged.

Sister Maria's insistence that Abby had been *inside* the hospital when her mother had plummeted to her death had brought back pieces of her memory, a memory she hadn't known had been shattered. Something about the way she'd recalled the accident was wrong—and had been for the last twenty years.

She *had* been inside the hospital. She remembered hurrying up the stairs, nearly running head-on into the tall nun who had warned her to slow down at the landing. But Abby hadn't paid any attention to the woman in the black habit with her stern expression and rustling skirts. She'd raced past and up the final partial flight, focusing on the doorway to 307 . . .

After that, her memory failed her.

Now, closing her eyes, Abby tried to call up what had happened then and why, oh, why, did she see her mother's broken body on the cement? A headache started in the back of her skull, pounding, warning her she wouldn't like what she found. Still she fought to remember. Gripping the edge of the counter for support, she forced her thoughts backward. If she hadn't been outside the car, on the hospital steps, not only had her memory failed her, but so had her family. Her father. Her sister.

For twenty years she'd felt something wasn't right about that day, but she'd been afraid to ferret out the truth, unwilling to peel the blindfold from her eyes.

No more.

It was time to stop protecting herself, to unwrap the layers of lies, deceit, and guilt.

Zoey, whether she wanted to or not, was going to help.

The night had been a bust. Montoya had spent his time talking to the students attending the vigil, double-checking with Courtney LaBelle's friends. Then he caught up with Father Anthony for a few minutes before the priest had to rush off, hell-bent, or perhaps heaven-bent in his case, to comfort Mary LaBelle's family. But Montoya didn't like him. Father Anthony Mediera was too smooth, too outwardly calm, too damned not-a-hair-out-of-place perfect for Montoya's tastes. The priest's faith felt worn like a badge.

Later, Montoya had stopped by Nia Penne's apartment to find her with her new boyfriend. Petite, to the point of being elfin, with white-blond hair feathered around a face Montoya thought was reminiscent of Tinker Bell, she'd politely answered a few questions, but she hadn't changed her story. Montoya noticed that the new man in her life was indeed sculpted, appeared strong, and for the most part, silent.

The boyfriend had stood near the fake fire, arms crossed over his chest, biceps bulging beneath a too-tight black T-shirt that showed off a slim waist and what Montoya figured were "abs of steel." His name was Roy North, his feet were a size twelve, and

Montoya intended to check him out. There was just something about Roy that was very territorial and angry and all muscled up on his own testosterone that bugged Montoya. And he hadn't been in Toronto last week with Nia and her friends.

As for Nia, she wasn't exactly the grieving ex-girlfriend. In fact, when he'd noticed the boxes scattered around the living room floor, she'd grinned naughtily and admitted that she was giving up the apartment and moving in with Bigfoot.

Tinkerbell and Sasquatch. What a pair.

So much for love eternal, Montoya figured, as he strode to his cruiser parked on a side street near Nia's apartment. For a fleeting second, as he returned to his car, he thought of Marta...beautiful, vibrant, full of sass and charm. He'd thought she would be the one he'd settle down with and that chance had been ripped from him. And yet, the sadness he'd once felt, the blatant out-and-out anger that ate at him, had slowly faded, and now, not even nostalgia clung to him. It was hard to envision her face, her dark eyes and long, curly black hair. When he did, her features blurred, as if washed by the rain still falling from the sky.

Another woman's face appeared.

A beautiful woman with whiskey-colored eyes, untamed red-blond curls, and a full mouth. Abby Chastain. Luke Gierman's ex-wife, the woman right in the thick of this investigation. Hell. She was the last woman Reuben Montoya should be attracted to, the very last, and he knew it.

But wasn't that the way it always went down? The whole forbidden fruit thing? How many married women in the past had attracted him? Flirted with him? How many had been engaged to other men? He'd never crossed that line, but he'd be a liar if he said he hadn't been tempted. Sorely so.

But this, with Abby, was different. She didn't flirt with him. She didn't pretend to be innocent and flash him glimpses of her body, nor did she play the naughty vixen to intrigue him.

Hell, she hadn't had the chance! He barely knew her. Had met her a few times under tense circumstances. He was just stressed out, that was it, and it had been a long time since he'd been with a woman. Too long.

Now, in the pelting rain, he unlocked the cruiser, slid inside, and pulled the door closed. Swiping the raindrops from his face, he turned on the ignition and wondered why he was already fantasizing about her.

She was out of reach and that was the end of it. He checked his mirror, found the side street deserted, and cranking on the steering wheel, pulled a one-eighty and drove into the wet, dark Louisiana night.

The damned gate was stuck!

How the hell had that happened?

Asa Pomeroy leaned out the window of his Jaguar and punched in the electronic code to open the gates to his estate. Again. Nothing happened except that he got wet. Again. Rain was coming down in sheets, sliding down the sleek windshield and drumming the top of his balding head. "Son of a bitch! Come on, come on." He punched in the code a final time and swore loudly. Then he tried the remote again. Clicked it several times but the damned gate still didn't move.

He had his cell phone with him, of course, but whom would he call? Vanessa was off at her mother's for a blissful week, the maid was gone for the night, the gardener-handyman was twenty minutes away. And he'd been drinking too much to call a cop. Any of his friends would take a full forty minutes to get here and they, too, would be tanked up from a night of drinking at the club.

No, he was on his own.

Which was usually not a problem. He was nothing if not efficient and capable. Hell, he hadn't spent two tours in Vietnam only to come back to the good old US of A to build, market, and ship a better weapon. He sold rifles, grenades, bazookas, ammo, and every weapon imaginable all over the planet and because of it was rich beyond his wildest dreams. All because of Yankee ingenuity from his father's side of the family, Southern charm from his mother's, and red-blooded American know-how, cast in iron from generations of his WASP ancestors.

Tonight, by God, no cheap-ass piece of Japanese technology was going to thwart him. He grabbed his Stetson, rammed it onto his head, pulled a flashlight from the glove box and slipped his reading glasses onto his nose, then stepped outside his car. Rain was running in rivulets, soaking his goddamned Italian leather shoes, the ones Vanessa had insisted he buy on their last trip to Tuscany. Jesus, what a waste of time and money that had been.

He was leaning over, peering at the backlit keypad, when he realized the dog hadn't come out to greet him. Without fail, Geronimo, upon hearing the Jag's smooth engine, would run pell mell down the long driveway and be waiting, tongue hanging from his mouth, on the other side of the gate. Once Asa pulled through, the big dog always raced the car up the long drive. Asa, without fail, let him win.

So where the hell was he?

Water dripped from the brim of Asa's hat. His half-glasses fogged as he stared into the darkness, through the iron gates and trees where, though the house was hidden, lights should glow.

Now, save for the glow of the Jag's headlights, where mist rose and swirled in the twin beams, there was only darkness.

He whistled loudly.

Nothing.

Something was wrong, he thought, and was just starting to sense that he'd been set up when he felt something hard and cold against his back. He started to whirl, but it was too late.

Zap!

Three hundred thousand volts of electricity jolted through his body.

His hat flew off.

He dropped to his knees.

Gasping, he tried to reach into his pocket for the knife he kept hidden there.

But he was confused, his body and mind at odds, and he couldn't so much as raise a finger. His brain ordered his hands to stretch into his damned pocket, but he couldn't move a muscle.

Disoriented, he saw a big man step out of the shadows to loom over him in the rain.

Panic grabbed Asa by the throat.

Someone, this guy and probably his friends, had planned this attack. Meticulously.

Fear cut through him.

His assailant was dressed in black, in some kind of tight-fitting body suit, his face covered by a mask. Leaning over, he had the audacity to hold his weapon up so that it was visible in the light from the car's headlights.

Still unable to move, to barely focus, Asa caught a glimpse of the stun gun and recognized it was one he manufactured.

Jesus H. Christ, what was this?

Then he knew. The guy was going to abduct him. To demand ransom in the form of millions. And he was going to kidnap Asa by using the very "self-defense" weaponry Pomeroy Industries manufactured.

Terror struck deep in his heart. Again he went for his knife. Again his hands failed him.

His assailant calmly set the stun gun against his neck and gave him another shot.

Electricity rocketed through him.

Another three hundred thousand volts.

Asa screamed.

Pain sizzled and popped down throughout his body. Despite all the advertisement to the contrary, the jolt stung like a son of a bitch. He writhed, flopping in the mud while his attacker slowly and calmly pulled out a roll of duct tape from his utility belt. Then he came up with a circle of fishing wire as well as a knife. Asa recognized that weapon, too. His attacker clicked open what appeared to be a Pom 4SF—a folding knife with a quick release and four-inch serrated blade—a specialty knife advertised in Pomeroy Industries' latest catalog for gutting big game as it could easily slice through gristle and bone.

A knife strong enough to eviscerate a man.

Fear turned his blood to ice.

He got the message.

Don't do this! I'm rich. I'll pay. Anything! He was screaming but only a garbled mewl came from his throat. He couldn't form words.

He tried to struggle, but it was no use. Helpless and without control of his limbs, he was flailing in the mud like a warthog in quicksand.

He glanced up at his assailant and swore he saw satisfaction in the eyes looking down at him through the slits in his mask.

But that was impossible . . . right? It was dark.

Who was this guy? What did he want?

Jesus, help me, Asa silently pleaded. He watched helplessly as first a six-inch piece of duct tape was sliced from a roll and slapped over his mouth, then his hands were jerked roughly behind him bound first by the same tape, and fortified with a plastic-coated steel fishing wire he recognized as the same type he used when he was trying to land a marlin. The tape would have been enough: the wire was some kind of statement.

All hope failed as his ankles were taped together, but no fishing wire used. Then a hood was forced over his head and tied at the neck. There were air holes so that he could breathe, but he was surrounded by darkness.

Just like in 'Nam.

He'd been captured by the Gooks. Held in a cage for nearly two weeks before he managed to escape. Well, he'd do it again, goddamn it. He'd fight back the terror, the bone-numbing fear, and beat this son of a bitch at his own damned game.

He was hauled to his feet by the collar of his jacket. He tried to fight, to spin away, but it was useless. He heard a car door open and his assailant pushed him inside, banging his forehead as he fell into what smelled and felt like the backseat of his Jag. His legs were pushed up so that they bent at the knees, then the door was slammed shut.

A few seconds later he heard the attacker climb behind the steering wheel, the car sinking slightly with the added weight, and then that door, too, shut. With a deafening click, all the doors were locked, the gearshift rammed into reverse, and then the perfectly tuned engine revved as they backed down the quarter mile to the main highway.

Asa's only hope was that someone would recognize his car.

But it was late.

Few vehicles drove this stretch of isolated road.

For now, he had to do whatever this bastard had in mind. No doubt it was money. He'd be held for ransom. Well, that was fine; he had enough cash to pay whatever exorbitant figure the kidnappers came up with.

He might lose a finger in the process.

Or an ear.

He inwardly cringed, but reminded himself it was worth it, if he could just get out of this alive.

Vanessa would willingly pay the ransom, right?

The board of directors at Pomeroy Industries included his children. They would be eager to fork over the cash, wouldn't they?

Hadn't he helped his wives and children, even his grandkids, for Christ's sake? He'd paid for braces, college, vacations, any damned thing his progeny needed, even the ones who disdained his wealth, claimed they needed only a "little something" to "get started" or to "find themselves." He'd shelled out for face-lifts and boob jobs and trips to psychiatrists. Health spas, new cars, even a boat; he'd come up with it, so those who owed him not only their lives but their lifestyles had damned well better offer up the cash to bail him out of whatever the hell this was.

Don't count on them, Pomeroy.

You've been in tough spots before and who was the only person who came to your rescue?

No one but your own damned self.

And the truth of the matter was, if he examined his life closely, he had a lot of enemies, and some of the worst were his own kin. Backstabbers, money-grubbers, liars, and cheats . . . all either having been married to him or with his blood running through their veins.

And then there were his series of partners, most of which he'd screwed over.

Was this his punishment?

Don't think that way. This is just some greedy, sick opportunist. You've dealt with worse across a boardroom table.

As the car purred down the smooth, winding road, some of Asa's disorientation cleared. He thought of his wife who didn't love him. His kids who didn't respect him. His two sons, both of whom were missing a screw or two, and his daughter, a gold digger like her mother. His grandchildren were just as bad and thought of him as their own personal ATM. His business partners who only pretended to like him because of his net worth.

Had one of those sons of bitches set him up?

Hot anger replaced his cold fear. He might be hog-tied now, defenseless. But that was only temporary.

Whoever the hell the bastard driving his Jag was, he would damned well get his. The idiot hadn't even checked his pockets, didn't know that Asa's own knife was, even now, resting against his thigh, right next to his money clip. If he got half a chance, Asa planned to use the Pom 3.5F, a deadly folding knife that would slice right through muscle and hide. Asa hadn't spent some of his army hitch with the special forces and not learned how to slip a blade between a man's ribs and slice the heart. It was just a matter of getting the jump on his attacker.

It had been years since he'd practiced killing a man, of course, but he was certain he could take the guy out. This time, the kidnapper had picked the wrong goddamned mark.

CHAPTER 14

"Asa Pomeroy is missing," Lynn Zaroster said as Montoya walked into the small kitchen at the station the next afternoon. He'd spent the day catching up on paperwork, going over autopsy reports, and interviewing witnesses, all the while waiting for the pictures that he'd taken the night before to be blown up. The bodies of Luke Gierman and Courtney LaBelle were being released to their families, the DA wanted answers, and Montoya felt no closer to knowing who had committed the double homicide than the day he'd walked into that cabin by the river.

Zaroster was carefully dunking a tea bag into a steaming cup of water. Montoya headed straight for the coffeepot.

"The millionaire?"

"Multi-multimillionaire, if *Industrialist* magazine can be believed."

"You read that crap?" Montoya asked as he grabbed a paper cup and poured a thin stream of coffee into it.

"My boyfriend does," she admitted.

"Wait a minute. Doesn't Pomeroy live in Cambrai?"

"Outside of the little downtown area. Kind of out in the boonies, maybe even the swamp."

He felt a tightening in his gut. He remembered driving past the elaborate iron gates securing the Pomeroy estate. "He lives close to Abby Chastain."

"Really?" she asked, tossing the used, wet bag of English Breakfast tea into the garbage.

"Yep. They're neighbors."

"How weird is that?"

"Weird enough." Montoya didn't like the feeling that was creeping over him. Didn't like it one bit. "What happened to him?"

"Don't really know. I just ran into Vera from Missing Persons in the ladies' room and she told me that the wife was out of town, came back this morning and he wasn't there. The bed was still made and apparently he never even pulls the covers up. A real slob. Anyway, both the maid and the gardener hadn't been able to get into the house, the automatic lock was jammed or something. It looks like maybe someone changed the electronic code according to the security guy who came out and checked. So the Mrs. calls Asa on his cell phone but he's not answering. At this point she's starting to get worried and then Asa's secretary calls from his office: Asa's late for a big meeting. After phone calls all around, including the cell again, his cronies, family members, and no one has any idea where he is, the wife called the station and is coming in to file a report...it hasn't been twenty-four hours yet, but it's not looking good."

"Where was he last seen?"

Zaroster, testing her tea, held up her free hand and shook her head. "I said I don't know anything. It's just gossip at this point. It's not our case."

Yet, Montoya thought uneasily, remembering how close the Pomeroy estate was to Abby Chastain's house. What were the odds that her ex-husband would end up murdered the same week her next-door neighbor turned up missing?

"Oh," Zaroster said, sipping from her cup. "I called my uncle up at All Saints."

"Yeah? And what did you find out?" Brinkman asked as he, hitching up his pants, strode into the kitchen and grabbed the pot of coffee, pouring himself the last of the dregs. "Don't tell me, the coven meets at seven every Sunday night like my aunt's bingo group."

"Yeah, that's it."

"And so, instead of homemade cookies and punch, they all bring their vials of blood for a little drinkie-poo?"

"Was Courtney's roommate *that* bad, or is he just being a prick?" Zaroster asked Montoya.

"You tell me."

"All I know is that my uncle said there's this big Goth movement up at All Saints. Nothing scary, just some kids into black hair, boots, lipstick, and white face makeup. It's not that big of a deal."

Brinkman snorted.

"But there are a few who take it a little more seriously."

"Like little Miss O, I'm bettin'," Brinkman said.

"Maybe. There's always gossip, of course, and there is talk of some vampire worship and blood drinking, you know, the usual college stuff."

Montoya laughed.

"What'd I tell ya?" Brinkman took a sip of his coffee and scowled. "Next thing ya know they'll be sacrificing virgins, except now that Mary LaBelle is already dead, they won't be able to find any. She had to be the last virgin in college."

"You might be surprised," Zaroster said, irritation showing.

"Yeah, right." Brinkman took a swallow from his cup, and his face drew together as if he'd just sucked on a lemon. "This tastes like shit."

"Then make a new pot," Zaroster advised and, when he started to open his mouth, added, "And don't give me any garbage about you not knowing how or it's a job better suited for a woman, okay?"

"Well, it is."

"I'm not in the mood."

He lifted a shoulder.

"How much of a baby are you? Look, the packs are premeasured." She pulled a sealed foil package of coffee from a basket filled with packages of tea, coffee, and smaller packets of sweetener. Then she held the foil envelope in front of Brinkman's nose. "Pretty damned easy. You flip one of these into the basket of the coffeemaker, add water, and push a button." She dropped the unopened package back into the basket. "And presto, in a few minutes, you've got fresh brewed." She skewered him with a don't-mess-with-me-anymore look. "Any cretin can figure it out, so I'm assuming someone with a B.S. in Criminal Law should be able to whip up a pot without too many problems. Oh, don't forget to open the pack first. You know, take the foil off."

Her cell phone jangled and she picked it up, then, carrying her cup of tea in the other hand, stormed out of the room.

"Whew. She must've gotten up on the wrong side of the bed," Brinkman grumbled, watching her backside as she disappeared around a corner. "Now that's something I'd give a week's pay to see, her gettin' out of bed with her hair all mussed." He took another sip and squinted at the thought. "Imagine her in heels and her shoulder holster. Nothing else." He sucked his breath in through his teeth. "I bet she's hot."

"Tell her that and she'll have you up on harassment charges so fast your head will spin. That is, after she's busted your balls."

Brinkman chuckled and Montoya walked back to his desk. He thought about Asa Pomeroy. What were the chances that the millionaire's vanishing act was connected to the Gierman-LaBelle murders? That was a stretch really. Or was it? Just because some rich old coot didn't show up for work, or hadn't slept in his own bed, didn't mean someone had killed him. And so what if his estate was close to Abby Chastain's property; that was probably just circumstance. It was nothing. No link whatsoever.

Nonetheless, the uneasy feeling wouldn't leave him as he checked his e-mail and waded through phone messages that had come in over the night and early morning. He picked up the phone and called Missing Persons. No harm in finding out all he could about Pomeroy.

Just in case.

"...the funeral will be at eleven," Luke's brother Lex was saying, "and I thought you might want to know. The service will be at St. Michael's. No casket. He wanted to be cremated. Oh, God, I can't believe I'm talking about this. It just really hasn't sunk in yet, I guess."

"I know."

"So...maybe we'll see you there."

"Yes," Abby said, "thanks for calling." She hung up her cell phone and sighed. The thought of the funeral was depressing. Not only would it be surreal to meet all the people who had known Luke in life and witness their grief, but it was just so hard to believe that he was actually gone, that he would be eulogized, that she would have to smile while everyone told all their "good ol' Luke" stories. And then there was facing his mother and father. "Not fun," she said to Hershey as she slid the phone into her pocket.

She'd been working in her studio all afternoon. Her digital camera was connected to her computer, which was set up on the desk. After digitally cropping the pictures, she printed those she needed, checked them again in case she wanted to change the parameters, then once she was satisfied with what would become the prints, she burned them onto CDs for her clients as well as kept copies on her hard drive and a separate CD for herself. She always printed out the final shots as well, then sorted and filed them.

She'd been at it for hours, barely taking off any time, except to get a cup of coffee or tea. Breakfast had been toast and peanut butter, then she'd spent a couple of hours packing and taking down some pictures from the walls, then removing the nails, using a hammer on the most stubborn ones. Afterward, around ten, she'd gone to work in the studio and she'd been too absorbed to break for lunch. The hours had flown by, and now, it was after eight. Her stomach growled, her back ached; she rubbed her shoulders and neck where a headache was starting. She only hoped she had a microwave meal in the freezer. She was stretching her back when Hershey, lying in the corner on her blanket, shot to her feet. Growling low, head down, she stalked to the door.

"Now what?" Abby muttered as all afternoon the dog had been nervous, wanting in, wanting out, barking at squirrels who scolded from the magnolia tree on the back patio.

The hackles on the back of Hershey's neck rose and her head lowered. Unmoving, she stared at the studio door.

"Give it up, Hersh," Abby said as she stared at her computer monitor and pictures of the Shippman wedding. She discarded the ones where the bride's expression was dour or the groom's cowlick showed prominently.

Hershey growled again.

"Stop!"

She studied the monitor again.

Every hackle on the dog's neck was raised. This time the growl was almost inaudible, but it was enough to break Abby's concentration. She finally gave in. "Okay," she said, refusing to be infected by whatever it was that made the Lab nervous. "Show me." She decided to call it a night and shut off the computer, then switched off the lights and opened the studio door.

The dog shot out like a rocket, barking and running back and forth along the back edge of the verandah, glaring into the dark trees beyond.

Abby felt a frisson of fear slide down her spine. Hershey was making her edgy, that was it, but she didn't need any help in that department. Ever since finding out about Luke's murder, she'd been nervous. And if she'd thought visiting Our Lady of Virtues would help her deal with the past, she'd been dead wrong. She hadn't slept well since walking through those forgotten hallways. Three images had stayed with her from her visit—her mother's locked door, the shutting of all the doors on the second floor, and the shadowy image of a man behind the third-floor window's glass. Even now, just at the thought, her skin pimpled.

She dead-bolted the studio, followed the short walkway to the house, and unlocked the door. Hershey was still growling, hair ruffled, eyes trained on the woods, when Ansel suddenly streaked across the patio and shot straight into the house. The big Lab galloped after the tabby, tail wagging furiously.

"Great," Abby muttered. She didn't know which animal she should throttle first. "You scared me half to death, Hershey." Angrily she turned the dead bolt. "You're supposed to be a guard dog, but you do not, and I repeat, *not,* have to protect me from Ansel, okay? Sheesh!" She kicked off her shoes. "Ansel is not the enemy. Try and remember that!" The tabby had hopped onto the counter and was perched near the window, his tail flicking in agitation, his pupils still black and dilated. Bristled up to twice his size, he hissed at the dog. "You knock it off, too. Both of you . . . give me a break. I can scare myself. Got it? I don't need any help from either of you!"

Abby scooped the cat from the counter and set him onto the floor. She opened the freezer door and found only extra coffee and an ancient pizza.

"Bon appetit," she said as she pulled the pizza out and preheated the oven. The pepperoni looked as if it had been made in the sixth century, the cheese showing little crystals of ice, the crust possibly freezer burned. But it was all she had and she figured she could get creative, slice up a tomato and onions. When she rummaged in her pantry, she came up with a tiny can of black olives. "Gourmet," she told the animals, then, as the oven warmed, dug in the cupboard and found a bottle of red table wine with no other information on it and a curled gold ribbon with a tiny card that said, *Thanks for the hospitality! Love, Alicia.*

Abby smiled, remembering Alicia's last visit. They'd discovered a little wine shop on Decatur, where they'd found the bottles of white and red table wine placed next to shelves of imports from Germany and France, and they'd loved the plain white labels with big black letters: WHITE TABLE WINE and RED TABLE WINE. No color, no foil, no fancy script.

"Don't you love this?" Alicia had said, holding a bottle by its neck, "It's so *un*pretentious, so *un*cool. Not wine-fashionable at all!" She'd rotated the bottle under the dim lights of the tiny shop, ignored the owner's pinched-mouth expression, and read, "'Smith Winery, Napa, California.' Smith Winery. Like, where's that?" Her green eyes had twinkled. "Do you think there's really a Smith Winery, or is it just an alias? You know, like when lovers supposedly sign into a no-tell-motel for a hot night of sex?" She'd lowered her voice. "Not that I have ever done that, mind you." Then she'd tossed back her head and laughed in that naughty, fun Alicia way. "We have to have this . . . and the red, too!"

They'd uncorked the bottle of white, seated outside on the verandah, listening to the sounds of the evening, picking at barbecued fish. Luke had called and said he was going to spend the night in town. "Work" he'd mentioned, "getting ready for a new format. I'll see you tomorrow. Love ya, babe."

Yeah, right. When Abby had hung up, Alicia had said, "He's such a loser, Abs. Divorce his ass and be done with it." She'd poured them each a second glass as the wind had sighed through the trees while a night bird had trilled. "But let's not let *him* ruin our night. That son of a bitch is so not worth it."

Oh, how right she'd been, Abby thought now. This bottle of red had been pushed into the cupboard, where it had collected dust for over two years. She'd made Alicia promise they would drink it the next time she visited, but that hadn't happened and now she was selling the place.

Time to uncork it. Who knew the shelf life of such a unique blend? She would open the bottle and call Alicia, tell her to pour herself a glass of wine, too, and they'd drink together while on the phone.

She opened a drawer to find the corkscrew. Her eye caught on Hershey standing frozen, not a muscle moving, eyes fixed on the darkened living room. Since she'd been working in the studio all day, the sun had set, and the house, aside from the kitchen, was dark.

"I'm not falling for this," she told the dog, thinking Ansel was hiding under the couch. Except that at that moment the cat hopped onto her kitchen stool and he, too, peered into the darkened part of the house. "Enough!" she said, but felt something, a shift in the atmosphere, and she hesitated. What was it? Something earthy and damp...not so much a smell as a sensation.

"Figment of your imagination," she whispered. Spying the hammer on the counter where she'd left it earlier in the day, she picked it up.

Yeah, like you're going to club someone to death? Get real, her mind taunted. *You, the woman who finds a moth in her house and captures it to release it outside.*

"Yeah, but I'm hell on hornets," she muttered, her fingers tightening over the hammer's smooth wooden handle.

Was it her imagination or did she hear something? The soft scrape of...what? A leather sole on hardwood? A door softly closing? She flashed back to the hospital with its ghostly opening and closing of doors. A whisper of fear, cold as a reptile's eyes, touched the back of her neck.

She held the hammer in a death grip.

Oh, God, don't do this to yourself.

Swallowing hard, she walked into the living room, quickly snapping on a Tiffany lamp. A rainbow of colors washed over the room, illuminating the dark corners.

No bogeyman here.

Hershey growled.

"You're freaking me out, so just stop it!" Abby said, irritated. For her own peace of mind she carefully, hammer firmly in hand, walked through the hallway, feeling her pulse increase and anxiety seep through her blood as she flipped on one light after another, opened closet doors, peered under her bed and the guest bed.

In the bath, holding her breath, she raised the damn hammer and, with images of the shower scene from *Psycho* flashing through her brain, scraped the shower curtain back in one quick motion. She cringed, but there was no one inside the tiled walls, not even a frightened, exposed spider scuttling into the drain.

"See...nothing," she said, her heart still pounding wildly, her stomach in knots.

There was only one other room on the first floor. She opened the final door to the laundry room and stopped short.

The window was open.

Her heart clutched.

She nearly dropped the hammer.

The window had been closed, hadn't it?

Her mind raced as she tried to remember.

She sometimes opened it when she did laundry to air out the room as the dryer, with its faulty vent, tended to heat and steam up the room. But she hadn't done a load today, didn't remember opening the window.

Think, Abby. Don't go nutso over this. You had to have opened it.

Fear brought nervous sweat to the surface of her skin, her fingers slick on the hammer's handle.

Don't lose it. You could *have forgotten to shut it last night when you did the load of towels.*

But she knew better.

Every night she double-checked the doors and windows, and though this one sometimes stuck, she always made sure it was closed.

But not necessarily locked, her mind taunted. Even after hearing about Luke's murder, she didn't always check the window latches, just made certain the windows were closed.

So why is this one open?

Try as she might, she didn't know. Stepping into the tiny alcove, she slammed the window shut, then tried to latch it. But she couldn't get the lock to hold. The window was too swollen from years of humidity. *Great,* she thought, knowing she'd have to jury-rig something to keep it closed—a board from the garage, maybe.

As she was deciding what to do, a chilling thought slithered through her brain.

Would she be locking the bad guys out, or would she just inadvertently lock some unwanted intruder inside? She still hadn't checked the upstairs. "Oh, crap," she muttered, turning around and walking directly to the end of the hallway, where a steep staircase led to her den.

She set her jaw.

She hadn't been upstairs in her office all day. Surely no one was hidden away in the converted attic. And yet she had to find out. She knew she'd never sleep a wink tonight if she didn't check every damned nook and cranny in the house. "Come on, Hershey, you started this," she said to the dog. Opening the door, she turned on the sconce that lit the stairwell. Then, still clutching the damned hammer, she mounted the steep, narrow stairs, hearing them creak against her weight, feeling the skin on her nape prickle with new dread.

This was crazy. So the window was open, so what? So the damned dog was going bananas? Wasn't that Hershey's nature? This Lab wasn't known for her intelligence, and she would hate to think what Hershey's canine IQ might be.

With each step, the temperature of the hallway increased, the heat of the day having risen to the rafters and ceiling of the attic. There were no windows in the room, only a skylight mounted in the sloped ceiling that she could crank open. Heart pounding, she reached the top of the stairs and snapped on the bright overhead light

The room, of course, was empty.

Aside from her desk and one old folding chair.

No bogeyman hiding up here either, just as there had been no monster under her bed.

"Liar," she accused the dog as she searched through the closets.

"False alarm." Hershey lowered her head, her tail barely moving, as if she were ashamed. "Well, you should be," Abby admonished. Dark liquid eyes rolled up at her in supplication. Abby felt a rush of regret. "Oh, Hersh, I'm sorry. You're just doing your job, huh?" She sat on the top step, ruffled the fur at the back of the dog's neck, and leaned close enough that Hershey gave her a quick lick on the cheek. "Doggy kisses," Abby whispered, petting the Lab all over. "They're the best." She was rewarded with another touch of Hershey's wet nose. "I love you, too. Just tone the guard dog thing down a notch or two, okay? Only let me know if there's real trouble here."

Don't criticize the dog. The laundry room window was open and you didn't leave it that way. Someone else pushed open the bottom pane. Either that or you really are cracking up.

Like her.

"No!" she almost yelled and the dog jumped. "Oh, Hersh, sorry." She wasn't even going to let that particular thought run wild. "Come on, maybe I can rustle up a doggy biscuit."

The dog, ever resilient, let out a short "woof" and streaked down the stairs. As Abby reached the main floor, she heard a soft ding, smelled the remnants of old meals burning, and realized the oven had finally reached temperature. The dog, barking, was at the front door.

"Oh, for God's sake. Now what, Hersh? You're not fooling me again, okay?" Abby called after the Lab. "No damned way." She took the steps more carefully, but as she reached the archway to the living room, a wash of headlights splashed across the walls.

Instantly she was wary again, the dog's behavior and the open window having scared her half to death.

Get a grip, Abby.

The Lab was already at the door as she heard the car's engine and the crunch of tires. Peering out the window, she spied a black Mustang wheel up to the garage. A second later the thrum of the engine stopped and the driver's door opened.

Abby caught her breath as she recognized the driver.

"Oh, no," she whispered, spying Detective Montoya behind the wheel. This was definitely *not* good news.

CHAPTER 15

Montoya, dressed in faded jeans, a black T-shirt, and a leather jacket, stretched out of his vehicle. He slammed the door and pressed a button on his key ring. The sleek car chirped and blinked its lights but Abby focused on the man.

His jeans were tight, his face set, his black hair falling over his forehead as he jogged toward the front steps. Stupidly, her heart fluttered. "God help me."

Oh, Abby, don't be an idiot. Do not go there.

She swung the door open before he pressed the button for the bell. Hershey bounded out, wiggling and wagging her tail, begging for attention. Yeah, some watchdog the Lab turned out to be.

"Expecting someone?" Montoya asked, and though there was a tension to his face, a bit of a grin flashed in his beard. The man possessed white, white teeth and a crooked smile, the kind, she supposed, that could melt a woman's heart. He took the time to bend on one knee and pet the dog, who responded by demanding more and more attention, wiggling and grunting in pure pleasure.

"Just you, Detective," she said, aware of the sense of relief she felt at the sight of him. Her nerves definitely needed soothing. And maybe she was just one of those stupid women who were hung up on tough-looking guys, men with an edge, who, if you observed a little more closely, had a twinkle in their eyes and a soft spot in their hearts.

Oh, for the love of God! What kind of ludicrous thought was that? Montoya is a detective. Period. He's working on Luke's homicide. End of story.

Yet as he offered up that smile again, sexy and boyish at the same time, his dark eyes seductive and naughty, she experienced a warm rush in her bloodstream. So there was a fun guy beneath the tough detective facade. Knowing Montoya had a sense of humor was even more dangerous. The last thing she needed in her life right now was a man, and of all the men walking this planet, Detective Reuben Montoya would be the worst choice for her.

A cop?

No way.

A homicide detective?

Even worse!

Get real, Abby.

And who are you to even think about choosing a man? The last one you were serious about just got murdered, remember?

"You were expecting me?" he asked. "Is that why you came to the door armed with a hammer?"

"What? Oh. No...I was just taking out some nails." Not a lie. That's what she'd done earlier this morning. Quickly, she set the hammer onto a table near the doorway. As Hershey ambled into the house again, Montoya climbed to his feet. Light caught in his ebony black hair and along the slope of his chiseled cheekbones; she wondered what it would be like to kiss him. She focused on those thin lips partially hidden by the thick blackness of his goatee and something caught in the back of her throat. In her mind's eye she saw him not only kissing her, but touching her, his mouth and hands skimming her body.

Whoa! Abby, stop it!

She couldn't. As they stood in the warm glow of the porch light: he, on the porch; she, on the other side of the threshold, there was a sense of intimacy in the air. Her silly overactive imagination ran wild with fantasies of making love to him.

Which was just plain ridiculous.

"Are you here alone?" she asked, though she was pretty certain of the answer. She stood on her tiptoes and peered over his shoulder, as if looking for a second cop.

"Flyin' solo tonight."

"What, no suave and debonair partner?" she asked, folding her arms over her chest. As if to protect her heart.

Montoya's grin was pure animal. "You're talking about Brinkman?"

"Such a gentleman," she said sarcastically. "He must win points with the women he works with."

"Not a lot."

"Big surprise, so where *is* my buddy tonight?" she asked, knowing she was flirting and unable to stop.

Montoya lifted a leather-clad shoulder. "Probably out irritating the populace and giving the department a bad name," he said. She looked surprised at his candor, and he added, "Okay, so he's a good cop. I trust his instincts. He's got my back, but hey, I do know the guy. Let's just say Brinkman and I, we don't bowl together."

She laughed, the tension of the night draining from her.

"I don't think I should be telling you this. It could get me into trouble."

"And that would worry you?" She didn't believe it, sensed that Reuben Montoya might thrive on stepping over the line for an occasional walk on the wild side.

"Not a lot. No."

"I figured as much." She stepped out of the doorway, silently inviting him inside. "So, Detective—"

"You can call me Reuben," he said.

"Does anyone?"

He chuckled. "Only my mother."

"And the rest?"

"Aside from my aunt, who insists on calling me Pedro because of my confirmation name, and my brothers and sisters who refer to me as Reu, everyone refers to me as Montoya."

"That'll work," she said. Less personal. "So, Montoya, you are here for a reason, whether official or not." She pushed the door closed. "You want to tell me about it?"

He nodded, following her inside. Looking at the cozy living room with its Tiffany lamps, antiques, and overstuffed furniture,

Abby decided she could think more clearly under brighter lights, maybe the dining room or the kitchen...

"Is something burning?" he asked.

"Oh, damn! No...not really!" She beelined into the kitchen and scared Ansel, who'd been hiding under the couch. The cat slunk into the dining room, looking furtively over his shoulder and letting out tiny little hisses. He hopped onto the seat of one of the chairs where, beneath the table, he could watch what was happening.

"Friendly," Montoya observed wryly.

"Ansel struggles with the concept of 'chill out.'" Again, Montoya's teeth flashed white against his black goatee and his brown eyes twinkled. "He's been a grouch ever since you brought Hershey here. Ansel's hoping the dog will somehow disappear. Or drop dead. That would work, too."

In the kitchen, Abby pointed at the freezer-burned pizza still sitting in its plastic wrapper on the counter. Her dinner. Which she'd planned to eat alone or with Hershey. Then there was the bottle of wine. Breathing invitingly on the counter. She hesitated before deciding to quit second-guessing herself. "I was making dinner, such as it is, before you showed up. It's...well, it's pretty damned pathetic, but...would you like to join me?" She felt a flush climb up the back of her neck and felt as silly as she had all those years ago when she'd impulsively asked Trey Hilliard to the Sadie Hawkins dance.

Montoya picked up the bottle of red table wine, smiled as he read the label. "I'm off duty," he remarked, looking up at her with those incredibly sexy brown eyes. "Best offer I've had all day."

"Really?" She couldn't help chuckling as she fished out a couple of wineglasses. "Geez, Montoya, you might want to rethink your life."

"Don't worry, I have." He poured the wine as she unwrapped the pizza. She opened a packet of pregrated Italian cheeses, the can of chopped olives, then quickly sliced the tomato and onion. "So," she said, sprinkling the cheese over the dry pepperoni, "about the reason you're here." She added the chopped onion and olives onto the top of the fresh cheese, then slid her beefed-up concoction into the oven. "Why do I have the feeling that you've come with more bad news?"

"Is there any other kind?"

"I used to think so," she admitted. "Now I'm not so sure, and the fact that you're here at nearly nine at night doesn't bode well, does it?"

"I guess not." He handed her a glass, took a sip from his own before resting a slim hip on her kitchen stool. As he did, his jacket fell open, showing the butt of the gun in his shoulder holster, and Abby was reminded that, first and foremost, Detective Reuben Montoya was a cop. He could sip wine, laugh, turn on the sexy twinkle in his eyes, even pet her dog as if he loved chocolate Labs to death, but he was still a homicide detective investigating the death of her ex-husband, a man who might still believe she was involved.

"So far, Detective, all you've brought with you is not only bad, but also disturbing news. What's on your mind?"

"Asa Pomeroy," he said and set his glass on the counter.

"What about him?"

"Haven't you been watching the news?"

She felt it then, that first premonition of dread. The sensation of relief that had been with her for the past ten minutes drained away. "No, I've been working. Alone in the studio." She hitched her chin toward the back door, then took a calming sip of the wine, which was surprisingly smooth. "I haven't even turned on the radio. What happened?"

"He's missing."

"Missing?" The little bit of worry grew. "Asa? My neighbor?"

"Since last night."

"You suspect foul play," she said and the world seemed to get just a little bleaker. If a man as rich and powerful as Asa wasn't safe, who was? No, no, her thinking was off. It was because of the wealth and influence of Pomeroy Industries that he was a target.

"We're not certain of exactly what happened, but since he's a neighbor of yours, I thought I'd stop and see that you were okay."

"Fine," she said. As the kitchen began to fill with the scents of melting cheese, warm tomato sauce, and baking onions, she thought fleetingly of the open window and the dog's growls and snarls.

"So there was no other reason that you were running around with a hammer?"

"I told you—"

"I know what you told me, but when you opened the door, you looked relieved to see me, and you were holding the hammer so hard the bones in your knuckles showed through your skin."

"You noticed all that?"

"I *am* a detective," he said. She couldn't tell if he was ribbing her or deadly serious. Probably the latter, considering the fact that he was here to tell her about Asa.

"Okay, *Detective,* you caught me. The dog acted like someone might be in the house, so I checked things out."

"With a hammer as protection?"

"It was handy."

"But you have an alarm system, right?" He twisted his head to the window cut into the back door. The gold alarm sticker warned any and all intended intruders that the house was connected to the sheriff's department.

"The house came this way. It's not wired to anything." She shrugged. "I'm not sure it ever was."

"Find out and connect it." All humor had left his face.

"You're serious?"

"Absolutely. As I said, we're not certain what happened to Pomeroy, but it doesn't look good." He gave her as much information as he had, and she listened in stunned silence. Both Asa and his car had vanished the night before, and it appeared as if there were some signs of a struggle at the gate to his estate. When the maid arrived in the morning, the automatic lock wasn't working. The police thought he'd probably been abducted and the FBI was already involved.

"All this happened right down the road?" she clarified, though she knew the answer.

"That's right. There's a chance that Asa could have just taken off and told no one where he was going, but it seems unlikely. All of the law enforcement agencies are involved, local, state, and as I said, the FBI."

"Because he's wealthy?" she asked. "That doesn't seem right."

"It isn't. But Pomeroy's high-profile and he owns property all over the South. His business is headquartered in New Orleans, but he's got warehouses and factories in Alabama, Texas, even as far away as Georgia. And there's a chance he might have been taken across state lines, we're not sure yet, but all the agencies are on alert. I work Homicide, and there's no evidence that Pomeroy's dead. But he's definitely missing. Since I've been to your house before, I volunteered to come and warn you and find out if you've heard or seen anything suspicious in the neighborhood."

"But you're off duty," she clarified again.

"That's right."

"So someone else could still come over . . . officially."

"Maybe. Depends on what shakes down. So tell me what you've seen or heard. It doesn't have to be something blatant, just something that caught your attention."

"I don't know. Nothing." She managed to find an oven mitt, but she was stunned, had trouble absorbing everything he'd told her. She opened the oven door and a cloud of spicy heat escaped. Carefully she slid the pizza from the oven. Melted cheese bubbled and dripped over the edges of the crust as she slid the pie onto a plate.

She thought about the times she'd been by the Pomeroy estate, either in her car or on foot. "I don't remember anything odd or suspicious," she said. "When I drive to my office, I go by there twice a day, once into town, once out." Scavenging in a drawer, she came up with a dull pizza cutter. Using all her strength, she pushed hard on the handle and forced the circular blade to slice the pie into eighths. "Then, I jog past the gates when I'm taking my run, but that's been spotty lately. Have you checked with the Stinsons? They live right across the street. Asa and Mark know each other through some kind of flying club, I think. They both have airplanes. Vanessa and Celia Stinson play bridge or golf together."

"Someone's already spoken with them. We're talking to everyone Asa knows."

"That'll take a while."

"No kiddin'."

She arranged the sliced tomatoes, found plates and a spatula, then set two pieces of pizza onto each small platter. Handing one to Montoya, she took the stool next to his but ignored the food. After hours of her stomach begging her for something to eat, she was suddenly not hungry. To think that Asa Pomeroy could have been abducted, only a few hundred feet down the road, was bone-chilling. Pomeroy's disappearance coupled with Luke and Court-ney LaBelle's murder killed her appetite.

"So you came here to find out what I knew about Asa Pomeroy or if I'd seen anything," she stated, not adding, *under the guise of caring*.

Stupid woman!

Montoya met the questions in her eyes. "I came here to warn you," he said, lifting a slice and taking a bite. "And to make certain you were safe."

A cold feeling settled at the base of her spine. "I don't even know Asa Pomeroy."

He nodded. "Tonight, that might be a good thing."

"I guess."

"Eat," he suggested. "It's good."

"It can't be."

He poured more wine and she finally sampled the pizza. He was lying. It tasted like raw onions on cardboard, but she ate it anyway.

He waited a few minutes, finishing his first piece, and said casually, "I heard you went out to the old sanitarium."

She nearly choked on the bite she was chewing. "How did you know that?" The only person she'd confided in was Zoey and she doubted her sister had picked up the phone and called the New Orleans Police.

Were the police tailing her?

If, so, why would Montoya bring it up?

"My aunt is Sister Maria," he explained, then washed down an-other bite with a swallow of wine.

"Oh." Heat climbed up the back of Abby's neck at the thought of trespassing on the grounds of the hospital. "So she turned me in?"

Montoya grinned, his smile disarming. "Nah. If she wanted to punish you, she'd make you get down on your knees and say the rosary from now until eternity. I called and asked about the hospi-tal, if anything was going on over there with the pending sale and demolition, and she mentioned that you'd been by."

Just my luck, to meet up with Sister Maria, the gossiping nun. She forced down another bite of pizza. "Did she say why I was there?"

"No. Even when I asked."

"So now you're asking me?"

He didn't respond, just stared at her.

"It's no big deal," she said, deciding to level with him. "Under the advice of a psychiatrist I went to a few years back, I decided to go to the hospital and confront my past, you know, walk the grounds where my mother spent her last days. She committed suicide on my fifteenth birthday, her thirty-fifth, by jumping from the window of her room...the closed window." She shivered and added, "But you already know that, don't you? My guess is you know a lot about me, more than anyone's willing to admit, and that makes me wonder why?" Growing angry, Abby pushed her plate away. It slid across the counter, nearly landing on the floor. She barely noticed. "So what is it? Am I a suspect? If so, in what? Luke's murder? Asa Pomeroy's disappearance? My mother's suicide?" Drilling him with her gaze, she said, "Come on, Detective Montoya, what's this really all about? And please, don't be reticent or try to spare my feelings. Didn't dear old Auntie Sister Maria tell you that confession's good for the soul?"

He smothered a smile. Wasn't intimidated in the least. Blast the man. "Maybe I just wanted to see that you were okay."

"You expect me to believe that? After you've had the Our Lady of Virtues spies checking up on me?" She couldn't keep the bite out of her words, but he wasn't offended. If anything, he appeared amused by her outrage. God, she'd love to shake some sense into him. He was just so damned maddening!

There was a part of her that was dying to believe that he had stopped by because he cared for her, that he had felt compelled to see her again, but that was just wishful thinking by a very feminine and silly piece of her. The more real down-to-earth side of her nature knew better.

This man was a cop. Period. He didn't trust her and she, now, didn't trust him.

"Believe what you want," he said, standing and wiping his hands on a paper towel he snapped from a roll on the counter.

"I will."

He tossed the used towel into the trash. "So everything cool here?"

Boy, he wouldn't give it up, would he?

"Except for a neurotic dog and a paranoid cat, yeah, everything's fine." She was tempted to tell him about the open window, and Hershey's growl-fest, but couldn't bring herself to do it. She didn't want to come off as some kind of scared little mouse of a woman, and besides, no one had been in the house.

She'd proved that, hadn't she?

He looked around the kitchen as if to satisfy himself. "Well, thanks for the dinner."

"If it could be called that."

Again, he flashed her that infectious, disarming smile, and if she let herself, and looked beyond his black goatee, she might see a dimple or two.

"It was the best invitation and dinner I've had in a long, long time." When she started to protest, he held up a hand. "Seriously."

"You're an easy man to please."

"Maybe." His dark eyes sparked and smoldered and she felt her breath catch in the back of her throat. "Come to think of it, maybe I am."

Oh, dear God. Her pulse was thundering. Heat curled in her stomach and spread to her limbs. What was it about this man that bothered her so? One minute he was so damned infuriating she wanted to strangle him, and the next, he was getting to her, teasing and flirting, and generally digging under her skin.

Which was *not* a good thing.

He was sexy as hell in his black leather jacket, faded, butt-hugging jeans, and irreverent attitude, and she guessed he knew just how to play a woman, something that should have turned her off completely. She warned herself to tread carefully; flirting was one thing, falling for a man like Detective Montoya was another thing altogether. He was still off-limits. Way off.

"Listen," he was saying as she walked him to the front door. God, she hoped he was unaware that she was sizing him up. "If you think of anything or see anything that you think just doesn't fit, call me." He slid her a glance that she could have interpreted a dozen ways. "You've got my number."

Oh, I wish, she thought. She'd love to know what made this man tick. "I told you. I don't know anything."

She opened the door.

Montoya hesitated a beat on the threshold.

For a full half-minute, he stared into the dark night, where the rain was beginning to lash the ground, and the wind was whipping the branches in the old oaks near the drive. "Listen," he finally said, turning to look her full in the face. Deep grooves cut into his forehead, and beneath his goatee, the corners of his mouth pinched downward. "Be careful."

Something inside her cracked.

She had trouble finding her voice. "I . . . I will."

"No, I mean it." He was deadly serious. One hand lightly touched her forearm, one rested over the deadbolt on the slim edge of the door. "Something's going on here. I don't know what, but I don't like it. Get that security system up and running. ASAP."

"You're starting to scare me."

"Good. That's the point." His expression didn't change. His dark gaze was intense, downright smoldering.

The back of her throat tightened. "Okay."

He slid a glance past her, to the interior and the table in the entry hall. "And the hammer's not such a bad idea. I'm not crazy about civilians with guns and guard dogs, but protect yourself." He frowned. "You might want a bigger one."

"Gun or dog?"

"Hammer."

"Like a sledge?"

"Yeah." He nodded and dropped his hand. "A sledge would work just fine." But he didn't smile as he hunched his shoulders against the rain. She watched him hurry down the steps of the porch, along the brick path to the driveway and into his black Mustang. Once inside, he engaged the engine, maneuvered a quick U-turn, and drove down the lane, his taillights fading in the rain.

"Did you hear that, Hershey? The hammer thing? As if. And he doesn't think much of your skills as a watch dog, does he?" She slid the deadbolt into place and walked into the bedroom, trying not to be depressed that he was gone. She barely knew the man, didn't trust him. But the house seemed suddenly empty without him.

Silly.

His warnings crept back through her mind. Maybe it was time to load the .38. She had ammo in a box in the closet.

She pulled open the drawer, intent on taking Montoya's advice.

But the gun was missing.

She blinked hard. No way! Luke's father's revolver couldn't be gone! She'd seen it only a few nights earlier, right?

So what had happened to it?

Shaken, Abby sank onto her bed, thought about dialing Montoya's cell, and decided against it. One more time, she looked in the nightstand drawer, then rolled across the bed to the other side and the matching night table. Nervously she pulled the drawer open, silently praying she would find the .38, that she'd forgotten where she'd last seen it.

No such luck.

The gun was missing.

And the window had been open.

Someone had been inside the house.

Someone had climbed inside and stolen Luke's precious handgun.

Her breath stopped in her lungs when she considered the possibilities.

The killer could have come inside, looking for something Luke had said was precious to him. Or some obsessed fan, who had heard Luke talk on the air about the .38, was either acting out of some fanatical obsession in righting the "wrong" she'd done his hero, or had thought the gun would get a great price on eBay, or the black market, or wherever it was that someone sold a weapon stolen from a famous person.

"Too bizarre," she murmured and too damned scary. Before allowing serious panic to set in, she spent the next half an hour tearing the bedroom and house apart, all the while hoping beyond hope that she'd misplaced the damned gun. But in the end, she found no trace of it.

So who had taken it?

And what were they going to do with it?

CHAPTER 16

The old man was waiting.

Which was just fine, he thought as he slid through the darkness and climbed the fence. His truck was parked behind the shed of the abandoned sawmill and he decided this was the last time he could risk parking so close to the Pomeroy estate.

Adrenalin crackled through his body and he felt more alive than he had since killing Gierman and the virgin. The threat was much stronger now that the cops knew Pomeroy was missing. The FBI would be called in and they would wire the Pomeroy mansion while waiting for a ransom demand that wouldn't come.

A sly smile crept across his lips.

They had no idea what was happening, not yet.

But they would tomorrow...he would see to it. He already knew how to contact them, and through whom.

As much as he loved watching the police scratch their heads and chase their tails, they were making things more difficult for him. With all the law enforcement agencies swarming around this part of the state, he would have to be careful. Very careful. That's why he'd snagged the gun today when Abby had been working in her studio. He'd watched her for over an hour, realized she'd probably spend most of the day in her studio, so he'd taken the chance. He'd known that soon things would become harder, especially as he intended to step things up, work more quickly. So he had risked sliding into her house and slipping the .38 from its hiding spot in her bedroom.

But he had indulged himself.

Despite the danger, he'd taken the time to lie on her bed, to drink in her scent, to imagine what it would be like to feel her body under his.

Writhing.

Sweating.

Wanting.

Faith's daughter.

His blood ran hot remembering what her bed had smelled like. In his mind's eye he'd seen her wild curls spread on the pillow, her lips parted and trembling, her body jerking upward as he'd thrust into her. Hard. Fast. Leaving her breathless until the perfect moment when he'd take her life . . .

Oh, how he would have loved to have surprised her today. He trembled with anticipation and his hands were slick on the steering wheel.

Be patient.

Her time is soon.

Now he opened the gate and eased his truck through then secured the chain again. The rain, which had been pouring most of the day, had lessened a bit, and he drank in deep lungfuls of the wet, night air. Stealthily, he drove onto the highway, eventually hitting the lights. With the police ever vigilant, it was time to act.

For nearly twenty-four hours, he'd let the old man think about his life. Long enough.

Now, it was time to end it.

"Damn it!" Gina Jefferson threw her pencil across the tiny room. It hit the wall, scratching the plaster beneath her award for being the 2002 African-American Business Woman of the Year granted her by the city of New Orleans. The pencil slid down the wall, landing behind the file cabinet. "Great, Gina. Smooth move," she muttered under her breath, angry at herself for letting her temper get the better of her. It was late, after nine, and she was the last employee still on the premises at Crescent City Center. She'd been here twelve hours, worked her tail off, and was as frustrated as she'd been in her fifty-five years. Feeling foolish, and glad no one else was in the room, she walked across the worn carpeting, tried to retrieve the pencil but couldn't. The file cabinet was a behemoth and stuffed full of client files, clients who would soon have to find a new facility for their mental health needs.

Unless she could pull a cash cow out of her hat.

She'd already knocked on most of the doors of the donors she could count on, over and over again. She needed a new list of wealthy philanthropists, if there was one. Using a coat hanger, she fished out the pencil, now covered with a long, sticky cobweb. Wiping it off with a tissue, she stuffed it into the cup on her desk, a gift from someone the free mental health center had helped.

"Lordy, lordy, give me strength," she said as she snagged her raincoat from the hall tree and slipped it on. The coat seemed tight tonight and she reminded herself that she was supposed to be on a diet, that she needed to lose at least thirty pounds, but she was too depressed to think about her ever-expanding waistline. Too depressed and too stressed. Some of her friends smoked when they were on edge, others had the good fortune not to be able to eat. She, on the other hand, found food a balm in times of anxiety, and right now she was pretty damned anxious. The center was going to close and soon if she couldn't find a way to raise the cash necessary to keep the damned doors open.

Through the window the night seemed darker than usual, but maybe that was just because she was so depressed. After months of fund-raising, hours on the phone, working round the clock, all her efforts seemed to have been for naught. The free mental health center would inevitably close its doors. Unless the coffers of some ka-billionaire or the ka-billionaire's charitable foundation miraculously donated thousands upon thousands of dollars to keep it open. Even then they would need more money, federal grants, and additional funds from the state or parish or city, all of which were tapped out.

Rotating the kinks from her neck, she snapped off most of the lights, then glanced through the glass doors to a spot across the street where twice this evening she'd noticed a man standing alone.

She was used to dealing with oddballs. After all, the center catered to those poor individuals who needed psychological and emotional help. The more serious cases were referred to the hospital, but most of the people they saw were troubled souls who needed some medication, or direction, or just to talk. One medical doctor and two nurses volunteered their time; the rest of the staff was made up of clinical psychologists or social workers.

In her fifteen years here, Gina had seen more than her share of strange people. So why tonight, she wondered, did she sense that there was something different about the individual she'd caught lingering on the other side of the street, just out of the circle of the lamp post's illumination?

A sixth sense?

Or just the fact that she was bone-tired?

There were lots of homeless people and drifters in this part of New Orleans. And the town had more than its share of oddballs and neurotics and druggies. As much as she loved New Orleans, she knew the dangers of the city streets. She'd been born and raised here, the oldest of seven children. Her father, Franklin, had been a boxer in his youth, a bus driver later in life. Her mother had raised the children and cooked not only for the family, but for people in the neighborhood. Then, with a small inheritance and encouragement from everyone she knew, Ezzie Brown had opened her own restaurant on the fringe of the French Quarter. All of Ezzie and Franklin's children, whether of legal age or not, had worked in the restaurant, busing tables, waiting, cooking, mopping the floors, and cleaning the grill, all the while learning the value of a dollar, and an appreciation for good jazz. A table made out of two doors stretched across the back room behind the kitchen and was set up as a long desk where, under the hum and bright illumination of fluorescent lights, every one of Ezzie's kids was supposed to do his or her homework. They were surrounded by shelves packed with jars of pickles, cans of tomato paste, sacks of onions, garlic, and hot peppers, all vying for space with the boxes of cornmeal and flour.

Now, Gina engaged the alarm system, tucked her umbrella under her arm, pulled her keys from her purse, and rezipped it, then, juggling her briefcase and everything else, she shouldered open the door. Outside it was a nasty night, wet and wild, water running through the dark streets, an occasional car flying past, splashing water, thrumming with music.

The scents of the city filled her nostrils, the smell of the Mississippi ever present. Lordy, Gina loved it here.

No stranger loitered in the shadows near the streetlamp.

She checked.

Breathing easier, she locked the door behind her, thinking of the restaurant where her mother, pushing eighty, still served the best Creole shrimp in all of Louisiana. Her parents had taught each of their children to be strong and smart, work hard, and love the Lord. No matter how tight money had been while Gina had been growing up, Franklin and Esmeralda Brown tithed faithfully to their church, sang in the choir, donated to the missions, and made their children do so as well. Never had a neighbor come by who had not been fed. If Christmas was lean, so be it; if the bus company laid Franklin off, then he'd work odd jobs until he was hired somewhere else. Throughout it all, the good times and the bad, her parents' rock-solid faith had never faltered.

Not even when their youngest boy, Martin, had been born. There had been problems with his birth from the get-go. Esmeralda, who had delivered six chubby healthy babies into the world, had nearly died in childbirth with the seventh. An emergency C-section and subsequent transfusion had saved her life, but the scrawny baby had been in distress in vitro and had been fussy and colicky for the first year of his life. Who knew if that harsh entrance into the world had been a part of the violence and temper that followed? Whatever the reason, Martin had always been different.

Always.

He'd been in and out of juvenile facilities, mental facilities, and later jail all of his thirty-three years. Even as he'd grown into a big, strapping man, he'd never completely emotionally matured. Twenty-two years younger than his oldest sister, Martin had given Gina her first glimpse of the struggles of those with mental problems. Though Martin tested normal, even intelligent in the standard exams, there was always something off. It didn't help that he possessed a hair-trigger temper coupled with a need for violence. As many psychiatrists as Martin had seen, including Dr. Simon

Heller at Our Lady of Virtues when the hospital had been open, he had never fit in.

People like Martin needed this center and needed it desperately! She couldn't let herself and the community down by not fighting for it to remain open.

Still clutching her purse, briefcase, and umbrella in one hand, she managed to slide the accordion-style grate over the door and locked it as well, then tested it by rattling the bars.

Opening her umbrella, she made her nightly mad dash through a gravel-strewn alley to her car. The Buick Regal, her pride and joy, was parked where it always was in the back parking lot, a sorry piece of asphalt. The wind caught in the umbrella and rain slapped at her legs, and again, she had that weird feeling that had been with her all day. She looked over her shoulder but saw no one. The alley was deserted, the traffic on the street thin and quiet.

So why the case of the willies?

There's no one out here, Gina, she thought. *Get over your bad self! You've done this hundreds of times, every night, like clockwork. No one's ever bothered you. You're just upset because the center is going to close unless you find a way to keep the doors open! You, Gina. Ain't no one else gonna step up to this plate!*

Walking briskly, she wondered how she was going to get the quick influx of cash. The trouble was, there just wasn't enough money to go around, she thought, fighting with her umbrella in the gusts of wind and rain.

But she needed one celebrity type to help out. Someone the public could relate to, someone they would trust and give generously to. She thought of Billy Ray Furlough, that nearly rabid televangelist. He managed to get people to donate weekly to his church and his catchphrase, "Lord, love ya, brother," was heard all over the country.

She'd never appealed to Billy Ray for money; there was something too slick, too big business, about him. But she might, after tonight's meeting, have to swallow her pride and, rather than call in, see him personally and try to fight her way through the obstacle course of receptionists, bodyguards, and yes-men to get to the preacher, the tall man who'd been labeled as possessing a "Hollywood thousand-watt smile." That phrase alone had made her want to throw up. She figured it was some spin doctor's idea of good press. These days, apparently, even preachers had a public image to uphold—an image that probably wouldn't need the world to know that the good preacher himself had worked through his own "issues."

Yes, she'd call on Billy Ray Furlough personally. And once again she'd approach Asa Pomeroy, another wealthy man in the city, one she could barely stomach. Pomeroy traded in wives for younger models on a regular basis, and he sold weapons to the highest bidder. And yet, he'd been known to donate hundreds of thousands of dollars if the cause appealed to him. And even Asa, the almighty, had a son who had battled his own share of mental challenges.

Again, she'd have to smile, ask sweetly, and bite her tongue.

You're a hypocrite, Gina. You hate preachers who are more about glitz and television ratings than God, and you despise anyone who makes money by selling arms.

But desperate times called for desperate measures.

Boy, did she understand that old bromide. Just last week she'd phoned her friend Eleanor Cavalier, who worked at WSLJ. Gina had wanted some on-air exposure, and she'd hoped to be a guest on Samantha Leeds's program, *Midnight Confessions.* Dr. Sam was a psychologist who worked at the Boucher Center off Toulouse Street and sometimes helped out here at Crescent City Center. The trouble was the program manager for the station had thought it would be more interesting for the audience if Gina appeared on Luke Gierman's show as well. Gina, fearing she'd just made a deal with the devil, had reluctantly agreed.

She figured now, with Gierman's murder, she was off the hook.

She walked through the parking lot to her car, fighting the umbrella, stepping in puddles that had collected in the potholes and feeling the water seep through her boots.

A night not fit for man nor beast, her father used to say and she realized then why it was so dark. The only security light for the entire lot had burned out.

How odd.

She had a bad feeling, again.

The long hours were getting to her. Every little thing made her jump tonight.

What she needed was to drive the five miles to her home, take a warm shower, pour both Wally and herself a glass of wine, and beat the pants off him in a game of cutthroat Scrabble. He'd be waiting for her, just as he had for the entire thirty-six years of their marriage.

He was a good man, had always been there through times of plenty and want. She reached her car and tried to slide her key into the lock, but just like everything else on this cussed night, unlocking the car turned out to be a problem. The lock was jammed.

She tried again. "Come on," she muttered between clenched teeth, her nerves strung tight as piano wires. "Oh, for the love of Mike!"

Flustered, she started to unzip her purse for her cell phone when she sensed something, nothing that she could see, just a dark premonition that made her turn, swinging the damned umbrella. Too late! Something cold and metallic was pressed against her neck.

She started to scream as thousands of volts of electricity sizzled through her body. Her legs gave way. Her arms flailed wildly. She couldn't breathe. Her thoughts scattered. It felt as if a million tiny daggers were touching her skin. No! She tried to scream again and only a garbled, faint noise came out of her mouth.

Quickly and adeptly, as if he'd done it thousands of times before, her assailant slapped tape over her mouth, grabbed her keys from the pavement beside her, peeled something off the lock of her car, opened both doors on the driver's side, and stuffed her unceremoniously into the backseat. Helpless, unable to move, she saw him scrape up something from the ground…her purse, then the umbrella. He tossed both items into the front passenger seat.

Panicked, Gina tried to get away, to force her jellied limbs to move, but it was no use. He was quick, and using the same kind of tape he'd pressed over her mouth, he bound her ankles as her legs still dangled off the seat, hanging out of the car. Once her legs were lashed together, he crawled half inside, painfully wrenched her arms behind her back, and wound tape over her wrists.

She tried to see him and wound him, to scrape some of his skin from his arms, but he was too quick, disguised in a black wetsuit or something like it. Who was he and why, oh, why was he doing this?

With all her might she tried to struggle, to fight, to save herself, but as many orders as her brain screamed, her muscles ignored. Her arms and legs were useless. A blindfold was swiftly tied over her eyes.

In less than two minutes she was trussed and locked into the backseat of her own car and he, whoever he was, began to drive. She felt the Regal's tires bouncing over the ruts and holes in the parking lot as he eased down the alley.

Throughout the entire ordeal, he'd been silent.

Deadly efficient.

Working with a cold brutality that drove fear straight into her heart.

It was as if he'd planned the attack for days, or weeks, possibly even months.

But why?

Who would do this?

Dear Jesus, help me! Tears burned behind her eyes and her entire body trembled. She tried to concentrate, to figure out a plan of escape, to, at the very least, fling herself out of the moving car, but just as the thought hit her brain, she heard the childproof door locks click down.

He slowed at, she assumed, the alley's entrance and eased onto the street, turning toward the river.

Oh, God, where was he taking her?

To do what?

She was shaking all over, tears tracking from her eyes, and she blinked hard, tried to get her bearings.

Think, Gina, think! Your cell phone! If you could just get to it and hit speed dial for 911.

Frantic, she willed her muscles to respond, but what good would it do? She was tied, her arms pulled behind her back, her shoulders aching in their sockets. Besides, her phone was in her purse and her handbag was in the front passenger seat.

Her heart dropped like a stone.

There was no escape.

There isn't unless you find a way! Don't give up, Gina . . . find a way out of this mess! Isn't that what you tell the people that you counsel, that God always gives you an opportunity, you just have to discover it and work for it? Then find that opportunity, now, before it's too late!

This is a test. God's test.

You can save yourself. The Lord will be with you.

She tried to stay calm, to keep her wits about her, to find comfort in her faith. *God helps those who help themselves.* What she could do was concentrate on where they were going. She couldn't see, but she knew the streets of this city like the back of her hand. The center was two blocks off Esplanade and he'd taken the alley to the west.

Now, he was driving slowly, winding through the city. She thought they were continuing west. Through the blindfold she sensed illumination, streetlights. She heard other traffic as well—tires humming, engines racing, people shouting—and then, as her Buick picked up speed, she knew they were on the freeway, but which direction? She waited for the sound of a bridge. A short one over the Mississippi River, or the bridge across Lake Pontchartrain that would go on for over twenty miles.

However, he'd taken so many corners before he accelerated onto the freeway that she was confused. Soon the illumination from the city lights no longer bled through her blindfold. She felt that they were on the freeway, but had no clue any longer which direction.

She was lost, hog-tied and alone with a would-be killer.

She prayed for her safety, but with each passing mile, her hopes for rescue died.

She knew the odds. This monster's motive wasn't money. Otherwise he would have stolen her wallet and jewelry and left her. Nor would he be demanding ransom as she and Wally lived modestly and had no money to speak of. She wasn't a rich woman. So if her abduction wasn't for money, his motive was darker, more frightening. Deadlier.

He wanted her body. To rape her or kill her or both.

She told herself that if she could get out of this with her life, she would be lucky. She reminded herself that no matter what vile or painful acts were to come, nothing else mattered but that.

Suddenly muted music, a lilting little jingle, rang through the car. Fresh tears slid from her eyes as she recognized the ring tone she'd assigned to her home phone. Wally was calling. Waiting. The wine poured, the Scrabble game on the kitchen table. Her throat clogged. She was probably only ten minutes late and he was already checking on her. Oh, blessed, blessed man. *I love you,* she thought, her heart squeezing as she conjured up his face, and remembered marrying him after high school graduation, making love with him for the first time in a tiny apartment on their wedding night. They'd sacrificed even then, forgoing a honeymoon to save money. The next five years they'd worked and gone to college, taken out loans and gotten scholarships. During that time they'd made the decision not to have children because they both wanted to help their large families, their siblings. Wally had become a teacher and she, because of her brother Martin, had decided to work with the mentally ill.

It all seemed so far away now as she lay in the backseat listening to the cell phone.

The phone quit ringing and her heart nosedived.

Don't give up on me, Wally. Please!

Ten minutes later the same song began to play from inside her purse. The driver ignored her cell phone. As if he didn't care. As if he wasn't worried.

Didn't he know about GPS chips? That the phone could be found by the cell towers where the signals were picked up, or something? She hadn't paid much attention to the spiel when the salesman had gone on and on about the value of the Global Positioning Chip which was part of her new cell phone, but now she only hoped that, however it worked, it would help.

Again the phone stopped ringing and she imagined the worry in Wally's voice as he left another message in her voice mail box.

Still her abductor drove. On and on through the night. Gina had no idea where they were but assumed from the lack of sounds of traffic and the time that had passed that they were far from New Orleans.

When the phone rang for the third time, she nearly sobbed. Poor sweet, brilliant Wally. He was probably worried out of his mind. But he would start looking for her and that was good. He would call the police, they would search for her car, and the GPS chip . . . oh, Lord, she'd never put her faith in technology before.

They drove for what seemed an hour longer before he turned

246 • *Lisa Jackson*

off the freeway and onto a smooth, curving road. The cell phone rang twice more...and she expected that Wally had started calling friends and family.

Finally, her kidnapper slowed the car. He turned hard to the right, and the car jostled and bumped, the sound of weeds or brush scraping the undercarriage. Dear God, where had he taken her?

Her heart was knocking as the tires slid to a stop. He cut the engine, then opened the car door and she smelled the heavy, loamy odor of forest and swamp. Crickets chirped, bull frogs croaked, and the wind swept into the Regal's interior, bringing with it the scents of swamp water and decaying vegetation.

She braced herself. This was it. Well, she wasn't going down without a fight.

The back door of the Buick was yanked open and she started to squirm and struggle.

"I've got a gun," he said. "Don't move." To reinforce his warning, he touched the cold, hard steel barrel to her thigh. He wasn't kidding. "And a knife." This time a long, cool blade slid down her leg.

She nearly lost control of her bladder. Now for certain she knew. He was going to kill her. With the gun, if she was lucky. There was no way out of this.

Lord, please help me. Give me strength.

He slid the blade of the knife between her knees and lower. If she could get some control of her muscles, she could kick up with both feet, maybe slam him in the face with her boots, but just as she thought of it, the knife sliced down hard and cut through the tape surrounding her ankles. She reacted, swinging a booted foot in a hard kick, but he caught her foot in one strong grip and twisted. Hard. Pain shot up her leg. Her knee popped. She squealed behind her gag.

"Bitch!" he growled, in a deep, disguised voice. "Don't you understand?"

Oh, God, yes, she understood. Pain screamed up her thigh. He was going to hurt her. Badly.

He pulled her roughly from the car, and though she was far from petite, he was strong enough to set her on her feet and prod her forward, the nose of his gun at her spine.

"Move." He pushed.

Had she heard his voice before? Was it familiar?

She inched forward in the blackness, her knee throbbing, her entire body quivering with fear. Her boots sank into the mud, but she plowed forward, refusing to cry out, determined to either find a way to thwart him, or die embracing Jesus.

All around her the smell of the swamp was thick and she imagined snakes and gators and all manner of beasts slithering through the night, none deadlier than the creature who had abducted her.

The toe of her boot slammed against something solid and she almost fell. "Up," he commanded. "Two steps."

Swallowing back her fear, she managed to climb the two risers, and as she did, she felt his breath on her neck as he reached around her. A screen door squeaked and he urged her again with the gun's cruel muzzle. Her boots clunked unevenly across what she assumed to be a porch.

Another door creaked open and her heart was hammering so loudly she thought it might explode.

"Inside!" The gun pushed urgently against her.

She inched forward. Even with the blindfold, she felt a new darkness, a closeness. Her every nerve ending was alive, her muscles tense, sweat covering her body. She was in a house, an empty house, she thought, her footsteps loud and reverberating against the floor. It smelled of dirt and misuse and something else, something acrid...urine?

Animal?

Or human?

Her stomach shriveled.

Oh, dear Jesus, were there dead people in here? Or were they alive, kept here against their will? A tiny bit of light pierced through her blindfold, a dim illumination. Her imagination ran wild as she felt him step closer to her.

"That's far enough," he said into her ear, and she felt the edge of a cold steel blade against her cheek. He was behind her, pressed tightly against her, and she felt a fear as cold and dark as any she had ever known.

He shifted, one arm around her ribs, the gun pressed under her breasts as he slowly and sensuously slid the blade of the knife down the slope of her cheek. Against her back, she felt his erection. The jerk was getting off on this!

Tears burned her eyes. All hope drained.

The knife moved lower, beneath her chin. To that soft, vulnerable tissue.

Oh, God... She quaked inside, her tears drenching the blindfold.

The blade pressed hard, moving seductively against the column of her neck, lingering at the soft spot between her collarbones. He was breathing rapidly now, short panting bursts against her ear.

Her knees gave out in fear, and had he not been holding her up, she would have fallen.

Jesus, give me strength.

Just when she was certain he would slice her throat, he moved and, as she gasped, cut the tape at her wrists. If she had known his plan, she would have been ready, but in the split second when she realized she was unbound, he shifted, holding the knife to her throat and forcing the gun into her hand.

She couldn't believe it. If she turned the weapon on him now, took the chance that she could kill him first, what did it matter? He was going to kill her anyway.

"Shoot," he commanded as his steely, gloved fingers covered hers.

What?

He aimed the weapon in front of her, pointed downward, and she heard another sound...a muted cry?

So there was someone else in the room.

"Shoot, Gina!"

Hearing her name made her want to throw up. That she was a part of this macabre, twisted act, whatever it was, made her stomach wrench.

The knife wiggled at her throat and she felt a hot, searing pain as he cut her.

"Shoot and end this."

Don't do it. Gina, don't...there is something horrible happening here, something worse than you originally thought.

Another muffled squeal.

From the area in front of her. The spot where he was aiming the gun. Dear Jesus, what was he forcing her to do?

She tried to jerk away, but the hand over hers tightened, positioning the heavy gun. It was wobbling in her hand, but he took control and squeezed, forcing her finger to pull the trigger.

Bang!

The gun's report was a crack of thunder.

Her hand flew up, but he held her tight.

A wail, muted by something, pierced the night.

Oh, Lord what had she done?

The smell of cordite and blood filled the air.

"Retribution," her attacker growled as he yanked off the blindfold.

Gina's eyes adjusted to the light, a small bulb at one corner of a large pine-paneled room. "Oh, dear Lord, no," she whispered as she saw what she had done. A big man with mussed white hair and a shocked expression was staring at her, the hole in his chest gaping, blood flowing.

She recognized him as someone she detested, the very man she'd hoped to appeal to for money, even if she would have had to grovel for it. A low moan of denial whispered over her lips as she watched Asa Pomeroy die. "No...oh, no, no, no."

Shaking violently, she shrank back, tried to drop the gun, but the monster was still behind her, his erection still hard as a rock. His fingers tightened over hers again. She looked down at the gun, a pearl-handled Colt .45, just like one of the pair her husband owned.

As she watched, withering in terror, he twisted her hand, forcing it upward to her own temple. Her throat closed and she silently prayed for forgiveness. *Lord, please, take my soul,* she silently pled. *Keep Wally safe... Wally, oh, Wally, I love you...*

CHAPTER 17

Maury Taylor looked at the note in his hands and knew it was pure gold. He'd overslept, run through the shower, thrown on his jogging suit, bought his morning jolt from one of those drive-through espresso huts, then parked his old Toyota in the lot across from the station. He hadn't had time for the morning paper, not today.

For the next hour, he'd sorted through the mail addressed to *Gierman's Groaners* or *The Luke Gierman Show.* He'd shuffled through cards, sympathetic notes, some stupid gifts including a tape of an old show—like the station didn't have them all?—the same old drivel. He was nearly finished when he'd found this gem in the pile and knew in an instant that his life had just changed forever.

For the better.

Big time!

The simple note had come to the radio station addressed to Luke Gierman, the dead man himself, and was encased in a plain white envelope with block letters and no return address.

Ever since Luke's death, the station had gotten bags full of cards and letters and notes. Not to mention hundreds of e-mail messages daily. The guy was more popular in death than life, and the ratings for his show were through the roof, which was just fine with Maury. The station manager was talking about making Maury the permanent host and eventually changing the name to something like *Maury Taylor Presents Gierman's Groaners*...it was a mouthful and would eventually become just the *Maury Taylor Show*, but, the eager station manager had assured him, they'd have to work on something a little memorable and personal. *Taylor's Trash Talk* sounded pretty good, but was too feminine. He didn't want to sound like some black chick...but things were looking up. Soon he'd get his due.

Too bad, Luke.

Ouch!

In Maury's opinion, Luke had been a real jerk. A pompous pain in the ass. Nonetheless, Mrs. Taylor had raised no fool for a son, and Maury, despite his feelings about Luke, had gone along for the ride, playing the role of idiot, laughing uproariously at things that secretly offended him, even pushing the groan button at a particularly bad pun or statement.

Hell, who wouldn't have taken the chance to be a part of a growing, popular show? Few people got rich being a radio jock, but Luke had broken through the barriers and, judging by the amount of flowers, cards, and calls that had arrived at WSLJ, touched a lot of people, who were either fascinated or repulsed by his show.

But now it was Maury's turn.

Because of this.

Maury read the single white sheet of paper one more time.

REPENT

A L

God, he'd love to read that one single word on the air, stir up the audience by suggesting he'd had contact with Luke's killer... imagine the ratings. His palms sweated at the thought. So the police would be pissed. Wasn't that what the station's lawyers were all about? He'd been flirting with jumping ship and taking a job over at WNAB, but first, he wanted to see how things were going to be handled here in the wake of Luke's demise.

So far, it was lookin' good.

And now he was holding the goddamned keys to the kingdom, if he dared use them.

What would Luke do?

That was a slam dunk.

Maury didn't have a second's hesitation. He walked to the copy machine in the backroom, nodded to Ramblin' Rob, a wiry old fart of a DJ who still played platters. Rob was drinking a potful of coffee while working the crossword puzzle, his usual routine before he went on the air. He challenged himself to finish it, then have time for a last cup of coffee and a smoke in the back alley before he sat down at the mike, playing requests from his stacks of old LPs. In this day of digital music, computers, iPods, and downloads, Rob was into "keeping it real," whatever the hell that meant.

Maury slid the note into the copy machine and pressed the start button. He did have one disturbing thought. What if the note proved to be a fraud? Just because he had a gut feeling about it didn't mean anything. He didn't want to come off as a buffoon. Not any longer. He'd played that role far too long as it was.

So how would he deal with that on the air later this afternoon... oh, hell, he'd just tell the audience about it, knowing the sender was listening, and then he'd bait the guy, force his hand. Maybe whoever wrote the note, whether he was a nutcase just looking for publicity, or the real killer, would respond. Especially if Maury jerked his chain a bit.

If so, the listening audience would go crazy. The buzz would be instantaneous. It wouldn't matter if the note turned out to be a fraud or not. He thought about how it would play on the air and nearly got a hard-on.

The wheels in his mind were turning faster and faster, like a train gaining speed as the Xerox machine spat out his copy. He grabbed it and the original and was heading out the door when Rob looked up from his puzzle.

"Hey! You hear the news?"

"What news?" Maury stopped short, irritated by the interruption, but curious just the same. He hoped that Luke's killer hadn't been found, not yet.

"The kidnapping."

"They find Pomeroy?"

"Don't know." The crusty old DJ pulled a face, all his wrinkles creasing more deeply. "No, I'm talking about Gina Jefferson, you know who she is?"

"The do-gooder? Involved in the Urban League, always clamoring to the city council about funding for her clinic, the woman who Luke wanted on the show so that he could publicly fillet her? *That* Gina Jefferson?"

"Yeah, that one," Rob said, obviously disgusted. "And, ya know, do-gooder isn't a dirty word. I know Gierman had a lot of fun knocking her, but she's a great lady. Done a helluva lot for the city and the homeless and, you know, the people who are a few beers shy of a six-pack. Anyway, she's missing, too."

"Missing? Like Pomeroy?" Maury said. For a second he felt a pang of fear for the woman, but then the wheels in his mind began spinning again. Even more rapidly than before. Somehow this would make a great show…two of the city's leading citizens missing, one a wealthy do-anything-for-a-buck industrialist, the other a bleeding heart who helped the downtrodden…yeah, oh, man, yeah. This was an incredible show in the making. "Was she kidnapped?" he asked and glanced down at his note.

Could this piece of paper have anything to do with the missing people? Hadn't Luke been kidnapped? And the girl, Courtney LaBelle?

"Appears that way. No one knows for certain yet. There hasn't even been a ransom note for Pomeroy and he's been missing, what? Two or three days?" Rob thought long and hard. "Makes ya wonder what the hell is going on."

The letter in Maury's hand nearly burned him. He walked toward the door, afraid Rob might get suspicious. No one could know what he was up to. Not the program manager, the station manager, or any of his other colleagues. "Sure does," he called over his shoulder.

Gierman's Groaners was airing in its usual spot in the schedule, but two other shows—"Luke's favorites"—had been slotted in, at a different time each day, causing a freaking nightmare for the program manager, but sending the ratings into the stratosphere and keeping Maury at the station, helping with the cutting, editing, and airing for hours on end. The idea was to find more listeners, and though a few had been pissed, e-mailing in that they wanted their regular program back in its allotted slot, the advertisers were thrilled and the general consensus was that Luke's regularly scheduled program, which was now Maury's baby, was at the top of the ratings. Even more of a success than when good ol' Luke was alive.

The irony of the thing was, Maury planned to keep Luke among the living, at least on the airwaves. When the show became his, he'd dedicate a segment to Luke, play some bit from a previously recorded program, and pay homage to the master. It kind of galled him, but it would work; Maury knew it would. Luke Gierman was going to become like Elvis was in death. More alive, more visible, more audible than ever.

And this piece of gold, this letter from the killer or whoever, was going to start the ball rolling. Maury planned to read the letter on the air, tell the listeners he thought it "might be" from the killer, but believed the letter could well be a hoax, sent by a fraud, thereby baiting the guy who wrote it, hoping the jerk would be stupid enough to call the show. Wouldn't that be the ticket? All Maury had to do was sucker the note writer in. Only then would he place a call to the police.

That should get the audience going. As he walked along the long hallway from the kitchen, leaving Rob still huddled over his puzzle and racing with the clock, Maury couldn't help smiling. Deep in his bones, he knew his time had finally come. He had a degree in journalism, for Christ's sake. He was tired of playing second string; it was time to join the A-team.

"You're kidding!" Abby couldn't keep the frustration from her voice. She was on the phone to the fourth security company she'd rung up today. Leaning against the desk in her small office in the heart of New Orleans, she slowly counted to ten and tried not to lose control of her temper.

"No, ma'am, I'm not," the gravelly voice on the other end of the connection assured her. "Our next free time is...let me see..." She heard pages flipping and wondered why Stan's Security Service didn't have all their appointments on computer. "...looks like two weeks from Monday, but something might open up. Ya never know. Trudie, our secretary, she'd know way better'n me, but she's on a break right now. When she gits back, she can tell you what's what. She should be back in ten, fifteen minutes."

"Thank you, I'll call back," Abby said and hung up. Who would have thought trying to get a company out to install a simple security system was tantamount to breaking into Fort Knox? She stared at her computer screen, where the latest edition of the Internet yellow pages was glowing, seeming to mock her with the list of security companies and system installers.

Why bother?

She was going to sell the place anyway.

Sean Erwin, the persnickety spiked-haired man who had said nothing nice about her place, was coming over for yet another "look-see" later in the afternoon. This time, along with his tape measure, he was bringing a list of dimensions of his furniture, and a sketch pad on which, he'd informed her, he'd plotted out the lay-out of his favorite pieces, the things he "absolutely couldn't live without."

She thought it was a waste of time, but had agreed to meet him after she'd finished working here in the office, where she'd made phone calls, paid bills, sent out reminders to those clients who were behind, and in general, caught up on her paperwork. She'd eaten lunch on the run, all the while trying to forget about Our Lady of Virtues and the weird sensation that had lingered with her long after she'd left the campus of the hospital. She'd also tried to push Luke's gruesome death and Detective Reuben Montoya out of her head.

Why the sexy cop kept messing with her mind, she really didn't understand. It wasn't as if she were looking for a man, for God's sake. In fact, until she moved to the West Coast, she'd planned to forget about dating, men, and sex altogether.

But the detective with his crooked smile, dark eyes, and nearly indecent laugh had managed to infiltrate her dreams and her waking thoughts as well. Which was just no good.

All things said and done, it would be far better for her to move and move quickly.

Before it was too late.

It already is, Abby. You're hooked. Face it.

Okay, then. Before she did something stupid.

Oh, honey, her mind taunted. *We're beyond that. Where Detective Montoya is concerned, you're well on your way to stupid central and you damned well know it.*

Laura Beck was furious.

She drove her Lincoln Continental with a Manolo Blahnik–encased lead foot. That wasn't really true, she thought ruefully. The leopard print sling backs weren't really Blahniks, but they were damned good knockoffs and they'd cost over two hundred bucks, so she wasn't happy that she'd have to walk through the rain and muck and chance ruining them.

Growing up a poor kid in Appalachia, she'd learned the value of a dollar at an early age, and it was only through smarts, grit, and yes, sleeping with the right men, that she'd come close to getting what she wanted from life.

So no low-life squatter was going to ruin the best deal she had going. No way. No how. She'd been in the diamond club of Respected Realty Company for the past eight years, selling over ten million dollars in real estate each and every year, in good times and in bad.

Now, she had a chance to buy out the owner of the realty company and she planned to expand the business to other cities. But even with all the cash she'd squirreled away, she still needed Asa Pomeroy's account to make it happen.

Damn the man, where was he?

Why the sudden vanishing act?

As she drove along the winding road to his hunting lodge, she had a premonition that he might be dead, and if so, lawsy-mercy, all of her plans would go up in smoke . . . well, unless she talked to his heirs. Fortunately the eldest son, Christian, hadn't been around for years, but Asa still had a couple of bitter ex-wives, a daughter who was an uptight bitch, and another son who was a blithering idiot and thought he was God's gift to women. Jeremy Pomeroy had come on to her often enough. Practically at every chance he got. A big bore of a man, Jeremy took after his self-involved daddy, though Jeremy hadn't been born with his father's brains or work ethic. And those kids of his! Holy terrors. Just the thought of Asa's grandsons set Laurie's teeth on edge. As bad as their swaggering, good-ol'-boy father and as cold as their mother, those two adolescent half-wits were damned scary.

She shuddered thinking how she'd had to put up with the entire Pomeroy family last Christmas, smiling and laughing at off-color jokes, feeling her butt being pinched by too-friendly fingers, getting caught under the mistletoe at every turn.

All because she wanted a piece of the Pomeroy fortune.

She and every other real estate agent in Louisiana.

She turned off the rural road and onto the long gravel lane that ambled through the estate, past century-old trees, and over leaf-strewn ruts. Brush and brambles obscured the view of the lodge from the road, but she noticed that the gates had been left open. Weird. Though the maid service and gardener didn't have the keys, they knew to close the gates.

It seemed as if nothing about this listing was going right!

"You can pull this off," she said then caught herself as she heard a bit of her Appalachian twang, the speech pattern she'd spent years disguising. It wasn't the part of the country that embarrassed her. Lord, some of the nicest people she'd ever known lived in the mountains and hollers of West Virginia, the breathtakingly beautiful country filled with God-fearing, music-loving, hardworking people. It was the poor part of her past that made her skin crawl and caused her to spend her life running from that poverty.

She glanced at her reflection in the rearview mirror. She still looked good, even though the big four-oh loomed just over next spring's horizon. Her hair was a vibrant red with perfect gold highlights, her green eyes wide and sexy, her body toned by a strict regimen of salads, low-fat dressings, sugar-free yogurt, and two hours in the gym every morning at five. Two cups of black coffee and she was wired for the day.

God, she loved her work.

But not when some idiots tried to sabotage it.

She'd gotten a call from a neighbor that there was a car at the lodge...and on tour day! At first she'd thought it was the groundskeeper who had been scheduled to clean up the place, but the neighbor assured her no work was being done on the estate and the car was not the usual beat-up green pickup. *Great,* she thought angrily. *Just...freaking great!*

She'd already had the interior of the place cleaned to a spit-polished glow, and her car was filled with two thermoses of coffee, a fruit platter, and a basket of mini-beignets for the other agents who were planning on driving all the way out here as part of the weekly tour. The first of the lot were due to arrive at the Pomeroy hunting lodge in less than two hours. How the hell was that going to happen now?

"Damn it," she muttered as she spied the old Buick in the drive. The neighbor had been right. Well, whoever was here was going to get the hell out.

Careful, Laura. Tread carefully. Remember what Mama used to say: "You can't tell a book by its cover." Maybe whoever is here is interested in buying the place. There could be an armada of Mercedeses and Porsches or Ferraris in this guy's garage.

No way.

The neighbor had called two hours earlier and Laura doubted a prospective buyer would hang out for hours just waiting. It wasn't someone here early for the tour and the Regal sure as hell didn't look like someone's idea of a hunting rig.

Strange.

She nosed her Lincoln close to the Buick and parked. Climbing out of her car, she felt the first little tickle of a run in her panty hose—dear God, why had she bothered today? No big deal. She'd strip them off and show off her legs. Carefully dodging puddles, she walked up to the Buick. It was unlocked. And empty.

So where was the driver?

Inside?

She looked at the large rambling old lodge with its steep roof, dormers, and pine needles collecting in the gutters. All the windows seemed shut. How would the Buick's owner get inside? The building was locked and secured with a real estate agent's lock box. Or had been. Maybe the maid had returned with another key. Or maybe she'd left not only the gate wide open, but the building unlocked as well.

That thought royally pissed Laura off.

The tiny run in her stocking crawled upward and moisture seeped through the sides of her shoes as she marched up to the door, ready to use her electronic release for the lock box and grab the key hidden inside.

But as she mounted the two wide steps, she stopped dead in her tracks. The lock box was missing, not hooked to the handle of the giant door of the lodge as she'd left it two days earlier. Damn it. What did that mean? Her gaze took in the broad porch and she made a mental note to sweep it off before the tour began. The past few nights' storms had pushed dry leaves and pine needles onto the hundred-year-old floorboards, and the damned lazy landscape maintenance man hadn't bothered to show up...oh, hell. She spied the lock box, its handle snapped clean through, propped against a post of the porch rail.

"Son of a bitch," she muttered, now not the least bit disconcerted about her twang.

She walked to the door, turned the knob easily, and pushed on the heavy oak panels. So much for security. The door opened as softly as if the hinges had been freshly oiled.

Strange.

Frowning, she took a step inside and had the instant sensation that something was wrong.

Well, no shit! The place is open!

"Hello?" she called out, the knockoffs clicking on the polished hardwood of the foyer. Smudges of dirt and a few dry leaves marred the shine. And there was something else. A hundred-dollar bill. Big as you please. Ben Franklin staring up at her from beneath a small table near the front door. "What the devil?"

Who had been in here and dropped a C-note?

The driver of the Buick?

The person who had broken in?

Glancing up the stairway, where hand-turned rails supported a gleaming banister, she yelled, "Anybody here?"

The rambling country home was silent as a tomb.

"Hello?"

She noticed a second bill in the archway leading to the living area...and another. Three hundred dollars. She picked up each of the bills and walked into the living room, where she saw more bills, a dozen or more, lying on the floorboards but they weren't pristine. They were smudged with dirt and...*blood?*

Her heart kicked. Oh, God. That's what it was, red stains smudged over Ben Franklin's face. Then she smelled it, that coppery odor that had accompanied her father when he'd come back from a hunting trip with gutted deer or from slaughtering the pigs... Yes, that's what she smelled. Blood and urine turning acrid, to sting the nostrils with the burn of ammonia.

She took two steps farther into the living area, where she could see the floor in front of the couch.

"Oh, *God!*"

Two bodies were lying on the floor. Obviously dead. A fully dressed, plump black woman on top of a bare-assed naked Asa Pomeroy.

"Jesus, no!" Laurie cried, backing up, nearly screaming out loud. "Oh, no, no, no..." She saw the bullet holes and the blood, pooled beneath Asa and streaking down the side of the woman's face. A pearl-handled handgun was still clutched in the woman's right hand.

No, not just any woman, Laura finally realized. As her brain kicked into gear, she recognized the facial features of Gina Jefferson, the woman who'd been reported missing earlier today.

Laurie gagged.

Throughout the room, hundred-dollar bills were scattered, littering the bodies floor and couch, catching in the breeze from the open door.

Laura stumbled, turned on the thin heel of her sling back, ran for the door. She lost one of her shoes in the process. She didn't stop, nor did she lock up, just leapt off the porch and sprinted to her Lincoln.

Inside, she turned on the ignition. The Lincoln's tires sprayed gravel as she tore out. Her heart was pounding and she felt as if every hair on her head had turned instantly gray. Asa's bloated face, his mussed white hair, the stain of blood, and his hideous beached-whale, white carcass, covered with the body of Gina Jefferson.

Her stomach curdled.

"Oh, God," she whispered and scrabbled in her purse for her cell phone. She dialed 911 on the fly, not stopping at the country road, just careening onto it and nearly hitting a pickup truck loaded with live chickens as she slid over the center line.

The pickup driver laid on his horn and shook his fist, but she barely noticed as the emergency operator answered. "Nine-one-one. Police Dispatch. What's the nature of your emergency?"

"I need to report a murder. A double murder!" Laura yelled, hyperventilating, her heart pounding, feeling for all the world as if she might pass out as the Lincoln streaked down the highway. "And...oh, God...you can stop looking. I've found Asa Pomeroy and Gina Jefferson. He's dead! She's dead! Oh, God, they're both dead!" she cried, fighting the urge to puke. She cranked on the steering wheel at the next driveway, stood on the brakes, heard the thermoses slosh and the tray of fruit and pastry slam forward against the front seat. For once she didn't care, just threw open the door and leaned out, heaving up this morning's coffee.

CHAPTER 18

"Pomeroy owns this place?" Montoya asked as he surveyed the crime scene. The 911 dispatch center had notified homicide as well as the FBI of the call they'd received. The operator had managed to pull the address out of a horrified Laura Beck, the real estate agent who had found the bodies and was now down at the police station talking to Brinkman.

It was late evening and dark. Lights had been set up, and the area roped off with crime-scene tape. Crowded inside this old hunting lodge, there were not only the crime-scene investigators but agents from the local field office, the sheriff's department, and the Louisiana State Police. Also, detectives from both the Cambrai and New Orleans Police Departments had shown up earlier in the afternoon, trying to work together and stay out of each other's way.

Bonita Washington, in a no-nonsense mood, had already barked at Montoya twice, first to sign the damned log and then to don covers for his shoes. He'd done both and held his tongue while Inez Santiago measured and took pictures. Another investigator dusted while a fourth studied the blood spatter.

The old hunting lodge was being examined board by board, trace evidence collected, the victims' hands bagged, not only photographs snapped but a video recording taken as well.

Everyone was tense.

No one cracked a joke.

They knew they were dealing with another serial killer in an area that had seen far too many.

This scene was staged identically to the Gierman-LaBelle murders with the one exception that Gina Jefferson hadn't been dressed in a bridal gown. In fact, it appeared as if she was wearing exactly what she had on when she'd gone missing. Her husband, Walter, had described her navy blue pantsuit and blouse to a T.

But Asa was naked as the proverbial jaybird. Not a stitch on. The clothes he'd been wearing had been left in a wrinkled pile near the fireplace: hat, boots, slacks, jacket, and underwear. Without so much as a drop of blood on any piece of the clothing. Nope. He'd been stripped before he was killed, rather than after. Just like Gierman.

The obvious difference in this scene was that over the bodies and the surrounding flooring, hundred-dollar bills had been strewn like snowflakes.

Why?

"Take a closer look at his body," Bentz said, motioning toward Pomeroy. "Check out the tiny bruise marks on his neck, close together, the skin red."

"Stun gun?"

"That would be my guess."

"What about her?" Montoya asked, hitching his chin at the corpse of Gina Jefferson.

"None found yet."

"So our killer only pulled out the voltage for Pomeroy."

"Right. But then he's a lot bigger than the woman and might have put up more of a fight. He had a reputation for being tough."

"Not tough enough," Montoya observed, frowning as he rubbed at his goatee. "If we're talking about the same killer, and I'd put money on it, he's changing his routine. This is different from how Gierman and LaBelle were handled. No stun gun marks on their bodies. And look here." He pointed to one side of Gina Jefferson's face, where a long thin cut sliced down her cheek and blood had oozed only to dry. "This isn't the same as the first scene either."

"Maybe these two weren't as compliant as the first. Or it could be that he's honing his skills. Something didn't work as well as he'd wanted the first time, so he improved his system, pulled out the stun gun and knife."

"Or he's getting off on his victim's pain," Montoya said, not liking that train of thought.

"We're already checking on who purchased a stun gun lately; maybe by the marks on Pomeroy's throat, we can figure out the make and model."

"That would help," Montoya agreed. "So what about the weapon that killed them?"

"We think it belonged to Mrs. Jefferson's husband, Walter. A few weeks ago, he came into the station and reported one of his pearl-handled revolvers had been stolen. Two were in the gun case, only one taken. From his den, while both he and his wife were working. I've got a call in to the officer who took the report and did the follow-up, but I doubt if we get much. Weapons are stolen every day. We'll see what the officer has to say, but the husband's a real mess, doesn't want to believe that his wife is gone, blames himself for the weapon being taken, the whole nine yards. Zaroster and Brinkman have already talked to him, gotten one of his brothers to come and stay with him, just in case he's so depressed he loses it and tries to do something stupid, like off himself."

"This just gets better and better," Montoya said with more than a grain of sarcasm. He scanned the interior of the pine-paneled room and stared at the money, still left where it had fallen, while the scene was meticulously photographed. "What's with all the cash?" There had been no hundred-dollar bills, or bills of any amount, cast upon the previous scene, though there had been a lot of feathers from the pillow strapped to Gierman. No pillow here that he could see. "How much is it?"

"Near as we can tell without moving the bodies, over six grand."

Montoya whistled. "Obviously the motive wasn't money."

"I talked to Pomeroy's wife. She says Asa kept five thousand locked in the glove box of his car at all times in case he joined up with a private poker party. Kept it in one of those purple velvet Crown Royal whiskey bags. But that was just his backup wad. He usually carried another fifteen hundred or so on him, in the gold money clip she gave him for Christmas a couple of years back."

"Is the money clip here?"

Bentz shook his head.

"You figure the killer took it?"

"If the missus can be believed, he never left home without it." Bentz shot him a look. "Wives have been known to be wrong about their husbands' habits when those husbands are off-leash."

Montoya walked around the bodies, viewing the death scene from another angle. "Let's just assume the wife knows what she's talking about. So, the killer takes the money clip but leaves the cash Pomeroy had in his pocket at the scene. The killer also somehow knows about the glove box stash and includes that in our confetti here. Either Pomeroy, maybe pleading for his life, told him about his money or the killer, or someone he works with, is close enough to Pomeroy to know about the cash in the glove box."

"Until we find the car, we won't know."

"The Buick out front belong to Ms. Jefferson?" Montoya glanced at Bentz.

"Yeah." Bentz nodded. He was avoiding staring for any length of time at the victims. Montoya remembered that Bentz always had trouble keeping the contents of his stomach down whenever he visited a murder scene.

"Anything taken from her?" Montoya asked. An investigator was prying the two corpses away from each other to check for lividity and take each body's internal temperature.

"Maybe. Mr. Jefferson swears she always wears a simple gold cross, one her mother gave her years before. On a chain around her neck."

"I take it, it's not there." Montoya glanced at the two now separated bodies.

"Not that we've found."

"Bingo," Santiago said, lowering her camera. She was looking at the base of a leather ottoman and the swatch of purple fabric that was peeking from beneath it. "Bet the Crown Royal Bag is under this." She took several more shots and, using gloves, moved the ottoman, then snapped off several more shots of the floor beneath the crumpled whiskey bag.

"Looks like the wife was right this time," Montoya said as Santiago slipped the purple velvet drawstring pouch into a plastic evidence bag.

Montoya had seen enough. He didn't understand why in each case the bodies had been positioned in a way to suggest the victims were lovers. What was the point of that? Skirting the central part of the crime scene, he walked with Bentz through the front door to the porch, where an officer stood guard, the sign-in log in his hand. Headlights and klieg lights were visible through the trees; the press was still camping out. Overhead the steady whoop, whoop, whoop of helicopter blades accompanied the beam of a searchlight from a local television station.

Bentz and Montoya lingered under the porch's overhang rather than be caught by the sweep of the searchlight or the cameraman's lens. "Courtney LaBelle always wore a diamond cross, and it was left in favor of the promise ring." Bentz looked thoughtful.

"As I said, our boy ain't about money." His back to the breeze that was carrying the scent of damp earth and rain, Montoya automatically reached into his jacket pocket for his pack of cigarettes. His fingers scraped the empty pocket liner before he realized what he was doing. If Bentz noticed, he didn't comment.

"Serial killers don't do it for the money. It's about power, ego-stroking, showing off, or some kind of personal mission."

"And they don't usually cross race lines," Montoya said. "Whites kill whites, blacks kill blacks. But now, it appears we've got three white bodies, one African-American."

"Usually. Yeah." Bentz scowled and jammed his hands into his pockets. "What makes you think there's anything usual about this case? Our guy has an agenda. This isn't random. So he might not fit the profile."

"Agreed." Montoya knew that statistically serial killers were usually white, male, and somewhere in their twenties or thirties. They may have been abused; they probably had a history of childhood violence. It wasn't true in every single instance, but it was the norm. However, there was always the exception to the rule, and Montoya wondered if this guy just might be it. "It's obvious he's trying to tell us something. With the things he's taken, the way he stages the crimes. Why are the men naked, the women dressed and

lying on top? Is he showing that there's sex involved? Or is he sig-
nifying physical or psychological dominance? Why make it appear
as if the woman killed the man, then turned the gun on herself?"

"If we knew all that shit, we'd have him." Bentz scratched the
back of his neck and gazed into the surrounding darkness. Another
chopper joined the first, and arcs of blue light sliced through the
night. He glanced up at the sky. "Give me a break," he muttered.

Montoya's cell phone chirped and he answered, "Montoya."

"Hey, it's Zaroster. You aren't by any chance listening to the
radio?"

"I'm at the crime scene."

"Take a break and listen to WSLJ, *Gierman's Groaners*. It could
be that the killer's surfacing."

"Got it." Montoya was already on his way to his cruiser, long
strides tearing up the ground, Bentz at his side. The sweep of the
helicopter's light zeroed in on them, but he didn't care.

"What is it?"

"Zaroster thinks the killer's contacted the radio station."

He turned the ignition to ACC, flipped on the radio, and found
WSLJ. Maury Taylor's nasal voice was on the airwaves.

"...that's right, so I'm not sure if this is the real deal, or a fake,"
he was saying. Every muscle in Montoya's back grew taut. He
hardly dared breathe he was concentrating so hard, glaring at the
radio's digital display. "I mean it doesn't take a brain surgeon to
send a simple, and I mean *simple,* note to the station here. Any
idiot can do that. So, if you're listening, A L, I don't get it. I mean,
I know that you're trying to creep me out and all, but I'm not all
that convinced you're the real deal."

"What?" Bentz asked softly.

"I mean, I'd expect something a whole lot better than this to
prove that you're the killer. So I'm going to assume that it's a fake,
that whoever you are, A L, you're just out for your fifteen minutes.
Sorry, Pa-A L, you won't get 'em from me. So, okay, enough with
cowards and fakes, let's get down to the topic of the night: Cheating on your spouse. If you can get away with it, who does it really
hurt?"

"Son of a bitch!" Montoya hit the dashboard with his fist. "The
killer's contacted him. That scrawny-necked piece of crap!"

"Maybe the killer's contacted him, maybe not. Remember who we're dealing with. Maury Taylor would sell his soul to the devil, then renege on the deal if he got a better offer and higher ratings were involved. This could all be just a publicity stunt."

Montoya, ready to spit nails, swore again. "Damn it all to hell, I think it's time to visit our friends over at WSLJ."

"Good idea. I'd better finish up here. Call me." Bentz glanced at the dash where Montoya's fist had hit. "Careful with the car," he said, climbing out of the Crown Vic. "It's publicly owned."

"Shove it, Bentz. Get the hell out of the car so I can go throttle that little dickhead."

Bentz slid across the seat, slamming the door shut behind him.

Montoya backed up then hit the gas, tearing down the lane, only to have to slow for the cluster of vehicles at the gate. Cop cars, lights flashing, half barricaded the drive while press vans collected as close to the crime scene as possible. Vehicles from rubberneckers lined the street, and knots of people stood and stared through the open gate, hoping for a glimpse of a victim or God knew what. Montoya wished they'd all go home. "Get a life," he muttered under his breath as one woman wearing a yellow slicker barely moved out of his way. She stared after him. He wondered vaguely if the killer was among the curious and had left instructions for the cops guarding the gates to check and keep track of anyone who wanted a closer look.

Once through the tangle of vehicles, cameras, klieg lights, and humanity, Montoya hit the gas again. He gripped the wheel as if he could strangle it and listened with half an ear to the police band. As the Crown Vic's tires hit the pavement of the country road, he switched on his lights. He was nearly an hour away from the city. He planned to be there in half that time.

Up.
Down.
Up.
Down.
His muscles screamed at the punishment, but he kept persisting, going through set after set of push-ups as he listened to the remains of the Gierman program. He strained hard and sweat ran

down his naked body, along the cords of his neck, and dripped from his nose.

Up.

Down.

Up.

Down.

The disk jockey was an imbecile. An insult to the human race, a pea-brain who was awkwardly, and so obviously, attempting to lure him into exposing himself.

It didn't matter. The important thing, the only thing that mattered, was that the note had been delivered.

Though the audio reception within the basement of the hospital was sometimes difficult, tonight the radio waves were getting through; he could hear the Gierman show with perfect clarity in this—one of the padded cells where those patients who had been out of control had been contained. It was a perfect room for honing his muscles. He was just finishing his daily routine—one that had been outlined by the armed forces—a regimen of sit-ups, pull-ups, push-ups, jumping jacks, and running in place. He had one elastic band he used for resistance as well as a set of graduated weights. A bench was tucked in the far corner. He worked out each day during the airing of the Gierman show. He'd intended to not interrupt his routine, but he couldn't help himself today. He would finish later, perhaps do an extra set, but for now, he drew himself into a sitting position and crossed his ankles. Naked and sweating on the mat, his elbows resting on his knees, he picked up a towel from the floor and blotted his body as Maury Taylor, thinking himself so smooth and sly, tried to bait him.

"... it doesn't take a brain surgeon to send a simple, and I mean *simple*, note..."

"How would you know, you idiot?" he said, swiping the sweat from his face. He closed his eyes and breathed in deeply, still smelling the bleach they'd used here when the hospital had been fully operational, when *she* had been alive.

"... but I'm not all that convinced that you're the real deal."

It doesn't matter, you cretin, they *will know. The police will understand. Don't you get it? You're just the sorry little messenger.*

He'd heard enough, so he snapped off the radio, satisfied his plan was working. Refocusing, he went back to his workout, did the other seventy-five push-ups, then finished off by lifting weights for nearly an hour, until his toned muscles screamed with fatigue and he was covered with sweat again.

Picking up his towel, he walked to the bathroom, an addition that had been here since one of the later renovations to the asylum. He had rigged up one of the forgotten showers, such as it was, and knew the old nuns would never suspect someone was on the premises because there was no heat involved; no electric bill to give him away. The water came from a well on the property, so no one would be reading a water meter, and the runoff and waste from his one toilet would flow into the same septic tank that was used by the convent.

He smiled at his supreme cleverness. The plan was foolproof and no one would be the wiser that he spent so many hours a day here. If the ancient pipes groaned in the hospital above, who cared? No one walked these nearly forgotten grounds but him.

Almost no one.

She had come, hadn't she? The daughter. The one who looked so much like Faith. He sucked in his breath at the memory. Though he should have slipped away before she caught sight of him, he'd wanted to let her know that he was around, had closed the doors on the second floor of the sanitarium quietly while she was on the third floor testing the door to Faith's room. So intent was he on his task, he'd nearly been caught by the nun. Jesus, that old bag had nearly ruined everything. Nearly. He had personal reasons to dislike outwardly pious and meek Sister Maria. Upon hearing her on the stairs, he'd had to slip into 205 while the nun accosted Abby on the floor above. He'd had to think fast, realizing he'd trapped himself when he heard Abby and the nun descending. He hadn't been able to use the stairs without running into them, but he'd known that when Abby noticed the closed doors on the second floor, she would search each and every room. His only chance of not being discovered had been the fire escape, and he'd quickly slipped onto the rusted grate, barely closing the window behind him before the two women had reached the second floor.

Over the hammering of his heart, he'd heard them opening and closing doors, pacing the hallway. He'd considered hanging from the railing of the fire escape and dropping to the ground, but instead had waited breathlessly. Fortunately neither Sister Maria nor Faith's daughter had checked the window on the far end of the hall.

If they'd spied him, he would have been forced to alter his plan and that wouldn't do. Not after waiting so long for everything to be perfect.

Now, he stepped onto the moldy tiles of the shower and turned on the faucets. Cold water misted and dripped from the rusted showerhead. He sucked air through his teeth and lathered his body. He closed his eyes as he washed, his hands sliding down his own muscular frame, just as hers had so long ago . . . and had he not taken her in a shower much like this? Oh, yes . . .

In his mind's eye, he saw her as she had been. He had come to her room and gathered her up, not listening to her whispered arguments, not caring about anything but having her. He remembered being barefoot and forcing her down the steps in the middle of the night to the shower room, where he'd turned on the warm spray and pushed her up against the slick wet tiles.

Her nightgown had been drenched, molding to her perfect body, the blue nylon turning sheer and allowing him to see her big nipples—round, dark, hard disks in breasts large enough to fill his hands. Lower, beneath the nip of her waist, was her perfect nest of thick dark curls, defining the juncture of her legs through the wet nylon . . . so inviting. She smelled of sex and want.

Even now in the cold spray he felt his erection stiffening as he remembered in vivid detail how she'd gone down on her knees before him, the water drizzling over her hair and how difficult it had been to restrain himself. Only when he couldn't stand her perfect ministrations a second longer without exploding had he hoisted her up and plunged into her.

He could still taste himself in her open mouth. "Faith," he whispered, remembering her tense fingers scraping down the walls, leaving tracks on the misty tiles in her want. He recalled the way she had opened her eyes, her pupils dark, her gold irises focused on *him* just before her entire body had convulsed. She'd clung to him then, had clawed into his shoulders as she'd held back a squeal of pure, violent pleasure, her slim legs clamped around his waist, her head tossed back, exposing her throat and those wet, slick breasts, her body bucking as hot needles of water washed over them both...

Oh, Faith, I vow, I will avenge you...your torment is not forgotten.

Shuddering at the vivid memory, he let the lather run down his legs, and then twisted off the faucets. There was so much to do. He didn't bother with a towel. The bracing feel of air evaporating the moisture on his skin snapped him to the present. It helped him focus, and he needed his mind clear now more than ever.

He couldn't become careless.

Too much was at stake.

Walking down a long corridor illuminated dimly by a few lanterns he'd left burning, he opened the door to his special room, the one where all his fantasies were born and replayed. Once inside, he lit candles, watching the flickering shadows dance on the wall and on the framed picture of her sitting on the desk. Faith. Staring at him with eyes the color of pure, raw honey. How he missed her.

Deftly he opened the old secretary and found his treasures. His most recent: the fat, old man's money clip. Pure gold and in the shape of a dollar sign. "Self-involved greedy bastard," he whispered, remembering with blood-racing clarity the fear in Asa's eyes as he'd stared down the barrel of the gun. He'd been filthy, had soiled himself, had been brought down to the most basic of needs, and still had thought he could buy or barter his way out of death.

It had been exquisite pleasure to help the black woman end his life. He remembered feeling her shake so hard she nearly dropped the gun. But he'd helped her, forced her finger to pull the trigger, watched the blooming surprise and horror cross Asa's face. Only when he'd been certain the old man had breathed his last, rattling breath had he forced her to turn the gun on herself. Oh, the joy in that...feeling her fear palpitating between them, knowing that she was praying to God even as the gun blasted!

Now, he fingered her necklace, holding it up in front of his eyes, letting the tiny gold cross dangle before him as it caught the candlelight. "You did the world a favor by killing him," he said, as if Gina Jefferson could hear him.

But the world didn't know it yet. Didn't even know that Asa Pomeroy and Gina Jefferson had breathed their last. Soon, though, the news would break, the police would scurry around, and plans would be made to bury the bodies.

Could he risk going to the ceremony for Gina Jefferson? The cop, Montoya, would be there, no doubt, pretending to pray, and all the while snapping shots of the grieving crowd just as he had at the virgin's candlelight vigil. He'd seen Montoya in the crowd, holding the camera and clicking off photographs, and yet he'd lingered, couldn't stop himself from watching the mourners, feeling their grief, his own body thrumming with the power of life and the pure knowledge that he was the one behind it all. It was he who had brought them to their knees. He who had meted out the perfect punishment.

The virgin had been the first.

The philanthropist the second.

But he was just getting started and he felt anticipation sizzle through his blood when he thought of the third...

CHAPTER 19

Montoya slid his cruiser into a no-parking zone, stood on the brakes, and switched off the ignition in one swift motion. Blood pounding at his temples, he stormed inside the building near Jackson Square that housed WSLJ.

Ignoring a pretty woman with coffee-colored skin and corn rows who sat behind the reception desk, he headed straight down the hall.

"Wait a minute." From the corner of his eye he saw her look up from her computer. "May I help you?"

Montoya kept walking.

"Sir, sir, you can't go down there!"

He heard the click of high heels as if she intended to physically stop him. Digging out his badge, he flashed it behind him and kept walking so fast he was nearly jogging.

"Officer, please!"

The inside of the building was a rabbit warren, but he'd been here before. He homed in on the glassed-in studio with its lights warning ON AIR. Through the window he saw the weasel, headset on, seated at a console, talking to everyone who was tuned into this edition of *Gierman's Groaners*. Disregarding the illuminated sign, Montoya yanked open the door, strode into the room, and glared at the skinny, balding disk jockey whose claim heretofore had been Luke Gierman's ass-licker. "You stupid, dumb son of a bitch!" Montoya growled, not caring that all of greater New Orleans and the surrounding parishes could hear him on their radios.

"Oh, look, what we've got here—a visit from New Orleans's finest!" Maury said. He was smiling broadly, as if he'd known Montoya would show. "Officer, to what do I owe the honor of—"

Montoya keyed in on the main power switch and slapped it. Lights blinked off and Maury's mouth fell open. "Hey! You can't do that!" Maury was beside himself, pressing buttons, reaching for the main switch.

"You've withheld evidence in a murder case and I'm taking your sorry ass downtown—"

"What the hell's going on here?" A big black woman strode into the room and he recognized her instantly as Eleanor Cavalier, the tough take-no-prisoners program manager for the station. "Detective, this program has to go on the air! Pronto." She shot Maury a look. "Turn it on. Go to commercial. There is to be no dead air. *No dead air!*"

Maury, looking for all the world like the cat who swallowed the canary, smirked at Montoya and turned on the appropriate switches.

"What the hell is this all about?" Eleanor demanded. As a crowd gathered around her, she spied Samantha Leeds, better known as Dr. Sam, the radio psychologist whose program *Midnight Confessions* aired later in the evening. "Samantha, take over the booth and handle the controls. You don't have to say much, just run the tape of a previous show for a few minutes."

Dr. Sam nodded, and there was a glint of amusement in her eyes. Walking into the studio, she whispered to Montoya, "Still getting into trouble, I see."

"Always."

She slid into the booth and Maury handed over the headset, then rammed a faded Saints hat onto his bald pate and ambled into the hallway, hands in his pockets as if he were taking a stroll along the Mississippi on a sunny summer afternoon.

Montoya glared at the man as Samantha settled onto the

barstool, flipped a few switches and adjusted the mike. She was already speaking to the audience as Maury finally found his way into the corridor.

"Your boy here is withholding evidence in a murder investigation," Montoya told Eleanor before the door to the sound booth shut.

"And you're breaking more than your share of laws yourself, starting with parking in the no-zone, then ending up with I don't know how many FCC violations." Uncowed, Eleanor Cavalier took a step toward Montoya. "Don't you flash your badge around here and bully your way around this station, got it? If you've got a problem with what's happening here, you can damned well talk to me or the station's lawyers." She turned furious black eyes on Maury. "Now what the hell were you thinkin'? I heard what Montoya's talking about and he's got a point. So, let's get down to it." She looked up, noticed the small crowd that had gathered, and said, "The show's over, people. Everyone get back to work." Her perfect eyebrows slammed together and she glared at each and every person who had made the mistake of letting their curiosity take them from their jobs.

They all scuttled away like bugs from beneath a rock. Satisfied with their reaction, Eleanor trained her fury on Montoya again. Her voice was steel as she said, "We'll talk in my office."

She motioned for Montoya and Maury Taylor to follow her, then led them to a small office where every book, recording, and file was in its place. On the desk was a brass paperweight in the shape of two golf balls . . . someone's idea of a joke.

"What have you got?" She skewered the smaller man with a glare as she rounded the desk and dropped into her chair, the seat creaking a bit.

"I got a note. Well, the station did. Addressed to Luke. Maybe from the killer." Maury shrugged. He and Montoya were standing like boys called to the principal's office. "But it could be a fake."

Her lips barely moved. "Get it."

He was gone for less than a minute and returned with a small white piece of paper and matching envelope encased in a plastic sandwich bag. Somewhat less recalcitrant, he handed the package to Montoya. "All it says is 'Repent' and then it's signed A L, both letters in capitals. I touched it, yeah, when I opened it, but when I figured it might be important, I was careful to put it where no one else would find it. I used a copy when I was on the air."

"Jesus, Maury, don't you have a brain?" Eleanor demanded. "Why didn't you tell me about this?"

"I'd just opened it before I went on the air."

"Right." She glowered from her chair.

"You should have called the department immediately," Montoya said.

"Hey, I'm tellin' ya. I just got it before I went on," the DJ insisted, but Montoya knew BS when he heard it. "I figured it wouldn't hurt to use it, might ratchet up listener interest, you know, maybe even flush the guy out."

Montoya wanted to throttle the twerp. "Don't for a second think you can 'play cop' on this. This is a police matter, and if you've screwed up my investigation, I'll see your ass in jail so fast, your head'll spin."

"You hear that, Eleanor? He's threatening me." Maury turned to his boss, some of his bravado slipping.

"I heard it. And I agree with the detective. You are *not*—do you read me?—*not* to mess with any police matters. And you"—she turned to Montoya, pointing a long, accusing finger—"have no right to bust in here like Wyatt Damned Earp. There is protocol to be observed, Detective, and I expect you to follow it. Don't think I'm not going to call your superior."

A muscle worked in Montoya's jaw. "Then make sure everyone here at the station follows that protocol you're so proud of," he growled.

She glared at him, her lips flattening. He saw he'd just stepped over a very thin line, but he didn't care. Let the brass call him on the carpet. Big deal. It wasn't as if he hadn't already worn a hole in it.

Taking the new evidence with him, he left the radio station and hoped to hell that whatever else that chicken-necked, dumb-ass radio jockey had done, he hadn't fucked over the investigation.

Zoey strapped on her seat belt and silently cursed the fact that, with the exorbitant amount of money she was spending on this airline ticket, a red-eye with a four-hour layover in Dallas, she'd ended up in the middle seat with a woman and an infant next to her on the window side, and a guy over six feet and topping the scales near three hundred—on the aisle side. The big guy couldn't get comfortable no matter how hard he tried. Every time he squirmed, his arm brushed Zoey's, and even though she wasn't a germophobe or anything, she just didn't like strangers touching her. Period.

She was even suspect of the blanket and pillow she'd found wedged between seats 13 A and B on her way down the aisle. But she needed to sleep and she hoped to hell that whoever had used the cheap bedding before her wasn't infected with lice, or cooties, or some major strain of flu or worse.

She had her iPod with her and figured she'd zone out for the trip. She needed to relax as much as possible, considering what she was going to face when she landed. All hell was gonna break loose. Able to read her sister like a book, Zoey knew Abby would flip out of control when she finally heard the truth.

Yep, this book was going to end bad, Zoey thought with a grimace. No two ways about it. From the phone call the other night Zoey had figured out right away that Abby wasn't interested in having her come visit or show up at Luke's funeral, but that was tough. It was time.

Zoey put stock in omens, curses, signs, and luck, and all the signs that she relied on had pointed to the fact that her secret had to be released. She felt that if not God, then the Fates were watching over her and would give her clues as to what she was supposed to do with her life. Other people often initiated the signs, just as Luke Gierman had all those years earlier, when he'd told her he couldn't stop thinking about her, that he'd had some cosmic revelation that forced him to follow her to her car on that warm May afternoon.

Though Zoey prided herself in recognizing bull when she heard it, she'd let Luke ramble on and on—finding him incredibly fascinating all over again. They'd been lovers before. She knew his chart by heart and realized that the planets were aligned for their union. *That* had been the sign—that and her own nightly dreams of making love to him . . . or at least that's how she'd rationalized it at the time. Even though she'd known he was engaged to her sister by then, that he'd promised himself to Abby, she'd been powerless to resist Luke.

Zoey had never felt good about herself since.

And now it was time to make it up to her baby sister.

Hadn't her personal astrologer recently told her that the heavenly bodies were situated in the perfect order? That now was the time to right past wrongs? Hadn't he hinted about the familial torment that had existed for two decades? Hadn't he suggested that now, before the stars shifted, she make amends?

And if the astrological viewpoint wasn't enough, there had been that other very strong sign: a recent anonymous letter. No return address. Block letters. Postmarked in New Orleans. It read:

COME HOME. HANNAH NEEDS YOU.

Now, that was a pretty clear sign. Had Abby sent it and was she ashamed to sign her name? Had she referred to herself by her middle name, the one their mother sometimes called her? The name of their maternal grandmother? Or had someone else sent the letter, someone who knew Abby well enough to use her middle name?

The final sign, completing the triad, was Luke's murder. How could she possibly ignore it?

Two things were certain.

It was time to return to New Orleans.

And it was time for the truth.

It had been twenty years since their mother had plunged to her death, and Zoey was sick to the back teeth of holding on to the secret she and her father had shared.

No more.

Abby was a big girl. She could handle the past. Hadn't she been trying to sort it out by herself? Going to the hospital on her own, wasn't that another sign that she was healing? And the insinuations Abby had made...

...we can talk about a lot of things before we have that drink, okay? Including Mom and the day she died. I think you know more about it than you've ever said... We're going to discuss it...

But now, Zoey second-guessed herself, something she rarely did. There was a pretty good chance that she should have come clean on the phone the other night, but she'd really thought it would be best to see her sister face to face before unloading the truth about the past.

At least she hoped she was making the right decision.

Zoey crossed her fingers, sent up a quick prayer to God, then asked the Fates to keep pointing her in the right direction, to help her be certain that she was making the right choice on this one.

The door to the plane closed and the flight attendants asked everyone to turn off his or her electronic devices before the jet pushed out of the gate. The big man next to her clicked off his cell phone and struggled to place it in his bag under the seat.

"Sorry," he muttered as he shoved things around and continued to brush against her.

She flashed him a smile that she didn't feel but her mind was on what she would face when she landed.

She couldn't believe Luke was really dead. Murdered, no less. A college coed had been killed with him. How sick.

Zoey had been keeping up with the reports and had called friends at a sister station in New Orleans who were convinced that the police didn't have any leads yet. Then there was this business with Asa Pomeroy, Abby's neighbor. What the hell was that all about? This morning she'd heard another woman was missing: an African-American community leader had seemed to have vanished. Though she wasn't certain, Zoey thought she'd heard the name before, a long time ago.

Gina Jefferson. Why did that name sound so familiar?

From the amount of information Zoey had gleaned on the Internet this morning, Gina Jefferson was a big deal in New Orleans, a woman who worked behind the scenes rather than in front, but who had gained recognition for her efforts supporting the mentally ill.

Was that it? Zoey wondered as the jet lumbered toward the runway. She thought hard, digging her teeth into her lower lip. Had Gina Jefferson somehow worked at Our Lady of Virtues or in private practice with her mother? Could that be? A social worker maybe?

A headache began to pound behind her eyes as the plane eased into position, then began to pick up speed, its engines roaring. Faster and faster, the jet tore down the runway and Zoey was pressed hard into her seat as the 737 lifted off, cutting into the darkness of the heavens and leaving Sea-Tac with its blaze of lights far below.

It would be worth it, she thought, a relief to finally put the past to rest. That was what Abby had wanted, wasn't it? Hadn't her sister said she needed to learn the truth and deal with it once and for all?

Jesus H. Christ, if Abby only knew what she was asking!

She will, Zoey, and soon. Steel yourself.

This ain't gonna be pretty.

Montoya drove through the pouring rain. His jaw was clenched. It had been hours since he'd dealt with that lowlife worm Maury Taylor, but he was still seething. He'd dropped the note off at the lab, then reviewed everything with Bentz and Zaroster that they knew about the four murders. Which hadn't added up to squat.

No news on the bridal dress yet.

No prints at the first scene, or on Luke Gierman's BMW, or Gina Jefferson's Buick, that could be identified outside family members or friends.

Asa Pomeroy's car hadn't yet been located.

No trace evidence that would help in locating the suspect ... at least not yet.

Size twelve boot prints at both scenes. The manufacturer had been contacted and was preparing a list of retailers who carried the common hiking boot.

Cell phones and personal phone records were being checked but so far had given up nothing.

The pictures he'd taken at the candlelight vigil were being pored over by the task force.

The black hair on the wedding gown was male and was now with the DNA lab. However, until they had something to match the markers against, it wouldn't mean much. Unless they got lucky.

Montoya sighed, turning over in his mind what he knew so far.

Each set of victims had been killed with the female victim's gun, then the scene was staged to approximate a murder-suicide. "Approximate" was the right word because it wasn't done well enough to fool the police. The killer probably knew that. He was toying with them, giving them a clue to his twisted game; Montoya just didn't understand it yet.

Then there was the note. If it proved valid, it suggested that Luke Gierman, to whom the envelope was addressed, was being instructed to "repent." One single word. And then the signature: A L. Who the hell was that? The department was searching databases and going over the notes from every interview taken on the two cases. Was it someone named Al, or Allen, or Aldren, or Alfred, or Alice . . . or was it initials? Everyone in the department had tossed out ideas, Bentz pointing out that two of the victims were Asa and Luke, and their first name initials could spell A L. Then there was the thought that it might mean Alabama. Maybe the killer had resided or had been born there. Turn the initials around and the other state abbreviation would be for Louisiana, their home state. Or how about LA, Brinkman had offered up, Los Angeles. "Tons of freakoids out there, let me tell ya. All that smog. Fries their brains."

Jesus, would the guy ever get serious?

A couple of the other detectives thought it might well be a hoax, but Montoya wasn't buying that. The single word, "repent," seemed somehow connected.

There was something religious going on here, he thought, otherwise why bother with the stolen cross . . . *but he didn't take the Virgin Mary's, did he?*

Hell.

At least it seemed Maury Taylor hadn't lied about no one touching the note but him; his were the only prints found on the single sheet of paper. There were others on the envelope, of course, and they were being checked against the letter carriers', but that was a time-consuming job. All the prints had been sent to AFIS and the glue under the flap of the envelope checked for DNA. If there was any, they would see if it matched the DNA of the black hair on the wedding dress.

Gina Jefferson and Asa Pomeroy's next of kin had been notified. Wally Jefferson had collapsed. The fourth Mrs. Pomeroy had taken it all in good stride, as had each of Asa's children. Not a particularly loving bunch, the Pomeroys, Montoya decided. All of the people interviewed had "no idea" who would want to harm the king of weaponry, the poster boy for the NRA; ditto for Gina Jefferson, who in comparison was a saint.

Black and white.

Yin and yang again...

But someone had wanted them dead. Some unknown enemy.

Someone inherently evil and incredibly dangerous.

Someone who killed people who were as different as night to day.

Someone far too close to Abby Chastain to make him feel comfortable. He scowled into the night, staring at the blurry taillights of the car in front of him. He'd been thinking about Abby a lot lately. Too much.

She was definitely starting to get under his skin. Smart, pretty, sexy—she was a woman who made others pale by comparison. He loved the deep throaty sound of her laughter, and the way her eyes rounded when he said something she didn't expect. He found himself thinking of her not as a witness or potential suspect, or even the ex-wife of a victim, but as a woman. Which was just plain stupid. He couldn't let her get to him. For all he knew, she could be involved in her ex-husband's death. It was a long shot, yeah, and he didn't believe it for a second, but he had to stay impartial, sharp, willing to look at all the angles and possibilities. So, too bad if she just happened to be hotter than hell.

Pushing thoughts of her from his head, he drove steadily toward his house, watching the wipers swish the rain from his windshield. He slowed as a traffic light glowed amber, then brilliant red, reflecting on the shiny, wet pavement. Two pedestrians, laughing and wearing cheap ponchos, jogged through puddles to the opposite side of the street.

His cell phone rang and he picked it up without looking at caller ID. "Montoya."

"Where do you get off breaking all kinds of policy and going on a personal rampage at the radio station?" Melinda Jaskiel, the D.A., demanded. Before he could answer, she added, "It's a damned good thing that Eleanor Cavalier is a personal friend of mine or your ass, as they say, would damned well be grass."

The light turned green and he stepped on it.

"Montoya, do not, and I repeat, do *not* screw up my case! We're going to nail this bastard and I don't want any high-profile defense attorney looking for his personal shot at fame to have any excuse to have evidence tossed because some cocky, hot-tempered detective messed it up. Do I make myself clear?"

"Loud and," he muttered, furious with himself, with the investigation, with the whole damned world.

"Good. Remember this." She hung up and he could still feel her seething through the phone.

"Goddamned son of a bitch," he muttered under his breath. He knew she was right, but it pissed him off just the same. Then again, everything about this case pissed him off. And he knew why. It all had to do with Abby Chastain. Each time he left her, he wanted to return. The other night with the bad pizza and so-so wine, it had been hard to peel himself away from her.

He'd found himself fantasizing about her, wanting her, thinking about wrapping his arms around her, saying to hell with the whole damned world, and kissing her so hard neither one of them would be able to think straight. He thought about stripping off her clothes, his thumbs skimming those breasts he'd only caught a glimpse of, kissing her throat, then tangling his fingers in that wild mass of red-blond hair as he ran his tongue downward.

His imagination ran wild: he saw himself tumbling into bed with her, both of them half-dressed, both so hot they were sweating and eager. He wanted to feel her anxious fingers on his skin as he thrust into her, not giving one good goddamn what anyone thought.

"Shit," he muttered, so caught in the fantasy that he almost missed his street. He gave himself a quick mental shake, forcing thoughts of the woman out of his mind as he parked in front of his house, a camelback shotgun that sat amid others that were identical. He'd bought the narrow house this last year and flat-out loved the shoe box design. He'd even taken to tinkering around it, fixing the porch, painting, adding some wrought iron, all that domestic crap he'd eschewed in his earlier years.

His home was painted pale blue, nestled into a pod of pastel colors that suited him just fine. He walked inside, tossed his keys onto a side table, picked up the remote, and turned on his television. Stripping out of his jacket, he walked through the connecting living room, den, and eating area to the kitchen, near the back of the house. He'd poured a lot of energy, elbow grease, and money into the rundown unit but it had been worth it, giving him an outlet, a way to work off energy from the stress of his job as well as give him a project to fill the few hours he had off with something constructive.

It had helped him get over Marta.

Throwing his heart and soul into the century-old boards, lath, and plaster of this railroad car of a home he had managed to firmly put the past behind him.

Grabbing a beer from the refrigerator, he twisted off the top while kicking the fridge's door closed. Now, his thoughts were about Abby Chastain. Abby and the case that had brought them together. A case that had taken the lives of four people, all from different walks of life.

Montoya rubbed his face, then took a swallow.

The suspect list was growing, but most of them were discounted the minute their names came up. He was still leaning toward Nia Penne's current live-in. Roy North was the right size and had black hair. His feet were size twelves, but his alibis were ironclad, unless Nia was covering up for her lover. So far, the police had no proof that Roy had been anywhere near Luke Gierman or All Saints College. And what would Roy or Nia have to do with Asa Pomeroy and Gina Jefferson? Nonetheless, Montoya wanted DNA from the guy. If a judge couldn't be convinced to issue a warrant, then maybe he'd have someone follow North, try to pick up a tossed cigarette butt or coffee cup or something with the guy's DNA on it, enough to compare it to the black hair found at the first scene and the saliva, if there was some, that would be collected from the envelope sent to WSLJ.

He took a pull from his bottle, then walked into the living room, where the news of Asa Pomeroy's and Gina Jefferson's murders was on every channel. The stations were talking about a serial killer stalking the streets of New Orleans again, and not only the public information officer for the police department, but also someone from the FBI, gave statements and took a few quick questions, all the while holding back information that only the killer would know about the murders, hoping to weed out the invariable nut jobs who pretended to be the sick-o called the station to "confess" and got off on the fame.

Sipping his beer as he watched, he knew that somewhere the killer, too, was glued to a television screen, reveling in the havoc he'd wreaked and the media and police department's attention. That's what it was all about: stroking a killer's damned twisted ego.

And the bastard would do it over and over again for the high, the rush of feeling superior, of dominating, and killing, then dancing away from it all.

"I'll get you, you sick son of a bitch," Montoya vowed. He drained his long-necked bottle. It might be far-fetched but he still believed the old hospital was somehow connected to what was going on. It was too late to call his aunt tonight. She didn't even have a phone in her room. First thing tomorrow morning, he'd dial her up and find out if she knew of any connection between Asa Pomeroy, Gina Jefferson, and Our Lady of Virtues.

In the meantime, despite his promises to himself, he snagged up his car keys again, threw on his jacket, and headed out the door into the wet night. Someone had to tell Abby Chastain that her neighbor had been murdered.

He decided he was the best man for the job.

CHAPTER 20

Abby couldn't believe what she was seeing and hearing on her television.

Asa Pomeroy and Gina Jefferson were *dead?* Killed in the same manner as Luke and Courtney LaBelle?

Sitting on the edge of her couch, staring at the screen, she felt sick inside. How could this be happening? What kind of lunatic was stalking the streets of New Orleans and making his way clear out here, far from the city?

The reporters kept speculating and talking, showing exterior shots of a hunting lodge owned by Asa Pomeroy, the latest crime scene. From there they flashed to the Pomeroy estate, just down the road from her, before panning on the Crescent City Center, a small mental health clinic that helped the poor and the homeless.

Something inside Abby pricked and prodded at her brain... Gina Jefferson worked for a mental health clinic. Had she once been a member of the staff at Our Lady of Virtues? Was that why the black woman with the even features seemed familiar? Or was it because, like Asa Pomeroy's, Gina's face and deeds had been a part of the local news for years?

Nervously she plucked at the arm of the couch, playing with the gold chenille pile without realizing what she was doing. What was it about the mental health worker she should remember?

As if a window were open, a sudden chill swept through Abby, cutting to the marrow of her bones. Something tugged at her memory, something important, but she couldn't quite latch on to it. The thought was just out of reach.

Yet she knew instinctively that it had to do with her mother and Our Lady of Virtues... *What was it?*

She glanced outside to the dark night and tamped down the sensation that someone was watching her, that deep in the thicket of oak, swamp berry, and buckthorn were hidden eyes, that something or someone malicious was peering into her house and studying her every move. "Stop it," she admonished. Still, she climbed to her bare feet and snapped every blind shut so tightly no light escaped. Now, no one would be able to see more than her silhouette on the blinds.

For once the dog was sleeping on her favorite spot on a rug near the cold, blackened fireplace. Ansel lay curled on the back of the couch. The cat's eyes were closed and he was purring softly, unaware of the turmoil Abby couldn't shake as she returned to the living room and flipped through the channels. She saw more of the same scenes: a helicopter shot from the air of the hunting lodge, taken before night had fallen, and another image of the old cabin where Luke and Courtney LaBelle had been found. Pictures of all the victims alive and smiling were shown and short bios reported, including the fact that Gina Jefferson had publicly harangued Pomeroy Industries, and Asa Pomeroy personally, for not giving enough to the needy, especially those with mental problems.

The two, according to the media, had often been at odds over Pomeroy's stingy nature.

Vanessa Pomeroy, a petite, perky woman, not a hair out of place, nor a tear in her eye, chatted easily about "the tragedy" of her husband's death. On the other hand, Walter Jefferson, so distraught and grief-stricken that he had to be propped up by a relative, was clearly undone, his face awash in tears.

"The poor man," Abby whispered and clicked to another channel, where the Reverend Billy Ray Furlough was standing in the middle of a crowd on the steps of his church. It was still daylight on the tape, so this scene, too, had been shot earlier in the day. The tape rolled and Abby, curled into a corner of the couch, watched in utter fascination as the charismatic preacher turned the horror of the day into his own personal revival meeting. He ranted and raved, gesticulated wildly, and prayed with a pious sincerity that could melt even the most stubborn atheist's icy heart. A natural-born public speaker, the Reverend Billy Ray had literally found his calling.

"Why is this happening?" he asked rhetorically as he faced the camera. "Why is God striking down some of our finest citizens?" A tall, good-looking man, with broad shoulders and a firm physique, he was somewhere in his late thirties, Abby guessed. Charisma practically oozed from him, with his clear skin, brown eyes, gleaming straight black hair, and white teeth that flashed disarmingly when he found the camera's eye. He wore his clerical collar with pride rather than humility and there was something about him that also seemed familiar, something she couldn't name, something that caused the hairs on the back of her arms to prickle.

"Perhaps we should not question God's wisdom. Let us not forget that God helps those who help themselves, and in our hour of grief, our time of tragedy, let us reach out to the Lord and tell him, 'Yes, Father, I will trust in you.'"

She flipped the channel, bothered by the display. It was almost as if the preacher were capitalizing on the tragedies, hoping that through his downplayed showmanship he could entice more people into his fold, more dollars into his church's coffers.

Don't go there, Abby. Who are you to judge?

Hershey's head lifted. She gave out a "woof" and Abby heard the sound of a car's engine as it approached. "Now what?" she wondered and again felt the uneasy sensation that had been with her for most of the evening. Padding to the front windows, she tilted one slat of the thin blinds and peeked through. Montoya's black Mustang slowed to a stop in front of her garage.

Good, she thought, relieved to see him slide from behind the wheel and slam the car door shut. Her heart did a quick little flip, which she completely ignored, but she couldn't stop a smile from curving across her face. Watching him, she noted again how his jacket stretched over his shoulders, the way his hips nearly rolled with his long, athletic stride, and how his jeans fit snugly but hung low on his hips. For once, his black hair was mussed and he shoved it out of his face as he climbed the two short steps and into the illumination of the porch light. Lines of strain were visible on his face, and his jaw was set in steely determination. Deep in his goatee, the razor-sharp line of his lips, drawn downward, gave him a stern, don't-mess-with-me expression that didn't bode well.

The minute he rang her bell, Hershey went nuts. Abby threw open the door and folded her arms over her chest. "Surprise, surprise," she said. "If it isn't Detective Montoya."

"I know." His mouth lost some of its hard edge. "I'm making a habit of this. Sorry." Was it her imagination or did his brown eyes grow even darker with the night?

"I don't remember complaining," she said, then mentally kicked herself for sounding so eager.

One of his black eyebrows cocked.

And she couldn't help herself as she gestured him into the house. "I figure you're just out here hoping for more of my fantastic home cooking."

"Yeah, that's it." Some of the tension eased out of his face, and he looked past her to the living room, where the television was still blaring the news of Asa Pomeroy and Gina Jefferson's murders. He stepped inside and Abby shut the door behind him. "So you do know about Pomeroy."

"It's awful."

"Amen." He walked to the set, standing not five inches from it, and stared at the screen. "Bastard."

"You'll catch him." She flipped the dead bolt. "Right?"

Montoya glanced up at her, his dark eyes deadly serious. "Damned straight."

"Well, do it soon, okay?"

"That's the plan."

From the couch, Ansel opened an eye, saw the stranger, and was instantly on his feet, back arched and looking as if he'd just stuck his tail into an electric socket. The tabby hissed, then sprang to the floor. With his tail drooping behind him, he slunk swiftly out of the room. "Not a fan of mine," Montoya observed.

"Of anyone else, save myself."

Montoya actually cracked a smile. "Have you tried Prozac? I'm serious. One of the beat cops was going crazy with her cat spraying and refusing to use the litter box, and she put the stupid thing on some kind of antidepressant."

"You're kidding."

He held up a palm. "God's honest truth."

"So, now you want me to get a fiercer dog and a sweeter-tempered, mellower cat?"

"I think any cat would fill the bill."

"Hear that, Ansel? The cop thinks you need to be replaced," she said, turning her head toward the hallway, where Ansel had disappeared. She smiled. "I think I'll stick with the pets I have, all the same." To reinforce her stand, she bent over and scratched Hershey behind her ears. "Yeah, baby, you have *nothing* to worry about." Glancing up at the detective, she added, "Loyalty. It's my thing." She saw something change in his eyes, a sobering, and she knew in an instant what he was thinking.

"Uh-oh," she warned. "Don't go there. The answer to the question cutting through your brain is yes, I was loyal to my ex. Disgustingly so. I said 'I do' and I meant forever, but in all those vows, you know, sickness, health, good times and bad, never once did I say, 'No matter how many affairs you have, I'll stick it out. It's okay. I forgive you.'" The minute she said the last three words, she felt a slight change in the atmosphere, and she remembered her recurring dream, the one where her mother, before she died, always whispered, "I forgive you." All Abby's lightheartedness fled into the darkest corners of the room.

"Something wrong?" Montoya asked and she jerked, brought back to the present, to the man with the searching dark eyes and protective manner. She yearned for that protection.

"Are you kidding?" She tried to make light of it, but her attempts fell flat. "A madman is running around the area, killing people, including my ex and my neighbor for starters, and I've got a detective checking up on me regularly. Lots of things are wrong."

"But it's good I come here."

"Yes...yes, it is." She swallowed and looked away from his intense gaze. "Come on into the kitchen and I'll buy you a beer...I assume you're off duty."

"Until tomorrow morning unless I get the call."

"What call?"

"That our guy has struck again." He was stone-cold sober.

"So soon?" What a horrible thought! She glanced at the television screen, saw the exterior of Asa's hunting lodge again, and silently prayed the terror would end soon.

"It wasn't that long between the two sets of murders. This killer doesn't seem to have much of a cooling-off period between attacks, and oftentimes serial killers escalate."

"Serial killers," she repeated, a shiver chasing down her spine. "Maybe this one's finished. Maybe whatever it was he felt compelled to do is now complete."

He sent her a look that spoke volumes. She saw her words as wishful thinking. He knew otherwise.

In the kitchen, she opened the refrigerator and dug out two bottles of Lone Star, cracked them both open, and handed one to Montoya. Ansel, hiding on one of the bar stools at the counter and frightened all over again, hopped to the floor and made a quick beeline down the hall.

"An improvement," Montoya observed. "No hissing."

"He's *really* warming up to you. Watch out if you sit on the couch—he'll probably hop onto the back and lick your hair."

"Something to look forward to," he said dryly.

Abby grinned at his look of disgust. "Actually, Ansel would never—but my girlfriend Alicia's purebred Siamese was really into it. Always wanted to 'groom' her."

"I'd say the cat has a few screws loose. Or maybe it was into the kind of gel or shampoo she used."

"Well, I guess we all have our personal idiosyncrasies," Abby murmured, far too conscious of the way Montoya's presence filled a room.

"Some more than others," he agreed.

They returned to the living room, where on the screen again, Billy Ray Furlough was ranting on about the wrath of the Lord and how everyone had to look inside him or herself to help stop the poor, demented soul who was committing these crimes against God and man.

"Can you believe this guy?" Montoya pointed at the screen with the index finger of his beer-holding hand. "He's already called the department several times. Wants to meet with the lieutenant and the detectives in charge to pray for divine intervention."

"So much for the 'God helps those who help themselves' theory that I heard him spouting a little while ago." She walked closer to the set. The preacher stared straight at the camera and offered a bold smile, one that suggested he was a strong leader in the face of adversity. "Hasn't his church been investigated by the SEC or the IRS or something?" she asked, trying to remember.

"Maybe, I don't know. He's pretty much off-limits, though, being the head of a religious organization. Believe me, he's buried so deep in tax lawyers, accountants, spin doctors, and I'd guess, makeup artists and hairstylists that it would take a backhoe to try and find him." He took a swallow from his bottle. "Just my opinion, though. I'm not speaking for the department." He rubbed thoughtfully at his goatee. "Odd thing though—I think his organization tried to buy the Our Lady of Virtues property."

Abby felt that whisper of fear, cold as death, scrape the back of her neck again as she sat in one corner of the couch, he on the other end.

"Along with a lot of other businesses and moguls, including Asa Pomeroy."

"Wait a minute...Asa Pomeroy? What? Did he expect to construct a munitions factory next to the convent?" she asked in disbelief.

"I think he wanted the entire piece of property, convent and all. And I'm not certain it was for a factory. It didn't matter. The nuns balked and the archdiocese passed on the offer."

"Why haven't I heard of this before?"

"I hadn't either. It happened a few years back," Montoya explained. "I only found out earlier today as I've been checking on the victims. Pomeroy seems to have a fascination with the place, though, mind you, he was an elder with the First Baptist Church in Cambrai. Makes you wonder why he donated so much money to the hospital while it was open. He's not exactly known for his philanthropy. I figure maybe he knew someone who worked there or was a patient."

"Like Gina Jefferson?" she said, trying to remember. "It's odd, but I have this feeling..." She frowned, forced her mind back to the day her mother died and the weeks before. "I think she might have been employed at the hospital."

Montoya ignored his beer and his facial muscles tightened. "I'll check it out."

"You think it's important?"

"Could be. Any connection between the victims will help us understand what's going on, who might be behind all this"—he gestured toward the television—"crap."

"Do you think there's some connection to the hospital?" she asked. "I mean, Clyde LaBelle was a doctor there, Asa gave money, Gina Jefferson may have worked on the premises..."

She felt his gaze upon her.

"What about Luke?"

She shook her head and tucked her feet under her. "That's where it all falls apart. Luke's only connection that I know of is that my mother was a patient—and died—there."

There was a moment of silence between them, then Montoya said, "I guess we'll just have to keep digging." He watched Hershey settle onto her spot by the unlit fire and suddenly asked, "Can we light that?" He indicated the dry stack of wood sitting in the grate. And then, as if he felt the need to explain himself, he added, "I've never had a house with a fireplace."

"Sure." She climbed off the couch, found the long, tapered barbecue lighter that she always used, flicked on the flame, then touched it to the paper and dry kindling beneath the chunks of pine and oak.

The paper caught quickly and the kindling, bone dry, snapped and sparked, hungry flames eagerly licking the dry wood.

"Oh, damn." Smoke began to billow and boil into the house and she reached quickly over the flames to pull the lever on the flue. With a rush, the fire burned more brightly and the smoke was sucked up the chimney. "Sorry," she said, feeling like an idiot, "I always do that."

"Are you okay?"

"No third-degree burns or singed eyebrows this time," she said and laughed. "Just this." She showed off the black soot on her fingers. "Give me a sec and I'll wash up."

It took longer than a second but she managed to clean the oily, black film from her hands, scatter some crackers onto a platter, and slice up some cheese, carefully cutting off a little mold from the end of the brick. When she returned, Montoya had kicked off his boots and was staring at the fire.

"Sustenance," she said. "Such as it is."

"Looks great."

"Well...it looks decent." She set the platter on the coffee table and took up her seat on the couch again.

Montoya grinned. "Beyond decent." Sitting low on his back, he cradled his beer between both hands and asked, "So did Luke know anyone named Al?"

"Al? Probably. Doesn't everyone?" When he didn't respond, she said, "Okay...let me think. He must have. Wait. Yeah. There was someone in college, someone I never met. Alan...Alan..." She snapped her fingers in rapid succession, thinking hard. "Oh, what was that guy's name? O'Brian! Yeah, Alan O'Brian. I think they might have been in the same fraternity. He lives...somewhere in the Northeast, maybe Boston now. I don't think Luke kept up with him. They both went to the University of Washington."

"Okay."

He seemed to be waiting for more, so Abby thought hard. "Oh, yeah. Later, Luke had a sailing buddy who owned a boat that he docked on Lake Union in Seattle. His name was Andrew Allen and I think some people called him Al or Allen, but Luke always referred to him as Drew."

Montoya rotated his bottle between his palms "What about you?"

"Do I know any people named Al?" she asked, and he nodded. "Well...I'm sure I've had clients or classmates when I was in school, but the only person I've ever called Al is my friend Alicia... the one who lives in the Bay Area."

"Where you're planning to move."

"When I sell this place, yes. Or if I ever do." She thought of Sean Erwin, who had come by earlier, moving furniture, measuring every room, window, and door, then taking notes. "So," she asked Montoya, "what's this all about?" But before the words were out of her mouth, she knew. "Oh, wait a minute. I get it. I heard part of the radio program today, I was in my car and just checked out what was happening at good old WSLJ. Luke's old program was running again, and Maury was talking about someone named Al, right? I'd just turned on the radio when someone showed up at the station and shut him down and Dr. Sam took over...hey, wait, was that you?"

The detective gave a quick nod.

Abby smiled at the thought of Montoya busting in on Maury's program. She could imagine the moron freaking out. "Way to go." She leaned over toward Montoya and clicked the neck of her beer bottle with his. "I think we deserve this drink."

He smiled. "Well, I know *I* do."

She laughed and it felt good to let go of some of the tension of the past week. "I'll have you know you're not the only one who's been working hard. While you were out fighting crime and keeping the streets of New Orleans safe from serial killers, I've been busy cropping wedding photos and paying bills. So, you tell me. Who has the more dangerous job?" She pointed the top of her bottle at him. "Have you ever seen the mother of the bride react when she sees a shot that shows off her double chin, or panty line? How about a candid one that catches her husband kissing the maid of honor?"

He laughed despite himself, his teeth showing white against his dark beard. Brown eyes glinted. "You're the one who should be wearing the gun."

She rolled her eyes. "Well, if I *had* one. Mine's missing." His smile fell away and she shrugged. "It was Luke's dad's .38. I kept it after the divorce, which really ticked my ex off. It was here the other day and now it's missing."

"For how long?" he asked, his expression suddenly hard.

"I don't know. Just a few days."

"You think you misplaced it?"

"No...I've looked for it. I don't know what happened to it."

"Who, besides you, has been in the house?" He set his near-empty beer on the coffee table, all of his attention focused on her.

Abby found his intensity a bit unnerving. He was asking all the questions she'd been afraid to ask herself. "No one, well, except a few people who've looked at the house."

"You've got their names, addresses, and phone numbers?"

"Just numbers."

"I want them."

"You think it's significant?" she asked, feeling that nasty breath of fear crawl through her again.

"These recent murders," he said, "in both cases the victims were killed with the female victim's weapon. In the first case, your ex-husband's murder, the gun was a gift to Courtney LaBelle from her father, for protection. In the second murder, the weapon was stolen from the Jefferson house, part of a collection the husband kept."

She could scarcely breathe. Panic swept through her. She shot to her feet, pacing before the fire. "You think the killer was here" —she pointed at the floorboards in front of the fire and tried to calm her racing heart—"in *this* house and he stole *my* gun so that he can kidnap me? Then kill me and some other person, a man, with that very weapon? Is that what you're saying?" She was nearly hyperventilating now, her breathing fast and shallow.

"I'm saying it's possible," he answered carefully.

"Damn it, Montoya, you're scaring the hell out of me." Hershey lifted her head, watching as Abby crossed her arms over her chest. Restless, she walked from one window to the next, thinking about the unseen eyes she'd felt, the open window she'd discovered the day she'd found the gun missing...oh, God. Was it possible? Had someone been in her house? Had someone stolen Luke's gun? Or had it been misplaced? "Then I guess I should tell you that when I found the gun missing, someone might have gotten into my house."

She glanced over at Montoya, who was completely ignoring his beer.

"Who?"

"I don't know. I don't even know if someone was inside. It was the night you came over and I had the hammer."

"You didn't tell me."

"I didn't know until after you left. You suggested I get a gun and I double-checked. As I said, earlier that day, Hershey went nuts. She was nervous and growled. I thought it was just the cat, but I searched the house anyway. There was nothing missing, I thought, and I'd locked the house, but I found the laundry room window open."

"You didn't leave it open yourself."

"No…"

"You should have told me."

"I was afraid you'd think I was an alarmist—one of those weak, scared little women I detest."

"Don't sacrifice your safety for your pride," he ordered, sounding so imperative that her temper rose.

"I'm still here, aren't I?" she snapped. "I searched the house and found no one, okay? It wasn't until after you left that I found the gun was missing. Since then I've been looking for it and" —she shook her head—"it's gone."

"I don't like it."

"Neither do I."

He was staring at her so intently, she had to look away. "So, tell me," she said, rubbing her arms. She felt chilled to the bone. "Who's this Al?" she asked, then suddenly she knew. "Oh, my God. He contacted the radio station, didn't he? The killer. Maury's been in contact with him! He called or wrote or e-mailed the station."

"*Some*one did. It could be a fraud. Lots of times people pretend to be the doer, just to get some attention."

"But you think it was the real thing," she guessed, glancing at him as she shoved her hair from her eyes. "That's why you're here and asking all these questions. You may not be on duty but you're still working."

"I'm not sure the killer sent the note." Montoya stood, stretching. "But it's possible and we're checking out every lead."

"What did the note say?"

She came straight toward him, her fear and distress dilating her pupils. When she turned her earnest face to his, Montoya's concentration shattered. He should have been prepared for the question. But he wasn't. Nor was he prepared for the onslaught to his senses brought on by this little bit of a woman with her quick smile, sharp wit, and deep-set determination. She was close enough that he smelled a whiff of some perfume, saw the tiny streaks of gold in her hair, gilded by the firelight, noticed the way the cords in her neck were visible. The FBI wouldn't like it if he spilled his guts about the note, and he didn't want to do anything that would remotely compromise the investigation. However, this, he thought, was a mitigating circumstance. She was missing her gun, for God's sake, and that single fact scared the hell out of him. So fuck protocol. The task force was just getting together. The message was only a single word, and who knew how many people at the station had heard or seen it?

"What did the note say?" she repeated.

"If I tell you, you need to keep this under wraps."

"Of course."

"I mean it."

"So do I, Detective."

"I'm serious, Abby, this could cost me my job or, worse yet, cripple the investigation."

"I'm serious, too. Damned serious. What the hell did the note say?"

He stared at her long and hard. "The only reason I'm telling you is that I have this sense ... worry that somehow this is connected to you. I don't know how, and I could be way off base, but that's what I feel." He saw the fear deepen in her eyes. "I'm sorry. But you need to be aware and alert. And cautious. I don't want you to be taken by surprise." Frowning, he ignored the warnings running through his mind, including Melinda Jaskiel's last order concerning protocol. It was all he could do to keep from taking her into his arms. "There was only one word: *Repent*—and it was signed by *Al,* or more precisely *A L;* both of the signature letters were capitalized." He watched as little lines of confusion appeared between her eyebrows, how her full lips pulled into a knot of concentration, how a shadow of fear chased through eyes the color of aged whiskey.

"Repent? For what?" Her gaze was troubled. "Sins? Whose? Why?"

"We don't know yet. But the task force is looking into it."

"Shouldn't this information be made public?"

"It will, when the officer in charge of the task force thinks it should."

She shook her head. "It means nothing to me and I don't know anyone else named Al or even with those initials." Her shoulders slumped. "Why the hell is this happening?"

"I wish I knew." And then he could restrain himself no longer. He wrapped his arms around her and pulled her close. When she didn't resist, he rested his chin upon her head and drank in the scent of her hair. "I'm afraid until we catch him, we won't know."

She shivered and held tightly to him.

"We will catch him. It's just a matter of time."

"Good."

He closed his eyes for a second, lost in the feel and smell of her. It would be so damned easy to kiss her. They both knew it, and when she looked up at him, the question was in her golden eyes. With their bodies pressed so close together, their hearts beating faster, it was all Montoya could do to slowly release her. He had to. But when they were at arm's length, he felt bereft.

She didn't argue, nor try to nestle herself close against him, though he thought he noticed a glint of desire ripple through her gaze.

Don't go there, Montoya. Kissing her would be a stupid move. Stupid. She's involved in all of this somehow ... remember that. She was married to one victim and could be the next.

His jaw tightened.

More to break the tension than anything else, he pointed to a picture on the mantel. "That you?" he asked, indicating a black-and-white head shot that was nearly identical to Abby, but just a little off.

"My mother."

"Really?"

"Yeah ... I think it was taken around the time she was twenty-five, maybe thirty."

"You look a lot like her."

"So I've been told."

"It's a compliment."

"Then, thanks."

She tried to hide a yawn. For the first time he noticed how tired she looked, how hard this was on her. "Look, why don't you go to bed."

"Now?"

"You look beat."

She glanced toward the door. "You're leaving?"

"Not on your life, lady. Not until you get a security system installed, a trained doberman pinscher, and an attack cat."

"But you can't just..." Her voice trailed off.

"All I need is a blanket and a pillow. I'll camp out here." He pointed to the couch. "Believe me, it's a lot better than some of the stakeouts I've been on."

"I...I don't know."

"You can throw me out if you want to, but I'll just park outside your door." He stared at her long and hard. "I'm staying, Abby, whether you like it or not."

"Thank you," she said simply.

The cop was there.

Had come late.

And stayed.

From his hiding spot in the trees beyond the veranda of Abby's house, he watched as the lights went out... all the lights, eventually even the bedroom lamp. He couldn't see through the drawn shades, but he noticed a soft flickering glow and smelled the smoke of a wood fire. It swept through the damp autumn air and reminded him of sitting by campfires as a child; fires he'd built, fires he'd watched alone. That same loneliness, that feeling that he was "different," "not quite right," "extremely smart—off the charts in his pure, crystalline intelligence, but you know, a little odd"—his mother's words, her way of explaining why he had no friends, why he was unlike his siblings—swept through him. He felt it again—that dark coldness of being alone. Segregated. Picked on.

Eventually he'd found solace being separate.

Then he'd met Faith.

And he was no longer alone.

Once more, he imagined her touch, her warmth, the feel of her lips grazing his skin...

But before he could sink into the delight of his memories, his gaze trained on the house. His jaw slid to one side. Rage burned through his veins, and his lips curled in disgust.

They were fucking.

He was certain of it.

Like a dog in heat, she was letting the cop screw her! Was even now probably writhing and wriggling beneath him, sweating, crying out, begging for more.

Fury and pain tore through his soul.

She was so much like her mother!

His stomach twisted. All over he felt tiny, little legs brushing over his body. His skin was suddenly crawling. As if a million red ants were marching over him, stinging and biting, turning his flesh to fire, creating a black rage deep in his soul.

She'd *betrayed* him.

Memories assailed him.

He remembered Faith's laughter, that throaty, heart-stopping chuckle that was meant only for him. Yet he'd heard it emanating from her room. Late at night. When she should have been waiting for *him*.

He'd tried the door handle.

It had been frozen. Wouldn't move.

Locked.

He'd been locked out.

Why?

He'd nearly called out, whispered through the panels. But then the other noises had reached him, the unmistakable sounds of rutting: the raw, guttural moans of animal pleasure, the crass, rhythmic creaking of the bedsprings, the swift intake of breath, and a muffled cry of satiated lust.

He'd smelled the scent of sinful sex seeping under the door.

Even now the sounds rang in his ears, a harsh, painful noise that pierced his eardrums. He remembered the vile odor of their excitement.

His teeth gnashed together so hard his jaw ached and his face twisted as if tortured.

So now the daughter was fornicating with the cop.

Bile rose in his throat.

He imagined her gold hair wet with sweat, her body so slick it appeared to have been oiled as she arched up to meet him, her breasts pointing toward the ceiling, full and aroused, dark nipples taut. Oh, how she would welcome the cop's hungry mouth, his long wet tongue, his sharp teeth. His beard would scratch her skin raw.

His heart was pounding with fury. And with lust as he mentally witnessed their coupling image. Oh, the things she did to him, the dirty, lurid sexual acts she would perform!

Tears filled his eyes as he thought of her beauty, of her tainted purity. He reached into his pocket and with gloved fingers touched the gun.

Her gun.

This weapon was his savior. And hers.

His right fist clenched around the cold steel of the revolver.

Your time is coming, he thought angrily. *And soon. Oh, yes, very soon.*

Closing his eyes, he conjured up her face. Beautiful. Innocent. Seductive. Playful. So much like Faith's as to be her twin.

And like her mother, this one had betrayed him as well.

In his heart he believed she was an angel.

But in his gut he knew she was a whore.

CHAPTER 21

The hospital was dark, the corridors murky, the stairs seeming to run upward forever. Abby hurried, carrying the box, wanting to surprise her mother. She had so much to tell her, so much to confide. She'd asked Trey to the dance...oh, my God...and wonder of wonders he'd said "yes!" Up, up, up, she climbed. But the package she was toting was bulky and awkward. It felt heavy in her hands, and as she struggled up the steep staircase, her euphoria seeped away, and the darkness of the old hospital seemed cloying. Her breathing was labored, her legs so tired, and unseen hands seemed to pluck at the bright ribbon on the gift.

Finally she reached the landing, where the stained-glass Madonna was glowing, hands folded, halo bright and shimmering. Abby paused to catch her breath, then started up the final flight to the third floor, only to trip, her feet flying out from under her, the package shooting from her arms. Desperately she tried to catch not only the box, but herself as well. She caught onto the railing, but couldn't grab hold of the gift. Twisting her neck, she watched in horror as the gold box, its fuchsia ribbon streaming behind, tumbled and bounced down the stairway, disappearing into the darkness at the base of the stairs. Into oblivion.

She started after it, but her mother's muffled voice stopped her.

"Abby? Abby Hannah?" It sounded as if Mom were very far away, calling to Abby from one end of a long tunnel. *"Abby?"*

"I'm coming, Mom," she said and knew that Zoey would bring the package. Hadn't they fought in the car about who would have the privilege of giving it to their mother? Let Zoey do it. Who cared? But as Abby stared down the stairwell into the inky blackness, she wondered where Zoey was. And where was their father? How long did it take to park a car?

"Abby!" Faith's voice was sharp. Frightened.

Abby spun around, heading up the final flight. From the corner of her eye she saw that the Madonna's image had changed. Not a lot. Not enough that most people would notice but Abby did. Instead of looking tranquil and serene, the Holy Mother's round eyes had thinned a bit, her angelic smile twisted a little wryly, as if she and Abby were sharing a private joke.

Frightened, Abby stumbled up the stairs. As she scrambled to the third floor, she heard the sobs. Broken, horrible sobs.

"Mom?" Surely it wasn't her mother crying! But all the other doors on the third floor were open, the rooms dark and yawning as if hiding unseen beasts who lay waiting in their dark depths.

The door to 307 was firmly shut.

She reached for the handle and pulled.

Nothing.

"No. Oh, no, please, don't—" her mother pleaded on the other side.

"Mom!" Abby pounded on the panels with her fist. Bam! Bam! Bam! One by one her mother's room numbers fell onto the floor.

Three.

Clunk.

Zero.

Thud.

Seven.

Bam!

As the final number hit the floor, the door burst open.

Abby stumbled into the room, where flowers withered in a vase. The mirror over the fireplace was shattered. Blood smeared the glass. Her mother was at the window... but not alone... a man in a white *coat and a shiny stethoscope had his back to Abby. His hands were on her mother's shoulders, pushing her backward, toward the window. Faith's dress was torn, one shoe kicked off.*

Help me, *she silently pleaded, looking over the man's shoulders.* Abby Hannah, help me!

Stunned, Abby found her feet, but her legs were leaden, refused to work. "Mama!" *she cried, stretching out her arms, trying desperately to reach her mother.*

The doctor pushed vigorously against Faith's shoulders. Shrieking, she fell backward, her body hitting the window with enough force to crack the long glass pane. It splintered slowly, but relentlessly. Try as she might, Abby couldn't stop her mother from falling.

The doctor shrank away, disappearing into the shadowy corners of the room as Abby propelled herself forward. The last frisson of glass shattered. Hot, moist air rushed into the room.

Faith, bleeding, clawed onto Abby's hand, linking fingers, pulling her close. "I forgive you," *she whispered.*

Together they pirouetted into the dark, dank Louisiana night.

Screaming, Abby sat bolt upright in the bed. She was sweating, her heart pounding, the dream so real that she couldn't breathe. "Oh, God," she whispered, pushing her hair from her face. When her eyes adjusted to the darkness, she saw her bedroom door stood open. She screamed again as she saw the silhouette of a man in her doorway. "Oh, God!" Her eyes rounded in horror as he moved closer. She shrank back, terrified, the dream still lingering.

"Abby?" he said and in an instant she recognized his voice, realized that Detective Montoya was with her. He snapped on the bedside lamp. He held a gun in his hand. He was dressed in low-slung jeans and nothing else. Seeing that she was alone, he set his weapon on the nightstand. "Are you all right?"

"You keep asking that," she said, trying to calm her racing heart, trying not to stare at Montoya's physique. She'd left him fully clothed on the couch after tossing him an extra pillow and sleeping bag.

"I, um, I, oh, Jesus." She leaned against the headboard and shoved her hair from her eyes with both hands. "I . . . I had that dream again." Shaking her head, she wondered if she would ever be free of that long-ago, painful night and the nightmares that stalked her. "Sorry... I didn't mean to wake you up."

He offered her a bit of a smile, the tiniest flash of white teeth. "It's okay."

She tried not to notice his strong pectoral muscles visible through black, swirling chest hair. And she attempted to ignore the fact that his abdomen was flat, just a hint of muscles visible beneath his taut skin. Drawing a long breath, she didn't protest when he sat on the bed next to her, nor did she argue as one strong arm slipped around her. She didn't even put up a fight when he drew her close enough that she could smell the male scent of him and hear his heart thudding in tandem with her own.

"Better now?" he asked.

"Yeah. I think so." She exhaled. "I hope so..."

His arms around her tightened, almost possessively, pulling her even closer. "Did you hear something? See something?"

"No...just a dream. The same one I've had for a long time. It changes a little each time, but..." She shuddered. "But it's always about the night she died."

"A long time for a recurring nightmare," he observed.

"That's why, on the advice of my most recent psychologist, I visited the hospital the other day."

"So it didn't work?"

"Not yet, I guess." She frowned as pieces of the dream teased at her. "But I think there's something important there, in my mother's room." She looked up into his dark, concerned eyes. "I know this sounds crazy, but it's like if I go there, I'll be able to put this all to rest," she said with a twinge of dread. "I have to go back."

"Why?" Swinging his legs onto the bed, he propped his back against the pillows, still holding her close.

"Because her room was locked when I was there last." Abby leaned her head into the crook of his shoulder, wrapped her arms around his chest, and fleetingly wondered about the wisdom of lying on the bed with him. "Here's the deal: No other room in that whole damned place was locked. Well... aside from a basement door. The exterior doors were bolted, the windows shut, but the interior doors were open. Except for Room 307. Mom's room." She looked up at him and saw the furrows drawing deep between his eyebrows. "Don't you find that odd?"

"Oh, darlin', I'm finding a lot of things odd," he admitted, and as their gazes held, she felt a shift in the atmosphere. She suddenly knew he was going to kiss her. Before she could think twice, he shifted, the bed groaned expectantly, and he drew her so close that she felt his breath mingle with her own.

This is wrong, she thought, but tilted her head up.

"Damn it," he muttered, and a second later, his mouth crashed down on hers. Warm lips molded over hers, one hand tangled in her hair, the other reached low and splayed over the curve of her spine, and she did nothing to stop him, to allay the onslaught to her senses.

Instead she closed her eyes and felt the wonder of his mouth, the gentle scratch of his goatee against her skin, the heat of his body against hers.

How long had it been since she'd kissed a man? Made love to him? She closed her mind to that train of thought and lost herself in the moment, feeling the urgent pressure of his lips against hers, the weight of his body as he rolled over her.

His tongue slid easily past her teeth, the tip touching the ridges along the roof of her mouth as he tasted her, touched her. She kissed him back, her own tongue exploring this man of whom she knew so little, this cop who at once charmed and irritated her half to death.

Don't trust this. It's nothing. Just two lonely people caught together in the middle of a long dark night. This isn't what you want, Abby, this is a nonrelationship and easy sex. It's not you.

And yet she couldn't stop. Wouldn't.

Think, Abby. About tomorrow and the next day and the next.

She ignored the rational, sane side of her nature. Not tonight. She wasn't going to follow the rules tonight. This loving was long overdue and she needed—oh, God, how she needed—some release. She kissed him as if she'd never kissed a man before, as if she couldn't get enough of him.

Nor could she.

Theirs was not a thoughtful joining, not a loving, tender exploration but a fierce coupling driven by need. His lips claimed hers, and she kissed him back with a hunger that tore through her soul. Her arms wound around his neck, and as his hands bunched her nightgown over her hips, fingertips skimming, palms caressing, she had trouble drawing a breath, difficulty thinking.

She could only feel, and she gave herself willingly into the exciting, nerve-tingling sensations.

Callused, practiced hands surrounded her breasts, thumbs skating over her nipples. His mouth was hard against her own, his kiss urgent. Demanding. She didn't think of right or wrong, of what doubts the morning light would bring.

She just wanted him.

Now.

Her body screamed for release while her mind begged to forget, for just a few hours, the horror of her nightmares, the pain of the past, the uncertainty of the future.

Tonight was theirs and she gave herself up to it, kissing him, running her fingers down the corded strength of his sinewy muscles, feeling the blood running through her veins heat with a deep, dusky wanting.

His mouth moved across her cheek and down her throat. Soft beard, smooth lips, and wet tongue brushed her skin. Deep within she ached, desire licking through her veins, causing a need so deep she was lost in it.

She let out a low moan as his hands scaled her ribs, fingertips teasing and touching, her nipples growing so tight they ached. He was stretched out over her, his legs pressed to hers, his erection hard and thick.

He kissed the circle of bones at her throat, laving the hollow, creating a heat that pounded through her brain, elevated her pulse, as he slid lower, arms surrounding her, hot breath whispering over skin he'd made wet with his tongue.

Love me, oh, please! she thought as his mouth found one breast and he teased and toyed, his tongue, lips, and teeth playing with her, tempting her, scraping her skin, causing her spine to arch and her fingers to sweep across the back of his head, holding him tight and forcing him to suckle long and deep.

"Oooh," she whispered, wanting more, desire pounding deep inside—a real, living thing that demanded freedom. She ran her hands over the muscles of his shoulders and down the sinewy strength of his arms. He was strong and hard. Had, no doubt, loved many women, fought many men, perhaps even killed.

He tasted her, tongue flicking over her breast, one hand pulling her hips to his, his fingers hot against her spine, the tips brushing the cleft of her buttocks.

She squirmed in delicious agony.

More!

Give me more!

Her fingertips slid down his flat abdomen, along the arrow of dark hair that delved beneath the waistband of those faded, sexy jeans.

She opened the top button and slid her fingertips past the worn denim. His stomach muscles contracted. Giving her more access to the warmth emanating between his legs.

"Careful," he whispered, sucking in his breath. "Dangerous territory."

"It's all dangerous territory," she replied and tugged. The buttons of his Levi's opened in a quick series of pops and she felt the smooth hardness of his erection, her fingers light as she brushed against it.

His entire body stiffened as he swore and slammed his eyes shut. Strong fingers shackled her wrist. "Abby," he said, his voice rough. "Maybe...we should think this through." He was breathing hard, his body straining, sweat slick and gleaming on his muscles.

"Why?"

"Because once we cross a certain line, there's no going back."

"You think I don't know this?"

"I'm in the middle of a murder investigation and—"

"Is that what you're in the middle of?" she asked, teasing, her breath hot as it blew across his bare chest. He let out a soft moan. "And here I thought you were in my bed, in the middle of making love to me. I wasn't wrong, was I?" She ran the fingers of her free hand up his sternum to touch one of his flat nipples. "I didn't get mixed signals." She kissed his abdomen, her lips wet.

"I'm trying to be noble here," he ground out.

"Duly noted."

"Abby—"

"What?" she breathed over his skin again, and the fingers around her wrist tightened for a second, then relaxed.

"Christ," he whispered. "If this is what you want, darlin', then it's what you're gonna get." He drew her up to him, held her face between his hands, then kissed her as if he'd never stop. His mouth was hungry and hard, his lips eager. The barriers down.

With her help, he kicked off his jeans. He didn't utter up a single sound of protest as she touched his hips, trailed her fingers along his rock-hard thighs, or cupped his buttocks.

His breathing audible, he moved slowly downward, kissing her intimately between her breasts, along her abdomen, and rimming her navel so exquisitely that she clutched the bedsheets in her curling fingers. His deft tongue and lips explored, while his hands kneaded as she writhed, sweating, panting, *feeling*. Hot, wanton sensations rippled through her and she wanted more...oh, dear God, so much more.

She parted her legs willingly for him, felt his ultimate caress as his tongue and lips tasted her, lapping, tickling, causing her to moan in sheer, incredible, torturous pleasure.

The first spasm hit her hard, jolting through her body, causing her toes to curl and her fingers to knot in the bedsheets. Again she rocketed, her body jerking. And again. Still he teased her, his hands kneading her buttocks, his fingers finding hidden spots, pleasuring her time and time again.

Her mind spun, and when she was finally breathless, she stopped him, pulled him up to her, and kissed him. "Your turn," she whispered into his ear, and he moaned as she lowered herself slowly.

She ran her tongue and teeth along his legs, feeling him squirm as his fingers twisted in her hair. She touched and kissed him delicately, sensing him hold back until he trembled.

"Abby," he finally whispered and pulled her to him, kissing her hard and rolling her onto her back. Then, with the lamplight giving off a soft golden glow, he slid her legs over his shoulders and, staring into her eyes, thrust. Hard. Deep. So far that she gasped.

Slowly he retracted only to plunge in again.

Quivering, she grabbed his arms and began to move with him, holding tight as he slid in and out of her, faster and faster. She burned inside and her breath came in quick short bursts. Faster and faster and faster they moved, until nothing in the universe mattered but that one spot where they were joined, the single area of intense friction that pounded and pulsed and sent shock waves to her brain.

His eyes closed just as she convulsed. A scream caught in the back of her throat. Still he came to her, pushing, pulling, hard and fast until she caught his fevered tempo again, her fingers digging into his shoulders, her head tossed back, her hair damp with sweat. Hotter. Faster. Wilder. Until her entire body bucked.

"Oh, God...Montoya..." she cried as he stiffened, his breath sliding through his teeth in a hiss, his head drawing back as if pulled by a string.

And then he collapsed, pouring himself into her, his arms surrounding her, his head falling against the hollow of her shoulder. "That's what I was waiting to hear," he said, his voice raw.

"What...?"

"My name and God's...at the precise moment of rapture."

Silent laughter caught in her throat. "How can you joke right now?" Her heart was still pounding out of control, her pulse in the stratosphere, the synapses in her brain still firing as afterglow tugged at her.

"Who's joking?"

"Bastard," she muttered and swatted at him with the back of her hand.

"From God to bastard in one fell swoop." He nuzzled her neck and she sighed in contentment, refusing to think of the morning and what recriminations the dawn would carry on its shoulders.

For tonight she would enjoy this fleeting feeling of love.

Let the morning bring what it would.

The Reverend Billy Ray Furlough was up late, in his study, his private sanctuary away from the world. Separated from the main house by a grove of tended willow, magnolia, pine, and oak, as well as an elaborate wrought-iron fence, his study was actually a suite of rooms complete with three car-garage, private entrance, lap pool, and interior full-sized basketball court. A little ostentatious, perhaps, but necessary, he felt, for him to spread the word of God.

Reverend Furlough never felt closer to the Lord than when he was sweating profusely and making that perfect basketball shot just to the right of the free throw line. It was his signature shot, had been since he'd been the leading scorer for the Hornets in college. He loved the game and for years the game had loved him. He'd played with a vengeance, with an angry fire that he had carried with him into his personal life.

It had been on the basketball court where he'd first seen the light.

One second he'd been leaping skyward and was completely air-borne, his fingers extended for a rebound, the next he'd been on the ground, in a jumble of players, involved in a freak accident that had broken his ankle and knocked him unconscious for over ten minutes. In that precious dark span of time he'd lived a lifetime, seen Christ's face, and when he'd awakened, had sworn that if he was allowed to heal—and play the next season—he would dedicate his life to God and His Son.

And so it was.

He'd healed, worked hard through hours of excruciating pain and physical therapy, and had received cards and notes from people he'd never met saying he was in their thoughts, swearing that they were praying for his full recovery. They had told him their private thoughts, offered good wishes, and to a one had asked the Lord for his complete recovery so that the Hornets, next season, could beat their arch rivals into oblivion.

And so it was.

He'd healed miraculously and sworn to all that it was not only through talent and hard work, but because of his promise to God. He'd vowed to take the team to the tournament for God, with God, and in His Holy name.

And so it was.

The Hornets had crushed their opponents and won the title of their small league. Billy Ray Furlough had played the best game of his life, stealing the ball, passing for assists, and putting forty-three of the eighty-five points on the board, including the final shot, at the buzzer, though the Hornets, at that point, hadn't needed the extra three points for a win. With Billy Ray's intensity, his fervor, his rage, they'd already slammed their opponents to the ground.

314 • *Lisa Jackson*

The crowd had gone wild. Immediately after the game Billy Ray, the MVP, a towel slapped around his neck, his hair wet, and his face alight with the glow of a champion, had been interviewed by a local news station. Still breathing hard, he'd stared straight into the camera's eye and dedicated the win, the trophy, and the title to God.

He'd received hundreds of congratulatory letters and phone calls. He'd been interviewed by Christian and lay stations for weeks.

But no pro contract had been offered.

No phone call asking if he was interested in a particular club in the NBA.

Nothing.

His college, was, after all, a small one; the Hornets' league not nearly as tough or as competitive as those of major universities. As for his injury, a bevy of doctors had declared him fit, tough, and stronger than ever. He still could play with fire and fury despite the two screws and plate in his ankle.

Only a handful of his closest friends had known of the pain he suffered after each game. His right foot, ankle, and calf felt as if they had been roasting in the fires of hell. He'd found relief not only from prayer, but from Vicodin and Percocet and whatever other prescription would help ease the raging, burning sensation that had made him grit his teeth.

It had been easy to find an adoring doctor, an alumnus of the college, to write him the necessary prescriptions . . . and he'd never abused the drugs, just used them to help control the raging pain and seething anger that accompanied it.

With no professional contract in the United States, he had briefly considered playing ball in Europe but knew he'd face the same problems overseas that he would have in the States. Then there were all the cards and notes he'd received and saved from the people who had reached out to him, the people who believed in him, the people who had asked for signed pictures of him, or wanted his old jerseys and basketball shoes. Adoring fans. Loving fans. People who believed in him.

He'd taken the lack of a professional contract as a sign from God to "play on Jesus's team." No fool, Billy Ray had realized that he could be a part of that team for the rest of his life, perhaps make as much money as in the NBA, but for substantially longer.

He could still be a star.

And so it was.

The same rage and dedication that had fueled him on the basketball court had helped him create a parish of thousands. No one knew where that rage came from, the lies his entire life had been founded upon. No one knew how betrayed he'd been when he'd discovered that his parents—two hardworking, loving people—had lied to him from the get-go.

They'd never told him he'd been adopted; never once mentioned that he wasn't of their own loins. He'd found out by a simple class in genetics when he took biology at fourteen. Blue-eyed people did not give birth to brown-eyed children... that was a simple biological fact, so either his mother had committed the sin of adultery or he'd been adopted.

Easy enough to find out, and find out he did.

Now he tapped his pen on the desk and scowled at the perfidy. How many times had he tried to forgive those poor simple people, and how many times had he come up short?

"Give me strength," he whispered as he sat in the study, darkness surrounding this part of what the negative press had dubbed his "compound." Let them say what they would. Who cared? Billy Ray believed that there was no bad press. As long as reporters were writing about him, people were hearing his name and that was what mattered.

He rubbed a hand over his eyes. He was tired and should turn in. He had an expansive bedroom here in the study—a king-size bed, huge flat-screen television, even a gas fire that could be flipped on with a remote. He spent most of his nights here rather than in the huge antebellum-looking house his wife had spent years building.

He dutifully stayed in the main house each Saturday night, slept in their marriage bed and made love to her as if he still cared. The next morning they always ate breakfast in that monster of a dining hall, dressed for church service, then left in separate cars, she with the children, he alone to drive to the church.

There had been a time when they'd been passionate. He'd even been so moved as to once have sex with her on that huge table, but that had been a few years back. Before she'd grown cold. Before she'd been so wrapped up in the children's lives that she had no time for Billy Ray. Before she'd relegated sex to once a week and had lain there, barely moving, a statue who, because of her wedding vows, let him rut over her.

He hated it.

Sex with one's wife should not feel dirty.

He had considered taking up with a younger, more vibrant, more *alive* woman than Aldora. He'd even flirted with the new church secretary, a recently divorced mother of two who wore high heels and tight skirts, and had a tendency to show a smile and wink at him when she talked.

So far, he hadn't stepped over that line.

Yet.

Had no plans to.

But...a man had to feel loved, not only by God, but by a woman as well. These days Aldora just wasn't holding up her end of the marriage bargain.

He felt a simmering anger as he unbuttoned his golf shirt and stared down at the words he'd scrawled on a yellow legal pad. He'd been working on his sermon all week, ever since hearing about Luke Gierman and Courtney LaBelle's murders. Their horrendous deaths presented an opportunity to bring more people to the Lord.

He'd already managed to get a lot of press over the killings; now he wanted more. Which was no problem. Asa Pomeroy and Gina Jefferson's murders had provided more grisly fodder.

Billy Ray had a feeling that this Sunday his church would be filled to overflowing. Fear brought out the piety in people. It was interesting, he thought, how his words of the Lord's wrath, of punishment for evil deeds, of fire and brimstone, were such a magnet for his followers. He'd found that the more harshly he spoke, the more he shook his hands toward the heavens, the more his voice boomed in fury, the more the veins in his neck throbbed with his convictions, the more the parishioners tithed. He even had a half-hour radio program on WNAB at nights and there was talk of television.

They all wanted a show.

Passion.

Wrath.

Power.

And above all else, a deep-seated love of the Lord.

Billy Ray had them all.

So this had to be a great sermon, about the wrath and love of an all-powerful God, about the compassion of Jesus and about . . . He looked up. Had he heard something? A footstep? He waited, his ears straining, and there was no other sound. Nothing but the wind outside, rustling through the dry leaves of autumn. He hadn't heard anything. He was just tired, his body reacting to a week of strain, of being "on" for the cameras, of showing his own sympathizing nature for the families of the victims, his own rage at the murdering maniac let loose on the streets of his city. Yes, yes, that was it. Picking up his pen, he began writing in swift sure strokes, his sermon spewing forth faster and faster. He would edit the text on the computer in the morning, clean up any mistakes. By writing his thoughts on paper, he let loose some of his anger, the pen nearly ripping through the top page as he scrawled on and on and . . .

Creak.

Again he looked up.

This time he was nearly certain he'd heard the squeak of floorboards. He leaned back and listened. "Anyone there?" he called, feeling a fool. His bodyguard and personal trainer had left hours ago and he'd heard the gates close behind Kyle's Chevy Blazer, seen the wink of the SUV's taillights through the open window.

Again there was nothing but silence.

He was just agitated tonight.

Perhaps he needed to pray. Dropping his pen onto the desk, he took in a deep breath. Then swiping his face with his hands, he leaned back in his chair, squeezed his eyes shut, and asked the Lord for inspiration, for clarity, for God's will to be spread through his sermon. For that's how it happened, the reverend believed. He was inspired by God, touched by Him as if the Father actually reached down from glorious heaven and placed His fingertips onto Billy Ray's crown. In that moment, God's thoughts entered Billy Ray's brain, sizzled through synapses down his nerves to his fingers, where the words—right from the Lord's mouth!—flowed onto the pages of this legal pad.

"Lord help me," he said aloud. "Let me see the light, let me feel Your presence, let me be Your mouthpiece..."

Again the noise.

Billy Ray opened his eyes.

He gasped and leapt to his feet.

There, standing before him, holding a Taser pointed right at the preacher's heart, was Satan.

Before Billy Ray could utter a word, Lucifer pulled the trigger.

Sister Maria sensed something in her sleep.

She rolled over.

A gloved hand clamped over her mouth.

Panic shot through her and she was instantly awake. Her room was pitch dark; it was long before morning prayers. She couldn't see her attacker, but he was strong.

Determined.

Angry.

She felt his fury, smelled his sweat.

A sickeningly sweet smell filled her nostrils.

Ether!

She recognized it from her days at the hospital.

No! she thought. *No, no, no!*

Sister Maria struggled. Tried to scream. Fought with all the strength in her body, but as she writhed and flung her useless arms upward, she breathed rapidly. Deeply.

The thick chemical wound its way into her lungs, dulling her mind, weakening her limbs, causing her eyelids to droop. She gasped, struggling for breath, but more of the noxious sleep-inducer was dragged into her airways.

Her movements turned sluggish.

She knew what was happening but was unable to fight the inevitable.

In the end, she gave up, her body going limp, the blackness oozing through her brain.

Forgive me, Father, she prayed dreamily, *for I have sinned...*

Chapter 22

Billy Ray Furlough wasn't going down without a fight. Blindfolded, gagged, strapped to a chair, he'd been left by his abductor somewhere that smelled of rot and dirt and dampness. He guessed he was near the swamp as he smelled thick, stagnant water, heard bullfrogs croaking and ominous splashes. He imagined alligators slipping through inky depths, only their eyes visible over the water's smooth surface, and he thought of cottonmouths or copperheads slithering down cypress trunks and roots to glide into the swamp water.

A chill ran down his spine, but as dangerous as the creatures of the swamp were, they were nothing in comparison with the man who had captured him. A tall, broad-shouldered son of a bitch dressed in a black neoprene suit and ski mask. He was deadly, swift, and determined to kill. Billy Ray knew it. He'd read enough about the recent local murders to understand that the man who had kidnapped him was the killer.

There would be no ransom demand of Aldora.

No negotiating for his release.

Not even the slicing off of an ear or finger to prove that he was abducted. No, there was only certain death. Unless he did something to save himself.

The Lord helps those who help themselves.

How many times had he blithely handed out that piece of advice? So now he had to take it. He had to help himself. He'd been left alone, so he had time to plan, time to get ready, time to figure out a way to save himself.

He wondered who the psycho was. Why had Billy Ray been chosen as a victim?

It made no sense. No one wanted him dead. He was adored by his parishioners and the news media alike. There was even a movement within his church pushing him toward local politics. But someone hated him. Someone with the balls to scale his fence and walk straight into his inner sanctum.

Yet bad as this was, at least Aldora and the kids were safe... right? The psycho wouldn't have gone back for any of his family, surely not.

But didn't this guy kill in pairs?

A man and a woman?

Assuming this was the same killer...maybe this nut job was a copycat, but whoever he was, he was strong and determined. Deadly silent. Without a word he'd walked into the study, stunned Billy Ray, and easily and efficiently trussed him up like a tom turkey before Thanksgiving supper. The only way Billy Ray could possibly get the drop on him was to pretend compliance, even fear, act as if he didn't yet have control of his body. Then he might just have a chance to overpower the man.

Maybe...but he'd have to be quick, surprise the creep. Even in as good a shape as Billy Ray was, this larger man was stronger, tougher. As soon as the Taser gun had sent Billy reeling backward and flopping on the floor like a landed catfish, his attacker had been on him, pinning him down, forcing his hands behind him, wrapping them in duct tape and doing the same with his ankles. A blindfold had been forced over his eyes, tape slapped over his mouth.

It had been over in a matter of minutes and then the brute had carried him fireman style into the garage, where he shot Billy Ray with the stun gun again. Hundreds of thousands of volts had shrieked through the preacher's body and he'd been tossed into the backseat of *his* Mercedes SL600.

The bastard had fired up the sleek car and breezed down the

lane using Billy Ray's own electronic gate opener to leave the estate. And all the while Billy could do nothing. *Nothing.* Never had he felt so powerless.

Lying on the smooth backseat, smelling new leather, Billy Ray had prayed, oh, how he'd prayed, for salvation. He'd had no idea where they were going. He'd lost track after the driver had turned west onto the main highway then north...probably on Gatlin Road, but after that, with all the twists and turns, Billy Ray had lost all sense of direction. Nor did he know why he'd been kidnapped. But he had a dark fear that this psychopath was the same one responsible for the deaths of four other people.

About a half an hour from the time he'd been abducted, he'd felt the car shimmy as it was turned too quickly onto a rough road. The Mercedes had bounced and lunged over potholes.

Within minutes, the car had stopped suddenly and the driver had climbed out. He'd opened the back door and given Billy Ray another shot for good measure. The rest of the abduction was blurry. Billy Ray was briefly unbound, stripped, then forced into a chair, his naked butt feeling a crack in the plastic seat. His hands had been tied behind him with tape, and his legs were strapped to the legs of the chair.

Then the assailant had said the first and only words he'd uttered since walking into Billy Ray's study.

Leaning close, his breath hot against the reverend's ear, he'd uttered, "The power of God be with you, Brother."

Billy Ray had felt a chill like no other.

Then his abductor had left. Billy Ray, shaking in his shackles, had heard the smooth sound of the Mercedes's engine purr off into the night.

At that point, he'd known he had to work fast. Either the bastard planned to return to torment, torture, then finish the job, or Billy Ray had been left here indefinitely to die of dehydration while the creatures who called this place home waited patiently.

He'd tried everything. Throwing himself forward in the chair, knocking it over, struggling to slide to whatever doorway there was, yanking at the tape at his wrists until his arms ached, kicking his feet so hard that pain screamed up his legs to his lower back.

With all his strength, he'd shoved and scooted the chair over the dirty floor. Dust and filth pushed into his nostrils. His left ear was scratched raw as he inched toward what he hoped was the door. Slowly the chair scraped over the smelly linoleum, past pieces of cloth, over tiny hard pellets that he assumed were rat feces. There had to be something...anything he could use as a weapon.

Minutes ticked by. He was sweating, his naked skin rubbed to bleeding where his shoulder pushed over the floor. Suddenly his nose ran into something soft...cloth of some kind? He explored with his face and felt metal, cool, smooth, attached to a thin, long... snake! *Sweet Jesus!* He scooted back rapidly, waiting for the sleeping serpent to coil and strike.

But he heard no warning hiss.

Sensed no movement.

Was it dead? Caught in a mousetrap? Lying on a pile of forgotten clothes? Why else the metal...? But smooth metal. Polished metal. Expensive metal? Out of place here...and the cloth hadn't been dusty or rotting. No foul odor had assailed his nostrils; if anything, he'd smelled a gentle musky scent.

His heart leapt.

Not a snake!

Not a damned serpent!

His belt. Right? *His* clothes? He'd found the spot where his abductor had tossed his pants and shirt after stripping them from his body. And the psycho had been in a hurry. Billy Ray had sensed that. As if the lunatic were running out of time. So the clothes had been left, along with anything in his pockets. Along with his Pomeroy Ultra pocket tool, the one his son had given him for Christmas last year. From needle-nosed pliers to a tiny saw to toenail clippers, the Ultra was a handyman's dream and boasted fifteen blades. Billy Ray needed only one. Any would do.

The other selling feature had been that the Ultra was easily accessible, meaning that with the push of a small lever, two of the most commonly used blades would flip out. He remembered his son, eyes shining, backdropped by the eighteen-foot Christmas tree. Garlands of greenery, lush poinsettias, tissue paper, and ribbons littered Aldora's gleaming hardwood floor, while his son proudly told Billy about the flip lever that made the Ultra "kind of like a switchblade of tools."

At the time Billy Ray had just smiled and thought, *Darn it, son, who needs that?* Now he was grateful for the function.

He worked feverishly, scooting the chair into position in front of his pants. Quickly his fingers searched through the pockets while his shoulders screamed in pain.

Breathing deeply, praying minute by minute, he remembered all of the pain he'd endured as an athlete: broken fingers, a crushed nose, bruised elbows, torqued knees in addition to his ankle. He could endure this. He would! Anger started to burn bright in his chest as he set his jaw and found one pocket. Good! He pressed onward, his fingers searching and coming up with...his lighter. Perfect. Carefully, he set it aside. It could come in handy. Now, the other front pocket. His fingers brushed over his fly, feeling the metal teeth of his zipper, then discovered the pocket. Straining, he pushed his hands downward into the lining. It had to be there! He always carried it with him! Sweat burned his eyes. Panic started to surge through him.

Then he felt it...the Pomeroy Ultra! It was hard to grab hold of, his fingers slick as they were with sweat, but with sheer guts and determination, Billy Ray grabbed the tool and, inch by inch, slid it from his pants. Eventually it was free...*Now, God help me,* he thought, his fingers trembling as he tried to open the spring mechanism.

The Ultra fell out of his hands. He nearly swore, but caught himself. He wasn't alone. God was with him. And yet he was angry at his clumsiness. "Give me strength," he muttered behind his gag and found the tool again. Closing his eyes behind the blindfold, he used a technique he'd learned long ago when trying to deal with his rage. He pictured the Ultra in his hand and, breathing slowly and calmly, rotated it until it felt comfortable. In his mind's eye he saw himself flipping the lever—where was the damned thing? There! He felt the nub and pushed.

Click! A blade swung free.

Hallelujah!

Thank you, Jesus!

God be with me, he silently prayed, *and give me the strength to kill the son of a bitch.*

In the last few hours of his darkness, Billy Ray had come to understand his mission. God was presenting him the opportunity to rid the earth of the monster who had abducted him. This was not only a test, but his opportunity to prove himself to the Lord. In so doing, he would not only save his life, and the life of whoever else the killer planned to murder, but also become more of a local hero. The press would eat it up. His parish would flourish. There would be a book deal. Even a television movie.

But he was getting ahead of himself. For now, all he had to concentrate on was somehow getting the upper hand, and he counted on his old buddy, rage, to help him through.

Because he was angry.

Furious and ready for revenge.

He began working with the Ultra, using the tool on the tape binding his wrists.

Come on, you sick bastard, he thought, fury searing through his veins, *I'm going to bring you down.*

Sister Maria was hauled roughly to her feet.

Her hands were bound behind her, but her assailant had cut away the tape that held her ankles together and untied her blindfold. He'd also draped her rosary over her neck.

"Move," he muttered from behind his mask.

Woozy and weak, she could barely walk. The muzzle of the gun in her back, and the urging of the brute of a man in black, kept her stumbling forward, through the darkness toward what? Torture, probably. Rape likely. And death certain.

As he pushed her forward, he swept the weak beam of a flashlight over the damp ground. Dead leaves formed a carpet over the soggy marshland. Cypresses grew tall, bleached like ghosts, their roots buckling the earth and delving into the standing water. She had no idea where in the swamps of Louisiana he'd brought her, but she was certain she was going to die.

Our Father who art in heaven . . .

He trained the flashlight onto a building, a single-wide mobile home that seemed as if it had been abandoned long ago; the siding had rusted, the windows broken out, the lean-to that had once been attached to it was now crumpled into a heap of grayed boards.

She thought of the vile acts he would commit against her, of the pain she would endure, and she accepted her fate, prayed for strength, for fortitude, so that she wouldn't break. She remembered Jesus and what he had endured upon the cross and only hoped that she would be able to handle what was to come with dignity, with piety, and be able to forgive this poor, tortured soul.

Up two uneven steps he pushed her, and she entered the dark interior, where she sagged against the wall. With the gun still pressed against her spine, he lit a lamp.

Her heart withered at the sight of the tiny space that had once been a living room. The interior was filthy from years of weather, vermin, and neglect. The smell of rot was everywhere and seated in a chair on the far wall, his legs bound to the rusted metal legs, his hands pulled behind him, was Billy Ray Furlough. He was naked, a blindfold over his eyes, a gag over his mouth. "No!" she cried, her voice muffled because of the tape over her mouth. Despite the weapon's muzzle hard against her back, she bent over and started to retch.

"Fuck!" Her assailant reached around her and tore the tape from her mouth just as her stomach emptied.

How could this be? Dear Father, no!

She was sobbing, crying, utterly destroyed.

No! No! No!

Tears ran down her face and she heaved again and again. She wasn't aware that her tormentor had left her, that he'd crossed the small scrap of stained linoleum to stand near her only child.

By the saints, how had the monster known? What did he want of her? Deep inside, her soul twisted painfully. Gasping and coughing, she looked over at the masked man who had abducted her and how pridefully he stood over her son.

She couldn't let this happen. Whatever this twisted mind had invented, she wouldn't let him harm her son, the baby she'd given away so many years before . . .

"Don't do this," she begged. "Ask for God's forgiveness and sin no more."

His body stiffened. "I'm not the sinner," he said slowly as he pulled off Billy Ray's blindfold.

Billy Ray turned glassy eyes at her and she realized that he, too, had already suffered. She would not look at his nakedness, but only into his dark eyes, so like his father's, a boy she'd known in her youth, a man long dead.

"You know each other," the abductor said in a gravelly, satisfied voice, and to her horror, she saw the recognition in her only child's features, realized that her secret had somehow been uncovered. "Mother and son."

Oh, Mother Mary.

"Both living lies."

Billy Ray's eyes turned toward their captor, and Maria saw something shift in his features, an anger in the flare of his nostrils, the narrowing of his eyes, and she knew then that he would do something stupid, something dangerous. She couldn't let it happen.

Somehow she had to save him. Even if she had to kill to do it. Murder was a mortal sin . . . her soul would go straight to hell.

So be it.

Billy Ray, pretending to be bound and still disoriented, couldn't help glaring at the woman who had borne him. Why was she here? The psycho had somehow abducted Sister Maria Montoya, the woman who had given birth to him and left him with parents too stupid to understand basic genetics.

There she was in her nightgown, looking old, tired, and scared, her rosary looped over her neck, her lips, now silent, moving mutely. He surmised she was mentally reciting the prayers of each decade of the rosary that was swinging from her neck. No doubt she was hoping for divine intervention.

She. The nun. Who was his mother.

Whore.

Hiding under the sacred habit.

Pretending piety.

He hated her, but more than that, he hated this man who was intending to take their lives with a gun that looked suspiciously like one from his collection, the nickel-plated Ruger he kept under the front seat of his Mercedes.

The psycho turned his back for just a second. In that instant, Billy Ray made his move. He leaped upward, his legs free, his hands unbound. With a strength he swore came from the Lord, he plunged the Pomeroy Ultra deep into the assailant's chest, just as the man spun.

Blood spurted.

The nun screamed and threw herself at the attacker.

With a roar, the psycho slammed the gun into the side of Billy Ray's face. Pain shot through his skull. His nose splintered. Billy Ray fell backward and lost his grip on the Ultra. His intention was to stab and stab and stab until the lifeblood flowed out of him, but his hands were slick with blood and the nun intervened, trying to force herself between the two, clawing at the man's face, *attacking* him with her bare hands.

No!

In an instant, the big man, his mask askew from the nun's assault, Billy Ray's weapon still protruding from him, smacked Sister Maria across the face, caught her as she began to fall, and forced his gun into her trembling, wavering hand . . .

Sister Maria gasped. *He was going to make her kill Billy Ray? No!*

She fought the brute, swinging her head back and forth, crying and screaming and praying in one horrible sound. But the psycho was strong—too strong. He aimed the weapon straight at Billy Ray's heart, cocked the hammer . . .

Billy Ray scooted backward, tried to get away.

Bang!

The Ruger fired.

Pain exploded in Billy Ray's chest. He blinked, stunned, and blood gurgled up his throat. He saw the psycho twist Sister Maria's wrist until she cried out. In slow motion and disbelief he watched the man place the muzzle of the gun to her temple and squeeze the trigger. Shuddering, Billy Ray closed his eyes and prayed as death claimed him.

The nun slumped in his arms. Carefully, he draped her body over the preacher's, leaving them entwined, mother and son, so different.

Pain seared through his body. He glanced down at the irritating knife still embedded in his chest and felt fury. The bastard had sliced him. Luckily the blade had hit a rib, so the damage was painful but not debilitating. He would remove the weapon soon, but later, when he was away from here. He couldn't afford any more of his blood being spilled.

He'd been foolish. Gotten careless. Hadn't given the preacher enough credit for being resourceful. Now, he stared down at the dead man. How had he gotten free? In the flashlight's beam he saw where the chair had been dragged to the pile of clothes. So the reverend had scooted himself across the room, somehow gotten the tool out of his pocket, freed himself, and then waited? Why not run for it?

Had he run out of time?

Not expected his captor to return?

Or had he wanted to be a hero, had he felt invincible as he was on "Jesus's team," as he'd so often said? The hypocrite.

Satisfied that he'd arranged them just as he wanted, he lifted the nun's head and pulled her rosary from her neck. Quickly he slid the holy beads into his pocket. Then he took the gun. Furlough's nickel-plated Ruger.

Silently he walked outside. Realizing there was blood on his shoes, he took the time to wipe them on the steps before stopping at the Mercedes and popping the trunk. He found the emergency kit, grabbed it, forcing himself to ignore the pain in his chest. Then he headed down a long path, to a dilapidated dock where pilings were settling into the bog. The rowboat was right where he'd left it hours earlier. He stepped inside and, using the flashlight, looked at the weapon still protruding through the wet suit. Checking the emergency kit, he found several gauze pads and sterile tape. Good enough for now. Gritting his teeth, he pulled out the tool. Blood started to flow and he quickly stanched it with the gauze. He unwrapped all five packs, layered the gauze pads, one on top of the other, strapping them down with the tape. He ached and bled from the jagged slice, but no vital organ had been perforated. He'd been lucky this time. In the flashlight's glow he stared at the weapon, a Pomeroy all-purpose handyman's tool scripted with the name "Ultra."

His jaw dropped.

Fucker!

He hated that Billy Ray, and now Asa Pomeroy, too, had gotten in this last word.

Well, it was too late for them.

Swishing the blade in the water, he cleaned the tool and dropped it into the box for the emergency kit. Along with the Ultra, he added the rosary and revolver. Quickly he grabbed an oar. Almost silently he began to paddle to the spot where he'd hidden his truck, not two miles from the preacher's study.

He'd have to work fast. Dawn would arrive in a few hours and he wanted to be far from the Reverend Billy Ray Furlough's compound when the preacher was discovered missing.

Besides, his work was far from done.

He wouldn't have much time, he thought as he dipped his oar into the water. *Stroke, stroke, stroke.* The pain in his chest throbbed viciously, but he pushed it aside.

He had others to take care of today.

His lips pulled into a rictus smile as he oared through the darkness. The beam from his small flashlight guided him through these familiar waters. He caught the glow of a gator's eyes as it glided past, and when he scanned the shore, he caught images of 'possums and raccoons staring after him. He breathed in the heavy scent of the water, rowing unerringly, just as he had as a child.

When he'd been allowed.

When the restrictions had been lifted...

His jaw hardened when he recalled how all that had changed. When *she* had been introduced to him. His lips curled as if he'd encountered a foul smell.

She, with her tinkling laugh, tiny voice, and iron will. A small woman even in the high heels she forever wore. A frail-looking beauty who caused men, even important men, to fawn all over her.

She'd changed things from the start. No more hunting off-season, no more late nights, no more eating in front of the television, no more "obnoxiously loud eardrum-splitting bass" and certainly not one more "disgusting, violent, and sick lyric."

His hands tightened over the paddle.

Stroke, stroke, stroke.

She, with her tiny, yapping dog and expensive horses...

His smile turned to a sneer as he considered the irony of it all:

the dog trampled by the horse; the sleek bay gelding rearing at a snake and tossing off his rider; the rider hitting her head on a large, knife-edged rock. By the time anyone had gone looking for her, the vultures had already been circling.

So now, he could breathe deeply of the thick bayou air, hear the insects thrum in the bulrushes, watch the moon rise over the dark, brackish waters. *She* couldn't stop him.

Stroke, stroke, stroke.

He guided his small craft to the side of an inlet. Hopping out, he dragged the boat to the shore, concealing it in the thick cattails and reeds.

Stripping off his boots for the sneakers in his backpack, he took several shallow breaths, then a few deeper ones. The pain was bearable. He stuffed the emergency kit into the pack before heading cross-country through a farmer's field, then on to the winding county road where he started the two-mile jog toward his truck.

Everything had been going so well.

Until Billy Ray Furlough had nearly outsmarted him, and the nun . . . who would have thought that meek milquetoast of a woman had the fire to challenge him? *Like a mother bear,* he thought, remembering his father's warnings before they would take up their rifles and begin the long trek to the mountains. *Do* not *get between a she-bear and her cubs. No matter what. If you make that mistake, shoot her. Quick. Before she has the chance to rip your liver out!*

Twice during his run, a vehicle had passed. Both times he'd dived into the roadside ditch and lain flat until the beams from the headlights had passed over his body, the illumination fading and taillights visible. Only then would he start loping again, his wound aching and leaden. He knew he was bleeding again, and he bit back an oath when he thought of being fooled by the preacher.

How could that have happened? He was the one with the genius IQ. Billy Ray Furlough was just a hot-headed, has-been athlete who'd found a way to make a buck out of his rage by using it as a tool to appear passionately pious. Correction: Billy Ray Furlough was now a *dead* hotshot has-been.

His truck was where he'd left it: at the diner where he was often a patron. It was a place that was open twenty-four hours, where truckers often stopped for coffee and pie; in the evenings it was beer and hard liquor. He was known in this place by name, and no one thought twice if his truck remained there longer than he did. He always parked in the thick of the rigs and semis that pulled in at all hours. He always showed his face, too, as he was coming and going: sometimes through the back where the bar was; sometimes the front of the restaurant. He made certain he was seen every two hours or so. People knew him to be a hunter and a fisherman, a guy who sometimes left his rig in the parking lot when he stalked game. He was teased, too, as no one ever saw him with a bagged deer, or even ducks, or fish in his creel. He always laughed at the ribbing, buying a round, and telling the regulars that it was more to be out in nature than anything else.

They believed he was an independent contractor—a sheet rocker. They thought he was oftentimes out of work.

No one asked too many questions and the cover worked just fine.

Now, he glanced around. It was dark by the truck, extremely so, even though the eastern sky was faintly lightening. Quickly and carefully he removed his sneakers, stripped off the wetsuit, then pulled on a pair of jeans. He was shivering. The gauze was bloody. He shoved his arms through a blue cotton shirt, buttoned it over the gauze, then pushed his arms through a navy nylon jacket.

He took a precious moment to pull himself together. When he climbed from the truck, he stopped to purchase a paper from the box outside. Pretending absorption in the headlines, he walked into the restaurant, which was bustling with truckers slurping down their first cups of java for the day. He waved at the red-haired waitress whom he knew was nearly done with her shift, then took a stool and ordered coffee, eggs over easy, crisp bacon, grits, biscuits, and gravy.

As he waited for his breakfast, he tried not to think about the killings, couldn't yet let himself go to that place between wake and sleep where he relived the thrill, felt the thrum run through his veins, got off on the memory of their deaths. No, not yet...he needed his wits about him. And he also needed to take care of his injury, but not yet, not until he'd set his cover deeply, made sure everyone saw him having a leisurely breakfast.

Scanning the front page, he noticed that all mention of Asa

Pomeroy and Gina Jefferson's deaths had been placed below the fold, though because of the funeral, Luke Gierman's picture was at the top of the page. Other related stories were buried deeper in the pages.

"Real sick-o behind that," a local trucker who delivered eggs said. He thumped the paper as he passed on his way to his favorite booth. The tag embroidered on his overalls declared that his name was Hank. "Can't wait 'til they catch that sumbitch and string him up by his balls." He nodded, squared the bill of his trucker's cap onto his head. "Yeah, I'll like to see that. I listened to *Gierman's Groaners* all the time. Can't stand the fact that his sidekick, what's the guy's name?"

Maury Taylor, you imbecile, he thought, but shrugged.

"Maury, that's it. A real jerk wad, that guy. Ridin' on Gierman's coattails. Hell." He rubbed his fleshy jaw, which sported two days' worth of silver bristles. "Don'tcha just hate it."

"Yeah," he said as his platter of eggs, bacon, and grits was placed in front of him.

"Sorry about the broken yolk," the waitress said. "New cook. You okay with that?"

No!

"I can get you a couple more."

Don't do it. Don't draw attention to yourself. Smile and act like it's no big deal that the cook is incompetent. "This is fine," he said.

"You're sure? It's no trouble."

"I'm okay." *Jesus, lady, back the fuck off!*

"Well, then I'll grab you a piece of pie. On the house. Pecan. Fresh baked."

He nodded and Hank clapped him on the back. "Have yourself a good 'un."

"You, too," he said, momentarily shocked by the impact. He struggled for breath. Then Hank's out-of-control gray eyebrows drew together over the tops of his thick glasses. "Hey, wha'd'ja do to yourself there?" he asked, pointing a thick finger at his shirt. "Cut yerself shaving?" Hank laughed but it sounded hollow.

He looked down. A red stain showed through his shirt.

He thought fast. "Chainsaw bucked the other day while I was cuttin' brush."

"Jesus Christ, man, you coulda kilt yerself. Gotta be careful with them things."

"Hit a knot." He nodded, pretended to show embarrassment that he couldn't handle a tool. "I had it stitched up at the emergency clinic, but I think I'd better go back in."

"Hell yes, you'd better go back in." Hank frowned, nodded curtly, then lifted his hat and smoothed his hair before pulling the brim down low again. "See ya 'round." Finally the old coot ambled back to his chair.

He zipped his jacket and ate fast, careful not to take one bite of the broken yolk. To appease the damned waitress, he even washed down four bites of pie with black coffee before leaving enough cash on the bar for the meal and a fifteen percent tip.

And all the while he silently cursed Billy Ray Furlough.

Well, the bastard got his, didn't he?

Dawn broke as he drove through the small towns to the back side of Our Lady of Virtues' campus. The truck bumped down an old forgotten road that had once led to a dairy farm, now long abandoned. He parked inside the barn, ducked through a hole in the fence, then headed down a path he'd walked years before, one that led to a private entrance to the bowels of the main building.

Once inside, he maneuvered through the maze of corridors and stairwells until he came to his private set of rooms, the ones he'd known years before and had reclaimed. Using his flashlight, he worked his way to an old surgery unit and there, in the drawers, found leftover bandages. Shrugging out of his jacket, he unbuttoned his shirt, then removed the soaking wads of gauze. As he took off the shirt, he saw that his blood was clotting, the flow had slowed considerably. If the bastard hadn't managed to slice him, had just left a puncture wound, then it wouldn't have bled so much in the first place.

Carefully, he cleaned the wound using cold water from the shower. He squeezed gel from a tube of antiseptic cream tucked into the reverend's first-aid kit. Then he ripped open packages of sterile cotton gauze patches—courtesy of the old hospital—and placed them directly over the wound. He secured the bandage with adhesive tape, then wrapped his chest tightly with a stretchy Ace bandage that he'd found still lying in one of the drawers. The whole place felt ready for business, as if it had just shut its doors yesterday. But it had been a long, long time.

Only when he was finished did he carry his backpack to his private room and light candles at his shrine. He unfolded the secretary's table, then reached into the pack and withdrew his new treasures. The rosary and revolver would go into one cubby together, shining blood-red beads wrapped seductively over the muzzle of the nickel-plated .357.

He fingered the other treasures, the watch and ring, the little gold cross and diamond-studded money clip...His collection was growing but it still had so far to go. Six items were locked away, but he needed eight more...all belonging to a special person, one of the chosen.

Opening a photo album, he examined the old pictures—the hospital, the staff, the patients, the nuns. There were other photos as well, for some of the players were not a part of the smiling group shots. Part of his mission would be to find pictures of them.

He'd chosen wisely, he thought. Spent years formulating and perfecting his plan. The fourteen men and women were not random. In a way, they'd chosen themselves, had they not?

He ran a finger down their faces, the ones that he'd marked with a red pen, and then he glanced up to the top of the secretary, where the framed picture of Faith Chastain stared down at him. He thought of her and their secret trysts so long ago...

And then as he heard the old pipes drip, and smelled the mold and death and darkness, he thought of the others...His mind reeled with the memory of each death, that pure moment, that heady feel of power, that potent sexual thrill...

He would hide.

Rest.

For a few hours, perhaps a few days.

"But not for long," he vowed, staring at the photograph of Faith. "Not for long."

CHAPTER 23

Abby stretched and opened an eye. Sunlight was slipping through the blinds, striping thin slats of light across the rumpled covers where Detective Reuben Montoya was breathing deeply. One of his arms was thrown over his head, his lips open just enough to inhale and exhale puffs of air. His black hair was mussed, giving a decidedly boyish look to his normally serious features.

Recalling the night's lovemaking, she smiled. Snuggling closer, she wrapped her arms around his torso, and spied the small gold ring in his earlobe. She kissed his temple, then nibbled at the tiny piece of jewelry.

"You've got half an hour to cut that out."

"You're awake."

"Very," he said in a low tone that seemed to throb through her.

In a quick movement, he rolled over, pinning her beneath him. He stared down at her. Then, he captured her lips with his and began rubbing her body intimately, touching all the spots that created heat to swirl and rise within her. Seconds later she joined in and they explored each other anew, rediscovering the passion that lingered from the night before.

She opened readily to him. As they made love, she closed her mind to everything but the pleasure that rippled through her body in deep, searing waves. It happened so fast it left her breathless and surprised by her own desperate response.

I'm falling in love with you, she thought but didn't let the words slip past her lips. No. She was enjoying this man, enjoying making love with him, but she wasn't in love. She wasn't about to mistake lust for love... yes, she cared for Montoya. She liked him. A lot. But that wasn't necessarily love.

Later, when their breathing had slowed, Montoya looked up to see Ansel staring down from the bookcase. "Pervert," he muttered.

"Maybe he's taking notes."

He grinned and rolled off the bed, searched a moment for his jeans, pulled them on.

"You're spoiling my view," she teased.

"Maybe you'll get another look later."

"I'll hold you to that, Detective."

"Fair enough." He reached for his weapon, still lying on the dresser, and stuffed it into his waistband. "How about I make coffee?"

"Mmm." She stretched lazily. "That sounds perfect." She lolled her head to one side and tossed her hair from her face. "And let the dog out, would you?"

"Yeah, right. Just after I bring you the newspaper and a long-stemmed rose." She watched him walk from the room, her mind's eye imprinted with the muscular V of his torso, the smooth muscles sliding beneath the skin of his back, the low dip of his jeans.

I could get used to this, she thought, lying back on the pillows to stare up at the ceiling. She bit her lower lip as images of their passion flashed behind her eyes. Pressing the heels of her hands to her eyes, she groaned aloud in embarrassed amusement. It had been so wonderful.

Hershey padded into the bedroom and hopped on the bed without an invitation.

"Hey, girl, how're you?" Sitting yoga-like on the bed, Abby petted the dog. She felt a light thump as Ansel landed on the foot of the bed. The cat gave the dog a wide berth, then settled next to Abby on a pillow and began to purr.

She heard cupboard doors opening and closing and yelled, "Coffee's to the right of the stove... upper shelf."

More banging. Then she heard the back door open, a few seconds of silence, then it was slammed shut.

"He's lost. I think I'd better go help, guys." Quickly she threw on her robe and padded barefoot into the kitchen, where Montoya had just discovered the coffee and grinder. "Some detective you are."

"Careful," he warned, his lips curving. "I'm still the guy with the gun."

She sobered slightly, remembering that Luke's .38 was missing. "Need a hand?" she asked, settling onto a bar stool.

"I think I've got it now."

"You're sure?"

Near-black eyes flashed in amusement and she found herself loving the way his hair fell over his forehead and the way his jeans settled low on his hips.

"Did you go outside?" she asked.

He nodded. "I checked under the laundry room window to see if there were any footprints, or any other sign of your thief. Nothing that I can see, but I'll have someone from the crime lab come out and dust for prints and double-check the ground."

"Doesn't there have to be a crime committed?"

"You report the gun stolen, and I'll pull a few strings. Then you get an alarm system."

"I'm working on that," she said. "So far the earliest I can get someone out here is next week."

"Try All-Security. Mention my name."

"You've got strings to pull there, too?"

"My brother Miguel works for All-Security. Has for years. I'm sure he can hook you up." He ground the coffee, and as the screeching whir wound down, Hershey let out a quick bark and, toenails clicking on the hardwood, raced to the front door.

The bell rang.

"Company?" he asked, glancing at the clock. "At eight?"

"I don't know..." Cinching the belt of her robe, she hurried to the door. Peering through the blinds, she saw Zoey looking back at her. Luggage was strewn over the porch and a rental car was parked in the drive near Montoya's Mustang.

"About time!" Zoey said, hauling in a roller bag, computer case, and oversized purse as soon as Abby opened the door. Hershey scrambled and wiggled wildly around Zoey's feet, as if she'd been missing Abby's sister for months. "Hey, girl." Zoey bent down and offered the dog some pets before straightening. "What's with the car? That's not your Mustang, is it? You didn't finally trade in the old Honda? Or did you inherit one from Luke, or..." Her words faded as she spied Montoya, dressed only in his battered jeans, his sidearm visible in his waistband, standing in the archway between the living room and dining room. "Oh...wow." Her gaze returned to her sister's. She cleared her throat. "A guy with a gun?"

"Zoey," Abby said, feeling a blush stain her cheeks and wondering where in the world this was going to go. "This is Detective Reuben Montoya. He's a *cop* with a gun and a black Mustang." Abby looked at Montoya and motioned toward Zoey. "Montoya, my sister, Zoey."

Zoey stepped forward and shook Montoya's hand. "I guess I, um, came at a bad time."

Montoya's dark eyes glinted and he slid Abby an intimate glance, then winked. "Trust me, it could have been worse."

"Ohhh..." Zoey looked envious.

Memories of their recent lovemaking flashed through Abby's mind. She could see Zoey melting under Montoya's charm. Just what she needed, her sister interested in her new man... *He's* not *your new man, Abby,* she reminded herself sternly. Managing a smile, she resisted the urge to link her arm through the detective's. "I think that was all the information my sister needs to hear right now."

"Let me take those." He grabbed Zoey's bags and walked unerringly to the second bedroom, as if he carried guests' bags through Abby's house on a regular basis.

Zoey raised an eyebrow and couldn't hide the smile stretching across her face as she watched him disappear. "Oh, Abby," she whispered. "He's—"

"He's the detective investigating Luke's murder," she said, cutting off Zoey's train of thought.

She looked surprised. "And he's here, with you? The ex-wife? Isn't that a major no-no? I watch those crime shows and the detective never gets involved with anyone close to the victim because it could—compromise the investigation." Her green eyes slanted. "Not that I blame you, though."

Sending her sister a warning glance, Abby said shortly, "Detective Montoya was just making coffee. You look like you could use a cup."

"You got that one right. The flight was the worst. I mean *the worst.* From Seattle to Dallas, I sat between a bawling baby and stressed-out mom on one side, and a big guy who couldn't get comfortable on the aisle. I was either retrieving 'binkies,' those pacifier things, or trying to shrink so the big man could play computer chess. Then I was hung up in Dallas and the next leg was worse. Mechanical problems, a new plane, no bin space, no food... speaking of which, what have you got?"

Montoya reappeared. He was smiling, obviously overhearing the tail end of their conversation.

"What?" Zoey asked.

"Nothing," Abby assured her as they headed to the kitchen, Hershey bounding in front of them.

"A private joke?" Zoey asked. "How long have you two"—she wagged her finger between Abby and Montoya—"been together?"

"It's not a private joke. More like common knowledge that my culinary skills are... limited." Abby adroitly sidestepped Zoey's question as she opened a cupboard. "So I've got toast and... peanut butter."

"Is it fat-free?"

Abby gave her sister a look. "It's peanut butter, Zoe. Plenty of fat and..." She picked up the jar and rotated it so that her sister could view the label. "... it's chunky. Pieces of real peanuts. Not the fat-free kind."

"I'll take it. Beats what I had on the plane, though, you know, you could have stocked up."

Montoya laughed.

"I see he knows you already," Zoey grumbled. As Montoya poured cups of coffee all around, she slid onto one of the bar stools. "I'm telling you, I'm going to eat this and then do a face-plant on the daybed. Wake me up an hour before the funeral and I'll pull myself together."

"It's at eleven." Abby found half a loaf of bread in the refrigerator, examined the slices for mold, then slid a couple into the toaster.

"Good. I can sleep a bit before the service and then catch up if I need more afterwards." She stared into her coffee cup. "I'm not looking forward to it."

You and me both, Abby thought.

A phone chirped from the living room.

"That's mine," Montoya said and strode out of the room.

Zoey, sipping from her cup, followed him with her eyes. "Nice butt." She turned her gaze on her sister. "As a matter of fact, pretty nice all around." Her eyes gleamed. "You should have told me."

"It's all new, I mean, *real* new."

Zoey gave Abby's state of undress and tousled hair the once-over. "Looks like you're pretty involved."

Abby didn't like where this was going. "As I said, 'new.' I'm not sure how...involved...we are."

"Run with it, Abs, the guy's definitely hot." She sipped from her cup. "But I don't know about the whole cop thing."

"I'm not marrying him, Zoe. We're just..." What were they? Not dating. "...seeing each other."

"Mmm." Zoey took a sip. "Don't blame you...not at all."

"What do you mean, 'missing'?" Montoya asked, his heart turning to stone.

The Mother Superior sighed. "I mean that we've searched the building, the grounds, everywhere. Sister Maria is missing. Her bed was obviously slept in, unmade, and...she's just gone. I hated to call you, but she spoke so highly of you and told me if ever something was wrong, I was to phone you first."

He was rapidly getting dressed, throwing an arm through a shirtsleeve, finding his socks and shoes.

"Who was the last person to see her?"

"I think I was."

"Where?"

"At the door to her room, sometime before vespers, we passed in the hallway...and...oh, dear."

"I'm on my way," Montoya assured her, a cold hammer of dread pounding at his skull. "Don't let anyone into her room or even in the hallway by the room. I'll be there in half an hour."

He threw on the rest of his clothes, strode into the kitchen. Abby looked up from slathering peanut butter on a piece of toast.

"I gotta go." He didn't have time to explain, but she looked so damned seductive in the white terry bathrobe that he couldn't stop himself from pulling her into his arms, kissing her hard, then releasing her. "Lock the doors," he said, already heading out the door. "I'll call later."

"Okay."

Zoey sat with the uneaten toast in front of her.

"My God, Abby," she whispered. "He's hot."

"You've looked everywhere?" Montoya asked, trying to keep his cool as he sat in the chair in the Mother Superior's office, a large wood-paneled room with a fireplace, broad desk, and windows that opened to the cloister.

"Everywhere in the convent. Everywhere she usually goes." The woman, about half of his aunt's height, was in her eighties, with papery skin, half-glasses, and eyes as blue as all of June. The lines around her lips were deep, but her mind seemed as sharp as it ever was. "Sister Maria is known to go on walks, alone. I've cautioned her against it, to take someone with her, but..." She sighed and shook her head slowly, making the sign of the cross over her thin chest.

"Have you searched the grounds?"

"Just around the convent here, but I've asked Mr. DuLoc to check the surrounding areas."

"Lawrence DuLoc, right? The groundskeeper?" Montoya remembered.

"Yes."

"How long as he been with you here?"

"Years...over ten, I'm sure. I would have to check the records."

"Would you?"

"We've never had any trouble with him."

"Does he live on the grounds?"

"A small cabin, yes, on the edge of the property, but really, Mr. DuLoc has been a godsend." Her eyes were fervent, and her chin inched up a bit, as if he'd offended her.

"We'll have to look into everyone associated with the convent to find Sister Maria. I'm sure you'll want to cooperate fully."

Her lips pursed a bit tighter. "Of course, Detective Montoya, but it's also my position to protect the people who live here."

"We'll both be protecting them." He stood. "May I see her room?"

The old nun nodded, took her glasses off her nose so that they swung from her neck on a chain, then climbed from behind her desk and led Montoya through the hallways to the second floor. She'd barricaded the room with a couple of chairs and opened the door without a key.

"The room wasn't locked?"

She looked up at him. "There is no need."

"Until last night."

He looked inside the tiny chamber. A twin bed was pushed against one corner, the covers wildly mussed, the sheet draping to the floor. His stomach wrenched as he imagined her struggle. The closet door was ajar and a few items of clothing—habits and street clothes—peeked through. Her small window was open a crack, a breeze sliding through. "You haven't disturbed anything?"

"No. Sister Rebecca, who usually walks with her to morning prayers, knocked on her door. When there was no answer, she went inside. Seeing Sister Maria was missing, she called me, and I came to her room. Then we went to prayers, thinking she would join us, but she didn't. When she didn't come to breakfast, we started looking more seriously. I spoke with everyone here and no one saw her after I did—which was around eight P.M. As I said, she didn't say or do anything that would lead me to believe that she was troubled. Then, I called you. She'd given me your phone number in case of an emergency."

There was nothing he could do officially until his aunt had been missing twenty-four hours. Nonetheless, he walked the perimeter of the convent, unofficially talked with a few of the nuns who were his aunt's friends, and was shown some of the rooms and hallways Sister Maria had called home for nearly forty years.

Anger burned through him. She hadn't been safe in a nunnery—the very place she'd found sanctuary when her own family had shunned her.

"You know my aunt well," he said, eyeing the Mother Superior as she escorted him to his car.

"As well as anyone, I suppose."

"Were you here when she joined?"

She nodded. "Yes." She smiled slightly. "I've been here a long time. I think some of the younger nuns consider me a dinosaur. T. rex, I believe."

He eyed the woman's birdlike stature. T. rex was quite a stretch. "You must know why my aunt came here in the first place."

She lifted a gray eyebrow as her lips pulled into a frown. "We're a tightly knit little community here. There are few secrets."

"Everyone has secrets."

She hesitated, then said, "And they should be kept private, between oneself and God. I know about her son."

They'd reached the pockmarked lot where Montoya was parked. He opened the car door but paused. "I don't know if my aunt's . . . if Sister Maria's . . . disappearance has anything to do with the old hospital," he said, "but I would like all the records for it. I need information about who worked there, who resided there, who visited often."

She looked up sharply. "The hospital's been closed for a long time."

"It's the records I'm interested in," he said. "They must still exist."

"That information is confidential."

"I'll get a court order. It will be granted. All you'll do is delay me and use up time." He looked at the little woman steadily. "I'm not sure how or why, but I think the double homicides that have occurred lately might be connected to the hospital. The information in those records might help me locate my aunt." He felt a little needle of guilt to think that soon after he'd spoken with Sister Maria, when he'd asked for information from her, she'd gone missing. "I asked her for some of this information and she gave me the confidentiality speech. Now she's missing. Is there a connection? I don't know. I need to find out."

"What are you looking for, specifically?" she asked.

He was surprised she read him so well. "I want to know exactly what happened to Faith Chastain."

Tiny lines grooved between her brows. "I don't know—"

"And I need to find Sister Maria."

She looked away for a moment, came to a decision. "I'll see what I can do. Despite what I may appear, I'm not a dusty old relic clinging to the 'old ways,' Detective. I understand about the world we live in and all its ills. But like you, I have a protocol I must adhere to."

"Thank you. I'll be back soon." He jogged to his car and drove like a bat out of hell to the city. As the miles passed, he called his mother and asked her to phone all the family members, find out if any of them had seen Maria. Then he dialed his brother Miguel at All-Security and explained that he needed someone to connect or rewire the alarm system ASAP at Abby Chastain's house in Cambrai.

"Hey, Reu, we're booked up for over a month," Miguel complained. "We bid a new subdivision and people are calling like crazy what with that nut of a killer running around. When business is good for you, it's good for me, too."

Montoya took a corner too fast, forced himself to ease off the gas. "This is important."

"They all are."

"I'd owe you."

"You already do, for life. Who is this woman anyway?"

"A friend, who might be in danger."

Miguel chuckled and Montoya heard him lighting a cigarette. "A new friend?"

"Yeah."

"About time you had a new woman friend," Miguel said. "Okay, I'll get to it the first of next week. Give me her address. Wait...I need to find a pen."

Once he was back on the line, Montoya gave Miguel as much information as possible, then mentioned that Maria was missing.

"From the convent?" Miguel asked.

"Looks that way."

"My God, a person isn't safe anywhere these days." He paused. "You'll find her, though, right? And she'll be okay."

"I hope so. Check around. With all the cousins, anyone she knew. I've already told Mom. I'll catch ya later." He hung up just as he was slowing for a light in the French Quarter. The sun, through a thin fog, sent rays of light along the streets and alleys.

It was Saturday and already warm enough that Montoya rolled down his window. Throngs of people were walking the streets, clogging the crosswalks or jaywalking through the city. He tapped his hands restlessly on the steering wheel. No one and nothing else seemed to be in a hurry. The Mississippi flowed steadily by, the scent of the river noticeable despite the aromas of baked goods and coffee emanating from shops or the odor of gasoline and car fumes that rolled through the town.

As he stopped for a traffic light, he noticed two young men, peacock proud as they sauntered across the street. He'd been one of those young toughs, he thought, noticing how low their shorts rode on their butts and how they swaggered. If it hadn't been for his stern you're-going-to-make-something-of-yourself-or-else mother and his athleticism, he might have never gone to college, never become a detective. Three girls in tight T-shirts and shorts walked by. The men's heads swiveled as if pulled on strings. One of them said something that the girls, one chatting on a cell phone, ignored.

The game goes on, Montoya thought, glancing at his watch. He drove past Jackson Square and St. Louis Cathedral, its three towering spires knifing upward into a blue sky currently blotted by wisps of lingering fog. People pushed strollers, walked dogs, laughed, and shopped, seemingly unaware that their lives were in danger, that a killer was stalking the streets, that the serenity of this morning was just a mask for something dark and terrible.

You have to stop him. You're a good cop, you know you are, so nail his hide and save Maria. For God's sake, Montoya, step it up. Don't let this bastard take another life.

He parked on the street near the station and strode quickly inside. On the second floor he ran into Lynn Zaroster. "Hey," she said as she was slipping off her jacket and hanging it over the back of her chair in her cubicle. "You heard the news? Billy Ray Furlough's missing."

He froze.

All his fears congealed. "You're kidding."

"Nope. The wife's already filed a report, though we think the last person who saw him didn't leave the estate until around eight last night. Apparently the reverend and the missus don't sleep together; he usually stays in his office on the property. It hasn't been twenty-four hours, but because of the recent murders, we're already all over it. Brinkman and Conway are on the scene along with someone from the local field office of the FBI."

"Shit," Montoya said, feeling sick inside. "My aunt's missing, too. From the convent."

"What?"

"My aunt's a nun. The last anyone saw her was yesterday around eight P.M."

"Oh, God." She grabbed her jacket. "I'll go out there."

"I was just there."

"Are you nuts! You can't investigate family members—"

"It wasn't official," he cut her off. "I was just the first family member called and I happen to be a cop. Yeah, I asked some questions. Yeah, I took notes. Yeah, I looked into her room. Yeah, I did tell the Mother Superior to keep it cordoned off. I figure we'll have to work with the local Sheriff's Department."

Frowning, she was already sliding her arms down the sleeves of her jacket. "You're already thinking that we'll find your aunt with Billy Ray Furlough."

"Yin and yang," Montoya said.

Zaroster gave him a long look. "Explain."

"Look at the two other pairs of victims: one person is directly opposite of the other. The woman is staged to look like the killer, fully clothed, diametrically opposite from the other victim as anyone could be." He felt bile crawl up his throat. "And that's the way it would be with my aunt and Billy Ray Furlough. Both involved with the church, one outwardly, ostentatiously, so; the other, a woman who became a nun to live a quiet, peaceful life with God."

"What is that? Principles of Taoism or some other Eastern philosophy?"

"I don't know."

She slid her Glock into her shoulder holster. "Maybe it's time to bone up."

The funeral had been excruciating. Abby and Zoey sat in one of the back pews with their father and Charlene, listening all the while the preacher extolled Luke's virtues. Mourners sniffled and a few close friends gave testimonials to what a fine all-around guy he was. She recognized some of his coworkers from WSLJ, a few friends that she'd lost track of after the divorce, and some mutual acquaintances.

Montoya had been there, too, observing the crowd, positioning himself near the church steps as people left. News crews had camped outside and several reporters brandishing microphones talked into cameras held on the shoulders of cameramen as the crowd dispersed.

She and Zoey had spent a couple of hours with their dad and Charlene until, after looking at her watch pointedly several times, the second Mrs. Chastain insisted it was time to go and dutifully wheeled her ailing husband to her Cadillac. Zoey and Abby helped her get Jacques seated, then managed to hoist the wheelchair into the car's voluminous trunk. "Careful of the paint," Charlene warned and Abby saw Zoey's jaw tighten. Afterward, on the drive home, Zoey muttered, "I wanted to bang the frame of Dad's chair against the fender of her damned Caddy. Who does she think bought that car? What a bitch!" Zoey leaned her head against the side window of Abby's Honda.

"It's not her fault Dad's in such bad shape."

"Yeah, well, it's what she signed up for whether she knew it or not. All part of the 'in sickness and in health' part of the vows." Abby didn't reply and Zoey sighed. "Okay, I'm cranky, I admit it. No sleep tends to upset my usually bright and cheery disposition."

Abby laughed.

"What?" Zoey grumbled.

"Bright and cheery? Give me a break."

Zoey let out a huff of air. "Maybe you've got a point." Yawning, she found a sweater in the backseat and wadded it up to pad her head before placing it against the side window again. "Mmm, better..."

"You sleep, I'll drive."

"You didn't talk to that cute new boyfriend of yours."

"He's *not* my boyfriend."

"Coulda fooled me." Again she yawned. "You know when a guy stays over, makes coffee, and kisses the socks off you before he leaves—that's usually an indication that he's a boyfriend."

"Did you see how he watched the crowd?"

"Like a wolf ready to pounce." As Abby drove onto the freeway, Zoey manipulated the sweater again. She closed her eyes. "Abs?"

"Mmm?" Abby checked her rearview mirrors and accelerated.

"I never slept with Luke, okay?"

"Zoey, that's a lie and we both know it."

"I mean *after* you were married. I know you think I did, but even I'm not that low." Zoey opened one eye and peered at her sister. She was dead sober. "I wouldn't do that to you, okay. Not ever. I don't know what Luke told you, but after you said, 'I do,' I said 'I won't. Ever.' And I meant it. As for before the wedding, okay, yeah, you know about that. But never once while you were married."

"Why are you telling me this now?"

"Because Luke can't lie anymore. He can't screw with your head." She sighed and twisted her neck so loudly it popped. "Being with Luke was not exactly my proudest moment, okay? I felt rotten about it forever. But there's nothing I can do about it now except tell you the truth. Luke came on to me a lot, but I didn't give him the time of day. Sure, I found him attractive once, but he was your husband." She hesitated. "Is there any chance we can . . . lay that to rest and start over?"

Abby hesitated, looked over at Zoey. Could it really be that simple?

Zoey still stared at Abby with her one open eye. "Deal?"

Luke was dead. It was over. So why not get on with her life? "Okay Zoey," she finally said. "Deal."

Chapter 24

"Look, I just wanted you to hear it from me," Montoya said as he drove to the station. He hadn't been able to catch up with Abby at the funeral, so he'd called her at the first opportunity. "Sister Maria is missing."

"What?"

He heard the anxiety in her voice. "I take it you haven't heard the news."

"No," she said, her voice breaking up as their cell-phone-to-cell-phone connection was weak.

"What's even more disturbing is that Billy Ray Furlough is missing as well."

"Oh, God."

"We don't know if their abductions were done by the same person who killed the others, but it doesn't look good."

"Oh, no," she whispered. "I'm sorry."

"Yeah, me, too."

"You'll find her."

Montoya nodded, switching lanes. "Yeah." He only hoped that his aunt would be located while she was still alive. His fingers tightened over the wheel and his guts churned when he considered the alternative. "I called my brother, Miguel, from the security company. They're going to squeeze you in."

"Thanks."

"And I'll be by, I just don't know when. Your sister is with you?"

"Yes. She's planning to stay for a few days."

"Good, and you've got the guard dog."

Abby laughed. Despite his sour mood, Montoya felt the corners of his mouth twitch. "Don't forget Ansel the alarm cat," she said.

"Oh, right. My buddy." He turned onto Chartres Street, close to Jackson Square, where a cluster of tourists had collected to listen to jazz musicians performing next to an open guitar case.

"Ansel misses you," she said and he snorted.

"Tell him the feeling is mutual." He pictured her face and the teasing light in her gold eyes and he felt better than he had since learning the news of his aunt's disappearance. "I don't suppose you've found the missing .38?"

"Not yet," she said. Her voice sobered, now coming in loud and clear. "But I haven't really looked for it again."

"I don't like it."

"I know."

The more he thought about the missing gun, the more worried for her safety he was. "I'll try to stop by later. In the meantime you let me know if anything, and I mean *any*thing, seems out of place."

"I will," she said. "Thanks."

He hung up, feeling vulnerable. Not only was his aunt missing, but he was worried for Abby's safety. Worried enough that, once her sister left, if the house hadn't been wired with a security system, he was going to ask her to stay at his place, here in town.

His conscience twinged as he considered that he had deeper, ulterior motives—motives that had more to do with sleeping with her than keeping her safe, but he dismissed those thoughts. First and foremost he was concerned with her safety. He knew in his gut that she was somehow in danger and he couldn't let anything happen to her.

Face it, man, a voice deep in his brain nagged, *you're falling for her.* His jaw clenched hard as he slowed for jaywalkers. The police band crackled. *And the last time you fell hard for a woman, you couldn't save her. All of your hotshot police skills and you were still helpless.*

"Son of a bitch," he whispered under his breath as he parked near the station. Though he hadn't been officially removed from the case, it was only a matter of time if his aunt's disappearance proved to be connected to the killings.

He locked his car and headed inside. He intended to plug his camera into his computer and print out all the shots he'd taken at Gierman's funeral. He then planned to compare them to the ones he'd taken at Courtney LaBelle's candlelight vigil. Her funeral was scheduled for tomorrow afternoon, so he would be in the crowd there as well. Surely the killer would show, to bask in the glory of the chaos and pain, to feel superior, to rub shoulders with the grief-stricken and the police to, in his mind's eye, relive the crime.

Come on, you bastard, he thought, climbing the steps to the second floor, *I'll be ready for you.*

"You received an anonymous letter that said, *Come home, Hannah needs you?*" Abby repeated, staring at her sister as if she'd gone completely mad. They were seated in a restaurant on St. Charles Avenue, located not far from Sacred Heart Academy.

It had been Zoey's idea to ride the streetcar and "get away from all this stress," once she'd taken a two-hour nap. Abby had wanted to stay home. She was tired and drained after Luke's funeral. But she also wanted to get to the bottom of the "secret" Zoey and her father seemed to share about the night her mother died, and Zoey had promised she would tell Abby everything she knew.

In the end, Abby had driven them into town, where they'd hopped on the streetcar, ridden down the oak-lined avenue, and ended up in this quaint Victorian home-turned-dining room. It was early evening. They'd been seated at a table near the window, where a view of the garden showed off a million tiny white lights winking in the lush vegetation and along the fence. As the waitress delivered a tall glass filled with bread sticks, Zoey dropped the bomb about the note.

"Here, I've got it with me." Zoey leaned over to scrounge in her purse. She came up with a plain white envelope. The postmark was NEW ORLEANS, but there was no return address.

Though the late afternoon was warm, Abby's skin turned to ice. "Didn't you think this was odd?"

"Yeah, a little." Zoey reached for a bread stick.

"A *lot*, Zoe. No one ever called me Hannah but Mom."

"Well, obviously *she* didn't send it."

"Precisely. So who did? Who wanted you here?"

"I thought maybe you sent it to me."

"You're kidding."

"I figured it was your way of getting me here without, you know, you having to swallow your pride." Zoey dipped her bread stick in a tiny butter rosette.

"If I had needed you here, I would have called. You know that."

"Then maybe...I don't know...maybe Dad sent it."

"Dad?" Abby picked up the note and shook it in front of her sister's face. "How would he mail it?"

"Maybe Charlene did it for him."

"Then why not just sign it himself? Why all the cloak-and-dagger stuff? Better yet, why not just phone? You know, like a normal person."

"Then I don't know," Zoey said defensively, but little lines of concern sprouted between her eyebrows. "Look, let's not worry about it right now. We'll talk about the damned note later." She snagged the paper out of Abby's hands and slipped it into the envelope just as the waitress reappeared.

"Are you all ready?" she asked pleasantly. She was plump, with rosy cheeks, her order pad at the ready. She glanced at Abby and added, "Or would you like a few more minutes to decide?"

Zoey, who had somehow scanned the menu, said, "I'll have the iceberg lettuce wedge, with shrimp, caramelized onions, and blue cheese dressing on the side...oh, and maybe a cup of the shrimp bisque."

The waitress turned to Abby, whose appetite was fast disappearing. She'd walked into the little restaurant famished and now her stomach was in knots. Who had sent Zoey the note?

"Abby?" Zoey said and glanced from her sister to the waitress. "Do you know what you want?"

I want an end to all these questions...all this secrecy...

Glancing down at the menu, Abby tried to focus. Was it her imagination or had several people at nearby tables stopped eating to stare at them? *Pull yourself together, Abby. Don't make a scene. You'll get to the bottom of this. So Zoey received a note with your middle name on it the same week that your gun was stolen and people are turning up murdered...* Her hands were shaking so she clasped them together in her lap.

"Maybe we do need a few more minutes," Zoey said.

Abby cut her sister a look, then ordered the first thing she saw on the menu. "I'll have the spinach salad, with barbecued shrimp. House dressing."

She waited until the waitress had disappeared before she turned furious eyes at Zoey. "You should have told me about the letter earlier."

"I wanted to wait until after the funeral."

"So you knew I'd be upset?"

"*More* upset." Zoey cast a glance to the ceiling, where paddle fans were gently pushing the warm air around.

Abby was finished with skirting the issue. "So when are you going to tell me about the day Mom died?"

Zoey stared down at the table.

"Zoe." Abby leaned toward her.

Zoey closed her eyes and shook her head slightly. She let out her breath as she picked up her glass of sweet tea. "All right... I wasn't supposed to tell you..."

"Why? What happened? Who said you shouldn't tell me?"

"The doctors. Your doctors, Abby. The ones you saw right after Mom's death."

There was an echoing roar in Abby's head, a sudden raging surf. She clenched her hands over her knees. "Tell me," she demanded, her heart nearly stopping.

Spying Abby's reaction, Zoey nearly changed her mind. "Maybe this isn't the place."

"Tell me!" Abby repeated more tensely.

"Okay, okay... You seemed to have had some kind of blackout that day. Because of the emotional trauma. Dad talked to the doctors who saw you after Mom's death and they said it's not uncommon. It's emotional amnesia and sometimes your memory comes back after a while and other times... it just doesn't." She took a swallow from her tea.

"Like in my case."

"Right."

"And in the past twenty years, neither you nor Dad thought I needed to know?"

"We were advised against it," she said simply.

"But it's been two decades!" Anger burned through her, but she tried like hell to push it aside. "Okay, okay, so what was different, Zoe? What is so horrible that I've blacked it out? What am I forgetting?"

"I don't know," she said, baffled. "It's just your memory isn't exactly right." The waitress refilled their tea glasses and Zoey waited until they were alone again. "You weren't just getting out of the car that day, Abby. You and I—we'd had a fight about who was going to take her present up to her. I won the flip of the coin. Dad was pretty angry that we were being so petty, as it was Mom's birthday and all . . . your birthday, too, I know. Anyway, when we pulled up, you got out of the car before Dad had even shoved the gearshift into park. You took off up the steps into the hospital at a dead run and disappeared inside before either Dad or I got out of the car."

Abby blinked hard, remembered that sultry twilight. "I wasn't outside?"

"No. When Mom fell out her window, you were already in her room."

The dull roar in her head grew louder. The restaurant's chandeliers seemed to sway. The lights out the window twinkled and faded into stars. She looked past her memory of that day—her false memory, as it turned out. Vaguely she recalled running inside, through the dark building, past a boy in a wheelchair who watched her fly by, and around a nurse pushing a tray of medications down a hallway. She tore past the grandfather clock that was beginning to chime out the hour and ran up the stairs.

"I do remember," she murmured in surprise. "I do."

Zoey looked unsure of herself. "Really?"

"Yes . . ."

She'd rocketed up the stairs, taking them two at a time, nearly plowing into the nun. She'd had to hurry. To be the first of Faith's small family to say "Happy birthday." It was their shared, special day. It belonged to them, and Abby, her heart pounding crazily from the exertion, couldn't wait to tell her mother about the upcoming Sadie Hawkins dance.

Up, up, up she climbed, her shoes pounding on the stairs, past the stained-glass window of the Virgin Mother on the landing and up a final few steps to the third-floor hallway that was empty, the lights already dimmed.

Breathing hard, Abby pushed open the door to 307 and raced inside. "Happy birthday, Mom..." she said, then stopped short, her good wishes dying on her tongue. Faith was standing near the window, not far from the rumpled bed. Half-dressed, her blouse open, her bra unhooked, a dark nipple visible, she wasn't alone. A doctor in a white lab coat, his stethoscope swinging from his neck, his hair mussed, was trying to grab her.

As the door banged into the wall, he spun. His face was red, a vein jumping in his temple as he pinned Abby with his furious gaze. "Don't you know this is a private room! You should knock before you just barge in!"

"But..." Abby, standing in front of the closet, looked past the doctor to her mother.

Faith was already rehooking her bra, swiftly covering up. Her fingers were working with the buttons of her blouse, but her gaze, looking over the shoulder of the doctor, was fixed on her daughter. Fear shone in Faith's gold eyes, tears glistening. Without saying the words out loud, she mouthed, "Don't, please..."

Her mother wanted her to keep her silence. She wanted her to hold the secret safe. And Abby hadn't breathed a word. Not ever. She hadn't even remembered that she'd been in the room. Now, she was shaking, feeling with surprisingly sharp clarity her mother's despair.

"Abby!" Zoey's voice was like a slap.

The memory faded, withering away, and Abby found herself in the restaurant again, her salad sitting upon the place mat in front of her. Zoey stared at her anxiously across the table. Her face was strained, ashen. "The waitress asked you if you'd like ground pepper on your salad."

"What?" Abby glanced down at the mound of dark green spinach leaves, pieces of mandarin oranges, bean sprouts, and succulent shrimp on the plate in front of her. She hadn't even been aware that she was still in the restaurant, much less been served. Dear God, she was cracking up! *Just like Mom.*

No!

Quickly she looked up at the waitress holding the huge pepper mill poised over her platter. She forced a tremulous smile. She was not like Faith. Not weak-minded.

"Pepper?" the waitress asked, probably for the third or fourth time.

"No, thank you," Abby managed, and with a last, curious look, the round little waitress moved on to the next table.

"What's the matter with you?" Zoey hissed. "Get a grip, for God's sake!"

"I remember..." Abby leaned over the table, whispering just loud enough for Zoey and Zoey alone to hear.

Zoey didn't pretend to misunderstand. She slowly set down her butter knife. "What happened?"

"She wasn't alone."

"I know that, you were there."

"No, not just me, Zoe. There was a doctor in the room and... and I think...Oh, Lord, I can't believe this, but I think he was *abusing* her."

"Abusing her?" Zoey stared at Abby as if she, too, had lost her mind.

"Molesting her."

"Jesus, Abs!"

"I know, I know, but as I recall, her blouse and bra were undone and..." She hesitated. "I can see his face, but..." She tried to think, to roll back the years, to call up his name, but nothing came to her, just the start of a headache that pounded through her brain. She drew a calming breath and glanced across the table. "Do you remember who was treating Mom? What the psychiatrist's name was?"

"There were lots of doctors and nurses." Slowly, as if she were acting by rote, Zoey dipped the ends of her fork tines sparingly into the small cup of dressing, then pronged her bite of lettuce and shrimp. "I don't know. She was in and out of the hospital a lot. The staff came and went."

"I know, but I'm talking about that last stay. Who was seeing her right before she died?"

"I can't remember, but Dad would know." She shook her head. "But he's so frail. I don't want to drag him into this."

"I don't think we have a choice, Zoe. I have a feeling that whoever that doctor was, he not only abused Mom, he might have killed her as well."

"Oh, now, come on...Now you're accusing this man of...what? Sexual molestation and...murder? You think he pushed Mom out of the window?"

Abby squeezed her eyes shut, tried to hold on to the memory, but it was slippery, skimming in and out of her consciousness. "Go visit Dad tomorrow. See what he knows."

"And what will you do?" Zoey asked suspiciously.

"Keep trying to remember." She ran her hands through her hair and regarded her sister. "You should have told me. I don't care what the doctors said. I needed to know. I still need to know."

"Nobody wanted you to keep having those nightmares."

"I had those nightmares because no one's been honest with me!"

"Okay, okay..."

They drifted into uneasy silence. Abby chased her salad around her plate with her fork. She now knew what she had to do, but she couldn't confide in her sister. Zoey would have a fit.

But armed with this new information, Abby was certain if she went back to the hospital, she would remember everything. If she wanted to learn the truth about what had happened to her mother, if she wanted to break the hold her mother's death still had on her, then she needed to step back in time...she needed to force her way into Room 307 at Our Lady of Virtues Hospital.

Only then would she really know what had happened.

Montoya pushed the stack of photographs to one side of his desk, leaned back in his chair, and rubbed his eyes. He'd been at the desk for hours. He'd been looking over each snapshot he'd taken at the Courtney LaBelle candlelight vigil, then later her funeral, and finally Luke Gierman's service. He'd do the same thing when Asa Pomeroy and Gina Jefferson were laid to rest.

So far he had a stack of photographs of people he hadn't yet identified. He'd separated that pile down, pulling out the females, then weeding through the men until he found those who were big enough to wear a size twelve. Even so, this could be a wild-goose chase. Who was to say that the killer had attended either service?

Even if the psycho had shown up, he would probably disguise himself...he could even come as a woman...albeit a tall one.

Frustrated, Montoya ran a hand around the nape of his neck, then climbed to his feet to stretch his back and legs. He had too much restless energy to sit at a desk for hours.

They didn't want him on the front lines till they knew more about his aunt. It was frustrating. Who better than he to search for his Maria? He knew he wasn't objective, but so what? No one wanted to find her abductor more than he did. Just as no one else was more concerned for Abby Chastain's safety.

"Crap," he muttered.

His family was going nuts. From the time Maria had gone missing, every aunt, uncle, and cousin twice removed had phoned him, either demanding answers or sharing their deepest fears.

None of which were any deeper than his own. With each passing second that Maria and Billy Ray Furlough were missing, he'd grown more certain they were victims of foul play. Every time the phone rang, he gazed at it uneasily, half expecting to learn someone had stumbled upon their grotesquely entwined bodies.

So far, that phone call hadn't come in.

Montoya expelled air from his lungs and tried to force the odd pieces of the murder puzzle into some sort of sane pattern even though he knew he was dealing with a deranged individual.

He reread the note from the killer.

REPENT
A L

Repent for what? What had Luke Gierman, Courtney LaBelle, Asa Pomeroy, and Gina Jefferson had in common? What sin had they all committed? And what the hell did it have to do with Our Lady of Virtues?

Again, he viewed the pictures of the crime scenes on his monitor. Why were the male victims stripped bare? Why the women fully clothed and lying over them? Why the precise staging? The FBI profiler hadn't come up with anything more than the usual... if a killer could be described as anything near "usual." The same old stuff, white male in his late twenties to early forties, from a middle-class or lower-class family, someone who was probably abused as a child, someone who set fires and killed animals before escalating to humans, someone who had a fascination with the police and law enforcement... Montoya knew the drill.

But this guy, his gut told him, was different. This guy had taken the serial killing game to a new level.

Since Montoya was sidelined from the case, Bentz and Brinkman had returned to the convent as well as visited Billy Ray Furlough's compound. The FBI—the agency in charge—was dealing with the worried wife and children, checking with friends, family, and members of the church, all the time waiting for a ransom demand that Montoya doubted would come through.

He leaned back in his chair and opened his desk drawer. He found a pack of Nicorette gum, unwrapped it, and popped a tasteless piece in his mouth. Craning his neck, he peered through the open door to Bentz's office, then glanced out his window, where gray clouds were weaving their way inland from the Gulf.

Soon it would be night again.

And Montoya was afraid the killer would strike.

What if the son of a bitch took Abby's gun?

He considered camping out at her house again, but he knew that, if he did, he'd end up in her bed. Their lovemaking had been hot, desperate, and addictive.

He reminded himself she wasn't alone.

Her sister was staying with her. And anyway Abby had her dog, and Miguel had promised to install a security system ASAP.

But her ex-husband's gun was missing and that made him crazy.

Maybe she'd misplaced it.

Or maybe someone had stolen it.

And maybe that thief was the killer.

He swore beneath his breath in frustration, changing the screen on his computer and studying a digital image of a map of New Orleans and the surrounding area. It was large enough to encompass all the places where the murders had occurred. Places where the bodies had been found were pinpointed in red. The places from where the victims had been abducted were marked in blue, and spots where their vehicles had been located were in orange. Also, each victim's place of employment and residence had been color coded. Montoya stared at the map, but try as he might, he saw no correlation.

He even played with the data, coloring everything that had to do with one victim, home, employment, abduction site, murder locale in one hue, then designating another for the second victim, and so on and so forth...but no pattern jumped out at him.

He frowned and shook his head. He was going at this all wrong. He looked at the crimes themselves. The commonality of the victims was twofold. First there was the obvious yin and yang of it all, victims selected based on the fact that they were diametrically opposed to each other, with good and evil being represented. The staging of the deaths represented the "good" half of the whole destroying the "bad." Then, of course, there was the link of each victim, however thin it was, to the old mental hospital. He still couldn't shake that.

He was still thinking about the old hospital when his cell phone rang. "Montoya," he answered.

"Hi. This is Maury Taylor, down at WSLJ."

Montoya's muscles tensed. "Yeah?"

"Well, you told me to call if I got another one of those notes. And I did. Today."

Montoya was already reaching for his jacket. "Don't do anything with it," he said. "I'll be right there."

"I thought I'd talk to the guy on the program again. You know, draw him out—"

"No!" Holding the phone in one hand, he thrust his other hand down the sleeve of the jacket, shaking his arm a bit to get the stiff leather over his shoulder holster.

"Look, I think I have the right to—"

"You have no rights where this is concerned. Got it? Don't touch the letter, don't open it and—"

"I already opened it."

The stupid little dick.

"I had to make sure it was from the same guy. Don't worry, I didn't touch it...well, not much."

"Listen, Taylor, don't do anything! You got it? Nothing!" He clicked the cell phone off and slid it into his pocket. Then he was out the door.

CHAPTER 25

The note read:
ATONE
L A W

As he stood in Eleanor Cavalier's office with the program manager and Maury Taylor, Montoya held the single white sheet of paper in his gloved hands. He checked the postmark—not only was it New Orleans, but the two notes had been processed through the same station. In fact, they were nearly identical. Montoya read the information over and over again, then added the new note into a plastic evidence bag.

"This is all you got?" he asked and Maury nodded.

"You're welcome to look through the rest of the mail," Eleanor offered, "but this is the only item that looked pertinent."

Through the plastic, Montoya read the note one last time. What was with the religious instruction? First REPENT, signed by A L. Then ATONE, signed by L A W. Was it a signature? He didn't think so. It looked like the killer was trying to tell them something, but what?

"I think I should be able to mention on the air that the killer is contacting WSLJ," Maury said in an obvious ploy to appeal to Eleanor's penchant for higher and higher ratings. "It's tantamount to a public service announcement."

"We'll decide that," Montoya told him.

"But it came to *this* station, *my* show. I should get to use it to make the public aware."

"Of what?" Montoya asked.

"Maybe someone close to the killer has seen this," Maury suggested. "They're unaware that their husband or best friend is the maniac."

"He's got a point." Eleanor tapped a red-tipped fingernail alongside her jaw. She was leaning toward the ratings spike, too.

Montoya managed to mash down his temper. "Okay, look, here's the deal. I'm going to take it in for analysis, have the lab and our handwriting experts and the cryptologist do their things with it. If we decide to make it public, you get first crack."

"I'm thinking an exclusive," Maury said, pushing his luck.

"If you can get the FBI to agree." Montoya shrugged. He hated giving the worm anything, but it wasn't his call.

"We have been complying with you," Eleanor pointed out. "I could recant all those nasty things I said about you to Melinda Jaskiel."

"Too late. Damage done." His cell phone rang. He glanced at the screen. "If you get any other letters, let me know. I'll talk to my boss and the Public Information Officer about an exclusive. They'll speak to the feds and we'll get back to you."

Maury looked about to argue as the phone rang again. He thought better of it as Montoya pressed the phone to his ear and walked down the long hallway toward the front door. Melba, the receptionist, offered him a smile and a wave, obviously through being miffed at him for rushing in and nearly throttling Taylor. Montoya figured that secretly everyone at the station was glad someone had knocked the cocky son of a bitch down a peg or two.

"Montoya," he answered on the third ring, shouldering open the door.

"Hello, Detective," Our Lady's Mother Superior greeted him, identifying herself. "I've talked with several detectives since I first called you about Sister Maria and I've given them all the information I had, including those personnel and patient records."

"Good."

"But there's something else you should know about, and it's personal." She sounded unsure of herself. "I need to speak to you. In person."

He felt it then, that little niggle in his brain that warned him when something was about to change. "You know, because of my relationship with Maria, I've been taken off the case."

"What I have to say is for your ears only. It requires the utmost discretion." Her voice brooked no argument.

He thought about the investigation and what his superiors would say about being a rogue cop, but when push came to shove, he didn't give a good goddamn what would happen to him. If he lost his badge, so be it.

He wouldn't do anything to compromise the investigation.

Unless it meant taking the killer out. He could do that and hang the consequences. Justice would be served and he'd save the state of Louisiana a pile of money in the process.

"I'll be there in an hour," he said.

"Thank you, Pedro."

"My name is Reuben."

"Yes, yes, I know that. But I remember Sister Maria liked calling you by your confirmation name. Please come directly to my office when you get here."

"I've got a stop first, but I can be there in an hour or two."

"That'll be fine."

He hung up, jogged to his Mustang, climbed behind the wheel with a sense of renewed urgency. The clouds had thinned and the spires of St. Louis Cathedral shone a bright, nearly angelic white. Music greeted him, a saxophone player backed up by a guitar, and along with the bustle of pedestrians and the hum of traffic, the mule-drawn carriages rolled past. Behind the levee, the Mississippi moved steadily toward the Gulf.

All in all it was a beautiful day in New Orleans.

And yet behind every smiling face Montoya saw a killer. Whoever the son of a bitch was, he was blending in. Of all the calls that had come into the station—people who were quick to report suspicious activity of their neighbors, friends, family members, or enemies—nothing had panned out. The phone lines had been jammed with callers, the 911 operators overwhelmed, but after all was said and done, not one report of suspicious behavior could be connected to the killer.

Maybe this new note would be the break they were looking for.

He stepped on the accelerator as he blasted to the station, his mind turning back to the notes. Could L A W be in reference to the law? The criminal justice system? Was the guy making a mockery of all the law enforcement agencies trying to bring him to justice? Or was there something more? Something that was close at hand, something he could almost grasp, but couldn't quite figure out?

There were a couple of obvious connections. L A W could be initials or the start of a name, such as Lawrence DuLoc, the care-taker at the convent. Montoya didn't really like it. It seemed too easy, almost a setup. This guy wasn't stupid. In fact, he was clever enough to steal weapons, abduct people, and leave the crime scenes with very little evidence for the police to work on. Still, since he was going to see the Mother Superior, he planned to ask some questions about DuLoc.

Montoya sped through a yellow light, then cut down a side alley. What if each letter was a symbol? Could the letter represent the victim?

L for Luke Gierman.

A for Asa Pomeroy.

W for... William. Montoya's pulse jumped. The Reverend Billy Ray Furlough's legal name was no doubt William. L A W... could that be it? Again it seemed almost too simple, but it made sense.

Dread settled in his soul. If his theory was right, it meant the preacher was already dead; otherwise the killer wouldn't have sent the note, right? And if there was one dead body, there was bound to be another, a female to complete the whole of the yin and yang. Montoya realized that if his theory was correct, there was little doubt that his Aunt Maria had been murdered as well.

Anger surged through his veins and pounded in his pulse. Never had he felt so impotent. Though he knew better than to per-sonalize the crimes, Montoya felt that the killer had singled him out, was taunting him.

Don't lose your cool.

Keep a calm head.

Remain objective.

Maria may still be alive.

He sent up a prayer as he slid his car into a spot close to the station. The streets were clogged with news vans, their white exteriors emblazoned with the names of the stations they represented, satellite dishes and antennae spiking out of the roofs. Several reporters and cameramen were taking position on the front steps—the station doors a backdrop for the segments they were taping. Knots of pedestrians had slowed to rubberneck.

Montoya ducked in through the parking lot door and headed to the second floor, where he was greeted with the clicking of computer keys, the smell of stale coffee, and the buzz of conversation. Detectives were interviewing suspects, discussing cases, or at their desks shuffling paperwork or talking rapid-fire into phones jammed between their shoulders and ears.

Zaroster was at her desk. He slid the note in its plastic evidence bag across to her. "Looks like our pen pal's back."

Zaroster eyed the note and whistled softly. "So we have another double homicide out there somewhere?"

"Unless he writes the notes first, then offs his victims."

She sent him a look that accused him of knowing better.

"Look, I've got an errand to run. Could you get this to the lab with a copy to the cryptologist?"

"How'd you end up with this? I thought you weren't supposed to be on the investigation."

"Maury Taylor at WSLJ called me. We're old friends. Go way back."

"My ass," she muttered, but took the note and said, "I'll get this to the lab and see how it compares to the other one."

He rested a hip on her desk. "How're we coming with all the evidence?"

"Oh, 'all' of it. Let's see, the lab is still working on the black hair, no DNA matches yet. The bridal dress was recognized by one shop owner as looking like a 'Nancoise' creation, whatever that is ... kind of like a cheaper version of Vera Wang, I guess. We're looking into it, trying to get hold of Nancoise herself to see if she has any records. No epithelials or trace that means anything. The boots are regular hunting stock, made by, get this, Pomeroy Industries, their clothing division, so we're making some headway there, although that particular tread hasn't changed in four years, so it's slow goin'. I did manage to find out something about the caretaker out at Our Lady of Virtues. Lawrence DuLoc? He's got a record, all stuff done about twenty years ago when he was a kid."

"What stuff?"

"Aggravated assault charge—that was dropped. Then later a domestic violence incident, again charges dropped." She shrugged. "Not much, but something. He's tall and wears a size eleven and a half shoe, but he's got alibis for the times of the murders. Brinkman's checking them out." She sighed and shook her head. "I talked to DuLoc. He just doesn't seem to have the smarts to pull off this kind of thing." She frowned. "You think he could be our guy?"

"Doesn't sound like it. Our psycho wants to outsmart us and then shove it in our face. Hard for him to pretend he's no Rhodes scholar. He wants us to know how brilliant he is."

"So . . . ?"

Montoya was already heading for the stairs. "So, we keep DuLoc on the list and push forward."

"You're not on the case," she yelled after him.

Montoya kept moving.

The pain was an irritation.

His hands clamped around the steering wheel and he felt sweat soaking into his neoprene suit. The first hint of exhaustion was pulling at him. Though he'd rested for a few hours, he could feel his body's need for sleep.

It would have to wait.

Until after.

His plans were set in motion, and he knew that soon he would feel that unique buzz that kept him going, that rush of adrenalin through his bloodstream that would carry him through and lift him up.

The damned wound bothered him. It hindered him more than he'd expected. Things weren't going as well as he'd planned, not as smoothly as they had been. Ever since he'd underestimated Billy Ray Furlough, and the bastard had plunged that stupid tool into his chest.

He gritted his teeth.

Carefully, he drove the white Lexus out of the city and into the wilderness. The vehicle handled well but stuck out like the proverbial sore thumb. Which was a problem. He glanced into the backseat, where his latest victim was shaking like a leaf, eyes blinking rapidly, mewling behind his gag, already pissing himself and causing the car to reek with urine.

You should be scared, you lazy little bastard...just you wait.

If the mewling got any worse, he'd use the ether or another shot with the stun gun.

He'd attended Gierman's service earlier today even though he'd known the police would be watching, monitoring all of the bereaved.

Imbeciles!

They were so easily outsmarted.

He'd walked directly past the cop taking pictures on the sly. *Snap, snap, snap.*

What a joke.

Pedro, the picture-taking detective. The defiler who had slept in Abby Chastain's bed.

Thinking of them rutting, he lost control for an instant, the Lexus wandering over the center line. No! He could not bring attention to himself. Fortunately there was little traffic on this back road. To calm himself, he flipped on the radio, heard some classical crap, then managed to find WSLJ. But *Gierman's Groaners* wasn't on the air at the moment.

Another aggravation.

Hadn't that stupid radio jock discovered the second letter? Why wasn't he on the air crowing about it? He checked his watch. It was early yet, darkness a few hours away, which made his job all the more difficult.

He'd drive this car to the spot where he'd ditched his truck. But first he needed to unload the shackled man in the backseat. The pisser.

The radio was playing some smooth jazz that caused him only more irritation. He snapped it off, warned himself to be patient. He'd waited twenty years. A few more hours wouldn't hurt.

His lips twisted at that thought. Just a few more hours and then the culmination...five of the seven would be disposed of—the most precious already dealt with. The other two couples were not in the area, and would have to wait . . . but he would need a cooling-off period anyway.

After tonight.

The pain in his chest eased a bit as anticipation sang through his veins. Soon he would feel that intense, incredible rush. He thought of the daughter, so much like the mother . . . only a few more hours . . .

The Mother Superior looked tired. Beneath her wimple furrows lined her brow and below her half-glasses were dark smudges. "This is difficult for me," she admitted, pointing to a manila envelope in the middle of her wide desk. "Those are the records you requested. Sister Madeline, bless her heart, knew where they'd been stored up in the attic and had Mr. DuLoc bring them down." She motioned to the boxes that had been pushed to the corners of her room. "I'm keeping them here, just in case you need anything else, but I think everything you want is in here." She tapped the large envelope with one unpolished nail, then slid it across the desk to Montoya. "There was a time when confidences were kept, where faith was not only essential but embraced, when there was more . . . order. But now . . . oh, well." She offered up the ghost of a smile. "I've thought long and hard and prayed for God's blessing and intuition, that He would help me understand the path I should take," she said. "In the end, He's left me with a difficult choice."

Pushing herself to her feet, she seemed to totter a bit as she walked to the window. She stared outside where a hummingbird was flitting through the hanging pots, seeking sustenance from the dying blooms. "I suppose I should have told you earlier. Your aunt confided in me that she had a son out of wedlock. She came here after the boy was adopted out."

Montoya watched the old nun finger her rosary. "I know."

She nodded, still staring out the window. "That boy grew up and became a local celebrity, an athlete, a scholar, and eventually a man of God."

"Billy Ray Furlough?" Montoya asked, stunned.

"So she told me."

Furlough was the right age, and if he thought about it, there was a bit of a resemblance between the flamboyant preacher and the Montoya family—the dark hair, burnished skin, and natural athleticism.

"When I heard that Mr. Furlough was missing as well as Sister Maria, most likely abducted on the same day, I thought I should contact you. And I didn't want to tell the other officers, not when I knew that Sister Maria would prefer you to know." She turned to face him, her back to the window. "You're her favorite, you know. Of all her nieces and nephews."

Montoya felt a fresh rush of guilt. He wondered if the killer knew that he'd murdered mother and son. Of course he did. These murders were not random. They were meticulously planned.

"What can you tell me about Lawrence DuLoc?" Montoya asked, deciding to cover that ground first.

"Mr. DuLoc is invaluable here, helps us immeasurably." She drew a deep breath. "He was a patient at the mental hospital. He had anger issues as a youth, though, of course, I shouldn't be telling you this." She turned her palms heavenward in supplication and barreled on, almost as if she were relieved to open the floodgates of her secrecy. "Yes, he was accused of some crimes long ago, but he has been with us for a long while. His work record is impeccable." She looked up at Montoya. "I will personally vouch for him."

"The department has to look at all the evidence."

"I believe your colleagues already questioned him." She walked to her side of the desk, reached across the glossy surface, and touched Montoya's hand. "Larry is not a murderer."

Montoya tended to side with her, but he didn't let on. "He's a tall man, right. Six-one or -two?"

"He's tall, yes," she admitted, straightening and folding her arms over her chest. "You can talk to him. Larry wants nothing more than to help you find your aunt. Larry DuLoc is a very devout man, Detective. His faith is strong." She motioned toward the window. "He's in the garden now."

"Thank you." Montoya hesitated, eyeing the nun. After a moment he asked, "And did you learn anything about Faith Chastain?"

She folded her hands. "She fell out of the window of her room on her birthday," she said, sounding like she was reciting a tired story. "The hospital was sued for not having the windows secured properly. The grating was defective."

"She fell through the glass."

She nodded. "Had there been metal bars, or the decorative grating across the lower part of the window secure, the tragedy might have been avoided, or so the lawsuit suggested."

"Who sued you? The State of Louisiana?"

Her smile was patently patient. "The State eventually got involved, but the lawsuit was initiated by the family. Faith's husband, Jacques. It never went to trial, of course. We settled out of court."

Montoya looked at her, feeling as if she was holding back. "Anything else about it?"

Mother Superior fingered the cross at her neck and seemed to be wrestling with an inner demon. Montoya waited and she finally admitted, "I suppose it doesn't matter anymore. It's been so long ago, and if it will somehow help you find Sister Maria, then..." She made the sign of the cross and seemed to whisper a silent prayer. "There was talk of abuse, or molestation—that one of our doctors and Mrs. Chastain were involved in a sexual relationship. At first the man involved denied everything. Then others came forward: staff members who had seen things they hadn't reported for fear of losing their jobs. When that happened, he said the affair was consensual." Her lips twisted downward in disgust. "Consensual? Can you imagine? With a woman who was suffering from mental illness?" Her nostrils flared angrily. "He was let go immediately," she said.

"No charges filed?"

She shook her head. "The family filed the civil suit for Faith's death, and that was the extent of it. Perhaps they never knew about the other." Her gaze slid to the floor. "Not the finest hour for Our Lady of Virtues Hospital."

"Who was the man?"

She met his eyes. "Dr. Heller was a brilliant psychiatrist. In many ways ahead of his time. But he cut corners, was a little sloppy, lazy, if you will." Her back grew even straighter, as if a rod held her up. This was difficult for her. "One of his worst critics was Gina Jefferson. She worked with us at the time."

"Did she witness the molestation?" Montoya asked, feeling that little frisson again. He sensed he was finally on the right track.

"I don't remember, but she was no fan of Simon Heller."

"Do you know where Dr. Heller is now?" Montoya demanded.

"No...I didn't keep up with him. He moved out of state. Somewhere west, I think."

"Dr. Simon Heller. Does he have a middle name?"

"Yes...I remember he was particular about the name plate on his door." She thought hard and Montoya had to force himself to remain seated. The clock was ticking. His aunt and Billy Ray could already be dead, and Abby's mother was somehow involved. She was the link. "Simon T. Heller, that's what was on his name plate. I can't remember what the T stood for. Theodore or Thaddeus, something like that."

"His name and social security number are in this file?" Montoya asked, holding up the manila envelope.

"Yes. And his picture, I think."

Montoya didn't waste any time, but opened the clasp, sliding out the yellowed pages. "Was Heller a big man?"

"Tall, but not big. Almost scarecrowish. One of the patients saw a picture of a praying mantis in one of the nature books, pointed to it, and said, 'Heller.'" She smiled despite herself. "That was unkind, but there was a nugget of truth in it, I suppose. He wore huge glasses and had extremely long legs."

Montoya found a small photo of Heller attached to his long-ago employment application. The color had faded but Heller's features were clear. He had black hair, a thick mustache, and glared out through huge, wire-rimmed, aviator-type glasses.

"He wasn't very old."

"Just out of medical school," the Mother Superior admitted. "Under thirty."

"Do you remember anything else about him?"

"He had an air of superiority about him that he tried to mask with bedside manner. It didn't work very often. He was a bit of a loner, and he ran, oh, my, how he ran. I think he did marathons, but...oh, well, I'm not certain. A lot of years have passed."

Montoya fingered the faded photograph. "Do you have pictures of everyone who lived here?"

"Just the staff, for identification."

"Was Heller still employed here when Faith died?"

"He was in the room with her," she admitted. "He witnessed her fall but couldn't save her. The molestation issue was brought up after her death. That's when he was asked to leave."

He gazed hard at the picture of an unsmiling man. His arrogance came through clearly. Montoya remembered the picture of Abby's mother he'd seen on her bookcase. A beautiful woman with a sexy smile—a smile her daughter had inherited. Faith had been Simon Heller's unwilling lover.

Montoya's gut twisted. What had really happened the day of Faith Chastain's death? Had her fall been a misstep? Or had Heller, maybe aware that the molestation issue was coming to light, given his victim a push?

The reverend mother cleared her throat. "Faith's daughter witnessed the fall as well. She ran in just moments before."

"Which daughter?" Montoya asked, but he already knew the answer. He'd witnessed Abby's nightmares.

"The younger one . . ."

"Abby."

"Yes, that's her name. Abigail, though Faith often referred to her as Hannah."

"Do you know why?"

"Oh, it's been so long ago, and though I did work at the hospital then, I can't remember. The daughter was just fifteen. It was her birthday as well as Faith's. Apparently she rushed in, saw Dr. Heller there . . . and that's all we know. Somehow Faith fell through the window. Hannah was so traumatized that she fainted. When she woke up, she remembered very little." Clearly disturbed by the tale, Mother Superior walked back to her desk. "I'm afraid that's all I can tell you."

"It might be enough," he said, meaning it. Simon Heller. Montoya now knew where to look. He just hoped he wasn't too late to stop another murder.

CHAPTER 26

Hidden in the surrounding forest, he watched her house. As it was still light, late afternoon, he kept back a long distance and was careful with his field glasses, making certain the lenses wouldn't reflect the sun's rays, alerting her. He'd also made certain he was downwind, so her stupid dog wouldn't smell him.

What a pain.

Everything was ready, the stage set. All he needed was the players, and two of them were in the house. He planned to wait until they fell asleep, but that was hours away.

Patience, he reminded himself. *Don't rush things. You've waited so long, another few hours won't matter.*

But he was anxious.

Eager.

And the pain in his chest was increasing, as if he'd somehow contracted an infection. Consequently, a headache pounded behind his eyes.

He was sleep-deprived, but was also too keyed up to rest. So he waited and watched.

The sister was half-lying on the couch, stockinged feet dangling over a padded arm, wineglass on the coffee table, remote control in one hand. That was good. *Drink up, Big Sister. Let the wine dull your mind, relax your body. Fall asleep early...oh, yes.*

374 • Lisa Jackson

Zoey would be easy to subdue.

But not so Abby...she was on high alert; he sensed it. As he watched her gather things from her garage and kitchen, then carry them to the car, he began to worry. It looked as if she had decided to leave. He couldn't have that. She'd packed a tool box, a crowbar, and flashlights.

Why?

His headache pounded and his agitation grew. He scratched at his chest through the wet suit until he realized what he was doing. *Calm down. Observe. She can't be going far. You've seen no suitcase, have you? No overnight bag?*

But it didn't mean she hadn't already packed one before he'd taken his position. Was she planning some kind of camping trip? With the cop? His stomach soured at the thought of them again, and he had to blink hard, clear his head. He couldn't let her get away, not now, nor could he risk being caught. Could he take them both now? What about the dog? Could he use the stun gun on each, or a rag soaked in ether? He didn't want to threaten them with a gun because with two of them, in his current condition, something could go wrong. They were both young, athletic, and unless they were frightened out of their minds, might put up a struggle.

The answer was simple.

He would disable the car.

Quietly, he slunk through the woods, keeping downwind, scaring up thrushes and a hare that hopped quickly out of sight. Pulling from his backpack the handy little tool that had caused him so much pain, he left the pack with his keys and field glasses on the ground, near the front of the house, retrieved the revolver, then sneaked to the open garage door, where the hatchback of her Honda was visible.

The door to the interior of the house was open a crack, and he wondered if the dog sensed he was near. Damned mutt. Pulse drumming out of control, he stealthily crept inside, careful not to step on the hoe and shovel that had been tucked into the corner near a wheelbarrow.

Silently he pulled out the tool and clicked open a sharp little blade. He was about to jab the tread of her front tire when he heard footsteps approaching. *Damn!*

He ducked down even farther, hiding between the car and the garage wall, his heart jackhammering.

No dog. No dog. No dog. His fingers tightened over the handle of the Pomeroy Ultra and sweat drizzled in his eyes. He noticed a spider waiting on a web near the floor where he was crouched, his head pressed to the cracked, oily cement. Hardly daring to breathe, he stared past the undercarriage of the Honda, to the far side of the car, where he watched her sneakers walk briskly. She opened the driver's door, and he didn't dare move a muscle. He heard a soft clunk against the door near his head and guessed that she had thrown something onto the passenger's seat.

Her purse?

Panic roared through him.

What if she was leaving now? What if she slid behind the wheel and half a second later the Honda's engine suddenly engaged? She would ram the gearshift into reverse and back out, leaving him exposed.

There was no way she wouldn't see him.

Nowhere he could hide.

In one hand he held the .38, in the other the multibladed tool. He hoped he wouldn't have to use either. Not yet. Not when he'd planned her slow, perfect death for so long.

He should have anticipated this problem.

He was slipping. Losing his edge.

But luck was with him. She started walking into the house again. He watched her feet, the frayed hem of her jeans brushing the tops of her Nikes, as she disappeared inside. The door closed with a soft click.

Instantly, he punched a hole in the front tire, then slid back for the second. One flat tire wouldn't do. She was resourceful enough to change it herself, so he nearly jabbed the rear tire for insurance but stopped himself...she would be suspicious if two tires suddenly went flat...no, he needed to catch her off guard.

He started to slink out of the garage and melt into the shadows of the forest again when he remembered that she'd tossed something into the front seat.

He walked to the front of the car, glanced through the Honda's side window, and spied a backpack. He froze. Was that the edge of her cell phone sticking out? Could he really get so lucky?

Quietly he opened the passenger door. Yes! It was the cell phone! Deftly and carefully, he plucked it with two fingers from just inside the unzipped pack, then he crept quickly outside. Only when he was in the cover of the woods, the damp swampy air tickling his nostrils, did he breathe again.

So far, so good.

His heart was pounding in his ears as he thought about the little car breaking down. If he could time it just right, he might even be able to catch up to her, come along, and play the part of the Good Samaritan.

Don't push your luck . . .

First the sister, then Abby.

Everything was on track again.

The afternoon nearly got away from Abby. She'd intended to leave Zoey at the house and then, in broad daylight, make a trek to the hospital, force her way inside, climb up the stairs, and using the crowbar she'd already packed into her car, jimmy open the damned door to Room 307.

But phone calls from Montoya's brother setting up a time for the security system installation, Charlene reporting that their dad was "resting comfortably," three potential buyers who set up times to view the place the next day, and a few clients who needed information "ASAP" had slowed her down. Even Alicia had called, and since they'd played phone tag for a week, Abby had spent half an hour catching up. All the while Zoey lounged on the couch, nursing a glass of wine, flipping through the channels where news reports about the killings and footage of Luke's funeral from earlier in the day were being aired.

"I thought maybe someone would catch us on camera since you were the ex-wife and all."

"That's sick."

"No sicker than going to the mental hospital again. For the record," she said, sipping from her stemmed glass of Riesling, "I'm against this."

"It's something I have to do."

"Does Montoya know?"

"No."

"Will you call him?"

"And say what? That I feel compelled to go back to where it all started? That I have to face the demons of the past, that I can't go forward with my life until I go backward?"

Zoey lifted a shoulder. "It sounds kind of like psychobabble to me."

"I have to do this," Abby said.

"Then go." Zoey threw up a hand in surrender.

Abby let out a long breath. "You and Dad lied for twenty years. That's a helluva long time. I think I can at least have a few hours to get over it and..."

Zoey finished her wine in a gulp. "So go, already. Exorcise your damned demons."

"I'm on my way."

Zoey stalked to the kitchen, where she opened the refrigerator, found the bottle, and pulled out the cork. "Maybe I'll take another red-eye home."

Abby glanced to the lowering sun. "I don't have time to discuss this now, Zoe. When I get back, we'll hash everything out, have a few glasses of wine together, okay? We'll drink and watch old movies on television if we can find a station that isn't consumed with 'updates at eleven' of the murders."

Zoey refilled her glass, then shoved the cork into the bottle. She sighed. "If this is what you have to do, fine. Sorry I'm being bitchy. I'm still fighting jet lag and I think I might be coming down with something. The woman on the plane right behind me coughed so much I thought she'd hack up a lung. It's probably the flu."

"There's ibuprofen in the medicine cabinet in the bathroom."

"This'll do for now." Zoey held up her glass and took a sip. "Unless you want me to go with you?" she asked reluctantly.

"Don't worry. I think this is something I should do alone."

"How about I drive with you? If you want to go into the hospital alone, I'll wait in the car."

"I'll be fine."

"Okay, then, but take my weapon with you."

"Your weapon?"

"Yeah, I usually have it in my purse, but because of airport security, I had to pack it. Just a sec." She left her glass on the counter, hurried off down the hall in her stocking feet, then returned seconds later holding some weird knife.

"What is it?"

"A cheaper version of the Pomeroy Stiletto. It folds up, but can be released by this little button here, see..." She demonstrated, her index finger pressing on the small red button. "Spring action."

"Aren't these things illegal?"

"All I know is: you can*not* take them on a plane. That's a major no-no, so I have to pack it." She closed the blade and slapped the little dagger into Abby's hand.

"Okay," Abby said, a bit uncertainly. "Thanks." She slipped the knife into her pocket. She was as ready as she would ever be; her car packed. She'd already tossed her purse, cell phone, camera, and for good measure, the canister of pepper spray she'd carried around for the better part of the last two years but had yet to use into the car. She'd also placed a crowbar, flashlight, and lantern in the back.

Hershey, spying her loading the car, whined and stood at the door, ready for a "ride." Abby hesitated. Should she take the dog? "Later," she said, patting Hershey's head. "Promise...or maybe 'Aunt Zoey' could take you for a walk."

"I'm not the dog's 'aunt,' okay? When you have kids, then sure, I'll be Auntie Zoe, but not for the dog."

"Whatever. I'll see you later. Build a fire, and have another glass of wine," Abby suggested. "If I don't show up in three hours, send the cavalry."

"I'll call Montoya."

"Even better," she said, thinking about calling him herself. But if she told him what she was doing, he would have a fit. Like Zoey, he wouldn't understand. Only he would be much more adamant that she stay home. Besides, he was busy—a detective trying to solve several murder cases, for crying out loud. His own aunt was missing.

Abby climbed into the Honda and backed out of the garage. What was the old saying?

Today is the first day of the rest of your life.

For her, it was the other way around. *Today was the last day of her previous thirty-five years.*

Tomorrow would be the first day of her new life.

"...that's right. Double-check Lawrence DuLoc's alibis and find out what you can on a Simon Thaddeus Heller. I've got his social," Montoya said, rattling off Simon Heller's social security number while driving one-handed and bringing Zaroster up to speed. "He was involved with Faith Chastain when she was a patient at Our Lady of Virtues. Let go, because of it. Then moved west, supposedly. Check with the FBI, they might have faster access to his records."

"Will do," she said before hanging up.

He cracked open the window and stared through his bug-spattered windshield. Had Heller returned? Was he wreaking his own personal hell on victims who had been close to Faith Chastain?...If so, how were Asa Pomeroy and Luke Gierman involved...or was it just a loose connection in their cases? Asa had a son who had been in the hospital, and Luke Gierman had married Faith Chastain's daughter, who'd just happened to be in the room when Faith died. Mary LaBelle was the daughter of people who had worked at the hospital. Gina Jefferson had been a social worker there.

When Heller had practiced at Our Lady of Virtues.

When DuLoc had been a patient.

He was closing in on the truth, he knew it, but it was still tantalizingly just out of reach.

He was nearly to the city when the phone blasted. He picked it up while negotiating a final turn before the country road became a highway. "Montoya."

"Zaroster."

"That was quick."

"It's not about Heller or DuLoc. I don't have an answer on either of them yet." She hesitated as Montoya watched the lanes separate into a split highway. "Look, I know you're off the case, but I thought you should know. Asa Pomeroy's car has been located, parked in the swamp south of the city."

Montoya braced himself; he knew what was coming.

"The car was spotted by a guy giving helicopter rides to tourists over that section of swamp land. He saw the car, knew it was out of place, then remembered the police reports and called it in. The first officers to arrive were from the local Sheriff's Department. Two dead bodies on the scene. Male and female, tentatively identified as Billy Ray Furlough and Sister Maria Montoya."

"Damn it," he growled, his stomach wrenching. Though he'd expected the news, it was still a blow, a kick in the gut.

"I'm sorry."

"That goddamned bastard." Rage tore through him. Tears burned the back of his eyes. Memories of his aunt, pictures frozen in time, slid behind his eyes. He recalled her as a young woman, full of hope and happiness, working with children, laughing at her nieces' and nephews' antics. There had been an underlying sadness to her, he'd thought, but she still had enjoyed her cloistered life.

"We'll get him," Zaroster was saying.

Montoya had no doubt. He would spend the rest of his life tracking down this psycho if he had to. Nothing would stop him. The monster would go down.

"Give me that address." He floored his car, turned on the lights, and drove as if Lucifer himself were breathing down his neck.

A flat?

Her tire was flat *now?*

"Great," Abby said, staring at the front passenger wheel of her little Honda. She glanced to the heavens and saw that it would soon be dusk. Great. Nothing to do but change the tire. Hopefully she'd get to the hospital and still have some daylight to work with. She could either change the tire herself—which would take a minimum of half an hour and God knew if the spare was any good—or she could call roadside assistance. That would probably take longer. Or she could take off cross-country. Though she was five miles from the hospital by road, she was probably less than a mile if she walked a straight line across farmers' fields and ignored the NO TRESPASSING signs. But then she'd have to stow her gear in her backpack, which wouldn't hold all the tools she wanted to take.

"Looks like Door Number One," she told herself as she found the jack and the instruction pamphlet about how to use it. *Maybe you should call the tow company and go back home—take this as one of Zoey's signs that you're not supposed to break into the hospital.* "Nope," she said aloud. Turning back now was *not* an option. She had to know the truth and she damned well had to know it tonight.

She should have gone with Abby.

Working on her third glass of wine and watching a sci-fi flick that she'd seen several times already, Zoey realized she'd made a big mistake. What had she been thinking, letting Abby return to that god-awful sanitarium by herself? She should have insisted that she ride along.

But she hadn't wanted to. The place was just creepy. She'd never liked it. Never wanted to go back there.

The dog, lying by the fireplace, raised her head and let out a soft little "woof."

Zoey looked up expectantly. Her heart lifted. Maybe Abby had thought better of her plan and had returned.

Hershey was on her feet. A low growl emanated from her throat.

No... not Abby. Something else. Zoey felt a shiver chase down her spine. "What is it?" she asked, turning down the television's volume. The dog, hackles raised, walked from window to window, looking outside. "Cut it out," Zoey commanded. What had Abby said, that Hershey was edgy... or was that the cat? Both of the animals seemed a little neurotic to her. "You're fine," she muttered and drained her glass of Riesling. "Give me a break." She pushed the volume button upward, flipped through the channels, and found an all-news station that was reporting on the serial killer terrorizing the citizens of New Orleans.

Who the hell was that guy and what was his deal? She thought of Abby and felt a jab of guilt. No one, especially a woman, should be out alone, especially after dark. She glanced to the windows and frowned. It was still daylight, but the sun was sinking fast.

"Crap," she muttered as the news switched to trouble in the Middle East.

The dog was still whining and growling.

"Fine. Go outside! Knock yourself out." Zoey pushed herself to her feet and felt a little tipsy, not drunk by any means, but she definitely had a serious buzz going. Driving was out. So was another glass of wine. The truth of the matter was that she was still tired, and the wine had only exacerbated the jet lag that had been with her ever since her red-eye flight.

By now the damned dog was going ape-shit at the back door. "Enough already," Zoey muttered. "Believe me, no squirrel is worth it." She unlocked the door, opened it, and the dog, barking and growling, bounded outside. Ansel, hiding on one of the bar stools near the counter, hissed in agitation, nearly giving Zoey a heart attack. She hadn't seen the cat. "Jesus. Give it a rest." Her heart was beating like a drum and from the hallway area she heard a clunk.

She was instantly wary. Was it the TV? She didn't think so.

The noise hadn't seemed to come from the living room.

Ansel hissed again and shot toward the dining area.

It's a damned zoo in here, she thought, unnerved. She listened hard, every nerve ending instantly stretched tight. But she heard nothing but the dog's angry barks and noise from the television.

She inhaled a calming breath.

The animals' neuroses were infecting her and she wished she could just climb into her car and take off after Abby.

She touched her numb nose. Nope, she didn't dare drive. Instead she'd call Abby, see that she was okay. Insist that she phone Montoya; that would work. She thought of the detective with his black hair, dark eyes, and bad-boy smile. He was way too sexy for his own good. Or Abby's. Maybe Zoey should phone him and tell him what her sister was up to. Surely Abby had to have his number somewhere around here...

Don't do it.

Don't call him.

Remember what happened with Luke?

You nearly lost your sister over him. Don't get involved.

The dog was still barking its fool head off. Zoey peered out the window cut into the door and saw Hershey barking and pacing around the edge of the house, near the laundry room. Whatever creature the Lab was stalking had probably darted under the house.

Great. What if it was a skunk?

She walked to the living room and found her purse. Scrounging through her bag, she glanced at the television. The Pope was on the screen, standing on some balcony and waving to a crowd of people filling a city square and spilling into the side streets.

She found her phone.

Creak!

What the hell was that? A door opening?

Zoey speed-dialed Abby's cell. She would not freak out. *Would not!*

She heard the connection and a second later a musical ring tone within the house. Had Abby forgotten her phone? Oh, no . . . Still holding the cell to her ear, she walked into the hallway. The music was coming from the laundry room.

"Oh, Abby," she muttered as she walked through the open door and spied the ringing cell on the sill of the open window . . .

Open?

Just outside that same window Hershey was growling and barking and . . . oh, God.

Every hair on the back of Zoey's neck rose. She clicked off her phone and turned.

Fear shot through her.

She nearly fainted.

A big man dressed in black filled the doorway!

She started to scream and saw the weird gun.

This is it! He's going to kill you.

Reacting on sheer instinct, she flung herself over the top of the washer and through the open window. She fell to the mud outside. Quickly, not daring to look back, she scrambled to her feet and began to run.

Where? Oh, God, where could she go? The rental car! She'd left the keys under the seat. She was sprinting by now, heading to the front of the house, realizing she still held her cell phone.

With trembling fingers, she disconnected the call and hit the middle button for 9-1-1. She heard a door open behind her.

Run, run, run!

She rounded a corner, the dog racing beside her.

The rental was parked to the side of the driveway. She heard the phone ringing on the other end.

Answer! she thought wildly, her bare feet sliding on the gravel. Oh, God, where was he? She glanced over her shoulder and saw him, not ten yards away.

Panic pounded through her.

"Nine-one-one Dispatch. What is the nature of—"

"He's here! The killer's here! In Cambrai. I'm at Abby Chastain's—"

She was at the car, saw the weapon rise again.

"Hurry!" Her fingers pulled on the handle of the car door.

And then he fired.

Montoya parked his car at the end of the lane where a police barricade was already being manned by two deputies he didn't recognize. He flashed his badge, wending his way through the other parked cars, avoiding the first news crew to arrive as he headed along the side of a narrow dirt and gravel road. This area of swampland was so deep in the forest that it was already as gloomy and dark as midnight, though there was still an hour before sunset.

The crime scene was orderly chaos. Officers were stringing tape around the perimeter and setting up lights; others were collecting evidence or taking pictures of the grounds surrounding an abandoned, single-wide trailer. A rusted-out car of indecipherable lineage lay in ruins beside the gleaming finish of Asa Pomeroy's Jaguar.

He knew he'd get some flak about being here, but he walked into the area as if he belonged. If someone challenged him, he'd deal with it. All he wanted was a look. Nothing more.

It wasn't that he didn't believe his aunt was a victim; he just had to see for himself what the psycho had done.

Near the Jag, Brinkman was talking with a couple of sheriff's deputies while Bentz and another guy from the Sheriff's Department were examining a path leading to a rickety dock. It looked as if the FBI hadn't arrived yet, but that was just a matter of minutes.

Right now, everyone was distracted.

It was now or never.

He walked up the steps leading to the yawning open door and stepped into the bowels of hell.

The interior of the old trailer was lit by the weird blue glow of klieg lamps and on the filthy floor were two bodies, entwined as previously: his aunt, in her nun's habit, draped over the naked body of her son, Billy Ray Furlough. If there was blood present, it was well hidden under the splatter of red and black paint thrown over the victims. On one wall, in violent red was painted:

THE WAGES OF SIN IS DEATH.

Bonita Washington, gloved and examining the bodies, looked over her shoulder. "You'd better sign...Montoya?" Her eyes rounded. "What the hell are you doing here?"

He didn't answer, just turned and walked out. He was halfway down the lane when Bentz caught up with him.

"Hold up!" he ordered and there was an edge to his voice Montoya didn't like.

He stopped. Turned. Glared at the older man. "What?"

"You know what," Bentz said tautly. "What the fuck are you thinking?" Montoya didn't answer and Bentz's eyes narrowed in the coming dusk. "Damn it. I'll have to report this."

"So do it. Do your job."

"Crap, Montoya, don't do this! We want this one by the book so we can nail this son of a bitch's hide to the wall. I thought we were clear on that."

"Crystal."

"Then get the hell out of here and don't come back." A muscle worked in his jaw as Montoya held his gaze. "Hey. I know this is hard, but let it go. We'll get him."

Not if I get him first, Montoya thought, his mind's eye sharp with the memory of his aunt's waxen lifeless face, the paint poured all over her body.

Montoya strode back to his car, anger pulsing through him. He thought about the message scrawled on the inside of the trailer: THE WAGES OF SIN IS DEATH.

That's right, you sick bastard, he silently agreed. *And you're one helluva sinner.*

Get ready.

CHAPTER 27

"God help me." Abby stared up at the old hospital and felt a chill as cold as the arctic sea settle into her bones. Twilight was beginning to steal over the land, dark shadows fingering from the surrounding woods, mosquitos buzzing loudly, crickets softly chirping, and as she stood near the fountain with its crying angels and cracked basin. She felt a presence, an evil malevolence, as if the building itself were glaring down at her.

It's just your imagination.

The dilapidated old building that appeared so menacing was just brick and mortar, shingles and glass. It wasn't haunted with the souls of those who had lived inside. It wasn't glowering down upon her, silently warning her that she was making the single worst mistake of her life. Nonetheless her pulse drummed in her ears.

"You're an idiot," she told herself as she summoned up all her courage. She couldn't back down now. Not when she was so close. Yet her heart was thudding, her nerves stretched to the breaking point.

This is where it all happened, she thought, eyeing the spot on the weed-choked concrete where her mother's life had ended.

Go. Now. Don't put it off any longer.

She made a quick sign of the cross, then hoisting one strap of her backpack over her shoulder, she skirted the building, cutting across lawns that had once been tended, where butterflies and honey bees had flitted, where a group of children about her age had stared at her as if she'd been sent from another solar system. She remembered their eyes following Zoey and her as they'd chased each other around the magnolia tree so fragrant with heavy blooms.

She'd thought them odd then, those kids, and yet her father had always told her to pity them. "There but for the grace of God go I," he'd reminded her...but she'd still thought they were weird. She glanced to the corner of the verandah where they'd always gathered and even now, when the flagstones were empty, she side-stepped the area and headed toward the back door.

But the ghosts followed her—if not the teenagers, then a little blond girl who never spoke and drew odd shapes in chalk over the rough flag stones; the boy who watched her every move and was forever pulling out tufts of his hair; the old lady who listed in her wheelchair, one arm dragging, her mouth often agape, her eyes wide and wondering behind thick glasses. She'd been a former beauty queen, Abby had been told, reduced by age and dementia to a hollow shell. Then there had been the boy on the threshold of manhood who had eyed both her and her mother in a way that had made her want to wash herself. How often had he with his dark hair and brooding eyes been in the hallway, near her mother's door, squeezing one of those stress relieving balls so slowly and methodically as he'd looked into Abby's eyes that she'd felt dirty? The sexual message had been clear; he'd been kneading a malleable ball, but he'd wanted to do so much more with his big hands.

She shuddered as she thought of all the tortured souls who had resided here, cared for by doctors, nurses, social workers and staff yet left adrift. Her mother was supposed to have been safe here; this hospital was to have been a place of healing, of comfort. Not pain. Not horror. Not molestation.

Abby rounded a vine-draped corner and sent up a prayer for her poor fragile mother. "Oh, Mom, I'm so sorry," she said aloud, her heart heavy.

I forgive you. Faith's words seemed to float from the heavens and Abby nearly stopped dead in her tracks. Is that what she'd meant? An icy finger of understanding slid down her spine. As she hurried along the broken sidewalk to the back of the building she thought of the monster who had abused Faith, the doctor who had slipped into Room 307, and under the guise of helping and healing had brought with him perversion and pain.

"I hope you rot in hell," she muttered into the gloom of dusk.

Light was fading fast, the sun disappearing behind thick clouds as it settled behind the trees, the threat of rain heavy in the air. Hurrying, she followed a broken sidewalk to the back door, which didn't budge. It was locked tight, just as it had been on her previous visit. But the window she'd hoisted herself through before was still unlatched and partially open. Sister Maria hadn't remembered to close it nor told the caretaker to see that it was locked. But then the nun hadn't had much time, Abby thought ruefully, as she didn't doubt for a second that Sister Maria was already dead.

She stared at the partially open window.

A stroke of luck?

Or a bad omen?

There was a part of her that was still afraid; still hesitant about this.

Her father's mantra whispered through her brain. *When the going gets tough...*

"Yeah, yeah. I know. Enough already!" She gave herself a mental shake and pushed back her fears. Nervously she dropped her backpack inside the window then heaved herself over the sill and landed on the floor.

She was here!

Deep within his sacred room he heard the quiet thump of feet hit the floor overhead. His heart rate accelerated and he took in a deep breath. He'd known she'd come. Lured by the past, Faith's daughter would return to the place where all her pain had begun. He licked his lips and blinked.

His pain, of course, had started much earlier.

As he stared at the walls of his room, he saw the writing he'd worked so diligently to create. Passages of Scripture, words of the great philosophers on sin, his own personal theories formulated by his own mother, reinforced at the strict Catholic schools that had eventually all kicked him out.

He listened hard. Heard footsteps. Of the daughter.

Deep inside he felt that stirring again, the lust he'd experienced for Faith Chastain, the wrath he'd felt knowing she was giving herself to the doctor as well.

The wages of sin is death.

How many times had he heard that from his mother as she'd sat by the window, Bible lying open on her lap, cigarette burning neglected in the ash tray, ice cubes melting in her drink. "He'll pay," she'd told her only son often enough. "Your father and his whoring new wife are sinners and they'll both pay." She'd taken a sip of her drink, her little tongue licking up a drop that lingered on her lip. "We all do." She'd looked over at him and there had been no hint of motherly love in her gaze. "You will, too. You've got his blood in your veins and you'll pay." Another sip before she rained on him that twisted sarcastic smile he'd grown to hate. "But then you already are, aren't you? The nuns at school have told me."

Now, he felt the same pulsing shame run through him as she'd ranted about the sins that had been pounded into her own head while growing up. Lighting another cigarette in fingers that had shaken, she'd focused on his transgressions. The nuns had told her he'd cheated in school, which had been a lie, of course, but she'd believed the sisters and to punish him, to make him consider his sinful ways, she'd locked him in a closet.

It hadn't been the first time.

Once before he'd been caught kissing a girl at school. Upon returning home, he'd faced a fierce, embarassed and angry mother. That time he'd been stripped naked, locked away for three days, left in his own urine and feces without water. He'd been ordered, as penance to write on the walls, *the wages of sin is death.* For the three days of his imprisonment he'd believed he would die in that empty closet that had once housed his father's guns.

He'd been released of course. Just as he always had been when his mother, reeking of alcohol, had finally decided he'd been punished enough. Then, always she would cry and beg for him to forgive her, bathe him, offer up new clothes, an expensive toy and kiss him … all over … while gently tending to the bruises and cuts that covered his body, scars from his efforts of trying to break free.

She'd been tender then, lovingly caressing him, assuring him that if he would repent and atone for his sins, he would find favor with God. With her.

Once after a particularly long stay in the closet, he'd felt not only fear, but rage. When he'd heard the locks click and seen that first blinding crack of light, he'd stood and walked past her, refused to let her touch him, and thrown her gifts of atonement back in her face. He'd threatened to leave her, to tell his father what she'd done. She'd shaken and cried but admitted that the man who had sired him had never wanted him in the first place. His father had paid for an abortion she'd refused. And later, after she'd given birth, had his father stuck around? Oh, for a few years, but after less than a paltry decade, the marriage had unraveled; his father had strayed and had abandoned them both.

At the time when she'd told him about this father wanting an abortion when she was crying and quaking, unable to hold her cigarette in her trembling fingers, he realized that this once she'd been telling the truth. His father had, indeed, abandoned them both for the whore.

He'd known then it was his mission to set things right, his own personal atonement for being unwanted.

And he'd eagerly taken up that sword of vengeance.

Hadn't the new wife died?

Hadn't he been looked upon suspiciously?

Hadn't he ended up here . . . locked away permanently until the hospital had closed and he'd been shuffled from one facility to the next, always a private institution, always peppered with nuns and priests and rosaries and crucifixes, always knowing his every sin was being observed and catalogued, never forgotten and never forgiven. He'd tried to stay true to his mission and not to follow his own urges. He'd tried to fight his own desires.

And yet . . . with Faith . . . he'd risked it all, condemning his soul to the depths of hell just to touch her and lie with her, to feel her sweet, warm body wrapped over his.

And now the daughter, who looked enough like Faith to be her twin, was here.

He glanced again at the words etched into the walls of this room. Above the passages he'd scratched into the walls, he carefully painted fourteen simple words for the fourteen victims, the sinners and the saints, those who would be punished, those who would do the punishing.

If only Faith were here...she would understand. She would soothe him. She would *love* him. But that was not to be. The lazy doctor had killed her. Fucked her, then, upon being found out by the daughter, pushed Faith, beautiful Faith, through the window.

His body convulsed as he remembered her scream, the sound of her body thudding against the concrete. Tears burned the back of his eyes. White-hot rage roared through his veins.

Faith's death hadn't been an accident as so many believed.

He knew.

He'd been there.

And so the doctor would pay for his sins.

Tonight.

Inside the hospital, the rooms were shadowy and still, twilight seeping through the windows that weren't boarded, the air stagnant with a thin rank odor. Abby felt the temperature drop, the atmosphere thicken.

No way, you're just freaking yourself out. Keep going!

She unzipped the pack and pulled out her flashlight. A part of her brain screamed that what she was doing was just plain nuts, that she was as crazy as some of the people who had once lived here, that if she had any sense at all, she would turn and make tracks.

Why not come back in the morning?

In full daylight?

With an attack dog, Montoya and a gun?

Because she wanted answers now.

Because momentum was propelling her forward.

Because she couldn't bear the thought of waiting one more instant.

Because it was now or never.

She lifted the backpack to her shoulder again. The fingers of one hand were curled around a crowbar, the fingers of the other hand gripping a flashlight. She swept the thin beam over the dusty floor boards, shining it on the windows. She spied rotted, peeling wallpaper and cobwebs draped from the corners of old chandeliers as she walked softly through the first floor. Every scary movie she'd seen where the kids split up and start inching their separate ways down dark hallways played through her mind.

Never had she felt more alone.

Never had she been more determined.

You have to do this. You have to remember.

The building groaned softly.

Abby bit back a scream.

It's nothing, just the settling of old timbers. You hear the same thing in your house.

She took two steps into the kitchen and heard another noise. Her heart lurched.

Scrape, scrape, scrape.

The scratch of tiny claws. She whipped the flashlight around, its beam jumping across old counters and the stove top to the rusted sink where she saw the furry back end of a rat sliding into the drain, its tail slithering like a tiny black snake as it disappeared.

"Jesus," she whispered, her heart knocking crazily.

Abby walked slowly, hearing her own footsteps, her own heartbeat.

She closed her eyes, thought she heard a soft cry.

Don't do this to yourself. No one's here. Don't let your fears run wild. Do not fall victim to your mother's paranoia.

Taking in a long, shuddering breath, she gripped the crowbar as if it were her only salvation. She swallowed back her fear but swore that if she listened really hard, she could hear the muted sobs and wails of despair from the patients who had suffered here.

Stop it. There is no one in this damned building, no one moaning or sobbing, for God's sake. Now, get going! It's nearly dark. Come on, Abby, get this over with!

Montoya floored the accelerator, ignoring the speed limit. He passed other cars and trucks, his jaw set, his pulse pounding in his temple. The image of his aunt's body laid upon Billy Ray's corpse burned through his mind and his fingers curled more tightly over the steering wheel. What if the monster had gone after Abby?

"Fuck," he growled, shifting down and passing a flat bed truck, spraying gravel as his back wheels hit the shoulder.

At a straight stretch in the road, he grabbed his cell phone and speed dialed her home.

He counted the rings, his dread mounting. "Come on," he urged. "Come on!" But no one answered.

Fear pounded through his brain.

So what? She could be out.

Rapidly he punched in the number for her cell.

The call went directly to her damned voice mail.

He didn't like it. There could be a million reasons she wasn't picking up, none of which had to do with the murders that had taken place, but he was still nervous as hell.

In his gut he knew that Faith Chastain's death had somehow led to the recent turn of deadly events. He just didn't know how, couldn't yet connect the dots. All he was certain of was that Abby was involved.

The countryside blew by in a blur of farmland and forest as he tried to keep panic at bay.

What the hell was the connection between Faith Chastain's tragic plunge from the third floor window of a sanitarium and the deadly events that were happening now?

The wages of sin is death.

Why *that* message? What did it mean?

Scowling through the windshield, his eyes narrowing on the burgeoning purple-bellied clouds that scraped the horizon, he thought of the first message received at WSLJ.

Repent.

For what? A sin? What sin? Slowing for a corner, ignoring the crackle of the police radio, fear chasing through his bloodstream, he tried like hell to piece it together. The second message played through his head.

Atone.

As in make amends? For what? More transgressions? What were they? What was with all the religious references? *Think! Put it together. You have to. Time is running out. And the killer is telling you something... it has to do with sin...*

Why were the two victims posed together?

What were their sins?

A muscle worked in his jaw and his head ached he thought so hard. He was close to the answer, he could feel it. Each victim had been picked for a reason...for his or her transgression. Against whom? The killer? Mankind? God?

Jesus, Montoya, figure this out!

He slowed as he spied the narrow bridge dead ahead. A motorcycle sped in the opposite direction, headlight glowing like one bright eye, exhaust pipes roaring as they passed mid-center on the span.

Montoya's brain was still focused on the damn notes from the killer.

The missives had been signed by Al W...no, A. L. W. There was a clue there. There had to be. What was the killer trying to say?

The obvious answer was simple:

L for Luke.

A for Asa.

W for William.

Why not the female victims?

No C for Courtney.

No G for Gina.

No M for Maria.

Why the bridal dress on the Virgin Mary? Why all the cash strewn around Asa Pomeroy and Gina Jefferson? Why the blood-red and black paint, the angry inscription on the wall of the scene with William and Maria, mother and son?

What were their sins?

And why was there so much rage evident at the last scene, so much anger? Such violence? When not at the others?

"Damn it all to hell." He flipped on his blinker and pulled into the oncoming lane, flooring it as he passed an old truck with a bumper sticker that said, *Honk If You Love Jesus.*

As he swung into the right lane again, he picked up the phone to try and call Abby one more time. He needed to hear her voice, to assure himself that she was all right.

Punching her speed dial number, he glared through the bug-splattered windshield, listening to the phone ring on the other end of the connection while his mind grappled with the puzzle of the case. Uneven pieces, sharp clues, poked at him, prodding him, taunting him that he couldn't put it together. What the hell was the twisted son of a bitch trying to convey?

What was the significance of yin and yang? Light and dark? Good and evil?

No!

Not necessarily good versus evil. More like sinner and saint!

He nearly stood on the brakes, skidding to the side of the road. As he pulled over, the pickup that had been on his bumper honked loudly as it tore by. Montoya's heart was beating like a jackhammer. Wildly. Crazily. Sinner and saint...Luke Gierman, the loud-mouthed adulterer and Courtney LaBelle, the virgin. Asa Pomeroy the greedy industrialist and Gina Jefferson, the philanthropist. Billy Ray Furlough, not Maria's son...no, that was only icing on the cake. He was an angry, fire-and-brimstone preacher, railing on the wrath of God, while Maria was a soft spoken, true believer, a woman who trusted in a gentle, caring deity.

Could that be it?

That simple?

His phone was still connected to his last call and Abby's voice, instructing him to leave a message, filled his ears. Oh, God, he hoped she was safe. He still felt as if she was somehow intimately involved in this horror.

As his Mustang idled at the side of the road, he instructed Abby to call him immediately, disconnected and speed-dialed the homicide department instead.

Seconds ticked by.

"Zaroster." Lynn answered on the second ring.

"It's Montoya. Are you near a computer?" he demanded, his mind running in circles as the first drops of rain hit the car's windshield.

"Yeah, right here. At my desk. Why?"

"I need a Google search. Or whatever search engine you use."

"Google. Sure...just give me a sec."

He heard her typing and about went out of his mind while he waited.

"Okay, got it," she said. "What do you want to search?"

"Start with the Seven Deadly Sins."

A pause. "The Seven Deadly Sins... Okay. . ."

The rain was picking up, splattering on the hood of his mustang, drizzling down the windshield. He flipped on the wipers as traffic rushed by. All the while he was impatiently listening to her type.

"Okay, I've got a lot of options here."

"Just go to one that lists them... use a Catholic website, if you can. Read them to me."

"Whatever floats your boat." More clicking. "Here we go. Got 'em," she said.

Adrenaline, fueled by dread, pumped through Montoya's blood. His knuckles showed white where he gripped the steering wheel.

"Let's see," she said. "We've got all the usual suspects here: Pride, Wrath, Envy, Lust, Gluttony, Sloth and Avarice."

"Okay. Good," he said, though his heart was drumming with fear. If what he was thinking was correct, if he'd finally understood what was happening, the worst was yet to come. "Years ago, when I went to Catechism, I learned about those sins. But there was more to it."

"Sorry, only seven."

"No, I mean, isn't there something about... virtues that counterbalance the sins?"

"Virtues?" she repeated. "You want to tell me where you're going with this?"

"As soon as I know," Montoya gritted out, dreading the answer. He heard the clicking of computer keys. "There should be seven of them."

"Virtues... as in Our Lady of Virtues?" she said and Montoya's fear only deepened.

"Yeah."

"Well, let's see..." More typing and a pause of a few long seconds. He thought he might go out of his mind. "Oh, here it is. Well, I'll be damned. Didn't know they existed. Shit. Look at this."

"What?"

"I've got a list of Seven Contrary Virtues listed here, one for each of the sins."

The heavens opened up and rain poured from the sky.

"What are they?"

"Well for pride, there's humility, for wrath, we've got meekness, envy's counterpart is charity, and chastity, of course, for lust. Then there's moderation for gluttony, zeal as opposed to sloth and generosity as opposed to—"

"Avarice," he said, throwing his car into gear again. Zaroster swept in a breath. "The letters. . . A, L, W? Avarice? Lust? Wrath?"

"Bingo." Why hadn't he seen it sooner? The clues were all there, the killer taunting him with the letters, not only for the victims' names, but because of their supposed sin or virtue. "I was just at the most recent murder scene and there was anger literally written all over that place. The other scenes showed no signs of rage. Just the opposite. Our killer is cold and clinical, so why the change? I thought maybe he was just unraveling, but then I remembered that Billy Ray Furlough was an angry minister and his given name, William, began with the letter W for Wrath. Contrarily, my aunt was the embodiment of meekness, her name was Maria—"

"M," Zaroster interrupted. "And Courtney LaBelle, our Virgin Mary, was C for Courtney, and Chastity to Luke Gierman's L for Lust. Jesus, how sick is that?"

"Asa Pomeroy's sin was Avarice," Montoya said thinking of the greedy industrialist, "and Gina Jefferson was the epitome of philanthropy or generosity."

"A and G," she whispered. "If you're right about this, then he's not even half way through. There are seven sins, seven virtues—"

"Fourteen victims." Montoya pulled a quick one-eighty, then floored the car again, the tires chirping as they hit the pavement. "And it all starts with Our Lady of Virtues Hospital."

"Shit! That's where Simon Heller worked," she said and he imagined the fury tightening the corners of her mouth. "He must be our guy. I just received a confirmation of his most recent address. Guess what? Heller moved back to New Orleans three months ago. Rents a place in the Garden District."

Montoya's heart dropped. Anger rushed through his veins. "Send someone out there." Maybe they could stop the bastard before it was too late.

"I'm on my way," she said and he imagined she was already reaching for her jacket and sidearm.

"Take someone with you. And tell Bentz what's going on."

"I will."

"Be careful, Lynn. This guy's dangerous."

"Don't worry," she assured him. "So am I."

Rain pounded the roof of the asylum.

Nerves strung tight as piano wires, Abby stepped past the stained-glass window at the landing where the gloom of the day hardly dared pierce the colored panes. Her throat was dry as sand, her pulse pounding in her ears. She strained to hear the slightest sound and squinted into the darkness that the weak beam of her flashlight barely pierced.

Up the worn steps.

Into the pitch black hallway of the third floor.

Her mother's floor.

Where Faith's life had ended.

Outside the wind whistled, driving the rain, causing the skin at Abby's nape to prickle. This was the very hallway where Heller had crept, where he'd lurked outside the doorway.

In her mind's eye, Abby recalled pushing open the door and finding him there, his big hands upon her mother, fondling her breasts, maybe pinching. Abby had gasped. He'd turned quickly, his face flushed and hard, his eyes glinting, a vein throbbing at his temple, his erection visible beneath his lab coat.

Her stomach had twisted in revulsion and only her mother's pleading eyes, looking over Heller's shoulder, kept Abby from screaming.

Now, Abby brushed the beam of her flashlight over the hallway. Every door down the length of the inky corridor was open, either yawning wide, or slightly ajar. But unlatched. Except for 307. That door was shut snugly.

It means nothing, she told herself, double checking as she slid the flashlight's thin stream of illumination to the other dark paneled doors and finding them gaping.

Just open the damned door!

Hands slick with nervous sweat, her skin prickling in dread, she slid the crowbar under her arm, then grabbed the doorknob. Closing her eyes, she gave it a twist.

The knob turned in her palm.

Easily.

Her pulse jumped. The last time this door had been locked.

She pushed.

The door swung silently inward, without so much as a sigh, as if the hinges had been recently oiled.

Fear drummed within her.

Something was wrong with this. Very, very wrong. Still, she took one step inside, the smell of antiseptic reaching her nostrils. She shined the beam of her flashlight over the floor of the familiar room, then swept the light over the walls and furnishings.

Abby froze, disbelieving.

Everything was exactly as she remembered it.

The iron bed, painted white, pushed into one corner.

The nightstand with a vase of fresh cut flowers.

The bifold picture frame with faded snapshots of Abby and Zoey as children.

The patchwork quilt in shades of rose and peach that Abby's grandmother had hand-stitched.

The crucifix mounted on the wall.

Time had stood still in Room 307.

"No," Abby whispered taking several steps farther into the room. Was that a hint of her mother's perfume over the odors of cleaning solvents?

It couldn't be.

Her mother wasn't here...

As if in fast rewind, her mind spun backward in time to that night when her life had changed forever.

She remembered rushing into the room, eager to tell her mother about the dance and Trey Hilliard...

"Mom?" Abby, breathless from racing up the stairs two at a time, nearly flew into the room. "Mom? Guess what?"

Her mother was near the tall window, twilight thick beyond the sheer panes. But Faith, partially undressed, wasn't alone. A doctor, Simon Heller, was grappling with her.

Abby skidded to a stop and stared. "Mom?"

Was Heller trying to push her through the glass, or save her from herself?

"Hey, what's going on?"

Heller spun. His face was red and screwed into a furious knot, spittle flying from the corner of his mouth. "Don't you know this is a private room?" he demanded furiously, his eyes narrowing under bushy eyebrows, the nostrils of his hawkish nose flared. "You should knock before you just barge in!"

"But..." Abby stared at her mother who was obviously embarrassed, working at straightening her clothes.

Faith couldn't hide her shame. Tears filled her eyes and her cheeks were flushed a bright scarlet. She gazed over Heller's shoulder to meet the confusion and disgust in Abby's expression. Mutely, she mouthed "Don't, please..." then out loud, "Abby Hannah, I'm so sorry."

Before Abby could reply, Faith spun, as if Heller had somehow whirled her and forced her to turn away. Her body hit the glass.

The window cracked with a sickening, splintering sound.

"No!" Abby rushed forward, trying to reach her mother, but Heller grabbed her arm, holding her back.

To keep her from saving Faith, or to protect her from falling?

"I forgive you..." her mother cried, her eyes wide and round.

The window shattered, clear shards stained red with blood as Faith tumbled through, her terrified scream echoing in Abby's brain.

"No! Mom! No!" Abby cried. She tried to rip herself from Heller's grip. She heard something—a swift intake of breath?—over the sickening thunk of her mother's body slamming against the concrete.

Horrified, tears streaming down her face, Abby stared through the broken glass to the cracked concrete and Faith's broken body. "No!" Abby wailed, disbelieving, yanking herself out of Heller's steely grasp. "No! No! Nooooo!"

Blood pooled beneath her mother. Faith Chastain's eyes stared sightlessly upward. The insects of the night continued to buzz and voices were suddenly yelling, screaming, barking orders, but Abby's mother was dead.

Sobbing, Abby stumbled backward, away from the horrid sight.

Another slight, nearly inaudible gasp from somewhere behind her.

Turning blindly, she saw that the closet door was ajar. Just a sliver. A dark crack of shadow. And within... the glow of malicious eyes.

Someone was watching this? A voyeur getting his jollies by viewing Dr. Heller force her mother into vile, perverted acts?

The eyes, sharp and hard, met hers in a moment of intimate, unthinkable understanding...

Dear God, she thought now, her head pounding, the vision of the past so real she could feel the moist heat of that damp Louisiana night.

The flashlight was quivering in her hands, its fading beam jumping around the room.

Her gaze swung slowly to the closet door.

Hanging slightly open, a dark crack between door and frame.

And from within, the reflection of hate-filled eyes.

CHAPTER 28

Abby held back a scream.

Her pulse thundered in her ears.

She trained her flashlight into the black gap and the weakening beam landed upon an old frightened man staring up at her. His hands were bound behind him, his ankles taped together, a gag slapped over his mouth.

She'd seen him before, she thought, as she stepped closer and the acrid smells of sweat, urine and fear assailed her. His eyes were wide and behind his gag he was screaming, yelling at her, the sound muffled.

She started to reach for the gag over his mouth, then stopped.

Of course she recognized him.

Twenty years had added wrinkles to his skin and bleached his hair to snowy white. But his features were the same. Hard-edged jaw, thick eyebrows, aquiline nose. With a sickening jolt, she realized she was staring into the petrified, blood-shot eyes of Dr. Simon Heller.

Her mother's abuser.

She recoiled at the sight of him. "You sick, murdering son of a bitch," she said.

He was anxious, shaking his head, yelling wildly behind the gag.

The bastard.

"I should leave you here to rot!" She wondered who had put him here? Who had bound and gagged him. Left him alone. New fear climbed up her spine as she grabbed a corner of the tape and yanked hard, the adhesive hissing as it ripped off some of his whiskers and skin. As far as she was concerned, he deserved a whole lot worse. He yowled and over the pitiful sound of Heller's cry and the rush of the wind, she thought there was another sound.

Something familiar.

A creak of floorboards?

A footstep?

She slid the crowbar into her hand, but it was too late.

"Watch out!" Heller yelled.

She whirled, swinging the crowbar wildly just as she felt something hard and cold pressed against her neck.

Crunch!

The iron bar connected. Hard.

"Bitch!" a pained male voice cried as he pressed on the trigger of his stun gun. Thousands of volts of electricity ricocheted through Abby's body. Rendering her helpless. Leaving her to flop on the floor, her crowbar skating to the far side of the room and smash against the baseboards.

She jerked wildly, unable to do anything more than look upward into the furious, flushed face of a man she felt she should recognize. "You goddamned little bitch," he growled, giving her another shot and rubbing his shin.

Her mind was misfiring. She couldn't control her limbs. But in the gathering darkness she recognized the angry slitted eyes glaring down at her, the same eyes that she'd seen long ago when he'd been a much younger man kneading his stress ball in the hallway or cafeteria or verandah, the same man/boy she'd discovered hiding in the closet watching Heller abuse her mother.

You sick bastard, she tried to say, but even to her own ears, her voice was garbled, only a series of indistinguishable grunts.

He smiled at her helplessness and his grin was pure, unadulterated evil. An unholy light glimmered in his eyes. She remembered how he'd kneaded that soft gelatinous ball, as if he were going to strangle it oh so slowly.

The spit dried in her mouth.

Christian Pomeroy!
Asa's son.
How could she have forgotten?
Oh God, not only was he going to kill her, but he was going to do it slowly and painfully, torturing her and somehow satisfying his own dark sexual fantasies.

She wanted to throw up and when he reached forward to stroke her hair, she tried and failed to turn her head and bite him. Instead she was powerless.

He knew it.

"Welcome home, Faith," he whispered.

What? Faith? No! She was not her mother.

"I've been waiting for this, for us, for a long, long time."

What the hell was this sick pervert talking about?

"The waiting is just about over."

Her stomach heaved as he leaned closer and she imagined he was going to place his slick lips on hers.

Instead, he gave her another painful jolt.

Drip.
Drip.
Drip.

The sound of water hitting the floor was steady and clear.

Where am I? Zoey wondered as she roused, groaning, every muscle in her body aching. It was cool and dank, only a small lantern flickering in the corner of a tiny cell-like room giving off any illumination. Her arms were forced behind her, her ankles shackled, and she could barely move.

Fear buckled through her.

Jesus-God, what was happening? She blinked and remembered the attack at Abby's house, how the tall, muscular man had chased her outside the little cottage to the driveway where he'd captured her. Vaguely, as if through a fog, she recalled that he'd been wearing what looked like a black wetsuit. He'd used some kind of stun gun or Taser on her as she'd tried to climb into her rental car. She'd been awake, but couldn't move or fight back as he'd gagged her, forced her hands behind her back, then wrapped duct tape around her wrists and ankles. As soon as he'd made certain she was no threat to him, he'd picked her up and thrown her into the back seat of her rented silver Toyota. He'd been strong and scary as hell, but as he'd lifted her, she'd heard the sharp hiss of his breath, felt him wince from the effort. He'd muttered an obscenity, as if the act of hoisting her up had caused him pain. Maybe he'd pulled a muscle.

She damned well hoped so.

But why kidnap her? Why bring her to this...this god-awful place?

Panic seized her and she looked around frantically, searching for a way of escape.

Drip.

There had to be a way out of her new prison, but her mind was out of kilter and thick. Concentrating, she focused on the lantern with its small flame that caused flickering shadows to climb up moldy, tiled walls. Not a window in sight. Just filthy tiles, a cracked concrete floor and a narrow door.

So what was with the drip from the ceiling, tiny drops falling to pool on the floor in an ever-expanding puddle? She glanced to the ceiling where a useless light fixture was protected by a metal cage.

Was she in some kind of prison cell? Or a closet...or underground? She thought of Abby and her fascination with the hospital, with her obsession with their mother's death.

Drip.

As the tiny droplet hit the pool, she knew.

With mind-chilling clarity.

She was somewhere on the vast campus of Our Lady of Virtues. Maybe even in the hospital itself...though she didn't remember any tiny cell like this. *Because you're underground! In a basement.*

No!

Adrenalin burst through her.

She had to get out of this prison! She hated basements. Went crazy when she was confined. And that lunatic, whoever he was, would be back. *Get out, Zoey! Get out NOW!*

She heard a terrified mewling and realized the sounds were issuing from her own throat. Clenching her teeth she fought back sheer, muscle-freezing panic.

God help me.

She took in a long breath.

Be cool, Zoey. You've been in tight spots before.

But not with a murdering psycho!

She didn't doubt for a second that he was the killer who had terrorized New Orleans, who had killed Luke and all the others . . . oh, shit . . . she had to save herself, *had* to! She was *way* too young to die, to face whatever sick torture he had planned.

So where was he?

And where was Abby? Wasn't she coming here? Dear God, had the monster already killed her? Zoey began to shake uncontrollably, tremors wracking her body. She prayed her sister was safe, that Abby had somehow outsmarted this creep, that even now she was running for help.

But deep down she knew the chances of that were slim.

Abby could already be dead.

Tears burned her eyes as she thought of her sister and how she'd taken Abby for granted. Oh, Abby, she thought, and began to tear at her bonds. She had to escape! It wasn't her nature to give up without a fight and this son of a bitch wouldn't know what hit him if she could just find a way to get the upper hand. Struggling with the tape restraining her, half expecting the psycho to appear from the shadowy corners, she scanned the tiny room.

Of course she was alone.

She listened hard, tried to hear any movement, but over the sound of her own frenzied heartbeat and shallow breathing, she heard only the sound of the lantern's soft hiss and the drip of water from the ceiling.

You're alone, Zoey. That's good. You have time. Make the most of it.

But the messages from her brain weren't firing quite right and she struggled to push herself into a sitting position. If she could only get rid of the tape around her arms or her legs.

You can. You just have to find a way. Come on, Zoey, concentrate. What do you know that will beat this guy? How can you find a way out of here?

The sick bastard who kidnapped you is a killer. THE killer. You can kid yourself all you want, but considering everything that's gone on recently, you know he plans to kill you just like the others.

Her insides turned to jelly and she wanted to break down and cry. This was so wrong. So unfair. Tears sprang to her eyes and she immediately gave herself a swift mental kick.

Bawling like a damned baby isn't going to help! Do something! Do it, NOW!

Using all her strength, she scooted toward the metal door, which, of course, was closed. She figured that if she could get herself to her feet and stand with her back to the door, she might be able to work the handle. Her wrists were strapped together and her shoulders hurt like hell, but she had no other option that she knew of. The thick iron door was the only way out of this room.

Slowly, she inched across the short span... she thought about the lantern, knew she could kick it over and maybe cause a fire, but how would that help? And nothing in the austere room appeared flammable. She would be trapped in this cell, with no one to come and save her.

No. That wouldn't do.

She inched over the filth.

Ignored the dirt.

Finally she was at the wall. She tried to climb to her feet, to push herself upright, planting her feet about a foot in front of her and pushing upward.

Once she fell.

Skinning her forearm, new pain searing upward.

Don't let this bastard get the better of you.

Cursing silently, she tried again. Only to slide down the wall, burning her arm.

Do this, Zoey. Try harder. Don't give up.

Her feet were bare, so she curled her toes, trying to dig into the cold cement of the floor, and managed to squirm her body up the door. Balanced, she attempted to push it open. To no avail. The slim handle didn't budge. Was locked tight. She tried again, hoping the old latch would give way.

Nothing.

Again, setting her jaw, she forced all of her strength into the handle, willing it to move.

It didn't.

Damn, damn, damn and double damn. She wanted to fall into a heap and cry.

She was trapped!

The madman had locked her up and would either leave her here to die a horrid, lingering death or would return for some other gruesome end.

She couldn't give up. Her only hope, she decided, was the lantern. If and when someone opened the door, she could kick the lantern with its kerosene, burning wick, and glass base at whoever unlocked the door.

Other than that, she was a dead woman.

"God *damn* you, Montoya!" Bentz growled, holstering his weapon. What the hell was his partner thinking? And where the hell was he?

Upon receiving Zaroster's call, Bentz had peeled off from the crime scene where Billy Ray Furlough and Maria Montoya were the victims. Leaving Brinkman in charge, Bentz had driven like a bat out of hell to land here at Simon Heller's house, a two-storied Greek Revival style home with huge white pillars, topiary in the front yard and a sweeping verandah.

Zaroster was already inside when he'd arrived, but the house had been empty. Bentz had barged in, shouting he was with the police and found Lynn Zaroster alone in the graceful old home.

"Something's definitely up," she'd told him and led him into a downstairs study where there were signs of a struggle.

A desk chair had been kicked over.

The computer monitor had been knocked to the floor and the screen had cracked.

Blood splattered a leather easy chair, where, it appeared someone had been working a crossword puzzle. The newspaper had scattered across polished floors; a pencil, too, had rolled up against the marble hearth of a fireplace, wire-rimmed glasses were broken and strung over a folded piece of the newspaper; a third of the answers to the puzzle had been filled in.

Zaroster had already checked the rest of the house, but Bentz, too, looked things over. Nothing in any of the other rooms appeared, at least at their first, peripheral search, to have been disturbed. The beds were made, dishes washed, no sign of anyone in the house. And Heller's vehicle was missing, a white Lexus SUV with California plates according to the DMV, not parked anywhere outside. Not in the single car garage, not in the alley, and definitely not on the oak-lined street. Bentz had checked.

But how had Montoya known about Heller?

That cocky forget-the-rules son of a bitch was a maverick. Montoya had enough balls to show up at his aunt's crime scene against orders, then had managed to sneak his way past all the guards to view the gutted mobile home where Sister Maria and Billy Ray Furlough had been killed and left. Then with barely a word to Bentz, Montoya had taken off on some personal vendetta. Not confiding in anyone.

Except, it seemed, Lynn Zaroster.

"Where's Montoya now?" he demanded, once he'd searched for the Lexus and had returned to Heller's den.

"At Our Lady of Virtues Hospital," Zaroster said and quickly recapped her conversation with Montoya and his theory about the killing spree being tied to the Seven Deadly Sins and Seven Contrary Virtues to Bentz. "But that's not all," she continued, "Montoya thinks everyone involved is connected either loosely or directly to that old hospital. We thought Heller was the killer, but—" she glanced around the mess in the doctor's den, "—it looks like he's another victim."

"Your theory is that the vics are killed using their name associated with a sin or . . . ?"

"A contrary virtue. In Heller's case, Simon Thaddeus Heller, I'm betting Sloth as the sin."

Bentz looked around the house. Other than the den, it was neat as a pin. "Doesn't look lazy to me."

Zaroster lifted a shoulder. "I'm just tellin' ya."

"I know."

"And this guy, he could have a wife or girlfriend or boyfriend or maid to clean up after him."

"Or the theory could be just a load of bull," Bentz thought out loud, but he was starting to buy it as he stared around Heller's house. Heller, who had worked at the asylum. Something about the way everything was falling together made Montoya's sins/virtues theory ring true. Still, Montoya had no business acting on his own, bending the rules to the breaking point. Possibly compromising the case.

As if you haven't, his mind nagged.

He ignored it.

They walked to the front door of the graceful old house with its expensive furnishings and original pieces of art, trappings that wouldn't help Heller now. "If Montoya's right, then our killer isn't finished."

"Not by a long shot. Let's go." She was already on her way to her car.

"Wait! You stay here. Secure this scene. Get backup. I'll go to the hospital. Call Montoya and tell him what's up. He won't pick up my calls but no way is he to go inside that place. Especially not alone!"

"You think I can convince him?"

"You'd better damned well try." Bentz was already across Heller's clipped lawn and at the curb where his cruiser was parked on the street. "Are you familiar with the riot act?" he threw out as he opened the car door and glanced over his shoulder through the rain.

Cell phone to her ear, Zaroster stood in the huge entryway of Heller's house. She looked up at him expectantly.

"You might want to bone up, cuz I'm going to read it to you letter by letter when I get back. You knew what Montoya was up to, so you, too, may have thrown this whole case in jeopardy. There is no room, do you hear me?—*no* room for this rogue cop shit." He slid behind the wheel, slammed the car door shut, fired up the engine, turned on the sirens and gunned it down the quiet street.

"Idiot," Bentz growled as he picked up his cell phone to call for backup and punched in the number for the station. He understood Montoya's motivations, just didn't like them. What the hell was the younger cop doing, messing up the goddamned case?

Zoey started edging toward the flickering lamp when she heard something outside the door. *Footsteps!*

God, please, let it be the police! Someone to save me.

Her heart pounded wildly, fear spurting through her blood as she heard the lock click loudly. Groaning, the door swung open.

Looming on the other side, his features shadowy in the thin light, appeared the embodiment of Satan.

Oh God! Please help me!

She scooted as far and as fast as she could from him, shrinking away until her back was pressed against the gritty tile and she had no where to go.

His grin was twisted.

Evil.

Leering.

She nearly fainted in fear as he stepped into the tiny cell.

"I thought you'd finally wake up," he said, his voice as smooth as oiled glass. "Good. I want you to know what's going on."

That sounded bad. She braced herself for another shot with the stun gun, but he walked into the room, hauled her roughly to her feet, then before she could react, threw her over his shoulder and held her by her bound ankles. Again she heard that hiss of pain as he straightened and she knew instinctively that he had a vulnerable spot somewhere. She just had to find it. To use it. To wound this psycho and somehow bring him to his knees.

As he carried her, his gait uneven, as if walking caused him pain, she squirmed, fighting and struggling, but her efforts were useless. He handled her easily, packing her in a firefighter's carry through dark, smelly corridors, past rooms where lanterns glowed. Her head was dangling behind his back, her hair falling over her face, but through the tangled strands she caught glimpses inside the rooms, quick looks at instruments of torture—electrical prods, surgical scalpels, straitjackets, hypodermic needles.

This place was a damned house of torture.

So she'd guessed right. The pervert had brought Zoey deep in the bowels of the sanitarium where Faith Chastain had been abused and molested, the asylum where she had died so horribly.

Now, Zoey feared, it was her turn.

Montoya slammed on the brakes in the parking lot of the convent.

Right next to Abby's little Honda.

"Hell." He'd instigated a Be-On-The-Lookout-For on the vehicle, but no one, as yet, had checked the private lot of the convent.

He hadn't called for backup and had ignored his cell whenever he'd seen Bentz's number appear on the screen. He didn't need a lecture. Or a command that he would have to ignore.

He wanted to confide in his partner, but couldn't drag him into this. Not until he was certain. Bentz would have to wait.

But Abby's car was a big clue.

A major clue.

He cut the engine and he slid from behind the wheel, then doubled up on his weapons by strapping a second small pistol to his ankle. He had a can of pepper spray with him and found a flashlight in the glove box. Once armed he started jogging for the gate.

His cell phone blasted and he checked the screen for the caller's number. Zaroster.

Dread grabbed hold of his heart. What if it were news about Abby? What if he was too late? He clicked on as he ducked behind the dripping hedge of arborvitae. "Montoya."

Zaroster's voice was hard. "Heller's place is empty and there are signs of a struggle."

"Shit!"

"My sentiments exactly."

"What about his car?"

"Missing. A white Lexus SUV. From the looks of this house and his car and everything, I guess life is good for the doctor. Or was. Bentz was here and we think Heller might be another victim. Why else the struggle in his own house? Looks like he was attacked in his den. We found blood and a pair of glasses smashed and broken, an identical pair to the ones in a picture of Heller that was on the mantel."

Montoya didn't like it. He'd thought Heller was the killer. If not Heller then who?

"Bentz is on his way," Zaroster continued as he eased through the gate. "With backup. And he's on the warpath. He told me if I got hold of you, you weren't to go inside the hospital."

"Too late. I'm already here. Abby Chastain's car is parked at the convent and my guess is she isn't planning on joining the order. I've tried calling her and she's not answering her cell phone. Did anyone get to her house? Check on her?"

"Not that I know of. Not yet."

"Damn." He knew the truth. Her car was *here*. *She* was here. He only prayed she was alone and not with the deadly psychopath who had already killed so many. Six victims that they knew of. Potentially eight more. Abby Chastain...What sin or virtue could she and her name possibly represent?

A for Abby. A for...Avarice?

Nope. Already used with Asa Pomeroy.

Chastain. C. Chastity?

Again, if his theory was right, Chastity was represented by Courtney LaBelle, the virgin...wrong again.

C for Charity? The virtue opposing the sin of Envy?

His heart skidded to a stop. That was it! But what about Heller? Simon T. Heller, another victim...S...for...sloth. But that didn't fit. The contrary virtue for sloth was humility.

Zaroster was still on the phone, trying to rationalize why he should wait for another cop to come along. "...local Sheriff's Department can send a deputy in a few minutes, I'd guess."

Montoya had heard enough. "Send them. Fast. But I'm not waiting. If Bentz doesn't like it, that's just too damned bad!"

"Bentz was clear about—"

"Bentz can cram it. I know what he said. You warned me. Your ass is out of the sling."

"It's not that, Montoya."

He didn't wait for her explanation. Didn't care. "I'll call as soon as I know what's up." He hung up, pocketed his cell phone, turned the ring-tone to vibrate, then followed the wet path. He ran, feet sinking into the soft loam, the smell of the earth heavy in his nostrils. Fear urged him onward. Dread caused every muscle in his body to tighten. He thought of Abby and what he might find.

Was the killer with her?

Was he already too late?

Or was this all a false alarm?

C for Charity...C for Chastain.

No!

What was her middle name? He'd heard it or seen it. Abigail Hannah Chastain Gierman. *Hannah! H* for *Humility!* Shit!

For once he hoped to God that his instincts were wrong as he jogged softly through thick brush and ever-increasing rain. It poured from the sky, drizzled down the tree trunks, plopped in fat drops from the branches.

He wondered if he'd ever see her alive again, then refused to think of the alternative.

You can't lose her!

Kill the bastard if you have to!

Kill him even if you don't.

He passed through a copse of sourwood, then spied, through the branches, the imposing, sinister-looking building of crumbling mortar and cracked bricks.

What atrocities had it housed?

What malignancies had resided in the dark hallways?

What heinous crimes had been committed in the interests of making raging patients docile, of keeping those who suffered from misunderstood diseases under control, or, in Heller's case, of making patients weaker and more malleable so they would submit to his lecherous needs?

With rain running down his collar and dripping from his nose, Montoya checked the doors.

Locked.

He tested the windows. Latched. Or boarded over.

And yet, he sensed someone was inside.

Damn it all to hell!

Time was running short. He could feel it passing and with it Abby's chances of survival. He had to find her. *Had* to. He searched the building again.

He didn't dare break a window.

Needed the element of surprise on his side.

Once more he jogged around the perimeter of the huge edifice, passed by the fountain where rainwater was collecting in the dirty basin, ignored the graffiti still visible through the plywood panels and eased to the back of the building, near what appeared to be the kitchen.

The door was locked, but close by, adjacent to a cracked cement porch, was a partially opened window.

And footprints.

Small footprints.

His heart nosedived.

Abby!

Without a second's hesitation, he levered himself over the sill and landed softly inside.

He prayed she was alone, but didn't call out, didn't let anyone know he was near.

Just in case.

CHAPTER 29

Abby could barely breathe. Trapped in the closet, her mouth taped shut, her ankles bound and her wrists pulled roughly behind her, she was forced to stare through the crack in the closet door just as Pomeroy had all those years before.

Why?

And why hadn't she remembered him?

Because you blacked it all out . . . you didn't remember Heller and you didn't remember Christian Pomeroy . . . get over it and figure out how to save yourself!

Night had settled into the room and Pomeroy, before leaving, had rigged up black blankets that he'd drawn over the window so that no light could seep inside or out. A small lantern had been left in the fireplace, burning quietly, giving off little light, just enough luminescence to bathe the room in a eerie, flickering glow.

She wasn't alone. Pomeroy had stretched Simon Heller upon the bed and chained him there, spread-eagle upon his back.

Abby shifted. Pain exploded in her shoulders. She couldn't move much. He'd tied her to a hook in the back of the closet and it was rigged in such a manner that the more she struggled, the tighter her arms were wrenched behind her.

She thought of her pepper spray, useless in her backpack, or the crowbar that now rested against the wall. Out of reach. Damn!

Don't give up. Think, Abby. Find a way out of this. He's not here. Now's your chance!

The closet was small with only one hook that held her bound and little else as far as she could tell. She'd felt the interior as best she could with her bound hands. There had been no other hooks, no nails protruding, but there was a board that ran around the inside of the closet, as if it had once been the base for a shelf. And it had a sharp edge. If she stood on her tiptoes and rubbed her wrists back and forth along the ridge, she might be able to cut through the tape. Maybe.

It was a long shot, but all she had.

Ignoring the burn of her shoulders and the fact that her calves quivered as she stood on her toes, she worked. Fast. Hard. Rubbing. Feeling the heat of friction.

Keep at it, Abby.

Rain pounded against the windows while the wind, picking up speed, screeched through the rafters. She rubbed harder. Faster. Her calves were on fire, her shoulders screaming in agony.

Don't stop!

Sweating, breathing hard behind her hated mask, she worked. Slid the tape back and forth chafing her wrists.

Then over her own racing heart and the rush of the wind she heard the sound of heavy tread upon the stairs, footsteps climbing to the third floor.

No!

Her heart, already beating out of control, kicked into overdrive.

Rub, rub, rub!

Did she feel the tape giving, if only just a bit? Or was it her own anxious imagination, her own desperate hopes?

Rapidly she worked, her shoulders shrieking in pain, her toes feeling as if they would break, her wrists hot and rubbed free of the skin where they'd skimmed the sharp edge of the board.

The footsteps came closer, following the hallway, pausing on the other side of the door to the room.

Oh, no! Not yet! Please God!

Abby swallowed back her fear. Sweat ran down her nose. She kept shoving the tape back and forth against the board, burning her skin. Faster and faster, pulling at the tape, trying desperately to stretch it though she knew the chance of breaking free was nearly impossible.

Keep a cool head.

The lock on the door to the room rattled and the door swung open noiselessly.

Abby's heart sank.

Through the crack in the closet door, a small sliver of visibility, Abby watched as Pomeroy lumbered into the room. He was carrying something, no, someone ... another woman ...

Oh, dear God, no!

All her hopes died as she recognized her sister.

Zoey!

Bentz floored it. He drove like a maniac through the pelting rain. The Crown Victoria's wipers fought hard against the deluge, slapping water away from the windshield as fast as it poured from the hideously dark sky. The tires of his cruiser hummed and cut through pools of standing water, hydroplaning a bit, yet he didn't let up.

No word from Montoya.

Of course.

Bentz had already alerted the Sheriff's Department. The bad news was that the parish's manpower was stretched thin, the result of a double car accident, one of the vehicles pushed over the railing of a bridge, the car plunging into the river, the other overturned on the shoulder. One driver was dead, life flight called for the passenger, the other driver and two passengers rushed by ambulance to a local hospital.

State and local law enforcement had their hands full.

He tromped on the accelerator.

The wind was howling, Spanish moss dancing eerily in the trees as he reached the turnoff to Our Lady of Virtues.

He set his jaw, kept his speed up. His siren was silent, his lights turned off.

He had a bad feeling about what was going down at the old sanitarium and thought it better, if he arrived first, to have the element of surprise on his side.

Rounding a corner he spied a fork in the road, one lane leading to the convent, the other to the hospital. He veered toward the old asylum and drove as far as he could, then, weapon drawn, climbed out of his car.

Of course the gates were shut. Locked tight. But not insurmountable. He'd been a wrestler and football player in high school and college. His senior year of high school he'd been the fastest in his class at climbing a thick rope that had dangled from the gym's ceiling. So what if he had twenty-five years and nearly twice as many pounds to deal with? So what if it was driving rain and the metal grating was slick? It was only a damned gate. Eight, maybe nine feet tall.

Piece of cake.

Abby nearly fainted as she spied Zoey.

What was the monster planning?

There was little doubt Pomeroy was the killer who had already slaughtered his chosen victims, pairing them as if they were involved in some sick ritualistic murder/suicide.

How, she wondered desperately, could she save herself, save her sister, save Heller? She looked over to the bed her mother had lain in twenty years earlier. The psychiatrist was stretched across the mattress, a fresh gag had been slapped over his mouth and he was lying face up on the quilt, quivering, his eyes round, his pants stained, bleating behind his mask like a lamb to the slaughter. She hated him, but couldn't just leave him to die. If she found a way to escape she'd have to try and save Heller, too, then bring his sorry ass to justice.

Pomeroy, limping slightly, unceremoniously dumped Zoey to the floor where she fell into a dazed pile, apparently unable to move. Her eyes rolled high into her head and Abby decided she'd either been terrorized, tranquilized or zapped with a stun gun.

Bastard! She saw the satisfaction in Pomeroy's eyes as he glanced at the closet. He was enjoying this. Getting off on his victim's vulnerability, on their terror.

Her sister would be no help.

You're on your own. Somehow, you have to trick him. He's too big, too strong, too determined to overcome physically . . . stay smart.

She knew little about him, just that he'd been in the hospital at

420 • Lisa Jackson

the same time as her mother had. He was Asa Pomeroy's firstborn, a child nearly forgotten when Asa had dumped Christian's mother, Karen, for his second wife and new son, Jeremy.

Wincing slightly, Pomeroy rubbed his chest and stared at Abby so hard her skin felt as if it would crawl off her body. He'd called her by her mother's name and the way he'd said it suggested that he'd been close to Faith; perhaps intimate. Lust had colored his gaze as he'd whispered, "Welcome home, Faith."

Her stomach heaved at the thought of what he'd done to her mother. Or had it been consensual? Oh, God...

Use this knowledge. Pretend you're Faith. Roll with his fantasy. Pomeroy won't want Faith to die again. Act as if you're your mother, for God's sake. Remember, he didn't kill her...Heller did!

From the corner of her eye she saw her mother's murderer, chained and scared spitless and she remembered in sudden vivid clarity how he'd pushed Faith out of the window, pretending to help her, restraining Abby from tumbling after, but definitely shoving her mother through the splintering glass.

As the lantern flickered and Zoey moaned on the floor, Pomeroy walked to the nightstand, opened the top drawer and withdrew two guns.

The first one was Luke's .38.

Oh, sweet Jesus. This psycho had been *inside* her house, creeping through the hallways, touching her things, sneaking into her bedroom, maybe touching her pillow or lying upon her bed. Again, her stomach convulsed.

Shaking, she was attempting and failing to stay calm.

Hang on, Abby. Keep trying to cut through the damned tape!

But her eyes were trained on her tormentor, fascinated and repulsed as Pomeroy took the second gun, a long barreled pistol, and held it in front of Heller's terrified face.

The psychiatrist flung himself away from Pomeroy, stretching the chains, rattling his handcuffs, trying to physically tear himself out of his bonds like a snared fox chewing its paw from the trap. Blood showed on his ankles and wrists and he was screaming wildly, bucking on the bed.

"You can't get away," Pomeroy said. "Your fate is sealed, Simon."

Heller was shaking his head.

"You killed her."

More frantic head shaking. Eyes as wide as saucers.

"I saw you. You pushed her through the window."

A squealing protest behind the gag.

"And even if you hadn't, the drugs you kept giving her were her murder sentence, medications that made her docile and willing, allowing you to abuse her at will." Pomeroy sneered down at his victim. "You're a sick man, Heller. And a lazy man. Instead of using your knowledge, instead of working to find a way to heal her, you took the easy, slothful way out."

Heller was crying now. Broken, whimpering sobs erupted through the tape fastening his lips together.

"And so you shall pay, doctor. You were the epitome of sloth, you see, and the only way to fight the sin of sloth is with the virtue of zeal."

Heller went still.

Sloth and zeal? Abby thought. What was he talking about?

"So I've brought you an angel of mercy. Someone who will destroy your sin of sloth with her virtue of zeal." He glanced down at Zoey. "I admit she's lost some of her zest for life, but that's short-lived and my doing."

Zoey looked dazed. Tried to raise her head but fell backward onto the floor, her muscles betraying her.

What kind of macabre, twisted fantasy was this whack job playing out?

In the closet, Abby worked at her wrists, ignoring the pain, sawing against the bracing board and all the while knowing they were fast running out of time.

He heard noises. Voices. Whimpers. Muted cries.

Montoya hated to think what he would find, but knew that the victims were still alive. Abby? Heller?

Up the stairs, not daring to make a sound, Montoya rounded a corner. He used his flashlight sparingly, quickly sweeping the small beam in front of him so that he wouldn't stumble. In his other hand, his Glock was drawn, ready to fire.

Rain and wind lashed at the building and the hallways were dark as night. The noises emanating from the third floor grew more distinct as he passed a ghostly stained glass window on the landing. He didn't pause, but climbed high enough on the steps to see the floor of the hallway, where he spied a ribbon of light beneath one door, the only closed door on the entire floor.

No doubt the thin line of illumination was seeping into the corridor from Room 307.

Where Faith Chastain had died.

Where he heard the rattle of chains and muted, petrified screams.

No time for backup.

As soon as he reached the doorway, he was going in.

The tape was giving way, fraying at the edges. Far away, over the sound of the storm, Abby thought she heard the thin, distant wail of sirens. *Oh, please, please.* In the dark, she kept running her wrists back and forth, silently moving the ever fraying tape over and over the sharp edge of the board.

Horrified, she watched as Pomeroy found a knife in the night table. Her heart froze in fear as he lifted the weapon, the long blade catching the golden light of the lantern.

She was certain he was going to slice Heller's throat, but instead he turned on Zoey, the dish rag lying at his feet.

No! Oh, no!

Desperately she worked at the tape, praying she could break through in time. But Pomeroy was swift. He bent down to Zoey and with a quick motion, sliced through the tape binding Zoey's wrists, then did the same with her ankles.

Why?

Was he letting her sister go? Because he had Abby? A woman who more closely resembled their mother?

Abby felt a second's relief until she realized that Zoey wasn't about to be freed. No, her sister, too, was a part of Pomeroy's sick plan.

"It's time to pay for your sins, Doctor," Pomeroy said with ultimate, chilling calm.

On the bed, Heller went wild. Screaming behind his gag, he writhed on the bed, rumpling the comforter, rattling the bedframe so hard that it jumped. Metal against metal scraped and clanged through the room, rising over the rain pounding against the windows.

Pomeroy hauled Zoey to her rubbery legs. "You, Simon Heller," Pomeroy said angrily, "are damned. You claimed to be a doctor, you swore by oath to help and heal. Instead you took the easy way out. You not only abused your patients but you suffered from one of the Seven Deadly Sins, the sin of sloth."

Abby couldn't believe what she was hearing. *Seven Deadly Sins? Sloth? He was rationalizing his crimes? Playing God?* How insane was he?

She watched in terror as Pomeroy wrapped one arm around Zoey's waist. Roughly, he pulled Zoey's buttocks close to his crotch and forced the long-muzzled gun into her hand. There was a smile on his lips, a satisfaction as he rubbed up against Zoey's rump.

Bile rose up Abby's throat. *Pervert! Sick, vile, pervert!*

Zoey rolled her eyes upward and caught Abby's eye in a moment of clarity.

In the heartbeat that followed, Abby understood. Zoey wasn't as far gone as she was pretending. But what could she do?

Nothing! You have to help her!

Abby worked furiously on the tape. Her arms were screeching in pain, but again she felt the thick tape loosening, the fibers within it fraying as her wrists chafed.

Pomeroy said, "And you, Zoey Chastain, firstborn of Faith, have the virtue of zeal, so it's your duty to rid the world of the slovenly."

Heller stiffened.

Pomeroy focused his hot eyes on Abby.

She froze. Had he seen her trying to free herself? Her heart drummed a horrified tattoo.

"And you won't be far behind, Hannah. You, who were humiliated by your lustful, adulterating husband." He cocked his head to one side and frowned, his eyes clouding. "Faith?" he whispered in confusion... "Faith?"

She nodded, hoping he would believe her, but the clouds disappeared and he shook his head as if to rid it of fog. "No...Not Faith. Hannah...for humility." He smiled suddenly as if all his synapses were connecting again. "Pride is certainly on his way."

Pride? Humility? Sloth? Zeal? Sins and virtues? What was this all about? And who represented pride? Someone whose name started with the letter P? She remembered the sins and virtues from her youth in private Catholic schools. But what did they have to do with her mother?

Virtues!

Our Lady of Virtues!

Is that what this was all about? Not that it mattered. Nothing did. Only escaping. Somehow turning the tables on this bastard. She had to do *something! Anything!* She couldn't stand by and end up a witness to cold-blooded murder.

"You know who I'm talking about," Pomeroy said, rubbing hard against Zoey's backside as he stared into the dark closet, searching for Abby's eyes. How demented was he? How far gone? "Pride? Your lover? Pedro?"

Bells clanged through her head. *Pedro!* Hadn't Montoya said that Sister Maria had called him Pedro?

"The cop," Pomeroy snarled.

Oh, dear God, this monster was going to kill Montoya, too!

"Now," Pomeroy said, and aimed the gun directly at Simon Heller's heart. "It's time."

Zoey was totally limp. Useless. Or was she? Through the tangle of her disheveled hair, she peered again at her sister.

Pomeroy aimed the gun.

Heller screamed behind his gag.

The killer pulled the trigger just as Zoey crammed her elbow into the big man's chest.

Bang!

The gun went off.

Heller shrieked horribly and went limp, blood pooling in his chest. At that second, Zoey rammed her elbow into Pomeroy's chest again and the big man sucked in his breath in a loud hiss. She kicked at his shins and he yowled in pain.

"Bitch. Zealous, overambitious bitch!" He turned the gun in her hand, forcing the muzzle to Zoey's temple. "Now it's your turn!"

* * *

Bang!

A pistol cracked, echoing through the hallway.

Muted screams followed.

Jesus, no! Abby! No!

Fear and anger rushed through Montoya.

He was too late!

Damn it, he was too late!

Weapon drawn, he flung himself at the door of 307.

The old lock gave way with a sickening crack and splinter of wood. Montoya shot through the door just as Pomeroy turned the gun toward Zoey's temple.

"Police!" Montoya shouted. "Drop your weapon!"

A gunshot!

Hell!

Bentz didn't waste any time.

Using the butt of his Glock, he broke a window on the first floor, cracking out the glass. He hoisted himself up, feeling razor sharp shards slice into his palms, then vaulted over the sill and landed on the parlor floor of the abandoned sanitarium.

As soon as he hit the floor, he grabbed his cell phone and speed dialed 911.

"Nine-one-one. What is the nature—."

"This is Rick Bentz. New Orleans Police Department." He rattled off his badge number and requested assistance, giving the name and address of the old hospital. "Gunshots at Our Lady of Virtues Sanitarium." He clicked off, jammed the cell phone into his pocket, then, weapon drawn, started through a decrepit old building that was dark as night.

Abby threw her weight against her restraints as Montoya burst into the room. The tape gave a little.

"Stay back!" Pomeroy warned, trying to hold onto Zoey, the muzzle pressed to her sister's temple as Montoya took aim.

Zoey's eyes were round with fear.

"Drop the weapon!" Montoya ordered. "Now!"

Pomeroy snorted. "Prideful to the end."

On the bed Heller wheezed and bled out, the light fading from his eyes.

Abby worked at her bonds. Unafraid. Determined.

"It should have been you," Pomeroy said, sliding a glance to the closet, inching backward toward the window, using Zoey, who was, with the gun pressed to her head, his shield.

"Stop!" Montoya ordered.

But Christian Pomeroy's eyes were trained on Abby and his lips quivered. "So beautiful."

"Stop or I'll shoot!" Montoya's face was set, his jaw hard, his eyes pinpointed on Pomeroy, his gun aimed at the tall man's head. "It's over."

"That's where you're wrong, Pedro," Pomeroy said in a calm voice that turned the marrow of Abby's bones to ice. "No matter what else happens, tonight is just the beginning."

"You're going down."

"And so are you."

Zoey flinched, throwing back her head and slamming her elbow into the killer's chest again. Pomeroy yelped. The gun in his hand wobbled.

Montoya fired.

Bam!

The bullet from Montoya's Glock ripped through the killer's shoulder just as Pomeroy squeezed the trigger.

Bang!

Zoey, blood gushing from her head, dropped to the floor.

The tape gave way, and Abby flung herself from the closet to the floor beside her sister.

Montoya fired again. *Bang!* And again. *Bang!*

Bullets ripped through the killer's torso. Blood spurted.

Pomeroy threw himself through the blanket covering the window. Glass shattered and cracked, bloody shards flying outward.

The blanket and Pomeroy hurled into the wet, dark night.

Behind her gag, Abby screamed.

Thud!

She heard the crunch of bones as he landed on the wet concrete far below.

Abby scooted next to her sister, lying on the floor, blood streaming from a wound beneath her eye. "You're going to be all right," she said as Montoya dropped down beside her and felt for a pulse at Zoey's neck. "You're going to be all right, Zoey...You have to be. Hang on...please, please, hang on."

Using Pomeroy's knife Montoya cut Abby free. Then he was on his cell phone, barking orders.

Everything was a blur in Abby's mind. Every muscle in her body ached and her mind spun as she had to fight to keep from blacking out. Through the open, broken window, wind and rain lashed into the room, the dark night warm with the scent of the bayou.

Sirens wailed, closer now, and she thought she saw the strobe of colored lights on the walls of her mother's room. People were shouting, footsteps thundering, and another man ran inside the room. She recognized him, she thought, maybe another detective? Bentz? But everything was surreal...trying to fade to black and Zoey...Zoey was lying unmoving, blood flowing down her face.

"Abby? Abby?" She heard his voice, looked into eyes as dark as obsidian...Montoya! Her heart swelled. He'd come for her. She forced a tremulous smile that fell away instantly. "She's in shock."

He held her close and said, "This is gonna hurt." Deftly he pulled at the tape over her mouth. It ripped and tore at her skin, burning, but she didn't care as she huddled over the still body of her sister.

"Zoey..."

"The ambulance is on its way," he said, holding her even more tightly. She drank in the scent of him, felt the power of his body.

"Zoey...not Zoey."

"It'll be okay," he said into her ear and she wished she could believe him, but here in this room, nothing was ever okay, nothing ever would be.

"Do you know who the killer was?"

She blinked and when she spoke it was a whisper, her voice raw. "Christian Pomeroy."

"Asa's son?" Bentz asked.

"He was a patient here once. I saw his name on the list," Montoya said, as she heard a lock being shattered somewhere on the floors below. Men filled orders, footsteps pounded and through the yawning hole of the window the whirl of helicopter blades could be heard.

"Life flight," Bentz said and suddenly the room was filled with people. Police officers. EMTs.

"Sir?" an EMT said to Montoya. The emergency worker was hovering over Zoey, pushing past them to take vital signs, hook up an IV, and try to stanch the flow of blood. "Move back. Please."

Another EMT, a tiny woman looked at Abby. "Is she all right?"

"I'm fine," Abby insisted, clinging tightly to Montoya and silently praying for her sister's life. She watched as Zoey was hoisted onto a stretcher and Heller's body was zipped into a bag.

"What about her?" Abby asked motioning to Zoey. "My sister? Will she be okay?"

"Too early to tell," the EMT said, "but she's stable." He took a second to stare at Abby. "We'll do our best."

"The guy outside? On the pavement?" Montoya asked.

"Dead," an officer replied, then hooked his chin toward the body bag that held Heller's body. "Like that one."

Abby shivered in Montoya's arms. Finally, the past could be buried. The future was no longer clouded by the unknown . . . or was it? What was it that Christian Pomeroy had said so cryptically, as if he had another secret, one that he hadn't shared?

She frowned. Surely he'd been lying. This had to be the end, and yet the killer's words, said with such conviction, echoed through her mind.

Tonight is just the beginning . . .

"It's gonna be all right," Montoya said, helping her out of the room where so much tragedy had occured.

"You're sure?"

"Yep." He kissed her crown. "Trust me."

EPILOGUE

"I don't think you need this anymore." Montoya plucked the *For Sale* sign off the post, then tossed it into a pile of leaves near the trash basket.

"You don't expect me to move?" Abby asked, teasing.

"Nah." He wrapped strong arms around her. "Well, at least not far."

He was right of course. In the past two weeks since the night that Christian Pomeroy had been killed, Abby had lost all incentive to move.

Her sister, Zoey, had spent a week in the hospital, then three days at Abby's house before declaring that she had to return to Seattle. Zoey's face still looked like she'd been beaten black and blue but the plastic surgeons had reconstructed the part of her cheekbone that had been shattered by Pomeroy's bullet, which had passed through the soft tissue on the other side of her face. She was looking at several more surgeries and extensive dental work in the future, but she was alive and wanted to be home in the Pacific Northwest.

Abby hadn't blamed her. She'd promised to visit and stay with Zoey during the next round of surgeries.

"Great. When this is all over, I'll be so damned beautiful," Zoey had insisted, refusing to let the thought of more reconstruction and recovery get her down, "Hollywood will be knocking down my door. I could even get a job with one of those entertainment programs, I'll bet. Mary Hart, move over!" She'd laughed, then groaned with pain. "Well, eventually."

As for Abby, she had no intention of moving away from Montoya, who had been with her day and night. Hershey, of course, was thrilled that Montoya nearly lived at their house these days, though Ansel hadn't budged in his out-and-out distrust of the detective.

Abby looked up at Montoya now, with the sunlight piercing through the canopy of branches overhead. Bright rays caught in his black hair and glinted in his eyes. Staring at him, Abby felt her heart swell. And she no longer fought the attraction.

After Luke's betrayal and her divorce, Abby had vowed she'd never fall in love again. But she'd been wrong. Dead wrong. What she felt whenever Reuben Montoya was around was five steps beyond exhilaration. As often as she'd tried to talk herself out of this ridiculous feeling of euphoria, she'd also decided it was time to trust again, to love again, to let the chips fall where they may. He'd asked her to trust him the night of Pomeroy's death and she had. He was definitely worth the gamble.

"You know, maybe I made a mistake," Montoya said, slinging his arm over her shoulder as they walked toward the cottage, Hershey bounding at their heels. As they passed the *For Sale* sign lying on the ground, he gave it a kick. "Maybe you do want to move."

"Oh?" She cocked an interested eyebrow. The man was forever surprising her. "So now, five minutes after taking down the sign, you're ready to put it up again and get rid of me?"

His grin stretched wide, showing off white teeth in his black goatee. "I didn't say that."

She cocked her head. "So what is this, some kind of back handed proposal?"

"I didn't say that, either!" He laughed and gave her shoulders a squeeze. "You certainly know how to take the wind out of a guy's sails."

She waited. Where was this going?

"So, okay, here's the deal: I have the opportunity to buy the shotgun house that's attached to mine. Mrs. Alexander is moving up north to be with her kids. She offered her house to me on a contract. It's a damned good deal and I was thinking about remodeling, you know, doubling the space, creating one bigger house out of the two narrow ones. So, I thought maybe you'd like to move in."

"Maybe," she said glancing around the grounds of her small cottage. "But I kind of like it here."

"Alone?"

"Not necessarily." She winked at him. "Why don't you move out here?"

"Oh, whoa. Plenty of reasons. Let's start with we both have work in town, so I thought we could live there, close to work and nightlife and friends, but also keep this place. You know, stay here when we wanted to get away from the city."

"Not too far of a getaway."

He drew her into his arms and rested his forehead on hers. The gold ring in his earlobe winked in the afternoon light. "It would be perfect," he said, his breath fanning her face, her heart suddenly trip-hammering.

"And that way, if things didn't work out, I could come back here."

"They'll work out." He seemed so positive. Yeah, maybe there was more than a little pride in Reuben Diego Pedro Montoya. "You know, they even have this pool down at the station. Bets are being taken. Bentz told me it's two to one that you and I'll be married by the end of the year."

"Is that so? Then you'll have to work fast, won't you, Detective."

"I've been known to," he said, and she felt that little jolt of lust seep into her blood again, reflected by the hint of desire in his coffee-dark eyes.

"I come with baggage," she warned, "and I'm not talking about what happened at the old hospital and all those old ghosts of the past."

"That's not enough?"

She punched him in the arm. "Noooo. I was talking about Ansel and Hershey."

He groaned. "I don't know. A dog and a suspicious feline?"

"And a zealous sister."

He laughed. "Is that all? No big deal. Come on, Chastain. Bring it on. What else do you have?"

"You're impossible," she said, giggling, and felt more light-hearted than she had in years.

"So I've been told."

"I'll consider the move," she said as they climbed the two steps of the porch and she heard a squirrel running rapidly across the roof. "But I can't promise anything."

As much as she'd loved being with Montoya these past two weeks, they'd been difficult as well. News reporters had called repeatedly as her name had been linked to Faith Chastain and Christian Pomeroy. Sean Erwin had been pissed as hell when he'd tried to buy the house for thousands less than it was worth and she'd turned him down. Maury Taylor was still milking Luke's death and the whole serial killer thing at WSLJ, and her clientele had grown exponentially with her newfound infamy.

In-depth stories about Christian Pomeroy, the rich, mentally ill son of a local millionaire who had "slipped through the cracks" in the mental health system had come to light in chilling detail.

At odds with a father who had abandoned him, Christian had used the very weapons Asa Pomeroy had manufactured to subdue and kill him. Grappling with neurosis caused by mental disorder and exacerbated by a religious fanatic of a mother who, it seemed from old records, had abused her son, Christian had probably killed the second Mrs. Asa Pomeroy.

Rather than face prison, Christian had ended up in Our Lady of Virtues Hospital where he'd hung out with a group of angry, sociopathic youths his own age, all with their own peculiar kinds of violent obsessions. While at the hospital, Christian had met and fallen in love with Faith Chastain, with whom, it was speculated, he had an affair.

Twenty years later he'd started his macabre killing spree.

Christian had died that night at the hospital, tumbling to his death just as his lover had twenty years earlier. Deep in the bowels of the old hospital, the police had found Pomeroy's lair, an old operating room that had been converted into bizarre living quarters for a demented individual.

References to sin and atonement, lines of Scripture, and religious quotes had been scratched into the wall. Over those rough carvings, Pomeroy had scrawled each of the Seven Deadly Sins in glowing paint and with each sin was its saintly equivalent, the Contrary Virtues written in an intricate hand with the same fluorescent paint that glowed eerily in the weak light from Pomeroy's lanterns.

There had been a cot and sleeping bag and an old secretary-type desk where Pomeroy had kept his treasures from his killing spree. Courtney Mary LaBelle's promise ring had been placed in a tiny slot next to Luke Gierman's Rolex, Asa Pomeroy's money clip had been surrounded by Gina Jefferson's gold chain and cross, Billy Ray Furlough's expensive revolver cloaked in Maria Montoya's favorite rosary...

Yeah, Abby decided, he was a real whack job.

It seemed that Christian Pomeroy had been plotting his revenge for years and that retaliation had been tweaked and molded by his mother's antiquated views of sin and redemption, creating a unique and deadly psychosis. He'd even dressed Courtney LaBelle in his mother's wedding dress, one he'd kept for years, and that a designer had identified.

The police had found fourteen names of his potential victims, along with their imagined sins and virtues, listed on a single sheet of paper tacked into the side of the desk. Six names had been crossed off: the six victims who had died in the first three staged scenes. Of the others, four names had been circled and had included Pedro Montoya, Hannah Chastain, Simon Heller, and Zoey Chastain. Pride, Humility, Sloth and Zeal. The remaining four people, none of whom she recognized—associated with Envy, Charity, Gluttony and Moderation—had escaped. Or so everyone thought. The police were still checking on their whereabouts.

Still, Pomeroy's dying words had haunted her.

Tonight is just the beginning.

Hogwash! He was dead. And she didn't believe he would resurrect.

So why did she still feel a little niggle of fear each time she thought of him? A coldness deep in the center of her soul?

Why did her nightmares now include him?

"Something bothering you?" Montoya asked as he shut the door behind them.

"Same old, same old," she admitted, but refused to dwell on Pomeroy and the horror he'd created. It was over. Done. *Finis!* "How about I buy you a beer?"

"Sounds good."

They walked into the kitchen and she opened the refrigerator door as Montoya's cell rang. He pulled the phone from his pocket and checked caller ID.

"Duty calls. It's Bentz," he said with a smile, then clicked it on. "Montoya."

Abby opened two bottles. As she handed a longneck to Montoya she saw his expression change during the one-sided conversation, his jaw tightening, the corners of his mouth pulling into a frown. "Nope, I have no idea," he responded. "It's news to me." He took a swallow of beer and listened again, his eyes returning to Abby.

Abby's guts twisted. Something was wrong.

"She's right here . . . . Yeah, I'll ask and get back to you."

"Ask me what?" she said as he clicked off. Her fingers tightened over the chilled bottle of Coors.

"It's about your mother."

Abby felt a cold breath of dread against the back of her neck. "What about her?" she asked.

"She didn't have any children other than you and your sister, right?"

"Right. Just Zoey and me." What kind of question was that? Her stomach knotted. She set her beer on the counter.

"And you were born by Cesarean birth?"

"No!" Abby shook her head.

"What about Zoey?"

"No. I'm sure not. I heard the stories of our births from Mom and Dad. And once I walked into the bathroom and saw Mom naked. No scar. Why?"

"Bentz was just going over the medical records for your mother, including the coroner's report," Montoya said, scratching at his goatee. "It seems she did have a scar that indicated she'd had a C-section. Bentz checked her other, previous medical records, none of which mentioned a pregnancy or birth."

"No way."

He studied her with those dark, warm eyes and she realized she knew very little about the woman who had borne her, the woman whose birthday she had shared, the woman who had slit her own wrists, the woman who had spent years in a mental hospital fighting her own set of demons.

"But that can't be ... Mom and Dad weren't even together ..." Abby said, hearing her own damning words as her insides turned to ice. Hadn't Faith had affairs with both Simon Heller and Christian Pomeroy? Wasn't it possible that she'd given birth to one of their offspring ... that Abby had a half brother or sister somewhere? A child sired by a killer? Her heart turned to stone. "I don't know," she admitted in a whisper. "I don't think so, but the truth is, I really don't know." She cleared her throat, fought back the denials she wanted to scream. "I ... I suppose anything's possible."

"Do you think that's what Pomeroy meant when he said 'Tonight's just the beginning?'"

She shuddered, hating to think of the consequences. "I—oh God—I guess we'd better find out." She detested the thought of it, just wanted to bury the past once and for all. Apparently, it wasn't to be. She took in a deep breath and met Montoya's concerned gaze. "So, Detective, where do we begin?"

Montoya thought hard. Took a long pull from his bottle before setting it on the counter. "At the beginning," he said, "where it all started." He held her gaze with his. "At Our Lady of Virtues Mental Hospital."

"Dear God, will this never end?"

"Of course it will," he said, managing a smile as he drew her into the strength of his arms. "We'll get through this together, you and me." He kissed her lightly on her lips. "You know, darlin', I have a feeling that Bentz just might win his bet after all."

"Really?" she asked, and despite everything she couldn't help but smile. She was with Montoya, the man she loved.

"Abso-friggin-lutely. Chances are by the end of the year, I'll be a married man."

"So who's the lucky lady?" she teased, her mood bright.

Montoya winked at her. "Why don't you take a wild guess?"

"Uh-uh, Detective. No guesses. I'm only interested in a sure thing."

"Well then, Abby, I don't think you'll ever be disappointed."

"Nor will you, Detective," she vowed. "Nor will you."

Dear Reader,

I hope you enjoyed *Shiver*. I love writing about Detectives Montoya and Bentz, so it's always great to go back to New Orleans and meet up with them again. *Shiver* is the third book in the series that currently is eight books, though I'm planning to write more, of course.

Meanwhile, I'm in the thick of writing a new stand-alone novel. *The Girl Who Survived* is a story that I've been thinking about for years. I can't even remember when the idea first hit me.

I wondered what would happen to a very young girl who survives a massacre of her entire family at Christmas. What if she were locked away in a closet by a family member to ensure her safety? What if she could hear the horror going down, but couldn't do anything about it? How would she live through the horror and aftermath? What would the psychological scars be? What about her survivor's guilt? What if what she perceived to be true was actually a lie? Or worse yet, had the figments of her own wild imagination created a false narrative about that horrible Christmas Eve?

The Girl Who Survived took years in the creation. I thought about it off and on while writing other books. It was one of the stories that just wouldn't leave me and was always there, just below the surface, waiting to be told. But it was fragmented with so many different twists and turns in the plot over the years. I was worried that this years-in-the-making story wouldn't come together with the different thoughts I'd had over the years, but once I met Kara, the heroine, the story came together. Damaged and different from many of my heroines, she nonetheless grounded the story. The odd thing is that had I written this book when I first considered the idea I'm sure it would be a different novel than it is today. So, it was worth the wait! Anyway, I hope you pick up a copy and enjoy reading it as much as I loved writing it.

As I mentioned earlier, once *The Girl Who Survived* is completed, I intend to jump right into the next New Orleans story with Detectives Bentz and Montoya! Yay! That story is another one where the idea came to me a few years ago, and I can't wait! It will be so much fun writing about my favorite detective team again!

As for the actual dates of publication for these next projects? I'm not sure at this point, but I'll keep everyone posted on my website, Facebook, Twitter and all the social platforms, so check in often.

In the meantime, stay safe and . . .

Keep Reading!

Lisa Jackson

Please turn the page for a very special Q&A
with Lisa Jackson!

The first book in the series, Hot Blooded, *came out in 2001. Do you remember where you came up with the idea for that book?*

Wow! That's been a while ago—20 years! But yes, I remember there were a lot of radio psychologists on the air at the time and I thought, "Who would tell their most private, innermost secrets to a live host with an audience of thousands of strangers?" Then I thought, "What if the wrong person heard the confession? What if someone dangerous used that information? How dangerous could that be?" That was the inspiration and I loved writing the book.

Was it your intention to write a series or had the plan been for Hot Blooded *to be a stand-alone novel? If that was your original intention, what made you decide to write a sequel,* Cold Blooded?

I thought, at first, that *Hot Blooded* was a single title, but then I fell in love with the characters and my editor suggested a sequel with the title *Cold Blooded.* A story was already forming in my mind, about a heroine who people thought was crazy because she saw a series of grisly murders as they were happening. I knew the cop I'd created, Rick Bentz, would be wary and suspicious of the woman while all the while fighting an attraction to her.

And after Cold Blooded *came out, what made you decide to keep going with the characters?*

Well, I know it sounds corny, but I fell in love with the characters and the city of New Orleans. My editor had originally suggested New Orleans for the setting of the books and I worried that I wouldn't be able to capture the feel of the city. I'm from the Pacific Northwest. So I traveled to Louisiana and spent a lot of time drinking up the culture, the romance, the history, the dark side and the fun of New Orleans and I just wanted to keep writing about Detectives Montoya and Bentz. They had more stories to tell.

Is there a book in the series that's your favorite?

Oooh. That's a tough one. I've always loved *Shiver,* so I guess that would be it. There was a lot of great backstory to the heroine's family and there was the darkly religious overtones to the book. So I guess, if I were forced to pick, I would say *Shiver*.

Which book in the series was the easiest for you to write?

That's another hard question. I think *Shiver* flowed the most easily. I really felt the characters and the situation.

And which was the hardest?

The hardest? Hmmm. I guess maybe *Devious* was the most difficult because I hadn't written a New Orleans book in a while and I had to double-check backstory information on the characters, to keep them all straight.

Do you enjoy writing a series or do you prefer writing stand-alone novels? What are the pros and cons of each?

I like each. Stand-alones are difficult because you start with a whole new setting and set of characters, so it's creating a whole new world. Contrarily, series are difficult because you have to keep track of everyone—their ages, relationships, and general info. With a lot of characters who have been around for a decade or two, that can get tricky.

Which character in the series is your favorite to write?

Oh, that's an impossible question. Though I relate more to Rick Bentz, I understand him better, I do love any scene with Reuben Montoya!

How long do you see the series going on for? There are rumors that you may be planning a spinoff series with Kristi Bentz and Cruz Montoya. True or false?

I'm not certain as to how many more books will be in the series, but I plan on several more. And yes, I hope to write a book with Kristi and Cruz because I think they are two of the most intriguing characters I've ever written. Each brings a certain sizzle to the pages, so

I see them working together in some capacity. That said, I have no book yet written for them, just an idea churning through my mind.

What are you working on now? And when will the next Bentz and Montoya book be out?

I'm finishing *The Girl Who Survived,* which is a stand-alone novel about a girl who survived the slaughter of her family. It starts out with Kara McIntyre, a child at the time, discovering that most of the members of her family have been brutally killed. It's Kara's testimony that sends her surviving half-brother to prison for the crime. Years later, he's released and just as he is more people start dying. It's been fun to write.

As for the next Bentz and Montoya book, it's set to be published sometime late in 2022 or 2023. As soon as I know the date and title, I'll post it on my website and Facebook, Twitter and Instagram, so keep checking!

Please turn the page for a sneak peek at
Lisa Jackson's newest novel
THE GIRL WHO SURVIVED
coming soon wherever print and e-books are sold!

CHAPTER 1

Mount Hood, Oregon
Twenty years earlier

Creeeaaak!

Kara's eyes flew open.

What was that?

She squinted into the darkness.

"Don't say a word."

She started to scream.

But a hand came down over her mouth.

Hard.

"Shhh!"

Marlie? Her sister was holding her down, forcing her head back against the pillows?

She started to struggle.

"Stop it! Just listen and don't say anything!" The warning was whispered against her ear. Hot breath against her skin. "Listen to me," her voice was urgent. This was no joke, not the kind of prank Kara had grown up with due to the antics of three older brothers. "Handfuls," her mother called them. "Delinquents," her father had said.

Now, though, it was just Marlie and she was freaked. "Just do what I say," Marlie warned. "No questions. No arguments. This is serious, Kara-Bear, so don't make a sound."

Why?

As if she read Kara's mind, Marlie said, "I can't explain now, just trust me. You're a smart girl. That's what all the teachers say, right? That you're way ahead of kids your age? So just do as I say, okay? Now, come on."

Kara shook her head, her hair rustling against her pillow, her eyes adjusting to the thin light. Whatever had scared Marlie so much could be handled. Mama would know what to do.

"You can't make any noise, okay? Got that?"

Marlie lifted her hand and Kara couldn't help herself. "What's—?" she started to whisper and Marlie's hand returned. Firmer. Pressing Kara back against the sheets.

"Just listen to me!" Marlie insisted through clenched teeth. Her sharp, desperate plea stopped Kara cold. Though Mama, at times, had accused the older girl of being a "drama queen," this time was different. Marlie was different. Scared to death.

Kara sensed it. She lay still.

"You have to hide. Now."

Hide?

"*Right now.* Do you understand?"

Wide-eyed, Kara nodded.

"And it can't be here." Marlie started to take her hand away from Kara's face.

"Why? Where's Mama—?" Kara said in a whispered rush. She couldn't help herself.

"Shit! Stop! Kara, *please!*" Marlie's hand was over her younger sister's mouth again. Harder. Forcing Kara's head back into her pillow. "No questions! They'll hear you!"

Who? Who would hear her?

Kara's heart was beating crazily. Fear curdled through her blood.

"Just come with me and don't say a word! I mean it, Kara. There are bad people here. They cannot find you. If they do, they will hurt you, do you understand?" Marlie's face pressed closer and even in their dark bedroom, Kara saw that Marlie's blue eyes were round with fear. She was dressed, in jeans and a sweat shirt, her blond hair pulled into a braided ponytail.

Kara shook her head violently.

"Okay. Now, this is the last time," Marlie warned. "Got it?"

Kara nodded slowly. Scared out of her mind.

"Promise you'll be quiet."

Kara swallowed against the growing lump in her throat, but nodded again.

Marlie hesitated a second, then withdrew her hand.

Kara didn't speak.

"Good." Marlie glanced out the window where moonlight played on the thick blanket of snow, then grabbed Kara's palm. "Come on!" She tugged, but Kara didn't need any more encouragement. She scrambled to get out of the tangle of bedclothes. They crept past Marlie's bed where even in the darkness Kara could see several neatly stacked piles of clothes piled over the rumpled coverlet. Even Marlie's boots were on the bed. Now, though, she, like Kara, was barefoot.

So her footsteps wouldn't be heard.

Kara's blood turned to ice. This was wrong. So wrong. She stepped on a toy, probably a Barbie shoe, but held her tongue as Marlie cracked open the door to the hallway.

Along with the scent of wood smoke from the dying fire, the faint sounds of a Christmas carol filtered up from the floor below.

Silent night—

Marlie peered into the darkness.

Holy night—

Taking a deep breath, Marlie squeezed Kara's hand and whispered, "Let's go." She pulled her younger sister into the dark, narrow corridor, past the closed doors of the boys' rooms toward the far end of the hall where the stairs curved down to the first floor, light curling eerily up from below, the massive doors to Mama and Daddy's bedroom just beyond the railing.

All is calm—

For a second, Kara's heart soared. Marlie was taking her to get Mama and—but no. She stopped at the last door before the staircase leading down, to the door that was always locked, the doorway leading upward to the attic and the warren of unused rooms above.

What?

NO!

All is bright.

Kara balked. She wasn't going up there! *No, no, no!*

She started to protest when Marlie caught her eye and sent her a look that could cut through steel.

Bong!

Kara jumped at the noise, her heart hammering.

But it was only the grandfather clock near the front door, striking off the hours, drowning out the music.

"Jesus," Marlie whispered under her breath and pulled Kara behind her as she slowly mounted the narrow wooden steps.

Bong!

"Marlie, no," Kara whispered, feeling the temperature drop with each step.

"We don't have a choice!" Marlie snapped, her voice still hushed as they reached the third floor.

She used her flashlight, its thin beam sliding over draped furniture and boxes, forgotten lamps and stacks of books, open bags of unused clothes. Her family used the extra space for storage, though, according to Mama, it had once been servants' quarters. "I wish," Mama had added, lighting a cigarette as she warned all of her "patchwork family" that the area was forbidden, deemed unsafe. "Don't go up there, ever. You're asking for serious grounding if you do. Hear me? Serious."

Her threat hadn't stuck, of course.

Of course they'd all sneaked up here and explored.

Though the area was declared off-limits, her brothers were always climbing up here and Kara had poked around the rabbit warren of connected rooms often enough to know her way around. But tonight, in the darkness, the frigid rooms appeared sinister and evil, the closed doors standing like sentinels guarding the narrow corridor.

"Bong!"

"Where's Mama?" she asked again, fighting panic.

Marlie glanced at her and shook her head. She placed a finger to her lips, reminding Kara of the need for silence, then pulled her anxiously along the bare floor of the third story.

This was wrong.

Really wrong.

At the far end of the hallway was another staircase, much narrower and close. Cramped. It wound downward and ended up in the kitchen. For a fleeting second, Kara thought they were going down the back way, which seemed stupid since they'd just ascended, but Marlie had other plans. She stopped just before they reached steps, at the small cupboard-like entrance to the attic.

Kara's bad feeling got worse. "What are you do—?"

Marlie pulled a key from the front pocket of her jeans and slipped it into the lock. A second later the attic door creaked open. "Come on."

Kara drew back and shook her head. "I don't want to." Marlie surely wouldn't—

"Don't care." Forcefully, Marlie pulled her through the tight doorway and yanked the door shut behind them.

"What the hell is this?"

"Don't swear."

"But—"

"Look. I'm saving you. Us." A loud click sounded as she flipped the old switch. Nothing happened.

"Shit," she muttered as they stood in the darkness.

"Don't swear," she threw back. " And saving us from what?"

"Shhh. Quiet. You don't want to know."

"Yes! Yes, I do! Tell me!"

"Look, it's . . . complicated." Marlie hesitated.

"And scary."

"Yes. And really scary." She pulled a small flashlight from her pocket and clicked it on so that they could see the stairs winding upward. The steps were steep and barely wide enough for Kara's foot, a rickety old staircase winding to the garret under the eaves. It was freezing in the tight space and dark as pitch.

"I'm not going up there."

"Of course you are. Come on."

This was bad.

Kara's skin crawled and though she wanted to argue, she didn't. The tone of Marlie's voice, so unlike her, made the ever-rebellious Kara obedient as she was prodded up the stairs. Marlie was holding the small flashlight, its weak beam illuminating the path.

At the top of the stairs, under the sloped ceilings where Kara was certain bats roosted, Marlie stopped, leaving Kara standing on the floorboards of the attic, while she hesitated one step lower, so they were eye to eye, nose to nose. She shined the flashlight near her face, distorting her features in shadow, creating an eerie mask much like their brother Jonas's face when he held a flashlight beneath his chin for a macabre effect as he told ghost stories.

But tonight was different.

Tonight wasn't a game. That much Kara knew.

"You need to stay here and wait for me to come back."

"No!"

"Just for a little while."

Kara shook her head. "I want Mama."

"I know, but I already told you that's not going to happen."

"Why?" Panic welled in her heart. "You're not leaving me here alone."

"Just for a little while."

"No!"

"Kara—"

"I'm not staying here. Why would you even say that?" Kara demanded.

"I just have to make sure it's safe, okay—?"

"No, it's not okay."

"Then I'll come get you. I promise."

"Safe from what?" Kara cried, freaking out. Anytime her siblings added an "I promise"' it was because they weren't telling the truth. "You said there were bad people here. Who?"

"I-I don't really know."

"What're they doing?"

"I'm not . . I don't . . . I'm not sure, but I know this, there's something . . . something really bad, Kara."

"What-what's bad?"

"I don't know."

"And it's here."

"I— Yes . . . please, just do as I say."

Kara suspected her sister was dodging the truth. "Where're Mama and Daddy?"

A beat. "Out."

"Liar." Why was Marlie lying to her?

"Kara—"

"What about Jonas and Sam and Donner?" Kara asked frantically. Her older half-brothers. They'd all been here earlier. She'd seen them at dinner and after. Donner and Sam had been listening to music and playing video games, maybe even drinking, and Jonas, the loner, had been in his room practicing his ninja moves or whatever it was he always did. Sam had kidded him, calling him Jonas Joe-Judo. Which Jonas hated.

Marlie said, "Everyone's gone."

"Gone?" On Christmas Eve? That didn't seem right. "Then what're you afraid of?"

Marlie licked her nips nervously. Her voice was the merest of whispers. "As I said, there's someone here. Someone else. Someone bad."

"Who? How do you know?" This was crazy. "But you just said everyone was 'out' and now . . . you're scaring me."

"Good."

"I want Mama."

"I told you she's not here!" Marlie's voice was still a whisper, but there was an edge to it. Like Mama's when she got mad or frustrated with Kara's brothers. "Just listen to me, okay? You're going to stay here for a little while, until it's safe, and then I'll come back and—"

"No!" Marlie was going to leave her here, in the middle of the night, all alone?

"—just for a while," Marlie was saying again, but Kara was violently shaking her head.

"No, no! You can't. Don't leave me!" Frantic, Kara clawed wildly at her sister. Why was Marlie doing this? Why? At seven, she didn't understand why she was being left. Alone. Here in this dark, horrid attic that smelled like mold and was covered in dust and probably home to spiders and rats and wasps and every other gross thing in the world. "I'm not staying up here alone, Mar—"

"Shh. Keep quiet!" Marlie's hands tightened over Kara's forearms.

"Please—"

"Listen!" Marlie's voice was sharp. A whisper like the warning hiss of a snake.

She gave Kara a shake. Her fingers dug through the long sleeves of Kara's pajamas.

"Ow!"

"Don't say a word, Kara-Bear. Keep quiet. You hear me? I'm serious."

"But you can't leave me here." Not in this cold, drafty space situated under the eaves of the cabin's peaked roof. "I'll freeze!"

"You won't."

This wasn't right. Kara might be only seven years old, but she knew this was wrong. All wrong. "You're lying!"

Marlie gripped her forearm so hard Kara dropped the flashlight and it rolled down the steps. Marlie's fingernails dug through Kara's pajamas and pinched her flesh. "Damn it," she swore. "For once, Kara, just do as you're told." And then she was gone, nearly tripping over the flashlight as she fled down the stairs.

Kara took off after her but was a step behind and Marlie reached the door first, slid though and shut it.

Click.

Kara grabbed the door handle but it wouldn't move.

Locked? The door was locked? Marlie had locked her in?

Fury and fear burned through her as she heard Marlie's swift footsteps as she hurried away.

No, no, no! "Marlie!" She rattled the door handle and pounded on the door, then as her rage eased a bit, thought better of it. This was no prank. Something was wrong. Seriously wrong. Something . . . evil. She swallowed back her fear and brushed aside the angry tears that had formed in her eyes. Her arms ached in the spots where her sister's fingers had clenched.

She wanted to scream, to yell, to beat her fists against the door so that someone would hear her, so that she could escape this sloped-ceilinged jail and breathe again.

But she didn't. Marlie's words, whispered like the sound of death, ran through her head. *I just want to make us safe . . .*

Shivering, she bit her lip and stared at the door, a dark barrier to the rest of the world. She couldn't just sit here and wait.

What if whoever it was Marlie thought had come into the house came up the stairs and found her?

What if he hurt Marlie? What if he *killed* her? Kara's heart wrenched.

Again she wished for her mother and father. They would know what to do. But they were gone, according to Marlie, and she wouldn't lie. Not about that.

Or would she?

Teeth chattering, heart knocking erratically, Kara waited, grabbed the flashlight and stared at the door, shivering and trying to hear something, anything over the wild beating of her heart. Her skin crawled.

She sat on the lowest step, clicking the tiny flashlight on, then off, watching its yellowish beam illuminate the back of the door for a second before she was swallowed in darkness again.

On.

Off.

On.

Click, click, click.

The light growing fainter each time she turned the flashlight on.

She couldn't just sit here and wait while the batteries in the flashlight died. What if Marlie never came back?

Kara wanted to rattle the door handle frantically, to scream and flail at the door, and reached for the handle again, her fingers curling over the cold lever. But she stopped herself. It would do no good. And probably cause unwanted attention. No, she had to be smart. She would find another way to escape.

Determined, she climbed up the rickety steps again to the attic where a single round window was mounted high above where the faint moonlight cast the dimmest of light through the dusty, forgotten boxes piled everywhere with words scribbled on them, some of which Kara could read: Books. Clothes. Office. Or marked with names: Sam Jr. Jonas. Donner. Marlie. Her sister and brothers. No box for her, the youngest, the only child of both mother and father. Not yet.

She heard the rustle of something, something *alive* in the far corner. Tiny claws on the wood floor. A squirrel? Or a mouse . . . or a rat?

She shivered and was sorting through the box again when she

heard it—a horrid, blood-curdling scream rising up from a lower floor.

"*AAAAHHHHHGGG!*"

Kara jumped. Nearly peed herself. She sucked in her breath as the horrid wail echoed through the house.

What was that? *Who* was that?

Marlie?

Mama?

Or someone else?

Thud!

The house shook.

Something really big had fallen.

Kara's mouth turned to dust and she blinked against tears.

Was it a body?

Someone hurt and screaming then falling?

Marlie?

"Mama," she mouthed around a sob.

Don't be a baby.

Pulse pounding, fear nearly paralyzing her, she forced herself to sweep the flashlight's thin beam over the boxes again and spied the one marked Office. It was closed, cardboard flaps folded but gaping. She shone the light inside and saw yellowed papers, an old stapler, envelopes, a tape dispenser and a pair of dusty scissors. She picked up the scissors and a paper clip that held some papers together, then silently made her way down the stairs to the door.

As she'd seen Jonas do at the locked bathroom door when she'd been spying on him, she took the paper clip, straightened it as best she could and slid it into the small hole beneath the lever. She'd tried it once before on Sam Junior and Donner's room and it had worked and now . . . she wiggled the tiny wire, working it inside the lock as she strained to hear any other noise coming from the other side of the door.

Come on, come on she silently said to herself, pulling the wire out once before sliding it back through the hole and twisting gently . . . feeling it move. With a soft *click* the lock gave way, and fighting back her fear, she took a deep breath, held her scissors in one hand and pushed the door open.